At the dawn of the twentieth century, New York City houses both the living and the dead. And when it comes to crimes of an otherworldly nature, it falls to the psychics and spirits of the city's finest secret agency—The Ghost Precinct—to serve justice beyond the earthly realm . . .

The ethereal denizens of New York owe a great debt to Eve Whitby, the young talented medium who leads the all-female Spiritualists in the police department's Ghost Precinct. Without her team's efforts on behalf of the incorporeal, many souls would have been lost or damned by both human and inhuman means.

But now Eve faces an enemy determined to exorcise the city's ghostly population once and for all. Albert Prenze is supposed to be dead. Instead he is very much alive, having assumed the identity of his twin brother Alfred, and taken control of the family's dubiously made fortune. With unlimited wealth at his disposal, Albert uses experimental technology to banish ghosts to an eternal darkness forever.

To achieve his vicious ends, Albert plots to manipulate Eve and twist her abilities into a psychic weapon—a weapon that not only poses a threat to spirits but to everyone she cares for, including her beloved Detective Horowitz . . .

Visit us at www.kensingtonbooks.com

Books by Leanna Renee Hieber

The Spectral City series:

The Spectral City

A Sanctuary of Spirits

A Summoning of Souls

The Magic Most Foul trilogy

Darker Still

The Twisted Tragedy of Miss Natalie Stewart

The Double Life of Incorporate Things

The Strangely Beautiful saga:

Strangely Beautiful

Perilous Prophecy

Miss Violet and the Great War

The Eterna Files trilogy:

The Eterna Files

Eterna and Omega

The Eterna Solution

A Summoning of Souls

Leanna Renee Hieber

REBEL BASE BOOKS
Kensington Publishing Corp.
www.kensingtonbooks.com

Rebel Base Books are published by
Kensington Publishing Corp. 119 West 40th Street New York, NY 10018

First Electronic Edition: July 2020
eISBN-13: 978-1-63573-060-9
eISBN-10: 1-63573-060-0

First Print Edition: July 2020
ISBN-13: 978-1-63573-063-0
ISBN-10: 1-63573-063-5

Printed in the United States of America

To the spirit world, may we always be a force for good...

Prologue

Manhattan 1899

Margaret Hathorn wafted along Fifth Avenue in her favorite ballgown, forever sporting the opulent fashion of the eighties; her skirts doubled with a fine bustle decked in bows and gathers, her dark hair pinned up with a few cascading ringlets.

To the living eye, the young woman was transparent and all in greyscale, but Maggie's favorite dress had been a bright rose as pretty as she'd once been praised to be. Glancing down at her rustling skirts, an undulating pattern hovering over the cobblestones, to her eye, the rose was faded but it still held a whisper of blushing color, a little slip of life.

At present, the wraith was on an important mission.

Looking in the front windows of opulent mansions, Maggie startled the occasional child who was looking out of them. The act, if she were honest with herself, gave her a distinct delight. It wasn't that Maggie wanted to be a terror, but she had to take her pleasures where she could. And Maggie had always liked to be seen; whether in an admittedly shallow life, or now as a more mature ghost.

For some, becoming a ghost wasn't a choice. But for Maggie, she retained every bit of agency she wanted. No, she couldn't pick things up or feel touch and embraces like she used to, but one adapted. At any point she wished, she could say goodbye to her loved ones, corporeal and non, and leave for that Sweet Summerland the Spiritualists spoke of; eternal rest in some wonderful Elysian Field. Someday. But not yet. There was so very much to do.

Death had rearranged Margaret Hathorn's priorities. Having been caught up in all manner of terrible things she'd unwittingly unleashed, she was murdered nearly two decades prior. Having sacrificed herself to save others, the act absolved her of torments caused by her ignorance. Her spirit lived on to make sure that Eve Whitby, the daughter of those she gave her life for, had a ghostly auntie always watching over her. It was Maggie and Eve's mutual mission to help make New York that much safer and brighter, instilling a spectral purpose she'd never had as a snobbish socialite.

The spirit paused before the target address. Every time Maggie tried to return to this terrible house, her spectral form quailed, as if the wisp of her that remained could not bear to confront this place of trauma again.

The Prenze mansion. Patriarchs of tonics and dubious cure-alls, the Prenze twins had made a fortune off chronic pain and symptoms of disease the medical profession had yet to cure. One twin, Albert Prenze, had died in an industrial accident at one of their London warehouses. Or so it had been said.

Albert was, in fact, alive, operating under a false name and acting from the shadows. Even his twin brother Alfred didn't know he was alive.

None of these details would be important to Maggie had Albert Prenze not made two things very clear: He was intent on destroying any ghost he could, no matter if they wished to haunt on and help mortals or not. And he was sure Eve Whitby and her Ghost Precinct of the New York Police Department was an obstacle in his aim.

Well, the man wasn't wrong; they were obstacles. And living and dead, they were about to fight back. Maggie just didn't know how. Thus, her research expedition.

Floating into the Prenze hedgerows, she waited. The thick, manicured branches around her made her feel safer, as if she were in the brambles surrounding an evil fairy-tale castle.

Again, Maggie tried to remember what exactly happened the night she'd disappeared. When Albert Prenze had tried to break what remained of her soul in two, never to haunt again. She'd been drawn to the mansion by the spirit of children that wanted her help. For whatever reason, she'd been able to get in that night, but never since. She remembered the electric lights had been odd, and perhaps a malfunction in what she now knew was an electrical blockade, snapping at spirits like a switch to keep them from coming in or out.

When she had gone inside, she did as the two siblings had asked and she managed to muster a small burst of physical force to send a collection of postmortem photography flying. In doing so, she'd roused the attention of their present nemesis. He had sent his houseguests out of the room, turned to her with a cruel sneer, and flipped a switch that tore her out of existence.

As if swatting Maggie from this memory, a ghostly, wrinkled hand slapped against the glass of the thin basement window. Maggie started, almost tumbling out of the hedge.

"Help us," came a desperate, elderly voice trying to travel the distance to her spectral ear. "He wants to kill us all. End us *forever*."

"We'll do everything we can," Maggie murmured back, unsure if she could be heard.

The sharp whinny of a horse as a driver cracked a whip was like an extension of the faint scream she heard coming from that cellar room. Looking behind her, she wanted to get the attention of the living, "Do you hear that? Can anyone help them?" But she couldn't.

So much was happening in New York City, so many people in their own little worlds and here in the finest part of town, everyone's little world was opulent and more important, it was clear, than anything that happened in anyone else's. These ghosts were alone, for all they knew, with no one but themselves to care.

"We care; we'll find you. Hold fast," Maggie said, doubting she could be heard from the hedgerows, but she had to say it. She had been abandoned before, in life, by society's finest, and it was the worst of betrayals because they of all people could have afforded to help her.

Maggie was startled by a presence appearing beside her, a dark-haired little girl in a white dress singed at the hem who immediately began exclaiming in a thick Polish accent, "They're trapped! I have to show them the way out!" The ghost of Zofia Berezowska was about to float forward toward the window when Maggie grabbed her and held her close.

The ten-year-old ghost that had died at work in a garment district fire had devoted her spectral life to helping the living out of myriad dangers, pointing the way out when smoke cleared or pushing something over to sound an alarm or summon help, fearless in rushing to the rescue.

"Zofia, love, not here." Maggie clutched the young ghost she thought of as a little sister even tighter, her voice breaking. "Not here you can't! Don't you know this place is dangerous? This is the Prenze mansion, the place I thought killed me!" The first time she'd been murdered was quite enough, and she didn't like the prospect of dying a second time.

"Then why are *you* here?" Zofia threaded her fingers through Maggie's. "I came looking for you. After losing you, don't you think I might look after you better than before?" They floated together, weightless but connected.

It had taken Maggie time to get used to how much touch was different in death. An embrace was half as full as the fortitude of life. Of course, neither she nor Zofia could touch the living at all beyond the caress of a cold breeze, so the ability for a spirit to have solid contact with another spirit was one of the comforts of this existence. Maggie tried very hard to appreciate her existence as one of floating, subtle, muted nuance. As it registered to her senses, death was full of gentle touch and quiet whispers. Death was soft and delicate.

The girls stared at the imposing mansion before them, the hands at the window, imploring, pointing. "That's more than I can bear," Zofia said.

"And that's why I'm back," Maggie countered. "I don't know how we're going to prove the evil of this house in ways that the living can prosecute, but this is now our sole focus."

"What if we could compel someone living to go in for us?" Zofia asked. "Someone who isn't Eve or any of the precinct operatives, seeing as they're known now by the family."

"That...could work," Maggie said, her mind already whirring. She'd taken note of several Sensitives in the city, not those as gifted as ran the Ghost Precinct she worked for, but ones who did see or sense. "We might find an ally I hadn't thought to utilize.... Good thinking, little one!"

Zofia looked up at Maggie proudly, and for a moment in those wide, dark irises of the child's eyes, Maggie saw the reflection of the fire that had signaled her doom. Even ghosts were haunted. The choice was theirs if they would let it entirely define them, or motivate them to a new mission.

There was movement in the basement. A form loomed in a dim doorway before darkness overtook the cellar level again. The ghostly palms withdrew from the barred windows, but the sounds of sobs overtook the exterior garden.

A murderer of ghosts, living like a king in the finest part of Manhattan.

"The Ghost Precinct has to root him out," Zofia murmured. "Force him into the light."

"I already have an idea. Tell the girls I'm off on an experiment and not to worry if I'm not back for a bit. Let's see if I can scare up some help."

Chapter One

Eve Whitby came to in a forest glade with no memory of how she'd gotten there.

Before her was a stone cairn, and from its foundation rose a single sandstone Gothic arch, the only standing evidence of a chapel that had never been built.

Eve recognized this sacred place, having been called here before to commune with the spirit world. This was a place that spirits called Sanctuary, and she must have sleepwalked to this precipice between worlds. Again.

The sky was brightening; dawn had broken on a cool, late autumn morning as the last months of the nineteenth century were shortening.

The realization of where she had wandered came with a wave of terrors: Where were her colleagues, and were they all right? As director of the Ghost Precinct, she was responsible for three young women, gifted psychic mediums. As leader, she was setting a poor precedent of wandering off unannounced, a rule she'd made her team promise they'd never break.

The last thing she remembered was trying to get to sleep after Albert Prenze, a man with no morals, a vehement hatred of ghosts, a terrifying capacity to mesmerize and compel his subjects, and a likely culprit of murder, had drawn her and dear Detective Horowitz outside into a confrontation, threatening them before disappearing.

She and Jacob Horowitz had parted ways after a breathless, private moment together, and her heart burned with a flame it had never before experienced while her mind raced with terrors of the present case. The combination of yearning and fear hadn't made for a pleasant night's sleep in her grandmother's fine townhouse. But, being so restless, she should have remembered rising, throwing a housecoat and wool coat over her nightdress and getting on a northbound train to exit outside the city limits on the Hudson River Line. But she didn't.

Jacob. Was he here now? Her heart spasmed. Whirling around, she found herself alone with only the pine trees and a few maples losing the remainder of their colorful leaves, one by one like slow tears, dripping from the tall eaves above her head. The last time she was at this precarious doorway where soul separated from body, Jacob had been there to catch her when she came to, making her feel safe, alive, delighted.

But there was no such comfort here now. There were only soft voices from unseen sources, echoing on the breeze.

Eve had grown up quickly due to necessity. Her nineteen years of life were entirely haunted. But that didn't mean she was inured to spectral chill or the threats brought on by certain paranormal experiences. There were things even seasoned minds and old souls should fear. The whispered phrase that distinctly emanated from the stone arch directly before her was one such thing; a recurring warning of late, from the spirit world to hers.

"Don't let anything in!"

The phrase repeated itself on the air. Eve crept forward and placed her ear against the cool grey surface, listening to the murmur of spirits, as if whispering on the other side of a door.

Then, a voice she recognized. A friend.

"Eve isn't 'anything'; she's my trusted ally in the living world," explained the voice of Episcopalian deaconess Lily Strand, a woman of the cloth whose ghost had devoted herself to the safety of children's spirits. Lily was Eve's guide through Sanctuary, a space outside life and death that had pieced together the souls of attacked loved ones, a service for which Eve would be forever grateful.

"Deaconess Strand," Eve called to the arch. "Lily. I don't know how I got here. Did you call for me again?" The pine trees rustled an answer she didn't understand.

A hand clamped on her shoulder, and she pitched forward through the archway, almost striking her head on the stone cairn covered in moss and ivy at her feet. She plummeted in a hazy fall.

Just as Eve was about to crash into a wooden doorway, she closed her eyes and braced for an impact that never came. She was wrested to her feet, gravity shifting, the world righting itself. Opening her eyes, the willowy, sharp-featured Strand stared at her, dressed in a simple blue sisters' habit. The deaconess released her grip on Eve's arms. They stood just outside what appeared to be a large cathedral when she'd just moments ago been in an empty forest clearing. Arches and spires soared away from them into oblivion. The building changed depending on one's general beliefs, familiar comforts or favorite architecture.

"There's an entity following you," Strand said sharply, looking around. Eve turned. Although there was nothing but a thick mist behind her and the vague outline of trees, a murky reflection of the forest beyond, the hairs at the nape of Eve's neck wouldn't settle.

"The man brings in his wake a terrible fear," Strand continued, "and promise of violence. In Sanctuary, we are all a bit psychic. The sacred space itself was made from the sheer force of spirit ages ago, made not from mythic creatures but human hearts. We *know* that man means us harm and I will not have it find us."

"Albert Prenze."

"Yes, he hates us. Not us specifically, but ghosts. And he's following you."

"Yes. My precinct has been working his case," Eve said. Strand opened the arched door of Sanctuary just wide enough for their bodies and hurried Eve in, closing it behind her to stand in a shadowy entrance foyer of grey stone arches and colored light. "His irrational hatred of ghosts stems from family torment. I don't know what purpose could be served by terrorizing you here."

"You've led him to us," murmured a voice from the shadows in a light African accent. A young woman stepped into the light cast by a bay of quatrefoil stained-glass windows over the front door, dressed in the same blue habit as Lily Strand, her brown face framed by the white of her wimple, her dark eyes wide and worried.

"Mara, please, Sister," Lily said in a low voice. "Eve has only ever wanted to help. That's why I called out to her in the first place. I trust this living one."

"You can trust my whole team," Eve insisted.

"But none of them know what we need *here*," the woman continued, anxious. "You can't know the ways in which we are vulnerable, and your presence only tears at our fabric."

"Mara, please, light candles if you fear a breach," Lily insisted.

The young woman glided away, small hands dancing nervously at the sides of her habit. Eve followed her, wanting to reassure her as she hurried away. She stepped forward under the archway of the foyer and into the nave, but Mara disappeared into a side chapel.

Eve glanced up at the stained-glass windows of the main sanctuary. The windows changed since last Eve had seen them; the structure altered itself in mysterious ways. She had recalled the windows featuring angels, but now human forms shone from them in all manner of dress, region, tradition, and time period. Was the light beyond their leaded images indeed darkening?

"My apologies," Lily said to Eve, following her gaze toward the windows. "My Sisters are uncomfortable for a living soul to come and go from here, and for the company outside. The growing storm. The threat that Prenze represents. Cruel hearts like his, forged by troubles I can't claim to know, seem to find purpose in disturbing the hard-fought peace of other souls. His hatred of spirits is most particular and personal. This places you in a precarious situation."

"You can't think *me* the enemy?" Eve asked in a pained gasp. She'd done so much for the spirit world all her life, taken it into her mind, listened to all its whispers when ghosts threatened to split her mind in two. She'd forsaken a higher education due to their pressure to keep them first, so she opened the Ghost Precinct and remained self-taught, she'd devoted her life—

Lily Strand put both hands on Eve's shoulders as if she could hear this runaway train of frustration.

"Of course not. I know you to be our biggest ally. It's what's around you. If Prenze is manipulating you here, it's likely to see if he can wedge in after you. If he were to get in..." Lily shuddered. "I worried enough about little Ingrid's body and the undertaker. But that disrespect was nothing compared to Prenze's abject hatred of spirits. I leave it to you and your gifted friends to stop him outside. I'll do what's necessary here on the inside. Though I will say, we need every living being who treasures spirits to lend us their love for the amount of protection needed."

Lily gestured to the nearest Sanctuary window. "These are the images of our helpers, gifted living folks who are attuned to the veil. Her Holiness, our foundress, asked Sanctuary's Living Light to reach out to those who can help us weather storms."

The nearest window struck Eve to the core; the leaded glass portrayed a woman in contemporary dress of light blue, but the rest of her was entirely without pigment. Hair and skin white as snow, her ice-blue eyes sparkled and her smile was kind. Radiant white light artfully shone from behind her in leaded strokes as if her whole body was lit. A stunning, ethereal vision. While Eve didn't recognize the woman, she desperately wanted to know her. One of Gran's earliest Spiritualist lessons had been to declare that powerful women were keeping ghostly balances steady all around the world; she and Eve were but two actors on a grand, mysterious stage.

"She's our best living asset, that one," Lily said, following Eve's gaze to the stained-glass portrait. "You're not the only gifted conduit to the dead, Eve." She gave a teasing smile. "And we need *all* of you here, at the end of an era, to be sure we're all not torn apart, to lend your lights. But as for you, go on; you've been here long enough. You'll have worried whoever came after you this time."

The deaconess returned Eve to the front door. Glancing out a beveled glass lancet window, she exclaimed, "Ah! It's the mortal whose faithful heart created this portal! Go on!"

Eve turned back to the nave to see several Sisters heaving great shutters over the Gothic arched windows, closing over loving, saintly looking faces from all around the world, battening down before a storm.

"It's getting worse, my friend," Lily said sadly. Thunder rolled in the distance. "Take care out there as we take care in here."

It was as if the whole spirit world shouted it at her in a thousand accusatory murmurs: *"Don't let anything in!"* Eve clapped her hands over her ears for the furor of it.

The deaconess heaved open the great wooden door, and as the light beyond blinded Eve and she raised her arms against it, the woman placed both hands on Eve's shoulders and pushed her forward into the brilliant void.

Eve fell again, that dizzying lurch and queasy pain distinct to this out-of-body experience, praying she'd come to again in one piece. She'd had quite enough of going unconscious and waking up without remembering the journey. For someone who loved to be in as much control as a paranormal life allowed, this was a fresh hell and terrifying new habit.

When she opened her eyes, would he be waiting for her? Albert Prenze? Had he been the one to drive her here, or was it her own unconscious, powerful desire to drink in the divine mysteries of Sanctuary mortals were not supposed to understand?

A shadowy figure suddenly obscured all ethereal light. She knew that form. It had been at her window. A torment. The astral projection of Albert Prenze's energy had been appearing to her of late, uninvited and unwelcome.

"I renounce thee!" Eve shouted to the enemy at the gates.

She snapped her energy out from her like a whip, and the figure vanished. Eve's knees struck a soft bed of leaves, pine needles, and moss.

"Hello, dear," came a familiar, kind voice from behind.

Eve, bent and kneeling, whirled her head around to see a tall, striking, and elegant woman of nearly seventy.

Regal and fierce, Evelyn Northe-Stewart stood before her: powerful psychic, paranormal counselor, medium, philanthropist, visionary, and most of all, Eve's best friend, ally, and grandmother. Wearing a magnificent House of Worth day dress with doubled green skirts and a royal-blue jacket with gold embroidery, her waves of white hair were swept up beneath a satin hat with flourishes, feathers, and tulle. Seeing the woman for whom she was named was like dawn breaking after a long, dark night.

"Gran!" Eve tried to run to her beloved mentor, but her body didn't cooperate. She fell on a bed of leaves. When one entered Sanctuary, it was the soul that went through while the body remained lifeless behind. The reconnection was dizzying. Eve empathized with Frankenstein's monster, waking up to an unwieldy body awkwardly made.

Rushing up, Gran brought Eve to her feet. The distinct lines of her face were distinguished and thoughtful rather than old or worn. A widening expression accentuated the deepest lines, those around her smile. "I know, my dear, that the detective came for you last time, despite all spirits' warnings not to. I know I can hardly make up for his handsomeness"— Gran added with a laugh—"*or* your attraction to him—"

Eve's face went red as she tried to stay stable on her feet. "I am—I have no such—"

"You're a gifted psychic but a *terrible* liar, Eve Whitby, and I raised you to be exactly so. I do see through everything."

Eve's twisting stomach had nothing to do with the fall from Sanctuary and everything to do with how much she cared for Jacob Horowitz, dashing detective and unexpected suitor. She had to change the subject lest he become her entire undoing. "Gran, how did you find me?"

"You're not about to leave my house unannounced and under mesmeric influence without my following. I was furious with myself the last time you tore out here on your own." She tapped her temple. "Ever since then, I've been fine-tuning our connection."

Eve grimaced. "That…shouldn't be your responsibility, I don't want to be a charity—"

Gran clucked her tongue. "My dearest namesake, you're being targeted by a villain and if I don't intervene, your poor mother… She'll never forgive either of us. Now come away from here." She fussed with Eve's coat, closing it more securely before guiding her out of the clearing.

"Now, when you were returning to yourself," Gran continued, "I know you weren't issuing a renunciation to *me*, my dear, so who did you see beyond? Did Prenze loom at you again?"

"I thought so," Eve murmured, brushing detritus from her skirts. "He vanished after I renounced."

At the edge of the wood Gran paused, looking back toward the glade. "That this place proved meaningful after all… I've tried my whole life to create and fund sacred spaces. That I made one just out of my *intent* for a chapel, carving out a link to the spirit world, is an honor. An awe-inspiring legacy." Gran frowned. "That someone should be trying to tear open what I have hoped to make transcendent, to hurt what should be hope, to intrude between the spirit world and the divine..."

"The Sisters inside Sanctuary are shoring up all the windows and bolstering their ties to living psychics around the world," Eve said. "They're very worried. They don't want me to accidentally let anything in. I was pushed back out, to you."

"We have to do better about shielding," Gran declared.

"And warding," came another distinctive voice from the edge of the wood. Eve turned to behold a striking figure. An array of golden silk accentuated the eerie, piercing quality of gold-green eyes. Clara Templeton Bishop was a powerful psychic in her own right, and she intimidated Eve fiercely. In her late forties, Clara was a woman of hard angles, sharp points, and careful boundaries. Her crepe hat and its gossamer veil were crowned with large, gold-painted thistles, as if her fashion served to deter anyone without a delicate, decorous touch from getting too close to spiny edges.

Hair in braids, a coil was carefully pinned to hang low over one ear to hide a terrible scar Gran had instructed Eve to never notice, which only made her wonder more. Gran and the Bishops were psychic veterans of international wars. Eve wished there was a way she could better honor their service. But like many who served, after a war, they didn't want to talk about it. Ever.

Clara was attuned to raw power; her gifts tapped into ley lines, the primal sources of spiritual energy. "The latitude and longitude of Earth's eldest spiritual energy," Gran once explained. Manipulating ley lines made Clara's body react in painful or epileptic extremes. But her sheer presence was as unmistakable and echoing as the ringing of some huge carillon.

"Mrs. Bishop," Eve exclaimed, her face again coloring. She wanted to impress the woman but always felt awkward in her consuming presence. "I didn't know..."

"When Evelyn ran after you, she instructed her staff to call me." Clara smiled pleasantly. "I do live just up the hill, you know. I suppose I ought to have a read on the both of you now." She tapped her temple as Gran had done, the psychic indication of tracking an important soul, like following mental footprints. It was Clara that Eve had gone to in order to find Gran when she was abducted at the beginning of their current case.

"I'm so sorry to be a bother," Eve whispered, dropping her gaze to the gravel path.

"No, it's good, really," Clara said brightly. "If I don't use my powers regularly, then when I do, they cause pain. Just like stretching a muscle, one must make sure their gifts remain flexible, lest I turn brittle and snap to bits." She turned toward Eve, her voice softening. Her intense presence didn't negate her kindness. "You force me not to turn away from the world but toward the better parts of it. Being tuned to you is no bother. Everyone's got a bit of a musical pitch to them if I put my mind to it." She stepped closer, cocking her head to the side. The tulle of her veil fluttered in the breeze as her silk skirts rustled against leaves on the path's floor. "You're *very* gifted and have a fair handle on your talents, so the note of your spirit is a pleasant one."

"Well, thank you," Eve murmured, cheeks scarlet, not knowing what else to say.

"What was *in* this wood with you, on the other hand, was terribly discordant."

"Did you see Albert Prenze?" Eve asked. "He's been dubbed 'the shadow man' by the spirit world. A hatred of spirits that began with his mother is now a dark obsession."

"I didn't see a negative, hateful energy, but I felt it," Clara replied. "I heard it. Once I was able to sense your spirit returning from across the veil, I could hear your renunciation, your banishing of him. You did a nice job shielding. I merely boosted your vehemence with my own energy."

"I greatly appreciate your support, Mrs. Bishop. I'm always trying to hone my gifts, but I've been stumbling lately. I'm sorry I wasn't strong enough to keep from being led here as if on strings. I don't know—"

"Not a single apology from you," Clara interrupted, lifting a finger. "You're still learning. No one can predict what will befall them in careers like ours. We are, by unfortunate nature, reactive. Circumstances push us into trials by fire."

Despite being the leader of her own department, Eve couldn't help feeling untrained and out of her depth.

Clara gestured up the lane. "Care for lunch? Our Sikh friends from the embassy were just visiting, and our kitchen is still benefiting from their generosity and knowledge. My energy work has become increasingly sensitive to eating meat of any kind; I can taste the death itself, so I'm grateful for vegetarian recipes. I'm trying to learn as many as I can."

Eve's stomach roiled, not the least of which at the casual mention of tasting death. "I'm sure I should eat, but I've no appetite for it."

Gran put one arm around Eve and reached toward Clara, grabbing the woman's thin hand. "Could I beg you and Rupert to come teach the girls how *better* to shield themselves?"

"Yes." Clara nodded. "A critical lesson. Your girls have what it takes, but you must be stronger. And Rupert's the very best in this regard."

Eve was surprised to hear Clara's husband's name. As far as Eve knew, he didn't usually involve himself in the paranormal; he kept to the business of embassies and ambassadors.

"Yes, Rupert too," Clara added, as if reading Eve's mind. Maybe she had. "Didn't you know he's a mesmerist?" Clara's tone implied Eve should have known better. "Go on to the train. The light is brightening and that isn't good for either of our eyes. I'll talk with Rupert. Tonight will be best. There's no time to waste in matters like these."

"Agreed." Gran gestured to the glade. "This dear place should be warded too, if you wouldn't mind, Clara. I worry for the thin barrier between worlds beyond if there isn't something helping it stay strong from our side and on our behalf."

"Indeed. I'll send Rupert to ward the arch. I'd best not be near the thin veil myself, but I agree it should be protected from disruption by darker energies."

Eve turned at a nearby sound. A delivery truck. Two workers in suspenders and shirtsleeves, caps low over their sweaty faces, with a large wooden spool on the side of the road ahead, were filling dirt over a line in shallow ground.

"What's that about?" Eve asked.

Clara shrugged. "Another telephone line up the lane? It's growing exponentially: technology, the sprawl of the city. Won't be quiet here much longer...." Clara's smile looked forced as she clapped her gloved hands. "Well then, go and ready your girls for our visit!"

With a whirl of golden fabric, Clara strolled off toward a line of bright maples in the end of their autumn splendor. Beyond those red and golden leaves lay the Bishops' home and a striking view of the Hudson River.

New York City loomed further down the line, and Eve knew she had to get back to protect it, whether it knew it needed her help or not.

Chapter Two

"I'm paying for a private compartment," Gran stated, patting Eve's shoulder and stepping up to a uniformed conductor. After she had a few quiet words with him, he gestured toward a compartmentalized car. Gran put her arm around Eve and walked her further up the platform. "The hem of your nightdress is hanging out from under your coat, and I just don't want people to think the worst of you, dear."

"Again…" Eve muttered. Another sleepwalking episode, another layer of distrust to add to her roster of recent mishaps.

"Your precinct colleagues are still resting and relaxing at my home as you left them," Gran continued, letting Eve step up the train car steps ahead of her. "We'll go there first. You will prepare them for tonight's lesson, which should be done at *your* collective home, to maximize the protective impact."

"Yes, Gran, thank you." Eve accepted her help to the compartment and sunk onto a cushioned bench. Gran slid the wooden doors with etched-glass flourishes closed and took a seat opposite.

Gran had the gentlest, most sensible way of explaining the next course of action. Eve might be the leader of the recently founded Ghost Precinct, but when Gran decided to give orders, Eve knew better than to disobey. Even if Gran might not have been granted the ability to see and hear spirits in the same constant, consistent way Eve was, her instincts were preternatural, her resources vast, and her experience lifelong.

As the train began rolling south, Eve stared out the curtained window and closed her eyes, the flash of bright sun through trees making her dizzy. Clara was right; it was prime light for a migraine if she wasn't careful.

She wished more than anything that when she got back, Jacob Horowitz would be awaiting her in Gran's parlor. Just seeing his handsome face, all striking angles until he offered a radiant smile, put her at ease. He was such a comfort. Her mind and heart reached out for him.

"Would you like me to call for the detective, then, your sweetheart?" Gran asked casually.

Eve's eyes shot open to behold Gran staring at her with maternal warmth. That was the trouble with being close to talented psychics: keeping secrets was difficult.

"Good God, was my mind really that *loud* about it?"

"Yes, sorry, I thought you'd actually spoken it." Gran laughed. "I didn't mean to be presumptuous—"

"Actually then, yes." Eve sighed. "When we return, once I've spoken to the girls, I should invite him for the lesson. He should know I sleepwalked again. I will need all my close associates to help me be responsible for my own whereabouts. How embarrassing."

"May I ask a question that I believe will affect your protections?"

"Yes…"

"Is he still courting you as a ruse to keep your and his parents from arranging unwanted marriages? Or have you indeed stopped fooling yourself that you don't care for him?" Gran asked. Eve sat back against the cushion of the carriage, frowning. "Again," Gran continued, "I don't mean to be presumptuous. What you say will remain confidential between us. But if your heart is tied to his, it may be used against you. We need to be aware of any vulnerability that may be exploited."

Eve blinked. Her breath caught in her throat. "He…would be used against me?"

"Much as I was used against you," Gran said gravely, referencing the abduction at the beginning of this whole, entwined, and complicated case. "I don't want to worry you, but I can't ignore my instincts. He needs to look out for himself as much as for you."

Eve sighed. It was almost too much to bear. When she and Gran had first dreamed up the Ghost Precinct, back when a seemingly unrelated sequence of details that several ghosts were fixated on—clothes, appointments, ledgers, property—ended up leading to the resolution of two unsolved murder cases, the spirit world had made their usefulness clear. All she had to do was listen, the spirits said, and their worlds would better balance the scales of justice.

That she and her loved ones could become embroiled in danger, the target of violence and deception, hadn't occurred to her. The awesome weight of responsibility fell heavy on shoulders that were too young to feel so weary.

She let the beauty of the surroundings comfort her, giving the great city ahead some of her worry, letting New York fritter her anxiety away in the course of its waking, bustling pace.

As they wound further south along the picturesque bend of the Hudson River, the distance between towns closed and the density grew until church spires and beaux arts rafters multiplied and coalesced in a blur of stories and ever-climbing structures testing the limits of architectural technology.

The city had changed so much in her nineteen years that she could hardly keep up. New buildings were springing up all along the distance between Sleepy Hollow and the northern reaches of what was now New York City, the five-borough consolidation having gone into effect the previous year. Trees were giving way to taller stories, new Bronx housing developments in brick and sandstone, fitted with exterior grandeur even if their interiors were less so.

And yet, undeveloped swaths lay between, New York ever a patchwork quilt of people, economies, architecture, disparate styles and languages, visible between shop signs, audible in shouts of delivery and connection, the world coming together in one city—not to melt away but to add another layer. New York was a never-static geographic, geomorphic wonder. Eve wondered how the spirits managed to sort it all out and not go mad from the pace of change as they remained distinct products of their ages.

There they all were: ghosts floating along in their greyscale glory, all in various states of intensity, some in sharp focus, others blurry, deepening the sense of time and change as their appearance and fashion were as varied as the personal stories Eve could only guess at. The dead wafted along their spectral paths, tethered to the living or to a place they loved, or to something still left undone, each with a different movement and motivation.

Between patches of buildings and population lay the incredible Hudson River Valley beyond: the backdrop of great scope and captivating heart, a magical place that made Washington Irving invent worlds here. But none of Irving's fanciful Knickerbocker notions or historical revisionism was a lie when it came to the beauty of the winding river or New Jersey's dramatic cliffs. Nature's grander scale offered Eve necessary perspective; her enemy was one small man who wanted to make himself far bigger. The whole world, and its spectral echo, was open for her to counter him.

Encouragingly, ghosts turned as she passed, nodding their heads. She'd set to rest many of late. Her service to spirits that had been silenced and desecrated had earned her a deal of respect in the realm that had once made her feel henpecked and assaulted. Becoming their champion had saved many souls. Finding purpose in this mission had saved Eve from being broken by youthful melancholy during spectral onslaught.

Elevated rail lines screeched overhead, and the clatter of carriages merging into a widening lane provided a cacophony that had been so absent in the forest glade. The city was pressing, a symphonic assault on all senses, and Eve didn't blame Mrs. Bishop for moving away from it as her own Sensitivities changed.

After alighting at the raucous Grand Central Depot and returning via carriage with Gran to her grand Fifth Avenue townhouse, by the light of richly colored Tiffany stained glass, Eve hung her coat in the entrance hall and spoke quietly. "Let me take a moment to collect myself before I speak with the team. I'm afraid they won't trust me after this, not after a second time," she said ruefully. "A leader can't be so unreliable and unpredictable as this...." She turned toward the stairs.

"Take your time. They'll still trust you. No one is perfect. And..."—Gran came close and cupped Eve by the neck, looking into her eyes—"perhaps I didn't do you any favors as you grew up, telling you that you were the most talented medium I'd ever known. Perhaps I gave you an unrealistic expectation of yourself. The level of your gifts doesn't mean you're infallible. Certainly not invincible."

Eve nodded, but the sentiment didn't make her feel better or more confident.

She turned at the top of the carpeted stairs and down the wood-paneled hall to a boudoir at the end of the upstairs hall designated hers when she was a child: decorated in a calming green spectrum of emerald brocades, ornate, floral, flocked wallpaper, and mint damask.

Glancing at the vanity mirror, she noted the grass stains on her dress from her stumbles by the archway. Feeling like a scattered mess didn't mean she needed to look the part.

Standing vigil in the corner of the mahogany wardrobe were a few staples Gran kept fresh for her, and she changed into a simple charcoal-grey linen walking dress with black ribbon trim, pausing to sit at the vanity table and adjust her thick black locks. Her generally sickly looking complexion had taken on more color these days since knowing Detective Horowitz. Just being near him brought out a rosy blush, but these fresh events shook her pallid once more.

Dashing the faintest hint of rosewater behind her ears and over her wrists, she chided herself not to fuss further. She had to prepare her team for tonight's instruction no matter her shaken confidence.

Returning to the wood-paneled hall whose upper wall was filled with art purchased from Metropolitan Museum shows, she was glad her grandfather was out yesterday evening at one of his innumerable soirees, all the better so he wasn't there to witness Prenze's unsettling visit. Grandpa Stewart had gone in the morning to his Met office, entirely missing the troubling events coming and going. He didn't worry for her like her mother did, but neither needed any fodder.

Crossing the upstairs hall, Eve found their youngest member Jenny at the other end, tucked into a small bed, recovering from illness brought on by psychic backlash from Albert Prenze, his energy and presence a contagion for the nine-year-old orphan. A cold compress lay on her forehead, a bowl of soup cupped in her small hands. A tray of china and a silver tureen indicated the girls had been taking care and dining in these rooms since last evening.

This small, sickly girl in a large fancy room reminded Eve of the moment Jenny arrived on Eve's doorstep a year prior, dead parents floating just behind the sudden orphan's shaking form. The ghosts asked Eve if she could take in their daughter "gifted with the Sight" whose cheeks were stained with tears. Eve did.

Feeling any better? Eve asked Jenny in American Sign Language.

A little, Jenny signed back and returned to her soup.

When Jenny lost her parents, Selective Mutism crept in to steal her voice. She could whisper on occasion if she worked hard to overcome the panic, but considering Eve's mother, Natalie, once suffered from the same condition also related to a childhood trauma, Natalie had raised Eve with sign as a second language and tutored Jenny until she was proficient as well. No one pressured the child to try to speak unless she wanted to, and the ghosts that involved themselves with the precinct interacted with her just the same. She would speak when she would and when she could. Everything in due time.

Jenny lay on one side of an adjoining suite with open pocket doors, Antonia and Cora having shared the other side during the night. Everyone must have slept fitfully as both women were now napping, one on a divan and the other on a settee. Eve looked at her team, and her heart swelled that she should be so fortunate to have such gifted mediums as these as colleagues.

Cora Dupris, leaning her kerchiefed head back on a velvet-covered divan, was the first member of the Ghost Precinct to find Eve, after a vision told her to leave her Creole family behind in New Orleans and join Eve in New York. Two years younger than Eve, Cora was focused, steeled, impressively mature, and kept Eve on her toes. Her psychometric powers of touching an object and seeing its past had grown exponentially, and the talent was critical in their cases. At the moment, Cora rested with her gloves on, a trick to keep her powers dormant when they weren't being used. All of them had been overtaxed of late.

Across the room, Antonia Morelli's tall, lithe form was draped over a settee with more grace than Eve could ever manage, her long, dark hair unpinned and hanging in a braid down her side. She, too, had come to Eve's doorstep, with her own circumstances in tow, having fled a family that could not accept her for who she truly was; a woman. As gifted a Sensitive as the rest of them, ghosts that were looking after Antonia's well-being suggested she seek out Eve in hopes of employment. The moment Eve greeted that feminine soul at the door, Antonia admitted that spirits guided her there. She proved herself in an immediate séance, seamlessly becoming part of their team. She was their resident scholar, always researching the latest trends in divination.

Their living precinct thereafter was fully formed. Gran remained the core asset that had suggested the entire Ghost Precinct idea to begin with, making the constant, incessant chatter of the dead into something useful. The shift had made a certain lasting peace with the spirit world as one of the primary yearnings of a ghost was to be seen and heard.

Little Zofia wafted into the room and floated beside Eve. "It happened again, didn't it?" the child asked. "Wandering off?" The child had an uncanny read on all of them.

"Yes," Eve said. "It's very worrying."

"You're not the only one." Zofia floated up to look Eve directly in the eye, her transparent form wavering slightly as a breeze from one open window at the end of the hall rustled the lace curtain behind her. "I couldn't find Maggie so I floated to where she'd gone before she disappeared."

"The Prenze mansion?"

"Yes. There are ghosts trapped on the ground floor. In the basement."

"Why did she return?" Eve asked, worried. "Did she know there were trapped ghosts?"

"No, that's new to us. She stopped me from going in to help."

"Good. Whatever Prenze is doing there is dangerous to ghosts."

Zofia looked down at the luxurious floral carpeting. "You know how I am, if I see someone who needs help... If I see someone who needs to get out... Eve, they can't get out, you know..." The child trailed off.

"I know you'd do anything, I know, my little hero," Eve said, reaching out to the cold air. "I don't know how you do it, face your trauma so bravely."

The ghost shrugged. "You choose not to think about the things you fear in order to do the things you must. I have to pretend a fire isn't a fire, even if I rush into them to help other children. Even though I know the blaze can't hurt me anymore, every time, I have to pretend the flames are instead feathers."

Eve put a hand to her mouth, eyes watering at this. "You are an inspiration, my dear."

Zofia smiled broadly, her greyscale cheeks dimpling, and Eve wished for a yearning moment she could have known the happy glow that must have brightened her once olive-toned skin. The thought that this girl could have ever been in the agony of death gutted Eve every time she thought about it.

As if intuiting her melancholy, Zofia patted her hand, which translated to little puffs of cold air. "Remember, I was lost to the smoke before anything took my body," she offered. "It's as if you sense pain and suffering, even if there wasn't any. I see it on your face every time. Don't let your empathy get away with you."

"My *wise* little hero."

Zofia smiled again before lifting a finger in the air. "Oh, I forgot! Maggie got an idea while she was looking at the cellar and wanted me to tell you not to worry if she's gone awhile, experimenting."

Eve raised an eyebrow. "Experimenting?"

"She wouldn't say on what."

"Probably because I'd tell her no," Eve muttered. "She never did commit to our procedures, especially not Preventative Protocol. I've had to give up on it. I like the idea of stopping things before they begin, but it creates quite the moral quandary."

"Maggie lets the mystery of spirit guide her," Zofia said, sounding so much older than her years, but then again, she was older than she appeared. "We can't always follow the rules of the living. Sometimes we must follow the wind."

And with that, the spirit vanished and Eve immediately wanted her back, to feel her, see her, try to take her hand. Privately, Eve hoped if she spent enough time with spirits she loved, perhaps she could easily step into their plane and give them a hug now and again. She'd keep trying.

Having gotten out of bed, Jenny put her soup on the cart stocked with provisions. Prepared for any eventuality, Gran kept her guest rooms filled with anything anyone would need, as if manning a grandly appointed fort during times of siege.

I bet Maggie's trying to find a different way in, Jenny signed, returning to the bed as Eve went to her side to tuck her back in. Putting a hand to her forehead, Eve noticed Jenny was warm but not dangerously so.

Eve nodded. *I hope she does it safely,* she replied in sign. While Jenny could hear just fine, Eve liked to keep up the practice of signing.

I was trying to read Prenze's aura when he came in to call on Gran, Jenny explained. *Everything was sickly grey. It wasn't Dr. Font's fault. His spirit didn't make me sick when he appeared. He's nice. When Albert showed back up alive, Font feared he'd accidentally covered up a murder.*

The doctor who had signed off on Albert Prenze's death certificate had visited Jenny in words and visions. Dr. Font's mysterious death in the Dakota building was a case Detective Horowitz had been working, and it seemed the doctor had gotten wrapped up in the darker side of the Prenze practice. Whatever Alfred Prenze had proudly built in restorative tonics, his twin brother Albert Prenze was now steeped in dark edges and cult dealings.

"We must call a séance for Font in the office," Eve said. "Until New York allows ghosts on the witness stand, he needs to give us something tactile."

As Eve was speaking quietly, she heard the rustling of fabric to the side of the room.

"Apologies for the late morning," Antonia said, her voice breathy and gentle. She put a hand over her mouth to stifle a yawn. "We all slept terribly. And if I'm not mistaken, so did you. I thought I heard pacing out in the hall."

"Yes." Eve gulped. "I didn't have a good night or morning either."

She debated not telling them. If they were asleep, they wouldn't have missed her, but Cora, who had also roused, after rubbing her eyes stared at Eve with an intense scrutiny. Eve had long ago promised them she'd never lie to them, that lies would not be tolerated in a team so close-knit. They were each tied to one another in energy, intuition, and life; a team that lived together in Eve's side of "Fort Denbury." Withholding would become an unraveling thread, and her Sensitives would sense it all.

Both of these women, full of their own special strengths and resilience, had Eve questioning herself, wondering if she shouldn't turn the leadership over to the stalwart Cora. At the same time, she didn't want either friend to face additional dangers by being at the head. She had always wanted to bear the brunt of any criticism or threat, and even more so now. The spirits had designated her to be the one to take a hit, and she had the most privilege among them to do so. But they all needed to be rallied, not to mention prepared for tonight's lesson in protection.

"My dears, I want to thank you for your tireless efforts, one day into the next," Eve said, standing up and shifting to be able to look at all three of her colleagues. "Each day has felt like a lifetime. You have not complained, or balked, and I am so utterly impressed by and bolstered by you."

"We're glad you push us to the limits," Cora said. "It proves what all we can manage."

"Yes, it does, and I hope you feel appreciated, because we'll need every strength and talent to counter a powerful adversary we can only take down with the utmost tact and discretion, by assembling all our pieces and proof. We'll regroup tonight, as there's more to learn and discuss...." She trailed off, swallowing hard, fumbling for words and stalling the inevitable. "Thank you again for putting up with what hasn't been my best week, in terms of my presence of mind, to put it generously." Eve's cheeks colored. "I...you know I can't bear it when I lose my composure, so I'm sure you can imagine how mortified I am...."

You're human too, Jenny signed, reaching out for a glass of water that was too far from her reach. Eve chuckled and brought it to her.

"Don't be hard on yourself," Cora said. "You've held up impressively, and I know you've done so battling migraines the whole time."

"Yes, but you don't know the latest..." Eve sighed. "I wandered out again, before dawn.... I came to at Sanctuary."

Cora exhaled. "Again?"

"I wish it weren't true. This time, Gran came after me. Clara Bishop too. She and her husband are coming to the house tonight to teach us about psychic shielding."

"Good. I want to know every possible trick," Antonia said with scholarly relish. "A healthy psychic life is one with myriad weapons in one's arsenal."

"They may bring wards of protection, too, so be prepared," Eve instructed. "I don't know what they'll need of us, so just follow their leads. I've a lot to learn from them, and, considering they were never allowed over for dinner, I'm making up for lost time."

"Why were your parents so strict about not allowing them by?" Antonia asked. "I mean, I know from your parents' trauma that they don't entertain and certainly don't *enjoy* the paranormal, but it's not like that's all anyone would talk about. Those of us who work in spectral realms don't live it every moment of the day."

Eve sighed. "I know. It always baffled me, especially considering the Bishops are so close with Gran. But I think it was the Bishops drawing my father back into a supernatural investigation, when he'd promised to walk away from anything of the sort. That, in my mother's eyes, must have been unforgivable."

"My parents won't speak of that time either, with the former Eterna Commission," Cora said, shaking her head. "Even Uncle Louis, when his ghost comes to visit and guide, he won't talk about his death or anything surrounding it. I know how maddening it is, Eve, to be curious, and to have your questions rebuffed. Those who wish to no longer be haunted sure do create ghosts out of their own anxiousness."

Eve laughed hollowly. "I'm glad you understand how it is to deal with supernatural veterans of other wars. All the battle scars they refuse to acknowledge. Thank you."

"You should have Detective Horowitz come to tonight's lesson." Antonia rose to pin her long, dark hair into a top bun with hairpins from the dresser and smoothed the faint hints of rouge on her high cheekbones. "He needs to know any tactic we learn, and as you've said, he seems to be gaining a bit of his own sixth sense. Maybe just about *you*, but he's intuitive." At this, Eve cleared her throat. Antonia chuckled. "I'll cook."

At this, Eve could see both Cora's and Jenny's shoulders relax at the offer. The team tried to share all tasks equally in rotation, but Eve didn't have to be Sensitive to know they barely choked back what she herself made. Antonia was a sorceress in the kitchen with even the barest ingredients. As if her scholarship wasn't enough; she excelled at the role of mothering them all.

Eve looked to Cora, silently asking permission to invite the detective. Cora smiled. "He is part of our team now, Eve. And he is a very good man. However, do sort yourselves out; settle what's unsettled because otherwise you're a distracted disaster and that's no good to us."

Called to account for her recent dramatics, Eve's cheeks reddened. She swallowed and nodded. "My wise friends. Take your time and I'll see you back at the house by dinner." It was only morning and there was so much yet to do.

Chapter Three

Mulberry Street Police Headquarters in downtown Manhattan, south of the bustling theatre district and north of the teeming financial district, was a multistoried building situated beside an infamous part of town rife with vice that seemed unperturbed by the law as its neighbor. For so many years the two had existed hand in hand, until now-governor Roosevelt cleaned up the corruption within. There were still cracks in the foundation of the institution, but like everything in New York, it was going through growing pains.

Showing her card at the front entryway, she had to hand over the new access document sent to all the girls by Roosevelt himself after they'd been targeted by threats.

Sending their Ghost Precinct entirely underground, these cards demoted the girls to research and records but allowed them access to any police building in the city. Eve chafed but didn't argue; having a secret job she was proud of was better than being erased from the books and taken off duty entirely. Even so, she still faced a frowning scowl from the patrol officer stationed at the door, as if her very presence in the building was suspect. She wanted her work to be welcomed as a way to ease the tension between the living and the dead, seeing ghosts as a "help, not a horror," but the force would need to accept living women as colleagues first. One step at a time. But she didn't feel patient about it, and she didn't feel she should have to.

Mulberry Street Headquarters' interior was less grand than its façade, and it became more worn the further back from the main entrance one got. So, too, did it get more raucous, the walls less stately and the floors plainer.

In the rear guts of the building were some small offices, converted storage rooms cleared out to house a growing but hesitant interest in new sciences, technologies, and manners of mental and physical study. Alienists were a new concept, studying the patterns and possible motivations of the human mind. The new process of fingerprinting was in the stumbling stages of becoming routine. Eve found the possibilities exciting and was glad when any department kept an open mind.

No one was more sensible about all methods and practice than the man whose office sat before her at the end of the hall, his door open.

Eve stared at Detective Jacob Horowitz, framed in the open doorway of his dimly lit room with its well-worn furniture and stacks of collected case material: papers, bound notebooks and the occasional item from a crime scene that the evidence room seemed to have forgotten but he never did.

He wore a finely tailored black frock coat, dark blue waistcoat, and crisp white neckwear tied in a loose knot. Not required to wear the uniform of a patrol officer on a beat, he dressed in elegant simplicity, a gentleman conducting interviews and professional business who could seamlessly disappear into a crowd from one clue to the next. To Eve, though, he would always stand out.

He looked up. His dark eyes, ringed in striking slivers of blue, suddenly lit. His frown of concentration vanished, his sharp-featured face shifting into a devastatingly handsome expression of delight. His smile nearly lifted Eve off the ground. The growing fire in his gaze at the sight of her made her toes curl in her boots.

They had become something that could no longer be ignored. Steady sparks struck between them had caught. They were now a conflagration.

But the work. The cases came first. As they should. But at some point, what they kept pushing aside might drag them over the edge if they weren't careful. It might become a necessity to let the fire breathe; putting it out didn't seem possible. Eve couldn't imagine dousing it.

Floating to his threshold, she wondered if she appeared ghostly in her approach.

"Hello, Whitby," he murmured fondly, gesturing her forward. "What brings you to me? I'm glad you're here, as I've a *lot* to share with you, but you look...well, lovely, but worried."

"Well...for a start, I want to see you, and I have something to confess."

At this, he rose out of his chair.

Realizing her voice had sounded more sensuous than intended, she continued at a stammer. "I mean...something happened today you need to know about, and you should come by tonight for dinner. And an instruction."

He came around to the side of the desk and approached her. "Are you all right?"

Reaching out, he cupped her elbow in his hand, running his thumb softly over the wool. He managed to touch her in the most caring of ways. Never possessively or too untoward, he won her with small, delicate gestures. Every one unlocked her further, and she feared she'd simply open; in trust and in desire. Her mind swam. Cheeks scarlet, she was grateful for his dim office. Her knees went weak at the thought of such surrender, and he reached out and cupped her other elbow in his hands, steadying her as he searched her for an answer.

"Yes, I..." Her eyes fluttered closed; the sensation of him so near and holding her in such a gentle touch was overwhelming. She debated about lying, but he deserved the truth. "You...affect me...sorry. I nearly forgot what I was going to say. I woke up...came *to*...this morning at Sanctuary again. Driven there, mentally, by Prenze. Whatever read and hold he gained on me through his devices, he's using it and I have to fight it."

"Why Sanctuary? What does he want with that place?"

"I suppose because Sanctuary is a place where spirits have ultimate control? He seems threatened by spirits. Maggie was one of his prisoners, and she escaped only by Sanctuary's intervention. I just have to make sure I'm not aiding the enemy by my own connection to spirits. Not having control over myself is the greatest terror I've ever experienced."

"I can imagine," he said, keeping that soft hold on her. "But you're strong."

"Sanctuary itself has a pull on me too; my soul feels bonded to the place, I just have to be sure if I visit it's on my own terms. So, that's what dinner will be about: psychic shielding and maintaining control." She dared look in his eyes. The fear and anxiety of the morning fell away. In its place, all their near misses threatened to bowl her over. She found herself blurting out, "Not that there...aren't cases when I wouldn't mind...losing a bit of control, I suppose. In the right place. With the right person."

"We'll have to do something about that," he replied in a murmur. A subtle shudder coursed down her body and an overwhelmed little laugh leapt from her lips. "But not now," he cautioned. "Not here. Certainly not in this zoo. I can't be seen embracing you, and I dare not close my door. The higher-ups remain unnerved by me, especially now that I've got other precincts cooperating with me, something they never manage to do well." He stepped closer. "And of course, we've a great deal of casework to do. But something has very nearly happened to us. More than once. I'm sure you know what I mean."

They'd had several, maddening, time-stopping near kisses by this point without *actually* kissing, and Eve felt sure he was thinking of each and every one of those missed opportunities as she did.

"And at this point," he continued, "we must plan for it. I don't want to get caught up in a hasty moment and regret imperfect circumstances. But if we don't...allow ourselves...a moment of affection..." He stared deeply into her eyes and then shifted his gaze to her lips.

"I won't be able to stop myself," Eve breathed.

"And, to be perfectly honest, I wouldn't stop you...."

Her arms itched to seize him, to run her hands through his gentle curls, to press against him so that she could drink him in, feel his wiry strength, press her forehead to his and imagine what he was thinking; one mind to the next....

"So...we'll be intentional, then," Eve said haltingly as noise from the hallway reminded them this was no place for passion, even if she could lose herself in his gaze indefinitely. "Soon." It was a promise that couldn't wait forever. But not here, Jacob was certainly right.

She stepped back, and they both took a deep breath. That she seemed to affect him in just the same way made her heart beat with a joyous thrum. Despite all the fear that came with her work and present cases, this fresh pulse was stronger. Yes, the work came first. Work now. Indulgence later: an earned, sweet reward.

He returned to sit behind his desk, safer to put a barrier between them to keep them from colliding against one another like magnets.

"What was that you were saying about dinner before we got distracted?" He chuckled.

"Please come to my side of Fort Denbury tonight, for dinner and a lesson," Eve said. "The Bishops will be teaching us how better to shield our minds from intrusion and the kinds of projection Albert Prenze has been inflicting on us."

"I'll happily go with you, but since it's many hours until dinner, there are *several* things I'm sure you'd like to see first."

He gestured for Eve to sit opposite him as he opened a file.

"I salvaged this before anyone stating that 'no Whitby works here' could toss it," Horowitz said, sliding a telegram envelope across the desk. "Since you've gone even quieter about your precinct than before, it seems this circled a bit before alighting here."

"Oh, thank you for catching it." Eve glanced at the otherwise unadorned Western Union telegram envelope and then opened the flap.

"If I'm in office," the detective explained, "I try to be present when the mail arrives. *They* call it snooping; *I* call it due diligence, making sure nothing comes in that my colleagues are eager to throw away for not wanting to deal with it."

"It's from Houdini!" Eve exclaimed. "I wrote to him about Mulciber's act, asking if he's seen it or if he had any thoughts about it." She read aloud:

Miss Whitby,
Writing to you on English tour.
Met Mulciber once. Set my teeth on edge. He's not right. Something's disturbed about that act but can't put finger on it. Levitation would be done by levers and angles. Mesmerism: harder to say. Not every audience is a plant. Some want to believe, to be mesmerized, to give over control.
Mulciber ran afoul of infamous, underhanded bookers now touring in England. Ask about Snare & Fiddle. M. swindled plenty. They're the ones still out for him, even though a third party was said to have intervened, they weren't paid in full.
Had a chat with A. Conan Doyle. He and I may start addressing sham acts that prey upon the vulnerable. "Spiritualist" liars when simply magicians. No betraying a magician's vow if none claim they're magicians. I'd be exposing their spiritual lie. Thank you for your inspiration.
H. H.

"Well, that's something," Eve said excitedly. They needed any association to crimes they could get, and she was pleased the magician had been so moved by her desire to see genuine Spiritualism lifted up and the charlatans revealed that he wished to take up the cause.

"I was in touch with Fitton to be sure that Jim Boot, Mulciber himself, was to be watched in custody at all times after what happened to Dupont," Horowitz explained. "Can't have Prenze coercing his associates to trepan themselves in custody. I'd planned on doing further interrogation, and now we've specific names to mention, with no time to waste. Shall we to the Tombs?" He rose to his feet and palmed two official-looking papers. "Then, after that," he added, brandishing the papers with a sparkle in his eyes, "I've more on the case docket if you'd be willing to spend the day with me."

"More than willing," she said eagerly, his smile contagious. Any moment with him was a joy, even if working on the most dreadful tasks.

"Good, then," he said, circling around toward her again.

He held out a hand for her. She took it, and he lifted her up and toward him and the magnetization returned. In this brief moment of closeness, she breathed him in, inhaling his freshness, a pleasant aroma of clean soap and a trace of mint. Her cheeks flooded heat again at the thought of tasting that mint, and as she looked away, he let go. Not here.

Out the office door at a clip, he looked back over his shoulder at her with a tantalizing smile. It was then that she realized how much he was enjoying the temptation of their closeness, testing the boundaries, teasing her at every tense turn, dancing around the edge of control with playful excitement. Driving her endearingly mad. She stared at him incredulously as she rushed to keep up down the long hall and out the headquarters' wide front door.

A few curious spirits bobbed along beside her as she exited the headquarters; she was grateful their chill cooled her blushing cheeks. Once outside, the spirits, like Eve, were accosted by the myriad sights and sounds of New York and were instantly distracted, especially at this curious Mulberry intersection of a finer neighborhood ahead and a vice-ridden area behind. The city existed all at once and on top of itself, constantly active.

A familiar form in shades of grey appeared at her side. "Take care where you're going; it's not a good place for young women," the elderly Vera warned in the street, drawing her floral shawl over thin, transparent shoulders. "The Tombs." The ghost shuddered.

Eve only nodded that she understood, not wanting the detective to think she was afraid of the prison. Her ghosts worried too much.

"What's your angle of attack with Boot?" Eve asked Horowitz.

"Lean on him about a positive identification of Montmartre as Prenze, and to see if he can confirm his involvement in the Arte Uber Alles group as an engineer and architect of suicide. We might not be able to get Prenze *directly* for murder, but by proxy, perhaps.... But now with Houdini's clue, we might do better offering Boot a plea and protection in exchange for information, especially if Scotland Yard wants anything to do with money owed across the pond, we might be able to dance around extradition."

"Smart."

"Once we've hopefully pinned down something damning, we've got an appointment."

"We do? With?"

"Officer Bills and the Irvington area precincts have been surprisingly helpful. All the pretty parts outside the city don't generally like working with our grubby metropolis, but I'm happy when an officer disproves the pattern."

He handed her two papers as they walked. Eve's eyebrows raised at the bold type across the page. "A warrant?"

"*Two* warrants," he corrected with a victorious smile, snatching the warrants back before she could read the addresses and tucking them in an interior breast pocket of his frock coat. "But first things first. This work is nothing if not due process one clue at a time."

Bordered by Franklin, Leonard, and Elm Streets, the Tombs was a massive granite complex of pure Egyptian architecture occupying an entire block, all courts and prison cells. The name arose from its ponderous appearance and funereal associations.

Moving in lockstep, they passed the main entrance on Centre Street, which gave way to a lofty porch supported by numerous stone columns, and turned toward the Bridge of Sighs, so named for the condemned prisoners moving along its path from court of special sessions to the prison itself. Without hesitation, they walked up to the barred and grated door on the Franklin side and, once inside the dark lobby, veered left toward the warden's office. Eve felt a shudder of unease, but she was sure not to show it.

Eve reminded herself that death was not quite so present here as it had been earlier in the century; executions were once held in the central interior courtyard, but since the advent of electrocution, such punishments were now outsourced to Sing Sing or Auburn. Still, many spirits haunted their last moments along the dark hall. There was nothing she could do for them, and thankfully none of them pinpointed her as a channel to try; the weight of guilt sifted them away from her carefully calibrated Sensitivities that tried to block genuinely negative or violent spirits.

These sad souls hung there as mere echoes of their final moments, not full-consciousness spirits like those who worked for the precinct. She said nothing of what she saw to Horowitz, and he didn't ask, only spoke to the front watchman and explained his business.

They were seen to one of the three hundred cells, arranged in tiers one above the other, a corridor through each tier.

Rude and lewd comments from the first few cells near the door—from inmates not expecting a woman to grace their path this morning—Jacob entertained none of it. A man who whistled at Eve through opposite bars as they stood before their quarry received a growling reprimand.

"Shut it or you'll regret it." The detective's tone was so ferocious, the prisoner actually turned away, startled.

Before them, Jim Boot flailed toward the front of his cell, reaching out with shaking fingers ragged from nail-biting.

"I didn't *do* anything, officer, ma'am," Jim Boot pleaded, slurring. He'd managed to make a mess of his sparse bedding; everything looked wet and grimy. Boot wobbled on his feet and gripped the bars. "I was just... *there*.... A body. Everything else moved around me; Heaven and Hell. I was just Purgatory...."

"Is he drunk?" Horowitz turned to the warden who had seen them to the cell.

The warden nodded subtly and matched the detective's low tone lest the other prisoners get any ideas. "Your friend Fitton was very clear that we were to keep him preoccupied and clear of any self-violence. Only way we could do that was keeping him...under."

"I suppose everyone chooses their own form of control or shielding," Eve muttered. "Perhaps that's how Boot managed it all."

"We don't have much time, Mr. Boot," Horowitz began. "We need your cooperation, and you'll fare far better if you give it to us."

"He'll find a way to kill me, you know," Boot said, tapping his head. "I've kept him out, drowned him out, but he's strong sometimes."

"Then you must be strong too, Mr. Boot," Eve said. "You're a commanding performer. We both saw you onstage. You can be that pillar of strength, guiding audiences through Heaven and Hell. Guide us."

Boot straightened and seemed to sober almost instantly; it was unsettling. "Thank you," he murmured. "All I wanted was just to be a performer. I...I fell in with folks I shouldn't have."

"Like Snare and Fiddle?" Horowitz asked. Boot paled and pursed his lips shut. "I hear you owe them."

"I do not. They were paid off."

"Entirely? Seems some folks in London aren't pleased with you. We've got it on good report from a source in your field."

"But...Montmartre took care of it."

"Montmartre paid your debts? To criminals?"

"He paid what I owed," Boot insisted. "And got me work."

"Performing?" Boot nodded. "And what about working with Arte Uber Alles?"

"They were devotees of the work and the art. I was just a figurehead. I just did what they wanted me to do, which was perform. I promise you, the darker stuff, the body parts in the set, the blood as paint... I thought things smelled a bit musty but I didn't know... I guess I didn't want to know...." Boot stared off into the distance.

"Did you ever know Montmartre by another name?" Horowitz asked. Boot shook his head. The detective reached in his coat pocket and withdrew a photo from a newspaper clipping, an article about the Prenze company from a few years back, featuring both twins. Jacob folded down Alfred and put Albert before Boot's face. "Is this Montmartre?"

"Looks mostly like him, but his hair is different. Glasses. Expression." Eve nodded; that checked out.

"Did you have any idea Arte Uber Alles was engaged in experimentation, in *suicide*, in mesmerism and coercion?"

Boot shook his head and began humming. He ran over to a small metal pail and reached in with both hands. Returning, the stink of cheap gin washed over them. "No, no, I was just working the stage."

"Would anyone in London, say, Scotland Yard, be wanting you for questioning regarding those Snare and Fiddle characters? You say Montmartre took care of it, you, but what if he didn't, at least, not entirely? Should we let Scotland Yard know you're in here for collaboration in the desecration of corpses, coercion, and violations of the Bone Bills? Possible accessory to murder? Would they like to trade for you, do you think?"

"They'll kill me over there, and I won't let him in *here* to take me over!" Boot cried, jabbing his finger to his temple. "I want free of this!"

Letting out a sudden shriek, in a bold, startling move, the prisoner slammed his own head against the iron bar between them, causing Eve and Horowitz to jump back. A spurt of blood erupted from the crown of Boot's head as he staggered back and fell down on the wet ground.

Eve looked back at the warden, who just shrugged, as if it wasn't the most jarring thing he'd seen today, or any day in the Tombs.

"Well that's a way to avoid questioning," Horowitz muttered. "If he babbles anything that might be related to what we asked him, please wire me directly." The detective handed the warden his card. The somber, unaffected man nodded. "If you have to move him somewhere padded so he doesn't strike himself dead, do. He's likely wanted for fraud or worse in England and I'm sure you don't want Scotland Yard interfering."

The warden shook his head, holding up his hands. "No, thanks. The more jurisdictions the more confusion."

A fresh yowl and sundry commotion, a furious clatter of chains against bars started up on the second floor of cells. The warden excused himself to tend to the disruption with a heavy sigh. "You can see yourselves out?"

They were glad to.

Exiting, Eve kept pace toe to toe; even though the detective was nearly a head taller, determination was as good a factor in one's pace as height.

"At least there's a solid identification of Montmartre as Prenze," Eve said. "That will correlate well with the Arte Uber Alles writings you collected from families in the Font and Zinne cases mentioning him, yes?" "Indeed. And with trails of money as well. We got something out of it." "What's next?" Eve asked as they walked east along Canal Street at their strident clip. The distinct, rich smells wafting out from Chinatown kitchens grounded her to an important intersection of the vibrant community.

The detective pointed ahead toward Broadway, the angling, ever-bustling central artery they most often used as their pathway uptown. They'd made a preferential habit of walking. Constantly hiring carriages was hardly financially sound, and walking was a way to still be alone, uninterrupted by the clutch of fellow passengers on the elevated rail or a crammed trolley car where Eve had to have a hairpin at the ready to defend against stray hands. Walking afforded two professional people who were having a hard time admitting how much they cared time to be together without the pressures of coming calling.

"Would you like to be more specific than generally leading me uptown?" Eve asked with a smile.

The detective patted his breast pocket. "One of these warrants is to get into Dupont's parlor. After Officer Bills processed Dupont's charge through the Irvington courts, he helped push for an extension of evidence gathering here. The second one is to gain access to Dupont's house."

Eve clapped her hands together. "Brilliant! We went into the parlor, the girls and I, unofficially, but we didn't dare try to break into the home. This is the key to getting anywhere with Prenze; tie him to Dupont's bizarre fetishes and the mysterious deaths of Dr. Font and the blood-let Mr. Zinne. What has Dupont been charged with, officially?"

"Theft and abduction with a few counts of desecration, which was a bit of a stretch considering the bodies hadn't been interred when the souvenirs were taken. There might be a few other charges depending on the Bone Bill statutes, but seeing as those went in to deter grave-robbing full corpses, I don't know if they'll cover blood or 'tokens.' Though considering Dupont's current mental state after the trepanning attack, none of his actions will likely go to trial. He'll be sent to the same island asylum as Heinrich Schwerin."

Eve sighed. "I hope that is enough to bring the spirits and people Dupont unsettled lasting peace. Good work on the warrant. I doubt anything is left behind as I'm sure Prenze has cleaned it all out, but one never knows. I'm still getting accustomed to a trained physical eye, not just my third eye, and looking at these spaces will do me good."

"It's a different way of thinking and seeing, but I know you'll be just as adept at changing the lens."

Eve smiled, touched by his confidence. Coming to consciousness at Sanctuary had rattled her so deeply, she allowed for Jacob's belief in her to reassert her own. This was no time to wither and crumble from within. That was their villain's hope. Psychological warfare waged its worst when the good and gentle were hardest on themselves. "Thank you for that."

"I'm grateful they never assigned me a partner at headquarters," Horowitz said, pausing as they hesitated on the next street corner for a joyful group of lady bicyclists in riding habits to fly by before crossing, continuing north.

"My friend Fitton would have been a great partner," he continued, "if he hadn't been reassigned all the way downtown, but it's worked out for the best." He glanced at Eve. "I'd like to think it's you who've become my partner, de facto, though I know you've a team and precinct of your own...."

"I can be both," Eve said. "I work well with my girls and I...work well with you."

"My liaison between worlds," the detective said with admiration.

Eve wanted to bask in his sentiment but remained angry at herself about her lapse. Hesitating a moment, she allowed herself to be distracted by watching the sequence of passersby from every walk of life, background, and identity, the city street the true equalizer of humankind.

"Did I somehow say something inappropriate?" he asked after many blocks of silence.

"No, no, I'm sorry. It's just that maybe I'm too much so," Eve responded ruefully. "Your liaison between worlds. That's likely what Prenze hopes of me. I think Prenze was pushing me to Sanctuary in hopes of gaining access himself, to do damage."

The detective frowned. "As Sanctuary is a place of rescue and respite for ghosts, I can imagine his hatred of hauntings would make him want to strike there, but if he can..."—the detective searched for the term—"astral-project himself, why not just try accessing Sanctuary on his own? Why involve you? Just to try to prove some sort of control over you?" The detective's frown deepened, a storm in his eyes.

"Yes, precisely that, I hate to say. Not only to remind me I'm under ongoing threat but to make me think I'm a danger to those I love and am called to serve. He wouldn't be let into Sanctuary on his own. The denizens are careful; they've a clear sense of a lurking shadow with malevolent intent. It's a broach of their rules to let me, a living soul, in as it is, and they're battening down their hatches. They were literally shuttering their windows against a storm."

"It's such a fascinating place, Sanctuary," Jacob said, recalling his experiences with her at that spiritual precipice. "I can't say I've actually been fully through *into* it, but trying to reach you there, when I grabbed you, lifted you, and bid you return to me, I was overtaken by a blinding light. For a moment I saw grand onyx columns, with arched capitals of gold, just like in my temple, and I could hear the most *beautiful* cantor singing. The vision was partial, vanishing when you came to at my side. But it was an incredible awakening to spectral occurrences that honored my culture in turn."

Eve sighed softly, following him as he turned onto Fourteenth Street. "It is a blessing to hear what you saw. I am affirmed that Sanctuary bends to the sacred architecture and rites most familiar to those who seek it. And it speaks so well of you Jacob, of your heart, that it opened light to you and knew you. Sanctuary did not see you as a threat. Lily Strand, my guide there, did say you were my tether, and that your heart was radiant."

He beamed, as if showcasing the very quality. Even despite all the fear and frustration of late, the fact that she felt so buoyant in his presence, that he seemed so happy in hers, was something priceless, unfathomable in its scope. Eve was stunned by the magnitude of alchemical magic happening in her heart.

They turned north onto Irving Place, and a chill washed over Eve in a wave.

The parade of ghosts was still there, marching around Dupont and Montmartre's Viewing Parlor for the Dead in a floating circle of protest.

Chapter Four

"Why are you still drawn to haunt this place?" Eve asked the parade, troubled by this lack of resolution. "I'm so confused."

Eve had sincerely hoped they'd put to rest the spirits haunted by what had happened in and around Dupont's work, but then again, the spirits so affected by the theft of body parts and tokens of their death were all children. The assembly remained of several adults and elderly souls. What *else* had the spirit world so unsettled about this place?

They ascended the stoop, reading the letters painted on the front bay window indicating funerary services and the viewing parlor.

The detective plucked a set of keys from his pocket and began trying each one in the lock.

"You managed to get a *key* with this warrant?" Eve asked, incredulous.

"Bills was so unnerved by Dupont's work he has proved helpful. He handed me Dupont's keys when we were at the theatre to separate the body parts from the stage set, thorough about the evidence of remaining parts. His cooperation with me, directly, insisting on me alone and not my superior, has me additionally suspect in the captain's eyes. But the people who *know* the case must remain the ones working it. So many things get lost in a hierarchy of ego and superiority."

Horowitz emitted a small laugh of victory as one long brass key turned in the lock with a resonant clang and the glass door swung open.

"Agreed. You're good about creating rapport, and the results follow. It's one of your best qualities," she said with a smile that he shared.

They entered the empty white entrance hall and the open, plain doorway that led into the long white-walled viewing parlor, empty save for the dais where a coffin would have been laid out for those who had become interested in separating death from their own home. "I was inside briefly with the girls so this part is familiar to me," Eve said. "Jenny broke in through a back window, and we looked around quickly before anyone could report us as intruders. We *didn't* have a warrant. In our haste I realize we didn't check the rear exit, and I didn't know yet to look for a box near the electric, keeping the ghosts out like in other venues."

"Then let's see," Horowitz said, and charged in, through the parlor and around to the back half of the building. Eve followed quickly.

Beyond a small preparatory kitchen left over from when the parlor had first been a home, they found a rear door with a dark shade over its window. The detective went out, Eve following to the small patch of struggling green surrounded by the backs of other buildings. Horowitz noted the fuse box on the exterior brick of the parlor and gestured to an additional small metal box beside it.

Eve reached forward and flipped open the lid to reveal the tines of metal and a sparking current snapping between them.

"Antonia broke the current of one of these boxes before." Eve peered closer. "If we can get something nonconductive, and break the wires there, it should disconnect it."

Horowitz picked up a broken plant pot and knocked the edge on the side of the wires, and with a click and scrape they fell to the side.

With a rush of cool air, spirits swept into the space. Eve followed the lead of the dead and the detective followed her. These older spirits were not dogging Eve like the children had been before their parts and tokens were found in Dupont's "reliquaries" and "art projects." In the wake of the spirits' chill came drops of rain falling from a darkening sky.

Reentering the parlor's hall, Eve watched the spirits swoop around, some five to seven of them, darting through walls and windows, experiencing the freedom of movement they'd not had when kept outside; but there was a focus to them—they were looking for something. A host of them went down a narrow stairs to the side of the kitchen, stairs Eve hadn't noticed before.

At the top of the winding stairs floated a distinct spirit that struck Eve with a sequence of memories. He was dressed in a dark robe and cap and had a long black-and-silvered beard; his skin was a dusky grey, which in life must have been a rich bronze. She'd noticed him before, floating outside of sacred sites but, not wishing to disturb his peaceful mien, Eve had never spoken with him, nor he to her.

He turned and floated down the stairs. Eve followed, Jacob on her heels, only to vanish at the bottom stair to leave them alone in a whitewashed room.

Downstairs, two narrow rectangular windows at the top of the cellar-level wall lit the room; coarse wooden floorboards were laid over a dirt floor. Set about the plain space were several wooden cabinets, most that looked like the base of a phonograph stand, two with wheels on tapered legs, one stocky and squat against a wall, and a few large wooden spools set against the far wall.

"These cabinets look like…" Horowitz trailed off as he looked into one of the wooden cabinets and examined the top tray. It was empty.

"The bases of the device attached to Gran during her abduction," Eve finished, opening another of the rolling cabinet bases. Nothing. "Devices then attached to me and Cora." She opened the door of the cabinet against the wall. Nothing.

"But only after we all were overcome by noxious gas." The detective finished recalling the events of that troubling night bitterly. Who had abducted them was unclear, but all roads pointed to Dupont and Albert Prenze as Montmartre. The detective moved to lift the large wooden spool shapes, but there was nothing in or on them.

"These spools look like they'd have held rope or, considering the devices, wire."

"Yes, wire," Eve confirmed.

The spirit in robes that had gone down ahead of them reappeared. When he saw Eve catch his eyes, he wafted closer to her. "I know you," Eve said. "I've seen you outside various sacred sites, since I was a child. What brings you here?"

"Dupont and Prenze have become notorious of the dead. They threaten spirits and living allies. We are united in the pursuit of justice," the man said in a thick accent, likely Armenian, Eve noted, from the Gregorian style cross he wore below his beard. She only knew this because Gran had insisted when she was a child that she learn as many icons and sacred symbols as she could, saying she'd encounter them all in the city's confluence and each had importance and power. As of late, New York's Armenian population was growing rapidly in hopes of escaping persecution abroad.

"I've seen you too," the man continued, adding warmly, "child of spirit. Any haunt remaining in service to life, to God, and to the city should learn the most gifted mediums of their age and take note."

"Thank you," Eve replied, moved by this outreach. "As I'm sure you know, prosecuting Dupont is under way, but Prenze…"

"We need proof, please," Horowitz added, taking Eve's lead, looking in the direction she was looking even if he couldn't see what she saw or heard what spirits said. "Tactile proof of wrongdoing. Anything you could point us to would help, spirit, thank you."

The ghost turned toward him with another benevolent smile. "Yes, child of Moses. I understand." He then pointed a long, robed arm at the wall nearest them, where the one cabinet not on wheels sat flush against the wall.

"The old priest is gesturing to this one," Eve explained, opening the door again to show the spirit that the cabinet was empty. The spirit gestured again, insistent, the arm of his robe like a shadowy wing.

"Then let's move it from the wall," the detective suggested, and they each took a corner of the heavy wooden piece that had been left behind likely out of expediency.

As soon as they moved it from the wall, a thin folder of papers fell to the floor and the detective rushed to pick them up. Eve looked over his shoulder as he examined the papers.

On top was a typed half page with handwritten names, indicating that Arte Uber Alles had a permit to exhibit an "unnamed art project" on the Brooklyn Bridge, with the year, 1899, but no date set. Another paper marked a transfer of property from the Zinne family to A. Montmartre: a warehouse of funerary clothes downtown near the water.

"That's the location Gran was abducted to, where we all were put unconscious!" Eve exclaimed.

"Now *this* is important proof," Horowitz said. "Thank you, spirits!" he said to the air.

Eve turned to the ghost, but he had vanished. Even if spirits weren't manifest, gratefulness carried to their world and Eve heard a soft chorus of "You're welcome" on the air and relayed the sentiment.

Another permit was for laying an additional telegraph line in Tarrytown jurisdiction, perhaps what Eve saw today. Did Prenze have property near Sanctuary?

Another paper was a receipt for wire from the Roebling Wire Company, many spools, and the next was for a bank account via the Chemical National Bank with its headquarters on Broadway, indicating that Arte Uber Alles had a new account as of 1896, the year Prenze supposedly died.

"Permit, receipt, property transfer, and account contract...." Horowitz listed off, peering at the addresses on each. "Places to inquire once we've continued sweeping this place."

"Neither Dupont nor Prenze as Montmartre could've known this was left behind, and I'd like to think that was through the help of the spirits," Eve said. "Though I confess, part of me is beginning to be paranoid enough to wonder if everything is a trap and we're just wandering where our enemy bids."

"If so and it leads to evidence, we use it to fight back," the detective replied matter-of-factly.

Eve kept sweeping the room, recalling Antonia had plucked a thin braid of hair from a baseboard upstairs and had left it on the grave of the child it belonged to, per the spirit's request. The recollection reminded Eve to look in every crevice and she did so.

Going back upstairs, Eve's eye caught on a small dark triangle on the baseboard a few steps from the ground floor. Using a fingernail, she separated the triangle from the wall, and with her fingertip slid a small, thin piece of metal up into view.

A tintype image. Likely from forty or so years ago, when the prephotographic medium was in its prime. The portrait was of a distinct, severe-looking woman in a black dress with a cameo at her throat.

"Good eye, Eve!" Horowitz exclaimed, looking at the image over her shoulder on the stairs.

Looking at the picture, Eve had a visceral reaction. She could feel a rush of information wanting to hit her all at once. At the center of her forehead, a burning sensation indicated there were too many spirits that this image summoned and that reactions were clogged at her third eye. She wavered on the step. Jacob gently steadied her.

"She hated him, and he her..." Eve murmured. "I *feel* it. The spirit world knows it too."

"Do you remember, the painting in the ballroom of the Prenze mansion?" Horowitz asked. "I think this is the same woman."

"Yes, it must be," Eve agreed. "The mother Albert had such contention with." Eve's ears perked up at a specific sound: a rustling, an assent. "She is at the core of his motivations." She tucked the tintype into the pocket of her skirt. She'd been sure all her skirts, for work or for everyday wear, had at least one. She didn't like the object being near to her, just a few layers of fabric from her skin, but the image was important. "Perhaps that volatility of emotion can serve us."

Returning to the parlor level, a woman in a plain dress, like the uniform of a schoolmarm, floated above the dais.

"Do you have anything to say to us?" Eve asked. "Anything would be helpful."

"All in black, everything in black, but never in light," the solemn woman said, and while her dress was simple and neatly kept, her silver hair was wild as if swept by a storm.

"Well, this place was a funeral parlor," Eve replied. "There's nothing unusual in that."

"But that's how we see him!" The spirit shuddered, her transparent form shaking. "The spirits, he hates us, and he stares at us, all in black, a void." The ghost's eyes widened. "He's planning something terrible, with all those things and wires and devices and we don't know how to stop it." "The shadow man? Is that who you're talking about?" Eve asked. A child spirit had described Prenze in such a way. The woman nodded. Something that rattled a spirit was of greater concern to the living.

"The shadow man wants to end us. Whispers and cries from places we can't access, spirits in great distress, imprisoned by his hatred." The woman swooped at Eve suddenly, her arms flailing. Eve tried not to flinch, but the rush of cold air made her blink back tears. "Help! Before he kills us all!"

"We want to help," Eve reassured the nervous old woman. "What else can you tell me?"

The spirit turned to look out the window toward a couple walking arm in arm under an umbrella. She reached toward them as if transfixed and didn't say another word, just floated with transparent arms outstretched, longing for some old suitor.

Eve sighed, seeing the woman's attention was lost to her. Horowitz was looking at Eve, patiently waiting for an explanation of what, if any, clues were shared.

"Taking lessons from the dead is admittedly a life of unreliable narration," Eve began. "But she said Prenze is planning something terrible. They want us to stop harm coming to ghosts. Like he harmed Maggie."

The fact that Eve hadn't seen Maggie all day troubled her, even if Zofia had mentioned she was off, preoccupied. Usually her best friend passed through, checking in, a consistent companion. Maggie was Eve's familiar, her spirit tether, guiding her through life. Losing her to Prenze's interference once made Eve nervous about any further absence.

"I wonder if those spools of wire, since dispensed, relates to the danger to ghosts, as Maggie seemed to think it was Prenze turning up the lights to a blinding level that…blinked her out, severing her spirit's tether to our world."

"I think you must be a connective piece, then. You and Gran," Horowitz said. "Cora too, those with psychic capacity. To do what he wants to do, he must need information from you; why else study you or hook you to the device?"

"I don't know. Whatever he did opened something; it was after that that he began the astral projection."

"Let's see if next door can be any more reliable than any of your ghostly narrators," the detective suggested.

Exiting the Irving Place address, Horowitz took a moment to lock the door after him before they turned toward Gramercy Park. Following the promise of trees ahead, they walked a block north and stood at the southeastern corner of the rectangular enclave of townhouses facing a gated green with a wrought iron fence to keep out anyone who didn't belong to the little district of old money that hid itself from the city's biggest industrial changes in the widening streets and avenues beyond.

The spirits that usually coursed around the neat and tidy green were still today, all floating in place, all staring straight at Eve. For them to be stock still was unnatural—stifling, even, to a Sensitive so accustomed to seeing them as reflective of the city's constant movement and restless nature.

Eve stopped in her tracks, the detective beside her, his hand brushing hers. After a moment he caught her hand and kept it, squeezing her palm as he tilted his head toward her.

"What is it?" her ever-attentive companion asked.

"All the ghosts are staring at me." Eve fought a nauseous wave of unease. "Their stillness is unsettling. Ghosts are creatures of movement and floating. Entities of eternal breezes. For the whole of the spirit world to be acting unnatural makes me wonder what Prenze is doing or perhaps what other changes are happening to affect them."

"Perhaps his electrical work, the monitors, the blockades—and more— are affecting their general freedom?"

"Perhaps…" Eve squinted at the spirits, which stared blankly back. She shook her head and turned toward the closest row of townhouses, Dupont's home around the corner from his parlor.

A breeze blew back the loose hair around Eve's face and Vera appeared again before her, white hair up in a bun with strands floating as if underwater. Her floral shawl that Eve had once seen in beautiful reds and blues in the fullness of Sanctuary was greyscale here, held taut over bony, folded arms. Born and raised in Mexico City, a talented artist, she'd spent her adult life in Manhattan. Her intense love of art and this city kept her soul as vibrant as her paintings.

"I was torn from here," she said, her accent light and lilting. "I tried to go in again, just as you stand, and from here I was ripped apart. Sanctuary put me back together, as it did Maggie. The same thing happened to her at the Prenze mansion. *Break* these devices of torture, Eve!"

"We'll do whatever we can," Eve promised, explaining to Jacob what the spirit said. "It's this house," she said, indicating the white sandstone façade with carved stone lions on either side of the stoop. They ascended. Vera hung back, hesitant.

Horowitz looked at the ring of six keys with a fob of a sacred heart stamped in metal, a sad reminder to Eve of all the little reliquaries Dupont had made from the parts of children. Jacob chose the most elaborate key, brass with a filigree pattern, and turned the lock that matched its pattern. Their reflection shifted in the etched-glass panel of the door as they entered.

Dupont's townhouse appeared just as empty as the viewing parlor, and as they stood in the house's parlor, similarly white walled and open, Eve noticed some of the same spirits that had been floating around the viewing parlor had come with them, looking in the front bay window.

"Let's disarm the blockade." Eve gestured to the windows. "They're here, looking in."

"Does it ever startle you, seeing them? I know you look upon the dead as your duty, but—"

"Always," Eve interrupted. All the spirits kept staring at her unnervingly through the window. "Just because one accepts a calling doesn't mean it can't scare you."

Jacob stared at her a moment. "Brave and honest," he said in admiration.

Eve shrugged. "If I wasn't at least a little frightened of the power of spirits, I wouldn't have built up my reserves, my shields, learned my limits. If I'd have just let it *all* in, without discernment, we'd never have met. I'd have been committed to some private asylum upstate." She turned and found her way to the back of the home.

Past a rear kitchen, the two exited onto an exterior landing. Eve gestured toward the electric box affixed to the brick outside where a similar blocking mechanism was mounted beside, and Horowitz did the same as was done at the parlor to remove it.

Spirits poured in; a floodgate lifted. Quiet at first, they took stock of the place, moving meticulously through walls, phantoms floating a foot from the floor.

"Greetings, spirits," Eve called. "Please direct us to anything of note."

At this bidding, Vera reappeared, her wrinkled face determined.

"No, Vera," Eve assured gently. "I would never ask you to revisit a site of trauma."

"No, no,"—she shook her transparent head, white wisps of hair flowing—"this place is an enemy and I want to vanquish it. This house." She clucked her tongue. "*Dios mio.*" The spirit sighed, floating toward the library, off the main entrance hall, gesturing with a bent hand that Eve follow her. "This room was the start of everything for me, with this case."

The library must also have served as Dupont's study. Umber-painted walls were broken up by tall maple bookshelves that seemed to have mostly been left alone. Books were stacked along the bookshelves, with gaps where perhaps Mrs. Dupont had taken some tomes of note or worth. A large leather chair and desk remained near a tall lancet window with stained-glass squares. Mrs. Dupont must not have felt the need to move what was obviously his, the man's actions and obsessions having estranged him.

"This was where little Ingrid Schwerin appeared to me," Vera explained, gesturing as she spoke, "just outside the house and then leading me into this hall. Just as the spirits of children begged for Maggie's intervention at the Prenze mansion, so did Ingrid want me to know her story here." The spirit shook her head. "I don't know how I was able to get in, past that blocking device to begin with. Perhaps Ingrid's tie to this place carved out a door for our souls. I launched her postmortem photograph from this desk into the hall, and that began the unraveling."

It was true; little Ingrid's spirit had led the charge toward what Eve prayed would prove ongoing justice. Their search continued.

Upstairs, the main bedrooms and boudoir, in earth-toned brocade wallpapers and wood paneling, were empty, a few small side tables and one bed left behind, and the spirits that had gathered seemed unconcerned for this floor. It was the uppermost floor they wanted Eve to see.

A silvery mass flew above, calling for Eve to follow as they passed through the ceiling.

Eve led the detective up a narrow flight of curving stairs to an arched top-floor hall with two small doors open into empty, cobwebbed rooms and one large door at the end of the hall, painted a bright red, an entirely unsettling and odd juxtaposition to the rest of the understated townhouse.

Three young spirits flew ahead, pointing to the arched, crimson portal. Vera hung back against the hallway wall, gesturing to the spirits as if what was to follow was for them to say, not her.

Eve recognized the souls, hovering at the threshold. They were three of the children that Eve had interacted with during Dupont's fetish. Eve recognized the boy of around ten or eleven at the fore; he had appeared in her office during a séance to glean information about Dupont's activities and the thefts of tokens from corpses.

"Hello young man," Eve said in a welcoming tone. "Giacomo, isn't it?" At this, the little boy brightened, nodded, beaming that he'd been remembered, and he and the dark-haired little girl beside him in a pale pinafore shared a smile. "I remember you were trying to get justice for your sister during the remainder of your too-short life and then, even after death. And is that you?" She turned to the girl.

"Yes, thank you, ma'am," the boy said. "This is Magdalena."

One of the reasons the dead so often cooperated with Eve and wanted her to listen was that she tried to make them feel important and recollected in a world that had often discarded them.

"I hope you two were able to find some peace, knowing Mr. Dupont had been arraigned."

"Yes, ma'am, but if you're here, then you know not everything's done with. And now that I'm here, I remember," the boy said ominously. "Not like this house would let me forget..." Eve took a moment to explain what she was seeing and hearing to the detective. The spirit pointed to the red door.

Horowitz approached, looked at Eve, and withdrew the six keys again, peering at the ornate double lock. He tried one of the remaining keys that didn't go to the front doors; eventually the slenderest key unlocked the base of the hefty iron lock and a second key above undid another latch, and the wooden door swung open on soundless, well-oiled hinges.

The room was triangular, one large window with a thick red curtain drawn aside, the view looking out over the shingles of the next rooftop, edges of the trees along the street coming into view beyond a small window ledge.

Inside were what looked like stage sets, which would explain the hefty red window drape as a stage curtain. Folded to the side were painted screens with various landscapes of field, sea, or forest. A mixture of props peppered one wall, a mixture of fantastical and liturgical things, a castle footing, a spear, a taxidermized peacock. An open trunk with a bunch of costumes spilling out. A small bookshelf held children's books with gilded spines.

A Bavarian scene was set at the fore, a crook, prop sheep, and large metal bell set to the side.

Vera pointed to it. "That's how Maggie described what her children looked like who asked for her help, little Grimm's fairy-tale children."

"Where *is* Maggie?" Eve asked Vera, who could only shrug, a sunbeam cutting through her silvery form, a contrast of luminosity, the sun highlighting dust motes floating amid the edges of the spirit's skirts. "I wish she were here to help make sense of this."

"This must be where Dupont did his private, postmortem photography," Horowitz mused. "Posing the bodies that had been left in his care?"

"This is likely all the staging for the collection that ended up in the Prenze mansion." Eve turned to the little boy and his sister. "Were you photographed as well as stolen from?"

The girl nodded, and gestured to her hair, indicating a lock taken at some point during the funerary process.

A third spirit that had hung back in the hall now wafted close to Eve, a wide-eyed child in a long robe with wispy hair. "This is how we were posed, so many of us," the child murmured. "Before we were laid out. Freshly dropped off. Barely dead a day in some cases. Before the stink could really set in."

"Art above everything," Giacomo muttered bitterly.

"Arte Uber Alles?" Eve asked. The children nodded. "Dupont spoke about a 'great experiment.' Were you a part of that?"

The three spirits nodded in unison. "There was testing," the waifish, robed child said, ominously pointing toward the wall.

Along both sides of the wall hung a sequence of long copper wires. Some were attached to discs like what had been placed on Gran's temples.

"Monitoring, or testing dead bodies? I don't understand."

Giacomo looked at his sister; she shook her head. The little brother spoke for her. "The process started here and then was perfected at the other parlor."

"What process?" Eve asked.

The boy sighed, as if trying to figure out how to explain it. "To try to block any of us ghosts. Some of us lingered on to see what he was doing with our bodies. He didn't want to be bothered; neither of them did."

"Who?" Eve pressed.

"Dupont and the partner. The shadow man. He helped with the devices. There's something behind the wall. Do you hear the hum? It goes up to the roof, to a wind device that powers the drum."

"There is a low note in the air, now that the spirits mention it," Eve said, bidding Horowitz listen.

"A low drone." He peered closely at the thin slats of stained wood along the narrow side of the room. Walking over to a seam in the wall, he fished out a curved metal hook from between the wood panels, and a panel slid out to reveal metal plates on the wall behind. The ghosts came close, peering too.

"It's all been about getting us to go away." Magdalena's voice was tiny and sad.

"Dupont's been mucking about with photographs for a long time," Giacomo offered, "but the experiments, all this wire and the metal and such, that's been about three years. Since the shadow man. We've been asking any spirit we see these questions. We know you need answers. We're trying to help you piece it together."

"Thank you, dear children," Eve said earnestly, looking at each spirit. "You're so helpful. You're right, we need answers, and proof. Each moment we're getting closer."

Vera's generally kind, warm expression was fixed in consternation. "These men." She shook her head. "If you don't want to be haunted, why act in a way that angers the dead?" Vera, floating in the doorway, asked the absent tenants, echoing the rhetorical question of this case.

"I'll let Bills know about this development," Horowitz said. "Those postmortem photos can be evidence, if we can ever recover them from Prenze's clutches."

They descended again to the main floor, and Eve peered at the only thing that had been left in the hall: a grandfather clock against the wall of the entrance hall that faced toward the open parlor arch.

"I can see why Mrs. Dupont didn't want to take this with her," Eve said, grimacing. The face of the grandfather clock was an eerie, smiling half-moon that looked more like a sneering caricature of a clown than a celestial body. She peered closer at it, seeing that there were smaller clocks in each corner that were set to other cities around the globe. Each of those small hands were spinning in an unnatural manner.

A cold dread crept over Eve at this sight, and it seemed the tall, carved wood sides of the large fixture trembled. The face of the clock suddenly careened close to hers, and strong arms seized her and swung her by the waist away from the clock and toward the other end of the hall, papers from the file scattering everywhere.

Jacob had moved, deft and nimble to swing her out of harm's way, covering her in a protective embrace as the clock crashed behind them against the balustrade and then to the floor in a terrible noise of clattering chimes and springing clockwork.

Looking up at the rear door window at a flurry of movement, Eve glimpsed a man in a black hat and a long black cloak leering for a moment before vanishing.

Prenze again and his blasted projection. The most unwelcome haunt, and now, able to manifest objects with force.

Jacob righted Eve, and she embraced him. "Thank you!"

The rear door swung open of its own accord, and they broke apart, both balling their hands into fists, ready to fight. But this time, there was a more welcome sight at the threshold. The spirit children reappeared.

"We'll help protect you," Giacomo, again at the forefront of the trio, said. "We'll try. If he can manifest force, maybe so can we."

"Thank you, Giacomo," Eve said, lowering her fists. "I don't want you to deny eternal rest on our account."

"We'll rest once all this is settled," the young spirit, hardened by a life and death of disrespect, declared. "These men disturbed us directly, but they've offended the whole spirit world now."

This echoed what Eve had heard from within Sanctuary.

"This isn't over until he's stopped his quest," Magdalena whispered, taking her brother's hand. Her breathlessness made her words all the more chilling. "He wants us all gone. And he must think you are one of the reasons keeping us here."

At this, Eve shuddered. It was true. It wasn't just that she was part of the inquiry into Albert Prenze, his family, his practice; it was that she tethered what he hated most.

The detective stepped around broken clock parts to pick up all the receipts and papers from their discovery to replace them in the file.

"I doubt after all this we'll be able to make headway at either of our offices," Eve said. "We should go on ahead to my house so we don't keep the Bishops waiting. We need them. Now that Prenze while manifesting can throw things at us like a damned poltergeist... We need shields."

"Lead on, then, Whitby." Tucking the file under his arm, the detective gestured toward the door. "Let us be schooled in the steeling of minds."

He rubbed his hands together, his tone firm as he continued. "But I'm going to request clearance on the Prenze mansion. The whole family needs to be watched. Tomorrow morning I'll scout locations. If I recall correctly, there are a few new hotels climbing up north of Longacre Square. We'll find one with a view of his property, procure a telescope and binoculars, and engage in some good old-fashioned surveillance."

He said it with such surety it actually gave Eve a surge of hope. Herein was a workable solution that avoided confrontation, something they couldn't do yet.

"Thank you," she said. "Sometimes the spirits make me unable to see the forest for the trees. I don't mean to not think like a detective, but sometimes my problem solving is all fantastical and forgets to offer up solutions in the practical."

"I had hoped we could pounce on something." Horowitz exited with Eve, locking the door behind him. "But we need a lynchpin. All the rest of this"—he indicated the papers under his arm—"will fall in around it. From what I know about casework, the more personal we get, the closer to the truth. We have to know what's going on in the family manse."

"Yes," Eve mused, withdrawing the tintype from her pocket, staring at a cruel face. "Mother dearest made a monster. But I doubt it was solely her fault. I hope we can *see* something to prove Albert's duplicity over Alfred, find some way to extricate him before Albert finally does him in. I wouldn't put it past him, to just take over."

"We'll need to know what's happening," the detective declared. "He can't be the one doing all the watching. Let's turn the tables."

Chapter Five

Fort Denbury wasn't terribly far south or west, two adjoining brick townhouses along Waverly Place, just off Washington Square Park. The nickname for the properties had come fondly from Maggie, and she, along with the other Ghost Precinct regulars, kept to Eve's somber-looking side out of respect for Eve's parents who lived in the one next door. Lady Denbury held a notable dislike of ghostly intrusion, a seemingly incurable tension between her and Eve.

Eve glanced up Waverly toward the edges of trees nearly leafless as autumn drew cooler. Her eye caught a few luminous forms floating a stroll along the stones, losing sight of vague outlines against the white of the Washington Square Arch.

"I'm trying to see if I can see the ghosts that catch your eye," the detective said, as if by being around her he might pick up on more of her talents. He'd started their acquaintance an unapologetic skeptic, but he'd grown more aware and able since they'd been working together and he seemed to be warming to the ghosts' chills.

"I can't help it here; I always try to see any that pass along the park, even if only an echo. I want them to feel seen and known. The bones below the park are so numerous and so forgotten in this now prized neighborhood, thousands piled together from the epidemics of the last century. They lie there all unnamed. No plaque, no memorial. The more recent dead of the city fear they'll be similarly neglected."

"It is good of you to honor the forgotten, Eve, in a way no one else I know can," Jacob said as they climbed her stoop, facing the black crepe mourning wreath she maintained on the outside of her door.

"The occasional spirit that floats across the bricks and paths are the only monument to that pit of bones," Eve explained, turning back to the edge of the park visible from her doorstep, "whispering to anyone who cares to listen that this is a place where hordes rest. I try always to hear the voiceless, in everything I champion." She shook her head, frustration rising in a wave of heat. "I don't want to lose track of that battling Prenze. I hate that this living man who was *supposed* to be dead is taking so much time away from the *actual* dead that need me to help them help the city. It's maddening."

"It is, and we'll stop him."

For all the ways that her Sensitivities made her feel volatile, the detective was a welcome force of balance and determination. She turned the key in an ornate silver scrollwork lock.

As Eve entered, she heard commotion in her parlor, the clinking of glass. Stepping forward into the center of the entrance hall, she looked through the open pocket doors to see Gran, backlit by a fire in the parlor's brick fireplace. She sat at the large circular parlor table that hosted séances when the girls chose to work from home rather than their offices.

Turning to the window at the sound of clinking glass, Eve was surprised to see Clara Bishop, already there and at work with curious glass vials in her hands. The distinct features of the birdlike woman seemed more pronounced by the gaslight sconces casting her dark blond hair in a halo. A flowing silver evening dress brought out the silver streaks in the braids coiled atop her head, especially the one that hung low to hide her scar.

Clara clinked one of the vials with her fingernail, and the material inside, soil or something of the sort, settled. Gran had spoken of wards before. This must be how the Bishops had crafted them.

"Hello Eve and companion," Clara said. "I'm protecting thresholds. Come in."

Gesturing beside her, Eve brushed her hand across Jacob's sleeve as she introduced him. "This is Detective Horowitz, Mrs. Bishop. He has been a part of all my recent cases and has also been threatened by Albert Prenze. He is a vital asset to my team, and I want him to learn any strategy of advantage and protection."

The detective bobbed his head. "Mrs. Bishop, a pleasure."

"Ah, yes, Detective." Clara cocked her head to the side like a songbird, listening. "Evelyn has said wonderful things about you, and your presence complements the young Eve stunningly. And that's not an easy feat seeing as she's so distinct a tone, she's *loud*, like me, but..." She gestured around her good ear, as if she were hearing something, and smiled. "You're harmonious."

Before Eve or Jacob could react to any of this, or before Eve could explain to Jacob that Clara heard energies like music, the force of nature continued. "Forgive my barging in and working ahead of you." Mrs. Bishop turned toward the furthest of the two front windows, where she sat down one of the vials against the window in the corner of the sill. "But there's no time to waste. A character like Prenze will stop at nothing, and I sense that he feels he is above capture or prosecution. Power drunk, wealth has afforded him being above the law, and this is vastly heightened by his discovery of his own psychic powers."

There was another clinking sound from down the hall, and as Eve turned her head toward the open downstairs door, Clara explained the noise. "That would be Rupert downstairs with your colleagues, who are showing him any place that they feel could be vulnerable to intrusion, psychic or otherwise. And thank you for keeping your ghosts at a distance. I don't mean to be inhospitable to them, but you know my condition...."

"Oh, of course, they understand!" Eve said, winking up the stairs when she saw Zofia poke a spectral head out from the top landing, the child eavesdropping from a safe distance.

Their absence was particularly evident to Eve as the room was far warmer than usual, the roaring fire notwithstanding. At any given time, at least three of their regular haunts were generally present, up to five if their resident spirit tethered to music felt like playing piano. Sometimes they'd attract seven full manifestations, not to mention those spirits that were simply and quite literally passing through.

Gran must have urged them out ahead of the Bishops' arrival. Not that Clara wasn't a gifted Sensitive, but due to her neurology, too many ghosts gave her seizures. Eve recalled her saying that there was "always a cost to these powers."

A visceral hope that there would be a cost to Prenze's powers hit Eve in a fervent prayer. As she'd indicated to the detective, her anger seethed. That a whole houseful of good, talented people cultivated protections when other worthy cases in the city needed their ear and attention was an egregious injustice. But that was the way of the greedy and selfish. Eve wished that immorally taking the talents and energies of others for personal gain was considered as criminal as theft of money or property.

"You'll want to reinforce the wards with your own beliefs and traditions," Clara added, clicking a fingernail against one of the vials. "Some find salt helpful, but..." She gestured outside. "From your descriptions, this is an astral projection of one unwanted, living man rather than what we would consider a demonic force. So"—she gestured to the vials then to Eve—"add to these vials any ingredient that you find resonant and synonymous with safety and fortification. I've lent some of my energy; you must bolster it and seal it with yours."

"What is in them?" Eve asked, sitting next to Gran at the séance table. Jacob took the seat to Eve's left, listening to Clara intently.

Mrs. Bishop gestured out the window toward Washington Square. "Soil from your park. As I know you respect the dead there, so too will they respect your protections. There's water from the confluence of the rivers, a leaf and petal from plants known to be protectors—juniper and ash. And a bit of ley line magic I've placed in there myself."

"Thank you, Mrs. Bishop, that's wonderful."

If Eve wasn't mistaken, the dark vial of ingredients held a slight, ethereal glow. Spirits must have been lending a sliver of their own light. Eve was accustomed to the nuances of a wider spectrum. Sometimes an object or a piece of clothing, a portrait, or perhaps someone's favorite chair had a slight glow to it that only the spectrally trained eye could see, a bit of living essence left behind in the inanimate. So it was with these wards. Light protecting life.

Something must have amused Jenny, as the little girl tore up the stairs into the entrance hall, snorting a giggle and smiling at Eve.

She gestured toward the man behind her. *He's fun and very kind,* the girl signed.

The tall and distinguished silver-haired ambassador was around Gran's age of seventy. He looked at Jenny as he ascended the stairs with a wistful smile; it was the first time Eve had wondered if the man had once wanted to have children but didn't or couldn't. Jenny was a wonderful addition to the patchwork family of friends and acquaintances that Gran had helped bring together, and there was something about the child that disarmed everyone and accentuated emotion.

"Hello, Eve," Rupert Bishop said warmly, turning to her at the landing of the main hall. "I'm glad to see you."

"And you, Ambassador."

Cora and Antonia rejoined the landing, and everyone gravitated to the séance table save for Clara, who stood near the window as if standing guard.

"Indeed, it is good to see all of you again," the ambassador said, gesturing at the girls. "It's been some time."

"It's been since you helped us into our offices," Cora offered. "And we spoke about my family."

"Yes!" Bishop said brightly. "How are your dear mother and father?"

"Still busy in New Orleans as private investigators," Cora replied. "They'd love to come visit if they can escape their clients." She laughed. "They're doing a lot of good, for many who dearly need it, but I wonder if they've taken any time for themselves in a while. Perhaps you could convince them; they're dearly fond of you both and I'm sure they'd listen to your advice," Cora said, turning to Clara.

Eve noticed Clara's eyes flutter a bit, and she recalled that Cora's uncle Louis, a ghost that was a great help to Cora and the precinct, had been Clara's lover long ago. Relations with Cora's father, Louis's twin brother, were also complicated. Yet Cora was rightly and unapologetically proud of who she was and where she was from. In part, Cora wanted to work in the Ghost Precinct because she saw Eve and herself as children of great talents continuing a spectral legacy to be celebrated, no matter if it brought up old pain.

Clara shook off whatever had passed over her and smiled at Cora with genuine enthusiasm, coming over to the séance table and placing her hands on her husband's shoulders. "Yes, we shall, Rupert; let's write to Cora's dear family straightaway for a long overdue reunion!"

"Wonderful!" Cora clapped her hands together. Eve wasn't sure she'd ever seen her friend so hopeful. It occurred to her then how much Cora had to give up at the age of seventeen, leaving her family and a city she loved to become a member of the Ghost Precinct, when all Eve had to do was go next door, or up Fifth Avenue to Gran for family connection.

Detective Horowitz watched all of them intently, and Eve was struck again by Clara's declaration of him as harmonious to her—how lovely. Eve couldn't deny the truth of it. He was a wonderful addition to anything she was involved with, and any room was far better for his being there. She turned to him, smiling. He reached out to briefly squeeze her hand, a small gesture that made Eve's heart soar. The detective then turned to Rupert Bishop attentively.

Once Clara took her seat beside her husband, the ambassador addressed them all, looking each one of them in the eyes. As he did, everyone leaned in and Eve was struck by how intense his gaze was, as if he were visibly pulling them forward.

"Now, my friends, we'll keep this simple, as the principle is simple, but very personal. Much like Clara has told you of the wards, shielding only works if it comes from the core of you and your inspiration. As for this Albert Prenze character and his mental manipulation, he may be trying to show you a grey nothingness, but that must be because there's a very scared and overcompensating person underneath that façade. His astral projection is a phantom cast in hopes of looming over. Lording over. The practice of astral projection was never meant to be used as a threat, but unfortunately here it is. Have each of you seen his form at the window?" "That's only been me," Eve clarified.

"Well, now that he's made it a point to interact with all of you, he may feel emboldened to terrorize you all. So, all must shield, not only from seeing the form, but from *any* manipulation."

"He did try to turn our own weapons against us," Jacob offered. "Eve and I had gone after him and there was a confrontation. Eve managed to break from his thrall, thankfully."

"But that's where his mesmerism went far beyond anything I expected," Eve said. "My hand was being moved forcibly before Jacob and I both fought back against his pressure."

Bishop nodded, his expression grave. "The power of persuasion ratcheted to a preternatural level. I wonder how he came to it." He rubbed his chin.

Jenny signed the answer to this query, and Eve translated to the assembly. "Jenny has been able to channel the spirit of Dr. Font, found dead in the Dakota of poison. He unwittingly signed off on Prenze's death certificate. Font says the day he thought Prenze died was when the path he was on took an even darker turn. Font presumes a nearness to death opened his mind, but not toward the godly and good. Quite the opposite."

"I see," Bishop said. "Trauma changes a body, for better or worse," he said, absently clutching one of his wife's hands as she pressed the braid over her ear with her other.

"Each of you is a sovereign state with distinct borders," the ambassador declared, pinning them again with his intense stare. "*Never* forget that. This man is trying to make you question your own boundaries. You must reinforce them. Protect yourself beyond yourself."

Bishop stood suddenly, towering over the table. "You do not end here," he said, tapping his forearm. "You do not end where your skin and bones contain you." He gestured the length of his arms, gracefully, as if opening wings. "Your energy naturally extends past you. Your existence is larger than your body."

He turned to Eve. "Now if you send energy…" Bishop made a gesture as if he were throwing her a ball. On impulse, she reached out and caught what did feel like some impossibly palpable thing. The ambassador's vibrancy was as potent as if it were a tactile object. "Energy can be received as Eve did, and I hope you feel it."

"I do."

"Good. Now return it to me?"

Eve closed her eyes, trying not to overthink it, but pushed forward what felt like a warm ball of light in her hand, giving it an intentional shove toward the ambassador.

"Very good," Bishop praised. "That, in a sense, is astral projection. Prenze is tossing a manifestation toward you to haunt you. Not to energize or support but to drain. It's a shame, because he could be using that energy to inspire, to comfort, to protect, but he is an inversion. You must extend your own energy out from yourself so that he cannot get close to you. You must push him back with the strength of your will. If you are shielding well, he cannot get in, to frighten, or to manipulate your minds."

"Shielding is *entirely* personal," Clara added. "It begins with a thought. The first step is connecting with what makes you feel powerful. Be it an image, word, liturgy, song, element, draw strength from it as *yours*. Breathe in and fill yourself with this strength on an inhale. For myself, I think of the air, the heavens, birds, divine creatures, and as I draw in,"—she breathed in deeply—"I think of angels unfurling their wings...." And then she breathed out, letting her arms stretch out in front of her. "And so, I extend..."

Eve could feel Clara's admittedly large, or as she claimed loud, presence magnify.

"Draw in your strength," the ambassador continued, breathing in, then out. "Expel that strength like a circular wall."

Eve and her colleagues did as instructed. The room grew smaller as Sensitivities expanded.

"Something to take care with," Gran added quietly. "Be sure that you're not expending from your own reserves. Intake from what inspires, powers, and uplifts externally. You have to use an outside engine to draw from an inexhaustible well. We are exhaustible creatures. We can't power constant protection from our own bodies alone."

"Draw in," Rupert Bishop instructed, breathing and extending his palms as he exhaled. "Press out. Extend your energy so that you create a boundary that isn't to be violated. I can't tell you what best protects you; that's yours to decide. Allow yourself more than one element or image." He let his words sit, as if giving the company time to calibrate. "And try again."

Eve closed her eyes. Gran had taught her these things in her youth, but she hadn't revisited the principles recently, and where she pulled her strength from wasn't always consistent.

Her instinct was to draw vitality from the fireplace crackling with life and raw power at the center of the parlor. In the core of her she imagined lived a lit candle, like the process of calling a séance to order. This would be her visualization. Beyond the firelight, she thought of everyone she cared about. The most important people in her life were in this room and next door. From this, her light would grow and glow. The darkness would have no room, pushed out of the field of vision, pushed away from her heart, sent away to the shadows from which it came....

The fire in her vision flickered. Her candle was snuffed out. Her mind's eye watched the smoke a moment before she felt Gran jolt in her seat, and her eyes snapped open to the movement outside.

A tall, dark form lunged at the window. There was a sound as if of cracking glass, yet no fissure was seen.

For a terrible moment, Eve wondered if somehow, in all this, she'd let him further in....

The young women gasped while Horowitz jumped to his feet. Prenze. The shadow man. The core of their trouble, now visible to everyone. Not just to Eve's gifted eye. He'd magnified his power and scope.

"He is but a vision," Ambassador Bishop reminded the startled group, his pleasant voice resonant and firm. "Yet you must *reject* this astral presence!" Bishop bellowed. Eve was moved by the ambassador's vehemence, the strength of his energy. These elders were the kinds of forces of nature Eve wanted to be. Eve threw her own aura out from her like a whip as had been practiced.

Out of the corner of her eye, Eve noticed Clara wavered next to her husband. Gently, subtly, attuned to every move his wife made and every sound of her breath, he placed his hand upon the small of her back, steadying her. That kind of partnership too... She realized she yearned for that as well, an intimacy in these matters.

Reliving how Jacob's gentle touch had felt upon her own back at the recent soiree, when he too had steadied her, she reached out and grabbed his hand. He turned to her, searching her face, as if asking how better he could help.

"I'm glad you're here," she whispered. He just nodded with a smile.

Everyone seemed to have utilized the shielding lesson as the figure vanished, lessening in opacity and then finally fading away.

There was a long, strained silence.

"How about some dinner?" Antonia asked hopefully. Everyone nodded and smiled.

Suddenly there was a terrible shriek on the other side of the door connecting Eve's townhouse to her parents'. Her mother's shriek. Eve jumped up. There was a clatter of chairs, running footsteps, and a pounding on the door between the homes.

"Eve! What's going on?" Her father shouted from outside that door, in a panicked, startled tone Eve had never heard. "Why is there a man floating at our window?"

Chapter Six

The assembled company looked at one another for a stunned moment and Eve and Gran, along with Horowitz and Ambassador Bishop, all went toward the door connecting the houses at the same time, the precinct mediums all on their heels. Only Clara hung back. Jenny hesitated at the threshold. As Eve unlocked the hallway door joining the townhouses, she glanced up her stairs to a luminous silver mass gathered at the top of the stairs. The elder spirit Vera had her arm around little Zofia, both hovering at the top of the landing. Eve held out her hand, indicating they should float their ground.

"Father, Mother, what's wrong?" Eve called, flinging open the door and running into her parents' entry hall that was much like hers in architecture, but opposite in color. What Eve kept in burgundy, black, and mahogany her mother kept in lavender, lilac, and rosewood.

Charging into the parlor, her host of colleagues behind her, Eve found her mother staring horrified out the parlor window, her father behind her, clutching her protectively.

"There was a man, there, at the window, floating like a ghost," her father said slowly. "But…"

"But he's not a ghost," Gran finished. "He's Albert Prenze, presumed dead, who is very much alive and our current enemy."

The team crowded to the window. "He's still there," the detective stated, pointing toward a shadow between the front stoop and entrance of a townhouse across the street.

The figure waved. His face, half-hidden beneath the shade of a wide-brimmed black hat, curved into a smile. How horrific. Hovering, threatening, wanting them all to know that he *could*. The audacity.

Eve turned to try to address her mother, but something on her face stilled her. Natalie Whitby was generally poised, collected, sometimes stern, always no-nonsense, but now…she looked like a terrified little girl. Cora and Antonia hung back while Jenny rushed to Eve, tugging at her sleeve. *Don't push her,* the little girl signed, gesturing to Mrs. Whitby's mouth. She gestured between them, and Eve began to understand; something about their shared history of Selective Mutism was suddenly in play, in addition to this startling turn.

Eve's mother looked between her daughter and Jenny and fled from the room. Eve made to run after her, but her father stopped her with a firm hand on her shoulder, gesturing back toward the window.

"What does he want and how can we get him to go away?" Jonathon Whitby asked.

"Albert Prenze is an unfortunately gifted mesmerist," Eve said, "wealthy industrialist and at the core of our current investigation. He is sending an astral projection I assume as a threat, perhaps to try to make us stop, out of fear, dragging everyone I love into it."

"Is he the one who kept you, nearly all of you hostage?" Her father looked at Eve, then at the assembled company, with a blank, searching expression. Jacob stepped up to Eve's side.

"We can't confirm it, but we suspect so," the detective replied. "Proving Albert Prenze's involvement in tactile ways remains our chief objective, but in these paranormal capacities, he is clearly aware of how little can be tried in a court of law."

The ambassador and Gran took one window then the next.

"Eve." Gran gestured for her to join them. "Push back," she demanded. "Virulently. With all you have."

Eve did, throwing her energy like a physical punch. The figure vanished, but she could almost feel an opposition before he did. She'd like to think he wasn't getting stronger, but it seemed he was gaining ground. She couldn't let that happen, not here.

"Remember, Eve," Gran said. "The truly evil are projectionists, not just here, where he is projecting his own image, but also, trying to intimidate your parents. Trying to get at *your* heart, particularly since we've been told by his twin that he hated his mother. The only way we're going to win against someone like this is to go at the heart as he tries to go at ours. But where he has no love, we do. I am sure that threatens him most. Go tend to yours. Strengthen your protections," Gran instructed.

"Ambassador," her father began, turning toward Bishop, continuing with clipped words. "How does this involve you?"

"Anything that threatens my friends and family threatens me." Bishop put a hand to his heart, over a burgundy pocket square. "I was teaching the precinct here how better to shield from psychic influence, projection, and manipulation."

"And we'll shield too." Her father's voice suddenly sounded not his own but some harrowed stranger. "We'll have to get back in that old habit, I suppose." Eve's heart sunk, looking at him. There was a haunted expression on his face that she'd rarely seen, but when she did, it filled her with overwhelming sadness.

"Go talk to your mother, please," he whispered, plaintive.

"All right..." Eve stepped into the hallway to find where she'd run to.

Gran strode after her, grabbing Eve before she could ascend the stairs, turning her around to speak softly. "Do you have any sense of what your mother went through in your early years?"

"No, because none of you will ever *talk* about it," Eve replied through clenched teeth. "At this point, silence is doing more damage."

Gran held up her hands in acquiescence. "It's not my story to tell and I'm a guilty party, but the distance between you two won't help you fight. Vulnerabilities will work their way in. Perhaps if you know *how* she suffered you'll be a better psychic warrior, for her sake if nothing else. Prenze doesn't have the strong foundation we have. Strengthen yours and we'll open wider his cracks."

Eve nodded. "Take care of everyone else a moment?"

"I shall." Gran exited back to the company as Eve ascended the stairs.

Her mother sat before her vanity in her boudoir, still as a statue, eyes wide and glassy. One lock of auburn hair fell from its pins. Eve had always thought her mother poised, stubborn, often quiet, but forever disapproving of Eve's Sensitivities as hardly ladylike, not fit for proper society. But in this moment, Eve saw the truth: her abject terror.

Eve came close and placed her hands on her mother's shoulders. They trembled below her fingertips.

She gingerly took the fallen lock of hair and pinned it again into the mass of curls atop her mother's head. A few grey strands were coming in around her otherwise auburn temples.

"This isn't just about the shadow of that man, is it?" Eve asked quietly. Her mother shook her head. "Gran said it's not her story to tell, though she has massive guilt about her part in it. What happened when I was a child?"

In a sudden, startling move, her mother jumped up, darting away. She began to pace before the window and wouldn't look at her daughter. Instead, she began signing in a flurry Eve had trouble at first keeping up with.

My old condition came back to me, then, when you were nearly two. I couldn't speak.

Just like I'm having trouble now.

Are terrible things just going to keep repeating?

Eve knew that when her mother was a little girl, she'd wandered out into oncoming traffic as a horse and carriage wheeled around a bend. In a split second, Helen Stewart, the grandmother Eve never knew, ran. She pushed her toddler daughter out of the way and was trampled to death before Natalie's eyes. She stopped speaking. It was only after meeting Jonathon Whitby that her voice began to return slowly and painfully.

Natalie now fought for words, and they came out quietly, stutteringly as she pressed her hands together and paced the room filled with white lace, etched glass, and lilac embroidery, delicate defiance against the darkness she'd lived through.

"You can imagine that…" Natalie began and had to stop, her breath coming in short spurts. She tried again after a long, shaking breath, struggling for control over herself.

"In 1882, you were nearly two, and your father…*and* your Gran…left… left us for England…to again fight demons. Jonathon…in danger…brought it all back. Old habits. Panic. Words fled. Terrified I'd lose him…after all. I thought we'd *won*. But evil returned. Prowling his old family estate. I didn't know if Jonathon would come back to us…or if the demons—" Her voice cracked at the word. "*Literal* demons, Eve!" She cried. "Not metaphorical." She pounded her fist against her hand. "Actual, dread, lightless shadows that snuffed out all light and hope. They'd…take everything I loved. The idea of raising you alone…terrified me. You can understand...why I… relapsed, then.… So, seeing a shadow, threatening, now…"

"I see," Eve said gently. "I don't remember you not speaking then. I don't remember you being absent. You didn't abandon me."

Her mother took a few deep breaths leaning against the doorframe and continued with more measured speech. "Your grandfather stepped in. I don't know how he'd done it with me when Mother, your grandmother Helen, died, but then again, there was always a strain with us too.…" Natalie chuckled sadly, as if she hadn't thought of that parallel before. "But your grandfather took days away from work, your aunt Lavinia and uncle Nat *doted* on you when they were in town. All while I…"—she clenched her fists, muscling the words—"tried to calm myself enough to say…just a few…even *one* word to you. I wanted to say *everything* and I could say *nothing*." She blinked back angry tears, stunning Eve with this hidden inner battle. Ambassador Bishop was right; trauma did dramatic things to a body.

"I managed a few whispers," Natalie continued. "But it was terrible. Rachel helped whenever she could, too. Between she and I, you understood that quiet. You didn't seem to be upset, even if at times you must have wondered." She stared at her daughter plaintively, opening shaking hands toward her. "I might not have been able to talk to you, but I was always able to hold you!"

Tears rolled down her mother's cheeks, and Eve, nearly bowled over by the emotional weight, rushed to embrace her tightly. There hadn't been many physical demonstrations of affection for some time now, since she began her career, but it didn't mean she wasn't still a daughter, and she resolved to be better about fondness.

"I never thought, for a moment, that I wasn't loved," Eve told her, speaking into her mother's lilac-scented hair. "I only thought that you didn't approve. Of my gifts."

"It's because..." Natalie wiped her eyes with an embroidered handkerchief plucked from her sleeve.

"I understand now," Eve reassured her.

"You might. In part. I know you think me cruel for having difficulty seeing Maggie, your dearest friend. But did she ever tell you how she died?"

Eve shook her head. "Not in any detail, no."

"She bled to death. In my arms. Gruesome and terrible."

"My God, I'm sorry," Eve gasped.

"Bet she doesn't want to think about it. But every time, her ghost reminds me of her last moments. I have every reason to be scared. To worry. Every nightmare too easy to recall." She tapped her head.

The silence. It had never been anger, nor anything Eve was doing wrong. Sometimes her mother just couldn't manage the words, she was the traumatized little girl who had watched her mother die, on account of her.... And that was only the beginning. To Natalie, the paranormal had been a deadly curse, never a gift.

Eve liked to think empathy was one of her strong suits, but here she'd entirely misread trauma as disapproval and she vowed never to make that mistake again.

"That man you saw today," Eve said. "It's a projection, one that's gone now. He's just a man, an angry man—"

"He reminds me of everything I *prayed* to leave behind," her mother exclaimed. "All your work comes so close..." She trailed off, and if there was a word she struggled with, she chose not to say it.

"There has been a distance between us, and there might always have to be a distance between us to protect you," Eve said, "but I am at better peace with it now."

"I don't want a distance, Eve." She shook her head, rueful. "I just don't know how to be close to...everything you do...without it...stealing my words again...."

A creak at the open door let Eve know her father was there listening. Then came his lovely, haunted face again. It made Eve's heart ache. When she spoke, it was to them both.

"I'm so sorry; I never thought this would spill over onto you when we were trying to contain it. Prenze is a bully. He wouldn't do this if he weren't scared of all of us, collectively. He should be scared, as we outnumber and outwit him." She spoke with confidence, but it was mostly bravado, trying to convince herself. She glanced out the window toward the street. Nothing. His form remained banished. Although, if he were listening, somehow, she'd want him to hear that.

Natalie shook her head. "I'll try to understand. Just...have patience with me."

She grasped her mother's hands in hers. "If you'll allow the same of me?"

Her mother offered a hard-earned smile. "Indeed. I am...very proud of you, I hope you know."

These words hit Eve as a blinding flash of light illuminating a deep darkness. She hadn't realized how much her parents' hesitation at her work and calling had made her feel as though they *couldn't* be proud of her. Eve's heart suddenly soared. For the most part, she'd been an obedient child who always hoped for approval. Her father came over, and the three of them shared a gentle embrace.

"I was horrified at what my absence had done," her father said, stepping back but keeping one hand on each of their shoulders. "I would never have wanted Natalie to have such a physical relapse. My guilt was crushing, but she didn't blame me, and Eve, you were so fascinated by life, you didn't seem to sense the sadness. I needed healing. And bless you, you both healed me. We've been so careful ever since, and *neither* of us knew how to talk about it."

Eve nodded. It was like a weight had been lifted from them all.

"I'm going to have to learn how better to shield and protect. With new techniques," Eve said. "Gran thinks a key to fighting this man, who long ago fell out with his mother, was in making sure I understood you. And regaining our strength. In thinking you never understood me, I never gave you any similar courtesy."

"We…know better now," her mother murmured.

"I must rejoin my team as we determine our next, and safest, steps."
After another fond embrace, she allowed her father to descend with her toward the more haunted half of the properties.

"What happened with the device your detective took to Bellevue?" her father asked.

"I confess, I don't know, I'll have to follow up with my—" She paused. The fact her father had called Horowitz "hers" and the fact she was about to do so in turn startled her. "With Detective Horowitz. How best should I speak with doctors about the sixth sense? We believe the experiments on Gran and me sought to measure our powers. Should I use the terminology in the journals you shared with me?"

"Yes, did you read them?" He eyed her. She eyed him back, wondering what he was getting at. He smiled. "You're notorious for getting fascinated by ideas and getting sidetracked away from doing any actual scholarship about them." Even as he laughed, she stiffened. "I do understand the ghosts must be terribly distracting. I didn't mean that as a slight—"

"I did read them, actually, and they'll be of great use when speaking with the doctors." She defended herself, when the reality was that she'd only skimmed them. She did admire her father greatly and wanted him to feel she took his work as seriously as she did her own but couldn't quite convince him of it because he was right: the ghosts always had taken precedence. They were why she'd had to discontinue her studies at Barnard. Spirits had driven the wedge between her family she was determined not to let grow.

"Well, let me know if I can help."

"Thank you," she said. Her father had never wanted distance, ghosts or no, and he seemed to crave moments of common ground as much as she did. She embraced him again at the threshold between their homes and shut the door behind her, shifting her attention wholly to her housemates and guests.

Jacob lingered in the parlor, discussing the warrants and the items found with the rest of the girls. Eve was grateful he wanted to keep them informed and aware, and they each were strategizing who would follow up with what.

Ambassador Bishop was at the armoire by the door, readying his wife's cloak and his own overcoat. As he did, Clara glanced at Gran who stood at the end of Eve's stairs, statuesque and grand, her expression far away, lost in intense thought.

"I confess," Clara said quietly to Eve, nodding toward Gran, the woman who had been Clara's own mentor and friend. "I've…missed her. I've missed this: a team, working together. I used to have one. If the spirits didn't give me such health troubles this would have probably been my place, my idea, my work." She looked at Eve with a piercing, honest gaze and continued with gentleness. "Not that I'd want to take it from you. You're incredibly smart and aware; you're far more talented, and wiser, far earlier than I was. I daresay you're the eldest soul among us. You're powerful. Don't neglect that in this. He's trying to make a show against you. Don't let him gain any ground. And remember, you can push back. Physically, psychically, mentally. It isn't just one way. You can project back if you need to."

This suggestion hadn't occurred to Eve. Astral projection was a talent she'd never thought to develop. She would be willing to make a bet that Cora would be better at it than she would be. As if the thought of her summoned her, Cora stood in the open parlor threshold, bobbing her head at the Bishops.

"Thank you for the illuminating lesson," Cora said. "I don't take it lightly. I'll share this with my family, give them your best, and keep learning."

"You're welcome, and good," the ambassador said. "Stay sharp, girls."

Once the Bishops had gone, Jacob came into the entrance hall. Cora exited, giving the two of them leave.

"I'd best be getting home," he said to Eve. She saw him to the door, and he lingered there a moment, hand on the doorknob.

"It isn't that I don't appreciate what I've learned, but again, tactile evidence," the detective said. "There are merits to what the Bishops taught, and I saw the presence at the window just as you did. I saw what our collective force could do in establishing boundaries and protections, forcing him out. But if we're going to get anywhere, we need to know what he's planning next in *this* plane of existence."

"Please know I never lose sight of what will ensure a conviction in *this* plane." Eve smiled. "No matter how esoteric an evening gets. Tomorrow at my offices the girls and I will begin with a séance of Dr. Font to follow up with his clues. You've a surveillance location to secure and accounts to inquire about. Meet you after lunch at your office?"

"Agreed. Until then." Jacob smiled. "You always keep things interesting, Eve; I'll give you that."

Chapter Seven

It was a bright day for the next set of dark dealings. Dressed in the stately police matron's uniform redone in black in honor of the dead, with a few alterations for style and preference, Eve descended to the small first-floor kitchen reserved for preparing lighter meals, put on a kettle for coffee and tea, pulled boiled eggs from the icebox, and brought bread and butter to the small dining room breakfast table, drawing the lace curtain to let a warm autumn light offset the creeping chill.

She liked to think she was attuned to her team, and as they each took a seat at the lace-curtained window, she took a good stock of each of them. The steady determination on Cora's face, Antonia's poised serenity, and Jenny's knit brow, focused as if listening to something important Eve could not hear—all this bolstered her. Her best leadership came when she trusted in the gifts of others, refocusing on talents other than her own.

It wasn't a directive that they wear uniforms to work; any modest, full skirt and well-kept shirtwaist would do, but today, the rest of the team had chosen to dress, an unspoken solidarity of closing rank against the rising threat, refusing to be silenced or shut down.

Eve had let them make choices about their uniforms, giving each the option of dressing in black as she did, to honor the dead, or in the dark police blue as matrons had done for nearly twenty years, or any somber, professional tone. As if echoing the greyscale of the spirits they served, they each had chosen a different charcoal wool in the plain matron dress pattern, darker to lighter from Jenny to Cora.

"Of our many orders of business," Eve said, pouring a round of coffee into china cups, "is reconnecting with Dr. Font." Eve looked at Jenny for permission to choose this as the next matter of course. Font's mysterious, suspect death in an empty apartment of the Dakota building had been one of the first ties between Detective Horowitz's case and what was unfolding for Eve and her team.

"Is this all right, my dear, as you've the strongest connection to him?" Eve asked the child. She nodded.

He may have once had a part in something bad, Jenny signed. *But his soul means us no harm. He was frightened by Albert revealing himself to us. I hope he won't be scared now.*

Eve shared Jenny's thoughts with Cora and Antonia, as learning sign was a process.

"Let's shield and get to work," Eve commanded, breathing deeply to extend her radius of protection. The girls did the same: a deep breath, and an expanded guard. Rising to gather her things, she tried not to think too much about the alarming fact that even ghosts were scared of the man waging a psychic war against them.

The Ghost Precinct offices were on an upper landing of an unmarked police building used for records and storage on Mercer, north of the Fifteenth Ward station house. Their title had been taken off the door and their work relegated to entire obscurity, under the guise of protection. The unfortunate truth of it was that their department was withdrawn to make the uncomfortable less aggressive; riding out those who derided their existence as "unholy."

Nothing, in Eve's mind, could be more sacred than communing with positive, helpful spirits, learning about life thanks to the afterlife. But Spiritualists were often misunderstood, no thanks to all the frauds taking advantage: magicians, not conduits of spectral messages.

The matron who served as a sort of reception desk at the fore of the building, directing those to records or those in the know to Eve and her team, nodded to them all; the sturdy and oft-sour-faced Marie McDonnell peered over the corner of her *New York Evening Post*, where a headline boasted:

PLANS FOR CITY SUBWAY ROLL FORWARD: The Dream of the 1850s May Soon Be the New Century's Reality!

The matron looked the girls and their uniforms up and down before snorting a chuckle. "*All* professional today, are we?"

"Never otherwise, McDonnell," Cora countered. Eve set her jaw and said nothing, sweeping up the wooden stairs to the next landing. The woman boasted that she was trying to toughen them up and thicken their skin for a man's world, but Eve didn't enjoy the matron's unwelcome gauntlet.

Even if the frosted glass of their office door no longer proclaimed their precinct name, it was their space nonetheless, carved out by Ambassador

Bishop, Gran, and none other than former police commissioner, now governor, Teddy Roosevelt.

Morning light pierced through the tall, narrow lancet windows of their office, illuminating dust motes and the occasional flake of coal ash floating like tiny spirits. Beyond, the sounds of business and leisure: the greetings of passersby on this fine day, the shouting hails for hacks or hansom cabs, the thump of papers delivered to stoops and landing beside the clattering of bottles in wooden crates, the unending push-and-pull, give-and-take of the city, its consumption and resupply, sound rolled and crested with the constancy of carriage wheels on cobblestones.

The spirits of the office floated in the same dreamy, hovering quality as the dust. Only Zofia and Vera showed up this morning at their opening hour, each taking a position by a file cabinet at the rear of the room. Maggie remained missing in action, yet again.

Cora excelled at bringing a séance session to order, focusing the minds of the team and opening the door to the spirit world. Eve needed her right-hand woman's piercing, calm quality now. With a nod shared between them, Eve rung a clarion little bell, forged with a holly leaf for a handle, letting the sound resonate in the space and bidding the mediums focus on the door that was about to open, relegating all other noise and distraction to the background where it belonged.

Tucking the clapper to the bell, Eve set it down on the burgundy tablecloth as Cora struck a match on a painted matchbox, given to her from New Orleans relatives, murmuring a Voudon blessing to *Bondye et les Mystères*.

"Spirits," Cora said in a clear, resonant tone, "heed our call for a specific gentleman to come illuminate us. One who came to us, wanting to tell us more."

Jenny lifted up both hands. The group paused any further sound, Cora letting little Jenny take the reins.

Selective Mutism was a complex condition that affected each person who dealt with it differently.

But in welcoming their intended target, Jenny offered a tiny whisper. "I'm here, Dr. Font. I'm here."

There was an immediate response from the spirit world. The Corridors between life and death opened, a hallway Eve knew well from her place as ambassador between worlds.

Jenny brought over a small slate, often used for automatic writing when one of them went into a trance. Instead the little girl turned the tables and wrote a note for the spirit in crisp white chalk: *Why did you tell me you were sorry, Dr. Font? Come tell us more.*

Clearly Jenny had used as much of her faint voice as she felt comfortable with and didn't assume her sign language would translate through the veil, but no colleague voiced the query, a reference to her prior communication with the doctor. Jenny's language was valid however she used it. For another medium to ask her question might disrupt the channel of the medium the spirit chose.

Eve glanced at her spirit assets against the wall. They nodded, an indication that an answer was forthcoming. Spirits didn't intuit others' thoughts in a psychic sense, but they tended to be a bellwether when another was about to appear.

The transparent, black-clad torso of a wild-haired man manifested over the table.

Jenny wrote on her slate again. *Speak to us, Doctor.*

"I'm sorry I couldn't stop him," Font murmured, his ghostly whisper raspy, adding to the haunted quality. "That I didn't know how terrible he'd become."

Jenny wrote a pointed question. *Did he kill you?*

The spirit nodded. "I suppose, in the end, I knew too much. But I didn't *know* that warehouse was a planted body, a poor soul lured to die through the lie of Arte Uber Alles. Art above everything for the sake of nothing." The spirit's words were bitter, pointed. "I was devastated by the loss of Albert, but that devastation was soon replaced by terror."

Scared to death? Jenny prompted on the slate.

"Yes, that's the last I told my relatives. I was having nightmares of a man outside my window. I thought Albert was haunting me, the greatest irony since he hated ghosts so much. I thought I failed him. I feared he'd terrorize me to the grave. I was led to the Dakota on a pretense of aiding a shut-in elder. When I saw him… Part of me was desperate. You have to understand, there had been a thrall about him, in life. Here I was seeing him again. And if I'm being honest…" The ghost went quiet, bashful.

Jenny motioned encouragement.

The spirit looked at the table below him, and the light of the candle glinted in his transparent eyes. "I suppose I fell a bit in love with him. But I could never have taken his attention away from his one and only love."

Jenny stared at him, and the rest of the mediums watched the exchange.

"Arielle. His only light," the ghost explained. "He loved his sister more than life. They were always close. Too close. It became uncomfortable. Perhaps driving her mad…"

Why did he kill you? Jenny wrote. *And how could we prove it?*

"You can't prove it. Not unless he kept a record of who he influenced. He was always persuasive, but he got too good at encouraging the worst. I'm sure my death appeared a suicide, thanks to the poison in my pocket and the state of my deteriorating health. It only took a little push; he always knew when those near him were vulnerable. Albert likely feared I was going to tell Alfred everything; the shifting company money, his obsessions with controlling the mind, the changes he was making below their very house in secret, his bond with Arielle... So, he poisoned me with one of his own tonics blended with acid and, I assume, made it look as though I'd just drunk myself to death."

The spirit circled the table in a floating curve as though he were the hand of a clock.

"After I died, I wandered detached, trying to piece together who I was and how I'd come to my end. One night I found myself outside his mansion. Everything came rushing back. He tried to stop me, but I escaped."

Jenny gestured for Font to explain how he'd done so.

"There was a device. The culmination of something he was studying when I met him. He was interested in spirit manifestation. What they were tied to and how an electric discharge could disrupt or make them disappear. He tried to vanish me using a trick of his electricity. He likely thought it worked; but I simply faded only to reappear later, and I had to piece everything back together again. He scattered me, and it took me time to remember why I still haunted this earth. It's why I didn't come to you sooner. But you..."

He floated down to Jenny's level to stare into her face. She stared back unflinchingly. "I was wandering in a dark corridor, and suddenly there was a shaft of light ahead of me and your dear young soul was asking questions, reaching out, and I wanted to answer you. I didn't know who you were, but I wanted to answer you and I want this cycle of misery to end...."

Eve's heart swelled with pride at this exchange proving Jenny a conduit of goodness. A good medium was like a lighthouse to a lost soul, a beacon warning them of the sharp rocks of death's listlessness, a point to focus on out of what could become an endless void.

Ideally, the dead were called to give the living answers, and the living who could hear them were called to ask questions. To mutually live into solutions. To right wrongs and heal wounds.

How can we end it, then? Jenny wrote. She exhaled slowly, her breath clouding in the spirit's chill.

"Albert's soul is lost. The key remains in Arielle and in Albert to stop his final aim."

"What aim?" Jenny whispered, her face determined even if she struggled with the words.

"To *end* ghosts as we know them," the spirit replied ruefully. "There's a phrase I remember him uttering when he first began designs with wires and sculpture, merging his aims with Dupont's dread art. 'Out from under the great arches, oblivion will fly.'"

Screwing up her face, Eve could see Jenny wrestling with words. Antonia reached out and squeezed Jenny's hand. "You're incredible, my dear. Take your time and comfort."

Nodding, bolstered by the woman who had become a soul sister, Jenny returned to her slate and chalk, demanding the next question of Font: *What does that mean?*

"I wish I knew. I'm not the only one worried nor the only one who has been hurt. And there's a host of hostages that will be happy to help give you proof, if only we can free them. Follow the money of Arte Uber Alles. You'll find bodies of sad souls strewn in its wake; you just have to know where to look. But for the living, try to get to Arielle. The bond between siblings may have begun as innocent, but it is now something different."

There was a scream; a dark shadow swooped over Font's face and the glow of him was obscured. The candle blew out, and the portal between worlds slammed shut, jarringly, so hard that Jenny, the most open of all of them, was thrown from her chair. Antonia reached out with lightning reflexes and kept Jenny's head from dashing against the nearest desk.

"Shield, everyone," Eve instructed. The women closed their eyes and engaged in their own private ritual. It was becoming more reflexive, but it still felt too ephemeral for Eve. She wished she could give them actual armor, not just mental acrobatics. "Prenze must have read him too, casting his dread shadow wherever anyone's looking too close," she added bitterly.

A sharp rap at the door startled them.

"Sergeant Mahoney looking to speak with you, ladies," McDonnell shouted.

Eve went to the door to let him in rather than shouting back. She wasn't sure what she'd get when she opened the door. She'd like to think of him as a budding ally, but considering the opposition he'd posed to their precinct at first, she'd proceed with caution.

"Sergeant, come in. Any developments since last we spoke?"

He took off his hat, his ruddy face reddening. "Yes. At least, I think so." He looked terribly frustrated. Eve gestured that he sit in the chair opposite the desk nearest the front of the room, her desk, and Jenny went to their modest refreshments tray where she'd set a steaming kettle of water. She readied him a cup while Cora and Antonia sat at the other corners of the room in their respective desks, attentive.

"I'd have come to you sooner but I couldn't remember it. Maddening, that." When Jenny offered him tea, he took it, thanking her with tender, palpable warmth before turning away. Eve recalled the sergeant had a daughter Jenny's age, a little Irish lass. He'd lost her. Jenny hadn't forgotten.

"I am concerned for Alfred Prenze's health, and by proxy that of his sister." Eve reiterated what they'd last left on: that Mahoney would try to root out discrepancies, try to learn more about Alfred's "bouts" of illness— likely drug induced—that she now believed were the times when Albert took over. She'd not yet revealed Albert as alive, as that was a danger for Mahoney to know, but a window into family inner workings could help bring proof of manipulation. "What happened that you couldn't remember?"

"Alfred asked me to do something, to look into an account. He went into his study and when he came back out, not fifteen minutes later, he told me not to worry about it. But he enforced that. Somehow. As if he tried to *will* it from me."

The officer scratched his balding head.

"Then it was like I didn't have it in my head anymore, what Alfred had wanted me to look into. But I've been trying to work at it, to pry it free. It was so much like when I'd black out from too much drink and see only pieces the next day. I hated that. I won't go there again." Mahoney shook his head vehemently. "I know what it's like to lose control, to have a need so big that nothing can fill it." He shuddered. "I don't want to go back to those days. To the drink. So I fought it off and remembered the list."

"That's wonderful," Eve encouraged. "Good work."

"Alfred wanted me to check to see if the Prenze London bank account had been touched, and when, and if that matched or predated his brother's will. He also wanted me to test every downstairs lock as he felt sure he was being kept from something downstairs."

"I'm glad that you remembered all this. It sounds very useful."

"It was like trying to find it again in a fog."

"I've an insight into why you felt so incapacitated by it, if you're willing to entertain something more fantastical."

Mahoney sipped his tea and widened his eyes. "Shoot."

"I believe that powers of mesmerism are being employed."

He raised a skeptical brow. "Influencing the mind?"

Eve nodded. "I doubt Alfred is doing it willingly; I think he's being controlled too." Her instinct was to see if Mahoney would come to Albert's involvement on his own, hopefully with independent proof. They couldn't be seen as leading witnesses or jumping to conclusions.

"I don't want to be under the influence," Mahoney declared. "Anymore. Of any*thing.*"

"And you don't have to," Eve reassured him. "You already discovered the key to fight back."

"And I'll be damned if someone is trying to do that to such a good man as Alfred."

"Then keep rooting around; something's rotten. See if anything affects Miss Prenze. Please take note of their regular routines and how they've changed. If you like, I can send you to someone who can teach you some strategies for blocking the influences."

"I'm not sure I want to see anyone about metaphysical stuff, miss; your lot is about all I can take," he said with a chuckle.

Jenny had gone to the largest of their windows and was gesturing to something outside. Two figures came through and hovered there, the panes making crosses through their bodies: a long-haired woman and a little girl in plain dresses, holding hands, staring lovingly at the sergeant. The little girl ran to Jenny, whispered something in her ear, and the two children shared a smile. Antonia put a hand to her heart.

I'm going to tell him something from his family, Jenny signed to Eve and then began writing a note. Eve knew better than to stop her this time.

When Mahoney had last been in their office it had been made clear that his daughter had died of illness and his wife had later committed suicide, but not before having been taken advantage of by a sham Spiritualist. It was not only why he'd begun drinking but also why he'd been so skeptical of the team, not to mention so loyal to the man who had gotten him out of his addiction: Alfred Prenze. Jenny had offered to Eve that they could do a séance for his family and reconnect them, but Eve had stilled her for a later time. This time the little girl was not to be dissuaded.

Jenny handed Mahoney a note. He read and his breath caught in a sharp intake. Tears fell from his eyes.

"Thank you, little one," he said through a sob, plucking a handkerchief from his breast pocket and wiping his face. "I…you couldn't have known my nickname for her; my "little lapwing"…so you…you must have a legitimate gift. I am…overwhelmed by this, by her words of love…and will ponder it in my heart."

The women were quiet a moment as he composed himself. Antonia had silently refreshed his cup of tea and glided back to her desk in the rear of the room. Mahoney's daughter waved to Jenny and ran off through the wall as if toward a playground or a carousel, something inscrutable in magic and play that many ghosts of children managed to retain, her mother blowing a kiss to her unseeing husband and trailing off after her sprightly charge. The room warmed.

He turned to Eve. "I'll trust you, then. Send me to your mentor."

"Ambassador Bishop. Call upon him at the British consulate where he keeps office hours. Tell him it's about shielding. You can share as much with him as you know; he has been an ally of this department from the first, liaising with Roosevelt in the earliest days."

Mahoney nodded. He turned back to Jenny. "Thanks again, Miss Jenny. May the angels be ever with you." He left, closing the door quietly behind him.

No one asked what it was about; they knew. Eve had seen the woman and child hovering around Jenny as she wrote, and she presumed her colleagues sensed Mahoney's family too.

"Trust him or no, it can't hurt to have other eyes and minds aware," Eve said after he'd gone, smiling fondly at Jenny. "You gave him healing, little angel, as only you could."

Antonia approached just as Jenny wobbled a bit on her feet. Empathic to the height of the gift, Antonia was highly calibrated to each of them, but with Jenny, it was unmatched, clearly her designated guide and guardian. Antonia's breathy voice was sisterly and stern as she ushered Jenny to a cushioned bench against the wall. "You've channeled *twice* today before lunch. You *must* take a rest."

Obediently, Jenny lay back and closed her eyes. That much mediumship at once was a lot for an adult body, let alone a pint-sized child, no matter how wise her soul.

"Now for what's next," Cora prompted.

Eve clapped her hands. "Horowitz is, as we speak, scouting locations for a Prenze surveillance outpost. There are several things to follow up on from the search of the properties. Cora, would you mind seeing if there's anything anyone could tell you about the Prenze London account Font mentioned? Follow the money. I'd call upon Ambassador Bishop to go with you and ensure access. I know you want more time with the Bishops to rekindle your family connections, and I want that to flourish, keeping our allies informed and stronger than ever."

Cora beamed, agreeing to the plan.

Antonia offered her own next step. "I'd like to conspire with Gran to see if there's any of Arielle Prenze's social circle to ask questions of, inquire how she's doing."

"Brilliant. Once the detective has a location secured, we'll all be tasked with rotation. Remember. Take care, and shield."

* * * *

As planned, Eve was to meet Horowitz in his office to follow up. She faced the usual eyeing at the front desk; the neutral police staff card signed by Roosevelt raised eyebrows; left so open ended as to her actual role. It may have removed the stigma and distrust of mediumship by removing the Ghost Precinct title for her safety, but her being a woman with ambiguous purpose did nothing for her standing in their eyes.

The detective had his lamp turned toward a missive he was typing out on a small, battered typewriter when Eve came around the hall. As if he sensed her, even through the din of the building, he looked up the moment she saw him and that smile continued to make Eve weak kneed and thrilled, the most pleasant sensation she hoped never went away.

"Right on schedule," he said, rising to his feet. "We've much to do."

"Did you find a suitable surveillance location?"

"I did. I arranged everything at the New Netherland. But before we go and see, there's an unfortunate development from the doctors." His face a bit grim, he turned to his desk and picked up a paper. "This was dropped off for me today by courier," he said, handing over a note on letterhead marked Bellevue Hospital. Eve read:

Dear Detective Horowitz,

It is with a great and perplexed sorrow that I write to you to tell you that the monitor box you brought to me has disappeared and in its place was left a threatening note: "This device does not belong to you. Have nothing to do with those who have unholy associations with the dead!"

It most certainly continues to be a police matter.

Since you first approached me with this device, Dr. Levi, whom I have since befriended as a colleague, said I should be the one to reply to you. I regret to inform you the device disappeared from his office.

What I can say is that we believe the machine was some kind of brain mapping device prototype. "Reading" the organ with electricity and a pattern. Terminology around these early ideas have used the term "electric encephalon," but these are the earliest days of an untested science. Both Dr. Levi and I are grateful for your showing it to us, and we hope you'll keep us informed if the device resurfaces or how else we might be of service.

Once Eve looked up after reading, Horowitz chose to take a hopeful tack. "I am glad for anyone at Mount Sinai and Bellevue to work together." Such positivity eluded Eve, and she slammed a fist on the desk. "The doctors made progress, and now it's gone again. Even our *solid* evidence vanishes!"

Her colleague nodded, his expression empathetic; but rallied, the picture of perseverance. "Let's take heart, however, now that not only the villains know about it, it's not solely their instrument anymore."

Taking his cue to overcome dejection, she remembered Gran's advice that protection meant not letting doubt and insecurity in. Jacob Horowitz was so good for her in this regard; his nature was optimistic and unflappable. Seeing her change of expression, he smiled. "That's my girl."

As someone who had always chafed against the idea of being "possessed" by any man, the way the detective said "my girl" was collegial. Encouraging. Awakening. The idea of being his was something that filled her with something she'd never felt, an invitation to intimacy that she'd never craved until they'd begun working together and gravitating ever closer.

A sharp rap came on Horowitz's partially open door, the officer peering in as if at the mouth of some mysterious cave.

"You Miss Whitby?" the officer asked gruffly, eyeing her. Eve sat straighter and was glad she'd worn her uniform. It didn't prevent her from being suspect in the average officer's eyes, but it did make them pause so as not to entirely dismiss her outright, especially with a message.

"I am."

"A…Reverend Blessing called to try to find you? Call bounced around a bit until we were told you might be here with this one." He gestured a thumb toward Horowitz.

"What's wrong?" Eve asked, immediately gathering her things, turning to explain to the detective. "Something has to be wrong for him to call."

The officer made a face. "Ask him yourself; he's still on the line. He wasn't making any sense so I figured I'd just try to come find you, I've got better things to do than deal with paranormal histrionics."

Eve tried to bite her tongue but couldn't stop herself. "Yes, *please* let me take this off your hands so *someone* can be granted a moment of respect around here!"

The man just snorted as she and Horowitz followed him into the captain's office, which was thankfully vacant. Eve was doubtful the captain would appreciate a woman on his phone, from everything Horowitz had said about him, let alone a woman talking to an exorcist.

For the reverend to actually use the phone was a concern. Gran had insisted her closest contacts and colleagues all have one installed, but he *hated* it. For a man who regularly dealt with possessions, he seemed more worried about technological demons than anything ancient realms could throw at him.

Eve asked the operator to be connected, and the line rang for what seemed like eternity before a familiar, rich baritone voice picked up.

"Hello? Eve, I hope this is you."

"It is, Reverend, what's wrong?"

"It isn't something for the telephone wires. It's something to be seen in person. Reverend Coronado is here. Something is wrong. He's staying with me until this…episode passes. Please come as soon as you can."

"All right…" She turned to Jacob, putting the bell against her collar to muffle her discussion with the detective. "He wants me to visit. It's important. Something's wrong with Reverend Coronado."

Horowitz nodded, plucking his pocket watch in silver etched with delicate filigree from his breast pocket and opening to the time. "We'll be there soon, then."

"It's very good of you to come," Eve said with a delighted smile. He didn't have to. The fact he was as amiable as he was adaptable, taking on the next problem with supreme confidence, was one of his many appealing qualities. Eve was losing count. She returned back to the telephone line.

"Reverend, we'll be by as soon as it takes to arrive from Mulberry Street. Detective Horowitz will be with me."

"Very well. Do prepare him for my work and world, will you? He didn't get the chance to see us in action the unfortunate last time our paths crossed."

"I shall. Until soon, Reverend." Hoping her sign-off sounded full of reassurance, she hung up the bell. The officer glared at them, but she offered him a genial smile.

"Thank you, Officer, for your time and facilitation!" the detective exclaimed, matching Eve's collegial tone.

The man harrumphed. Eve and Jacob, in a unified front of positivity, refused to let this man's sourness make them cross in turn. They held their heads high as they exited into the hall and out onto the street.

Eve pointed further west to pick up a trolley uptown along the west side.

"The reverends are exorcists, if you recall, Coronado under Blessing's mentorship. They're Protestant—Episcopalian to be specific—so they're hardly what the Vatican would send, but what they do is known and appreciated, and much more accessible as they aren't beholden to Rome's limitations."

"Reverend Coronado. Yes, I recall you and he speaking fondly. To be fair, we'd all been put unconscious; it does addle the mind. But as I recall, you two did seem to be a bit breathless together," the detective said with a wide grin.

Eve scowled. "Why are you smiling about it?"

"What, would you rather I be jealous about it?" He leaned forward. "Do I have something to be jealous about?"

"What, no, I...I just..." Eve gestured awkwardly as she sputtered. "I... don't know why it bears comment, is all. I mean..."

"He is, as I'm sure is universally noted by anyone he meets, extremely handsome," the detective stated matter-of-factly, "and I find it *terribly* endearing that you're not sure what to do with beautiful people."

Eve rocked back on her heels. "Oh? Well, I find this conversation *terribly* mortifying."

He laughed. "All this to say that I notice you, Eve Whitby. I notice your dear, open heart and the fact that you have moments of breathless—"

Eve clenched her fists, interrupting him with an exasperated squeal, her face surely as red as the firehouse door they passed en route to the trolley line. "*You* make me breathless, Jacob Horowitz, I'll have you know!"

She darted toward the stop ahead as if running away from him. With a delighted chuckle, he pursued her.

"I wasn't fishing for a compliment," he said, catching up with her in a few easy strides, "but I won't complain about receiving one."

She eyed him a moment, knowing the fact he could see her blush made it impossible to cool it, her skin a terrible traitor to composure. The color might as well be a tattoo at this point, unable to conceal the mark whenever he was around.

"And to be very clear," the detective continued with that disarming smile that had made her breathless in the first place, "I wasn't being jealous. I find jealousy unbecoming. I was, honestly, teasing you. But that's really not fair."

Eve looked down at her hands, pressing them together so she wouldn't fidget. "It...*isn't* fair," she murmured. "I...I'm no good at this, talking about such things with people I...well—"

Her inelegance was, quite truly, saved by the bell of the trolley pulling up to the stop. She fumbled for coins in her reticule, but by the time her trembling hands found them, Jacob had already paid and slid into an empty bench, holding her place next to him.

"I hope you don't mind dogs," Eve said, eager to change the subject. "They're friendly. The place may be a bit of a zoo. He's rescued as many animals as he's shepherded souls."

"Why, that's wonderful!"

Glad for the detective's enthusiasm, Eve continued, relieved to offer information rather than disastrously flirting. "Reverend Blessing was one of Henry Bergh's greatest supporters when he founded the American Society for the Prevention of Cruelty to Animals. I think that's where he met Gran, at a gala. One of them mentioned spirits and they've been best friends and spiritual comrades in arms ever since. He took on sheltering and fostering dogs as a part of Bergh's initiative, particularly greyhounds, rescued from harrowing racing conditions. Of the many I've met through the years, they're well behaved, albeit excitable."

A few blocks uptown and across the park from Evelyn Northe-Stewart's fine home was a modest brick townhouse adjacent to a slightly finer rectory, serving an Episcopalian church whose grand spires and front entrance could be accessed from the next avenue over.

"The reverend is a supply pastor to congregations all around the city and to shut-ins, places where a black man of the cloth is welcome, mind you," Eve said with an edge she knew Jacob would understand and, unfortunately, empathize with. "He meets the city's needs, always has. But he's getting old. He needed someone who could offer the same kind of flexibility, cultural access, and spiritual gifts. Coronado, with another year to go in seminary, showed up on his doorstep, much like Cora showed up on mine: in a sequence of visions. Fate led them each to their calling."

She lifted the brass door knocker and let it go. A sequence of barks followed. A few creaks of floorboards later, a white-haired, dark-skinned man with a smile that could light up a whole city opened the door. Three long noses poked out from around him, emitting soft little excited whines.

"Come in, friends," he said, and tugged on three collars lest any of them think twice about leaping out to race a streetcar. "Back, you fiends," he warned the dogs lovingly.

"You remember Detective Horowitz?" Eve prompted as Reverend Blessing shut the door behind them. "Hello, puppies," she whispered, bending so that they wouldn't be tempted to jump up, as they covered her face with kisses and the bunts of happy, nudging noses trying to find her hands to hurry her petting them.

"Reverend, good to see you again." Horowitz extended his hand.

"And you, Detective," Blessing replied heartily as the men shook.

Eve was delighted to see that there was a new dog since last she'd visited, admittedly too long ago, a tall, brindle-brown creature who was perhaps the most excited about fresh company.

"And hello, new friends," Horowitz said, grinning as he bent beside Eve and subjected himself to a round of skittering toenails, small little jumps and circles, and a few well-placed kisses right on his nose. They allowed this fondness to continue a few moments before Eve stood and the dogs took to sitting and looking up at them with trained, albeit straining, grace.

"Thank you for coming on such short notice," Blessing said before lowering his voice. "I don't dare return him to the seminary. I don't want his colleagues to see him like this."

Eve leaned in, matching his tone. "Like...how?"

"I..." The reverend stepped closer and whispered, "I think he's possessed."

Eve stared at Blessing and managed to suppress a laugh. "But...*you're* the exorcist! With all due respect, Reverend, why did you call me?"

"Because you were asked for by name and then there wasn't another word." Blessing folded his arms. Eve's blood chilled, and whatever laugh she'd held back died in her throat. He nodded his head toward the hall. "Come with me."

Following through the entrance hall of the modest residence, they were led to an open, arched door and into a small parlor with goldenrod painted walls. Floor-to-ceiling bookshelves were interspersed with religious paintings. A few wooden chairs were set about a tea table, near a brick fireplace with logs but no fire, and a piano against the far wall. Wooden shutters were open to the midday sun, and several lush pots of ivy plants sat along the sill.

Reverend Coronado was lying on a long, well-worn leather bench. Yes, he would be considered universally handsome, if not exquisite. His clean-shaven face was serene, his short, black hair was all mussed, and his priest's collar was partially undone, a jolt of starched white springing out from his buttoned black collar, but the moment Eve entered he opened his eyes and shot to his feet.

"Eve, darling!" He rushed to her and embraced her, kissing one cheek then the other and grasping her shoulders. "Oh, my dear, it feels so amazing to be able to *touch* you after all this time!"

At this, Detective Horowitz coughed. Loudly. Eve's face went an immediate scarlet.

"Oh, Lord," Reverend Blessing uttered, passing a hand over his face at the threshold.

"Reverend Coronado," Eve began hesitantly, stepping back. "I'm not sure you're feeling very well. Is there a reason you're being so familiar and enthusiastic with me?"

"Don't you recognize me, your *best* friend?" The reverend's voice was still his own, his same rich, musical tone with a slight accent from his early years in Mexico City, but his delivery was hardly his usual cadence, it was more that of...

Eve narrowed her eyes and took a step forward, leaning in. "Maggie?"

"Yes!" he said as if that were entirely obvious.

"Maggie! What are you *doing*?" Eve exclaimed.

"Practicing!" the reverend exclaimed, in Maggie's distinct exasperation whenever she'd done something and thought Eve too slow in catching on. "We need to get into Prenze's home, and *I* can't go in as a ghost, because of whatever he's done to the place, and none of *you* can go in as you're compromised, so we need a willing target!"

"And Coronado was willing?" Eve could hear her own pitch rising. "To be *possessed*? Maggie, you know we have protocols—"

The reverend batted his hand as Maggie's ghost did whenever she wanted Eve to stop worrying. "We're in a new world with this terrible Prenze, and we *have* to think ahead of him."

"Why didn't you *ask* me?" Eve said, reeling. "This is a bold step. To say the *least*."

"What safer way to conduct a test possession than by starting out possessing an exorcist?" Coronado countered.

"The ghost has a point," Horowitz stated, staring at the two of them with blank surprise.

"But Maggie..." Eve tried to keep her calm and her patience, but it was difficult given Maggie's impetuous nature, and speaking to her through the admittedly—*devastatingly*—handsome Coronado was an additional trial, her conversation with Jacob having made it all the more pointed.

While always wanting to be helpful, Eve wasn't sure Maggie thought everything entirely through or considered the many complications. Sighing, Eve steepled her hands and tried again. "Maggie. Listen to me. What if we can't get you out?"

"What part of *exorcist* are you missing here, my dear?! Do you doubt these fine men's talents?" Speaking through Coronado, the ghost sounded appalled.

"Of *course* I don't doubt their talents, but what if, during exorcism, you're sent somewhere, Heaven, the Corridors, Sanctuary, and you have a hard time coming back?" Eve asked. "We've no protocol for this, no precedent..."

"I'll peel away from him just as I tumbled into him," came the reply. "What if you were to call her out like you would in a séance?" Blessing suggested, still standing in the doorway. "I'll lend a few prayers for extrication."

Before Eve could do anything, Maggie seemed to wrestle inside the gorgeous man; a sudden shroud of eerie light overlaid upon his shuddering body.

"You don't have to be quite so *dramatic* about it, Miss Hathorn," Coronado said quietly through gritted teeth, fighting to regain himself amid this takeover.

A shimmering form of white begin to separate from his handsome face. But then suddenly the priest's eyes shot open and his arms went out.

"Eve, before we part, will you do me a favor?" Coronado asked. Eve raised her brow, and before she could answer, he threw his arms around her, speaking softly into her ear. "I've missed embraces most of all. I wanted to feel this again. Especially after I nearly died *twice*, it made me pine even more keenly for my tactile days."

He drew back, cupped her face, and leaned in. For a panicked moment, Eve wasn't sure what anyone was going to do next. Jacob darted forward with a hissing intake of breath, clearly ready to extricate her. But the priest placed a friendly, chaste, soft kiss on Eve's head and loosed a small laugh that was entirely Maggie's way. Coronado stepped back. Jacob did too, but his brow remained furrowed in clear consternation.

"Thank you," Coronado said. In that moment she wasn't sure who was speaking; it could have been either of them. The reverend didn't seem to be fighting Maggie, and the earnestness was clear. Only then did Horowitz release the breath he'd held.

"Promise you'll tell me before you do something so bold again, Maggie?" Eve pleaded. "We've been worried about you, again, this whole time."

"Eve, I'm sorry. I went to see the Prenze mansion and there were spirits in the basement. Trapped. They put their hands on the cellar window, pleading for release. It nearly drove me mad with anger and desire to help. What I fear Prenze is doing, in that basement prison, is exploiting the dead's fear of death. The *final* death. The obliteration of the spirit. Sending a soul not just to an undiscovered country but a nonexistent one. He tried to destroy me and in a way that could never be reconstituted. That's the ultimate evil, to not only kill but to entirely wipe away!"

It hadn't occurred to Eve how much of a vendetta Maggie had against Prenze. She hadn't empathized enough.

"I don't mean to doubt you, Maggie, but especially with Prenze, he'll punish *all* of us. I have to be responsible for *all* my operatives, whoever is inadvertently dragged into this too, like the reverends. And you can't use Coronado to spy on Prenze anyway! If Albert Prenze was indeed responsible for abducting Gran and toying with the rest of us, the reverends were both there; all of us were knocked cold, so you're going to have to find someone else less suspicious."

"Of course." Maggie scoffed. "This was merely practice for the next feat."

"And what's—*who's* that?" Eve cried. "I know you think not telling me your plans will strengthen dramatic tension, but that's *not* how a police department works, dear!"

Maggie did take her existence a bit too theatrically. Perhaps she'd learned too much from the Veil family. "You must tell me what you plan to do next," Eve continued. "If it is another possession, you'd best be careful and ask for permission."

"Well…we'll see about that," Maggie replied through Coronado airily. "Who I have in mind is a critical piece of the puzzle. If I can work with her, she'll unlock everything. But now that I know I can possess, I can seek her out and see what we can do together. So, I'll be right with you.…"

There was another shake and shudder that worked its way through the reverend's body, as if he'd touched a live electrical wire.

"Actually"—Coronado laughed nervously, perhaps his own unnerved intonation mixed with Maggie's—"I do think I need a little help here. Don't exorcise me so thoroughly that you banish me, mind you, but perhaps a little shove from the Book of Common Prayer. I don't wish to tear at this poor man," the ghost said with a sigh. "I rather like him. Do tell him so, as I'm not sure he can hear me."

At this, a choked laugh escaped Coronado's mouth. Shaking his head, his cadence returned to his own to counter to the ghost. "I can hear you, Maggie, and I confess…I rather like you too, unconventional as your new friendship may be," the priest said. "Let me be sitting down this time, as when you took me the first time, I was nearly bowled over."

"Maggie is rather a force of nature." Eve grinned. "And thank you, Reverend, for being so wonderful about this. I'm so sorry for this inconvenience."

"Don't be," he said himself, beautiful eyes searching her with the utmost honesty. "It's…one of the most incredible experiences of my life."

A quiet moment followed where no one knew what to say.

Blessing stepped forward to stand close between Eve and Horowitz.

"Detective, all my life I have been shoulder to shoulder alongside Jewish brethren fighting for justice and freedom. All traditions are welcome in matters of care and well-being. If you would like to take part, you are welcome to offer any *berakhot*, any prayer or blessing you feel would suit this…admittedly unique situation."

The detective nodded solemnly.

Closing his eyes and holding out his hands, Reverend Blessing began a psalm. Once he had recited the psalm, and invoked peace and quietude on behalf of all souls, he withdrew a small metal dispenser, a vial that allowed a small spritz of holy water to anoint the surroundings. Water splashed gently on Coronado's face and the reverend closed his eyes, serene.

"I will not utter a renunciation," Blessing continued in his clear, commanding tone, "as this presence with us is no demon, no evil, but a family friend. Merciful God, guide Margaret Hathorn out from the body of our colleague Reverend Coronado so that she may return to us in her ethereal light, and our brother here regain himself. Lord, *Adonai Eloheinu*, hear our prayer."

"Hear our prayer," Eve echoed.

Jacob added a congregational response, "*Baruch Adonai ham'vorach l'olam va-ed.*"

"Come back, Maggie," Eve continued gently, reaching out her hand. Coronado reached back but hesitated.

Light worked over his body; the image of his face shifted, two faces superimposed, uncanny and unnatural. He winced, a slight moment of pain. There was a moan of strain, as if trying to wrest something heavy free.

A silver, luminous hand separated out, one above the other.

"That's it, my dear." Eve coaxed her lifelong friend forward.

Reverend Coronado stood stock still as Maggie's cold, transparent palm hovered over Eve's and the rest of her followed, breaking free in an ethereal extrication that caused the reverend to shake violently.

Blessing stepped forward to steady his colleague. He walked Coronado back to the bench and helped him sit, and he slumped against the wall. Moisture beaded his brow. Blessing withdrew a handkerchief from his coat pocket and offered it to his friend before stepping back to stand next to Eve and Horowitz.

Maggie floated before the reverend, bending to sit as if next to him, floating an inch above the leather cushion. He turned to her, a complex set of emotions on his handsome face.

"Can you hear me, Reverend?" Maggie said, searching Coronado's face, her hands folded over her chest as if in supplication.

"I can, Miss Hathorn," the reverend replied.

"I'm very sorry to have troubled you," Maggie said. "But thank you so much for being so lovely about it."

"I'm…I'm not upset," the reverend said earnestly. "I…don't know that there could be a more profound closeness between two souls." He reached out to Maggie, cocking his head to the side in wonder as his hand passed through hers instead of taking it, as it seemed he would have wished to. "Thank you…for your closeness, Margaret Hathorn, forgive me for being so bold, but…haunt me again?"

Maggie's colorless, silver cheeks became a darker grey. A ghostly blush.

"I…it would be my honor, Reverend," she replied, biting her lip.

Suddenly Eve realized they were in the midst of an unexpectedly intimate moment and she felt the intruder. Glancing at Jacob, the detective's eyes were as wide as if he had walked in on something he shouldn't have, felt terribly awkward, and didn't know how to walk back out of it.

Reverend Blessing cleared his throat across the room.

At this, Maggie snapped to an alertness, shifting back away from her new fascination and emitting a nervous giggle as Coronado sat back, utterly dazed.

Everyone was clearly happy to be interrupted by the patter of feet, the dogs returning in a greyhound whirlwind to break the tension.

"Maggie," Eve called.

"Yes, dear?" Maggie floated over, a dreamy look on her face.

Eve had never seen her deathly friend so happy. It pierced Eve's heart. Maggie had fallen in love once, a terrible complication on account of Eve's father. Maggie had never actually had a love of her own, none of the thrilling connections and heart-stopping chances that Eve had begun having with the detective. She suddenly wanted more of the world for Maggie, and perhaps something like this was a window into life, and a chance to obliterate a spirit's regret.

"I promise I won't just disappear again," Maggie said, as if she knew what Eve was about to admonish.

"I believe you. I know you get an idea in your head, and you're your own woman. I'm not your mother, but I would dearly appreciate knowing your plans."

"Arielle Prenze is my plan, Eve; isn't it brilliant? If I possess her to unlock the secrets of that house, if I possess her to *gain* secrets and trust, we free the trapped spirits and foil whatever Prenze's dastardly plans are, including releasing her from his thrall, if she's indeed gone along with his plan as the woman who helped abduct Gran when this all started."

"She wants to possess Arielle Prenze," Eve explained to Horowitz.

"Well, that's a quite good idea as a way into the family," the detective offered, shifting toward the cooler draft in the room. "I say good luck, Miss Hathorn. Miss Prenze hasn't been seen in some time, according to the patrolmen in her precinct I spoke with while scouting our surveillance location. I don't know how you get in to see her let alone *into* her...."

"All the better if she wants to get out!" Maggie gestured dramatically toward the company. "I leave that opportunity for you clever lot to manufacture; then I'll swoop in and we'll learn what makes these odd ducks tick. I am telling you, we shall be heroes!" And with that the ghost flew out the window.

Everyone blinked after her silvery form, the room returning to normal temperature. Eve ran a hand over her face. "Well, no one can say we lead uneventful lives or that our company is not colorful, even in greyscale."

"Are you all right?" Blessing asked his mentee.

"Yes...a bit thirsty. But...yes," the man replied, dazed. "I've a lot to think about."

"I'm sure." Blessing retrieved a glass of water from a decanter across the room and brought it to the man's side. He turned to Eve and Horowitz. "Thank you for coming."

"Of course," Eve said. "If there's anything else that relates to our case, we'd be grateful for your thoughts. We'll show ourselves out. Please rest and take care, Reverends, both of you," she added gently.

Coronado simply smiled at her.

Outside, once they'd hailed an enclosed carriage to their next destination, Jacob seemed to be weighing something to say as they sat down and started off. He finally blurted it out. "I'm sorry, I'm sure I shouldn't have been affected by his holding you so close, but...I...was."

Eve's stomach was again lifted by butterflies. "*That* was Maggie, using the poor man as a puppet," Eve countered. "I know this work tries the senses."

"He didn't seem to mind," the detective said with a small chuckle. "In fact, everyone seemed to be enjoying themselves. Hardly the scene I could have predicted in regard to a possession."

"I am glad I could give my dearest friend *and* the good reverend some comfort, that's all." Eve turned to Jacob, leaned close, and smiled. "You can tell, I hope, the differences."

The detective furrowed his brow as if he didn't understand.

"There's everyone else, and then..." Reaching out, she ran a soft, slow caress over his cheek; then her fingertips moved to graze his throat, and as she did, his eyelids fluttered closed and his mouth parted with the slightest sigh. "There's *you*..." She rested her hand over his heart.

He reached up to grasp her hand with his own, pressing her hand to his chest so that she could feel the swift pace of that dear heart within. Leaning back against the cushion of the cab, he turned to her, his eyes wide, open, searching, warm, and overwhelmed. This achingly tender sight made Eve's heart falter. His next words made her stop breathing.

"The range of feeling on any given day in your world—the shift between emotional, spiritual, psychological, and paranormal happenings—isn't something I'm accustomed to. But then again, Eve Whitby, you have me feeling any number of things I've never felt before.... Every day is new and unexpected." He leaned a bit closer to her. "And what on earth will be next...?"

Eve panicked and rejoiced in equal measure as the distance between them narrowed.

The carriage jolted suddenly in a near collision with another driver, and they nearly knocked their heads together before being jostled about. The driver hurled a few choice Gaelic curses.

As Eve gasped for breath, Jacob glanced out the window and sighed with a weary laugh. "And...we missed our stop." He rapped on the carriage roof.

Eve threw open the carriage door, fanning herself with her hand even though it was hardly warm out. She stood on the baseboard of the carriage and looked out upon the picturesque display before them.

They had stopped at the northeast corner of Central Park and Fifth Avenue in all its grandeur, from the park's unfolding length uptown, to the magnificent buildings anchoring the blocks surrounding the park, to the finest ladies and gentlemen strolling around the exteriors, parading in and out doors onto carpeted stairs. The work of the gilded age was laid out before them, and all the city's spirits couldn't seem to stop staring at wealth's parade either.

As she paused, her foot on the baseboard, Jacob jumped down and raced around the side to help her down, grasping her hands and holding her close, not just to balance her, but clearly for the excuse of being able to touch her. His arms didn't just steady her, they enswathed her.

Only the driver's distinct "ahem" had them breaking apart and rummaging in pockets for the fare. The driver sped away with a distinct snort of "lovebirds."

Jacob stared at Eve as if he were coming to from a dream.

They had to do something about their attraction. It had become positively absurd; their distraction was incapacitating and if they didn't do something about it soon, it would affect their work for the worse. And what would solve this problem? Even the mere thought of the possibilities had Eve swooning, and she nearly lost her footing on the cobblestones but regained herself before being humiliated by weak knees.

"Lead the way, Detective. We do have work to do," she said, chiding herself aloud.

"Indeed," he agreed, holding himself to the same.

He gestured ahead of him, to the New Netherland hotel, which had just opened within the year, a grand, Romanesque building as was the present fashion, a whole seventeen stories tall, climbing above its surroundings, the lower stories in brownstone and the rest in buff brick, with stone and terra cotta detailing. Nothing in this part of town went without lavish flourishes, whether in architecture or in fashion.

"New, higher buildings going in want views of the park, both hotel and residential, so we've a bit of an angle, before current construction blocks that section." He gestured southeast, where Eve recognized the small corner of curated green hedgerows, pressed on all sides by towering sandstone. "There is our house in question. The ground floor will be impossible, but the upper floors prove visible. Fitton is already installing scopes. We can scale fire escapes, if need be, for vantage, allowing us quite a scale."

"Amazing!" Eve exclaimed. "I'm *so* impressed you put this all together."

He held out his arm. Eve took it.

"*Monsieur, madame*," the uniformed bellman said at the top of the hotel's carpeted stairs. Horowitz bowed his head in a nod, and Eve did the same, and then the doors were opened for them.

"You've all this set up, with knowledge of coming and going?" Eve murmured as the bellman eyed them. Their clothes clearly weren't fine enough for the clientele here, but the mustachioed man at the reception desk nodded at Horowitz warmly.

"The front desk knows there are several of us with the police," the detective explained quietly, "trying to assess a witness vantage point. I mentioned I may be conducting interviews. They know everyone, including us, wishes to remain discreet. We're on the sixth floor; the elevator is this way."

"Good."

The lobby was grand, all marble and brass, and Horowitz led her through the lobby to a gilded, caged elevator car, the operator offering the detective a genial "sir, miss," to them both, pressing the sixth-floor button, clearly aware of their business and hardly as wary about it as the front door. The cage rattled closed and lurched up the shaft.

Once they were released into a red-carpeted hall, Horowitz led Eve to a suite of rooms in the corner, knocking on the door at the end of the hall.

The man who opened the door was a pleasant, dark-haired, olive-skinned young man in uniform.

"Good to see you, Officer," Eve said to Horowitz's friend Fitton, a studious, pleasant, extremely helpful presence in several instances, his close colleague from his first days on the force until he'd been transferred further downtown.

"And you, Miss Whitby," he said, showing Eve into a richly furnished suite with hardwood floors, with sets of doors that opened to further rooms, allowing for more of a vantage point toward their target.

Fitton gestured to the windows facing the park and downtown. "As you can see, we're set up." Telescopes were set through the slats of two of them, two pairs of high-grade binoculars on the console table near the wall, pencils and notebooks between.

"Incredible. Thank you." Eve turned to Horowitz and whispered, "How do we have the budget to rent this?"

"We don't, but in preparing for surveillance I checked to see if any hotel owners were trying to curry favor with local police. This was one. What moral quandary the management may be in to warrant the need for favor is a mystery that will have to wait another day."

"That's *clever*," Eve said, additionally impressed.

A figure came around the open doorway of the rear set of rooms, dressed in a simple cream dress of lace and linen, her dark hair up in a simple bun.

"Oh, my goodness, Rachel!" Eve exclaimed and rushed over to the Whitby family friend who had meant so much to Eve since childhood, embracing her enthusiastically before stepping back to sign, *You're here too!*

Rachel happened to be a talented medium in her own right. While deaf, she could hear spirits and communicate through writing and sign.

A lip-reader is useful in surveillance, Rachel signed in reply.

Eve whirled to Jacob, who was smiling proudly. "You really did think of everything!"

Plus, the more time spent together, the more familial power I can have on your behalf, Rachel signed. Glancing at her second cousin Jacob, then at Eve, she added, *Because if I've anything to say about it, you two are meant for one another—*

"Thank you," Eve interrupted her unexpected declaration with a cough and turned away.

"What was that?" Jacob asked, eyeing them.

"Nothing, just fondness, that's all."

Eve turned away toward the windows, bending to gaze into the telescope. It was trained and focused to the upper floors of the Prenze mansion, which offered up several key vantage points. "It's exceedingly clever of you to have deduced this angle, Jacob," Eve said, watching a man in a hat and long coat enter a room and draw back a curtain in a large open bedroom with ample light and gleaming floors.

"It isn't perfect," the detective replied. "One floor down might get us even more, but it's what I could get today; we'll see if we can shift down tomorrow."

Even from the first moment, this uncertain enterprise did not disappoint.

The bottom half of a four-post bed with its curtains open was visible, a velvet chair beside it. A frothy gown was splayed across the bed, and petite, pale feet were moving restlessly in the diaphanous layers, as if kicking while dreaming.

"That must be Arielle Prenze, the younger sister," Eve said. She watched as a man in a long coat and a dark hat bent over the form, and it seemed as though he were dabbing something at her mouth; only the slight hint of her jaw could be seen, tendrils of red hair splayed to the side. Perhaps bidding her drink or pressing a tonic to her lips.

Grabbing a pair of the binoculars, Horowitz stood beside Eve and pressed the lenses between the slats of the shutters hiding their activity from view. Even though no other building near them rivaled the height, they could still be seen from below if anyone truly cared to look. "Sedated and barely stirring."

Eve stepped back and signed to Rachel that she'd like her thoughts, pointing her to the other telescope to see if she could glean any words, though the angle wasn't perfect. But if he sat, it might be. She picked up a notebook and went to the south side of the room, closer to the objects of interest.

Eve returned her gaze to the telescope and was drawn to the movement from one set of the high-ceilinged rooms to the next. A light was turned brighter, and she saw the same man in a long coat mixing what appeared to be a solution into a clear glass and offering it to the lips of someone in trousers and shirtsleeves. Presumably, Alfred Prenze.

Another figure in trousers paced in the background. No maids or other attendants could be seen anywhere; no other activity, movement, or light could be seen around the parts of the darkened house visible from their side.

"Proof of the family being drugged," Eve declared.

"While you and I have a good sense that's what's happening, we'd need to prove it as a form of control and coercion. A doctor could simply be administering them Prenze tonics."

"Yes, tainted with poisons to control them. Possibly to poison them both. What if he kills them? We have to rescue them," Eve said.

"Unfortunately, we can't just come calling and demand to be let in. Even getting this surveillance approved was a battle."

"We'll say we want to see Alfred Prenze, that we have an appointment, and then search."

Horowitz shook his head. "Without a warrant? Surely at this point Albert will answer the door as Alfred."

"It will undermine your case if you move too soon," Fitton agreed from across the room.

"Too soon?! Too soon—when we've all been attacked by this man."

"In no way we can prove in a court of law," Horowitz reminded her gently.

Sighing, she clenched her fists. "I can't bear seeing these people trapped."

The spirit world felt the same way. It manifested in growing pressure on her skull. There would be a migraine through the night, no doubt. Whispered moans of a worried world glanced off her ear, causing sharp pains at her temples. Rubbing the back of her skull, she remembered what Maggie said.

"The basement," Eve said. "Look in the basement windows. Maggie reported…" Eve trailed off as she saw, in one of the cellar windows that wasn't blocked by a hedge, a darting flicker of white. One spirit, perhaps several, pacing. The unmistakable form of a hand pressed up against the glass. "Yes…something's trapped there just as she said."

"I'll put in the request today for a search warrant," Horowitz said. "I just have to think of the best grounds. I can't promise anything."

"We saw both twins with our own eyes for the first time," Eve said. "I wonder if the query put to London and Scotland Yard can more easily open inquiry. Have you heard back?"

The detective shook his head again. "I'm not sure there's been time to, but I hope I'll get a response soon."

Several spirits, from what I can see and sense, in the bottom cellar, Rachel signed, reporting from the other window. *Only there, nowhere else inside.* Eve signed her thanks.

Horowitz crossed over to Fitton and began discussing possible routes of correlation to justify warrants, going back from Gran's abduction onward.

Zofia and Vera appeared on either side of Eve, a sudden rush of cold air frosting Eve's breath. "Six figures from what we've counted, trapped in the cellar. We can only get so close before whatever buzz and hum of the blocking device grows too powerful."

Eve thought of the postmortem photography that had set so many things in motion and wondered if any of those pictured souls were part of the cellar collection; perhaps some of the spirits related to Prenze were trapped there too, part and parcel of his source of spectral hatred.

"*Dios mio*, I can't bear the thought of it, after being torn from this world by Dupont's device." Vera shuddered, folding her rose shawl tighter over her bony shoulders, the fringes of the floral fabric lifting in spectral weightlessness like seaweed. "Damn these men and their torture of spirits. I know you can't prove what they're trying to do to us, but...thank you for fighting for us," Vera said quietly. "I'm not sure you've heard that enough. I know the battle has aged you into an elder woman from such a young age, but...thank you."

Eve hadn't realized how much she needed bolstering for her mission and purpose, having felt so vulnerable, manipulated, and undermined by Prenze, so Vera's words nearly brought tears to Eve's eyes. "It's what I'm built for," she replied quietly.

"Still, even the born warrior should be celebrated for bravery," the old woman replied. Floating along the perimeter of the room, looking down at the streets below, she clucked her tongue. "All this wealth. All this excess. All the golden calves. It makes the spirit world heavy. It makes your job harder."

"Where is Maggie?" Eve asked.

"Still waiting for a moment to get in," Zofia explained, gesturing toward the mansion. "To get to Arielle."

Eve shook her head. "I can't believe she wants to go back in there."

"Any more than you can believe I would go into a fire?" Zofia countered. "Why are we still here if not to help? It is literally our only reason for being."

"You are still loved, and that is something too," Eve said softly, reaching out toward the little girl's face.

"Yes," Zofia said with a smile, pressing the wisps of her cold cheek to Eve's warm hand.

"Well, if it isn't a familiar face," Horowitz declared, peering through his binoculars. Eve squinted through the telescope. A man stood at the window, looking drawn and haunted.

"If it isn't Sergeant Mahoney," Eve muttered. "Well, so much for trust. He did come to the offices with concerns; we told him the truth and our cautions. I'll hold out hope he's on reconnaissance and trying to protect Arielle and Alfred, but I'll believe it when I see it."

"He looks worse for wear, though," Fitton commented across the room. "He and I shared a dispatch for a time. Perhaps I can look in on him."

"Please do," Horowitz agreed.

Eve watched as curtains were drawn over each four-post bed, presumably Alfred's, then Arielle's, and the man in the long coat walked out as Mahoney, his steps hesitant, followed.

There was movement seen briefly through the hallway window but nothing more.

Suddenly an eye was on the other side of the telescope and Eve jumped back with a cry. Maggie floated through the wall, laughing.

"You're terrible, you know that?" Eve gasped. "What's your read on the spectral front?"

"I cannot get in to Arielle Prenze, and whatever slip in their system that allowed me to get in that one evening has been fool-proofed since."

Eve thought about how they'd disabled the boxes at the chapel and the Dupont residences. The Prenze system might be more elaborate, but affecting the power might work.

"How about Mosley? Could we coordinate with Gran's electrical wonder of a friend? Couldn't he…disrupt the line, however he does what he does? Would that offer a window of escape for those trapped and you a moment to get inside?"

"That's a perfect idea," the ghost replied. "I'll bring it to Gran straightaway."

"Wait until I can get the girls here so that we're scheduled on rotation," Eve said. "I should get back to them. Everyone was on errands today, all of us trying to find a way in."

"I'll see if there's anyone at headquarters I can persuade to start us on at least an official interview. We might be able to summon Alfred Prenze down to the station, but I'm sure Albert would show instead and foil it all. We could try for Arielle, even if to force a reply of illness, creating a trail. Fitton, you good for a bit yet?"

The officer nodded.

I'm a night owl. I'll see what the place looks like at the witching hour, Rachel signed. *And I'll sleep here in the far rooms when tired.*

Eve relayed this plan, and everyone agreed and said goodbyes.

"Come," Jacob said, opening the door for Eve. "I'll escort you back down to your fort."

"It's maddening to watch and not be able to rush in," Eve said as the gate of the gilded metal elevator closed on them and they jolted to a descent. "To just end this all now."

Jacob nodded. "Believe me, it's the hardest part of the job. When you know something is wrong, when you know who is to blame—but if the law is to be upheld, it requires things we don't have yet. But we're getting them. We won't be stopped from exploring every avenue."

They were walking back toward the hub of activity around the elevated line when a large industrial delivery wagon wheeled too close around a corner, causing the two to have to jump out of the way. The driver shouted insults at them even though it was his recklessness, nearly causing another collision with a baby pram.

Eve thought about her mother being shoved out of the way by her grandmother, and a pang of Natalie's revisited trauma coursed through her. Helen Stewart was a sometimes ghost that would hover on the edges of their homes, never quite making her presence fully known, knowing how much the death itself still haunted Natalie. This moment was an uncomfortable echo to her family's past.

"Was that close call his doing, or our paranoia?" Eve gestured to the careening cart ahead.

"I can't say. Intentional or not, he's going to keep coming at us one way or another," Horowitz said, without dread or fear, just simple fact. "And we're going to have to keep going."

She tried not to envision a barrage of dangers, anytime they went anywhere being on guard for spectral sniping. It was no way to live; they had to gain grounds for arrest. They sat on a bench at the top of the trestle.

The detective watched her, not pressing her for a reply, but patiently expectant.

"I trust my allies," Eve said, trying to match his fearless tone, balling her fists so he couldn't see her shaking; the tremors a result of anger as much as close brushes with danger. She didn't want to be rattled anymore. She was a woman of strength and purpose, and she was being eroded by a predator. "I *have* to stay connected to strength," Eve said.

"I don't think you're ever disconnected from it, Eve," the detective replied. "You're the strongest woman I've ever met. Even if you don't always think so. That, too, is strength. Vulnerability is necessary to learn, truly feel and be human. It's underrated as a tool for growth. If you find yourself doubting, it's a chance to rebuild confidence from an even sturdier, wiser foundation."

Eve slowly moved her hands to close over his folded ones atop his knee. She didn't mind the passersby of all kinds; no one paid them any attention, and she was slowly becoming less self-conscious. "You are so wise and so dear," she murmured, looking at their enfolded hands.

"When are you most at peace?" he asked softly. "Because you should find some. You've been chasing clues since I've met you. It is important to take moments to relax and enjoy life.…"

Eve kept staring at their hands. "Well, when do *you*?"

"Oh, no." Jacob laughed. "No more countering me with questions so you're never called to account to answer your own. That's one of your most common tricks, and I am wise to it now."

"But I want to know," Eve said sheepishly, smiling and leaning toward him, their heads only a few inches apart. "I want to know so I can, perhaps… help bring peace to you, too."

"Green spaces. I walk through every park this city has created. And I read. There's always music. I love a good symphony at Carnegie Hall."

"Oh, yes," Eve said excitedly. "I adore concerts, but I can't remember the last one I attended! Also, a whole day lounging in Central Park. I haven't had one of those in ages."

"Then these are promises." He slowly turned his hands below hers, opening them so that her hands slid against his palms and he folded his fingers over hers, his thumbs gently caressing the backs of her hands. Eve shivered at the exquisite sensation. "What else kindles your fires of happiness? One of the reasons there are so many celebrations in Jewish tradition is that we know that to keep a spirit strong against persecution, there must be joy. Joy is undefeatable."

His words hit her deeply. The train screamed into the station, and they boarded, taking to the least crowded section of the interior, a little corner with a bench for two.

"What else?" Jacob insisted. "Speak to me of joy."

"Dinner with my team," she said as they sat. "My girls, my family, savoring Antonia's delicious cooking, sharing favorite heroes and heroines in books…" Eve blushed. "And…"

"And…"

Clasping her hands, she bit her lip, forcing herself to look at him. "Being with you. Being with you kindles *such*…joy. I've never felt anything like it."

He beamed a gorgeous smile. "Then that settles it. Tomorrow, Eve Whitby, I'm taking you for a day in the park and a concert at night. You're going to give me the whole day. Our case will unfold as it must; none of the offices we must make inquiries in will be open tomorrow and no warrant to go into the Prenze mansion can possibly have come through."

Leaning closer, his voice was a gentle caress. "Please, Eve. If I have the distinct honor of making you happy?" He released her hands and lifted his own so that they hovered over each of her cheeks. His eyes, brown gems ringed in blue, glistened, searching hers, his voice matched by the gentle touch of one palm cupping her cheek then the other, his thumbs grazing her temples then the edge of her ears. "Then I must do my part to strengthen and steel you against anything that would wish to harm you. I won't let anything get through me. Let us be joyous together." Overcome by this promise, Eve couldn't help herself. She had to do something intimate, unmistakable. She turned her face in his hands and kissed the inside of his palm. Jacob breathed in sharply.

"More...tomorrow..." he said, his words strained as she opened her lips and breathed against his palm. "When I have you all to myself... When we make a point of this, not just a collision of pent-up notions."

Eve dared to meet his gaze once more, her lips still grazing his hand. At the sight of his smoldering, hungry expression, a bolt of desire thundered through her, head to toe. Gently, he lowered his hands and folded them in his lap.

Knowing full well they teetered at a tempting, dangerous precipice from which they could not retreat, they were unable to say another word for the return trip downtown. Looking out the window, Eve's heart raced as fast as the spin of the train wheels as the cars swept between the upward climb of city buildings and chugged above passersby a story below.

Exiting a stop before he did, she rose as the station neared, bidding him a fond, quiet farewell, unable to look at him for fear she'd simply fall against him if he looked at her that way again.

Jacob stood and grasped her hand before she exited. "Tomorrow, Eve Whitby," he repeated, his words an intoxicating spell. "Eleven. Meet me at the southwest corner of Central Park."

"Yes..." she murmured. The rail rang its bell, and Eve stepped out onto the platform as they watched one another, wide eyed, excited and nervous as the train rolled away.

"Ah, *amor*," Vera murmured in an aching sigh, appearing before her as she exited the platform and down the metal stairs.

Eve folded her arms, offering the elderly ghost a sideways glance as she stepped onto the busy street. "Were you spying?"

"No, dear, I find that rude. I can feel it in your heart. There was such a burst of fondness it drew me to you as if it were a summoning spell. Let these old hands bathe in that light, in the memory of love."

"I caution you against the word *love*, Vera, there is something between us, yes—"

Flying away, the ghost cackled a fond laugh, and Eve's vain protest was defeated.

Eve took a few turns in Washington Square Park before returning home, trying to cool her cheeks and settle her nerves.

A shadow framed in the monument arch sobered her.

Lethargy swept over her, and the notion of wanting to give up overcame her, making her limbs feel like lead.

Perhaps the vulnerability Jacob opened up in her had allowed her shielding to lapse. She closed her eyes, pictured the candle of a séance table, drew in a sense of fire and light, and radiated that outward in a violent, lashing vision of release.

The figure vanished but the exhaustion remained.

Eve climbed the stoop to her home. Her team was already eating dinner when she entered, and her stomach growled the moment she smelled a pepper-pot delight.

"We saved you some celery stew," Antonia called from the dining room. "Come sit and have some before it's too cold for comfort."

"Bless you, dear heart, we would all be malnourished waifs without you," Eve said, sweeping over to kiss the crown of Antonia's head, noting the pleasant aroma of peony blossom from her freshly cleaned and rebraided hair. Gestures of affection and compliments were always met with Antonia's gamesome hum of delight, a sound that lifted Eve's tired spirits.

"All right, my dears," Eve began, renewed by her company, taking her place at the side of the dinner table. Jenny reached up and squeezed Eve's hand, and Eve turned to her, clasping the child's little hand in both of hers as she eagerly inquired of them, "Tell me about your day; I anticipate our updates will be intense. Mine certainly are!"

"It was right to suggest Ambassador Bishop escort me to the bank. That man does unlock people." Cora shook her head, laughing. "His power of persuasion is breathtaking to behold. Taking the tack of investigating international fraud, we soon found accounts indicating holdings related to Arte Uber Alles. A file is being prepared for him and will be sent to his post at the British embassy. Bishop thought that was best, to take the target off our home and office, and relate this to Prenze's time in England."

"Very good work," Eve said. She could see her right-hand woman blossoming under the direct influence of the man who had saved her father's life. Cora's refreshed, vibrant spirit was stirring and humbling to behold.

"Thanks to his encouragement," Cora added proudly, "I've begun practicing astral projection as the Bishops advised and encouraged. Besides, with you teaming up ever more consistently with the detective, I have to take on certain new mantles. I was hurt, and I missed you at first, but…"

Eve looked at her, furrowing her brow, trying to discern if Cora meant this with an edge. There had been an initial frustration, then adjustment, as Eve's and the detective's cases merged. Cora had seemed to be gaining peace with this, but perhaps it was going in stages.

"I see the way of things. And I like the new challenges," Cora said, and Eve saw the true leader that Cora was, innately, shining through. "In projection, I like that I am not confined to this body, and that this skin, as beautiful as I think it is but as conditional as this nation thinks it is, is not all that holds me." Antonia sighed wistfully. At the sound, Cora turned to her. "I'll teach you," she promised, and the dear friends smiled, their bond growing ever stronger.

"How did you do it?" Eve asked.

"I looked at a map of the city and tried to place myself there. Outside Prenze's home. It was difficult, but I managed to place my energy in front of the Vanderbilt mansion. I could see passersby. I will get better at it."

"I know you will," Eve said. "Again, well done." Cora beamed at the praise.

A pang hit Eve's heart, but she quelled it in the instant as it was selfish to be jealous about her team having incredible experiences without her. But if she were honest, she did like being at the center of everything, just as Cora had said. But just as Cora had also warned, she couldn't be her team's everything. Eve chose to rotate between her team and the detective's work, moving between worlds, so did she then have to let her team be bolstered by other talented associates too.

"I've been to see the surveillance locale," Eve said. "Horowitz and Fitton got it all set up, with my dear Rachel Horowitz too, talented medium that she is, on hand for lip-reading. Our turn in rotation and discernment begins Sunday afternoon."

The women seemed excited about this new aspect.

"Does Gran have a gossip strategy in place?" Eve asked Antonia, and in response she laughed, a tinkling, lovely sound.

"Of course she does, and she's already been employing it. Her friend closest to the family is worried for Arielle, confirming she hasn't been seen out since her gala." Antonia leaned in. "Gran even let Jenny and me come calling with her!" Antonia blinked back tears that threatened to smear the faint makeup that heightened her delicate features. "She made sure I looked my very best and daintiest and I…never had anyone for that…."

"Oh, my friend, I'm so glad…" Eve said, moved by these moments where her colleagues had time with vital mentors and family figures, especially Antonia. Eve had to remind herself that they were all, herself included, still young and needed elders as much as they needed each other.

"Arielle and Alfred appear to be sedated by a figure that must be Albert," Eve relayed. "I saw Mahoney there at the house. I'm hoping it was on our suggestion to watch, report, and act if need be, but the fact he wasn't stopping Albert, if that's the case, is suspect."

"I'm not sure I can trust him," Cora reminded the team. "His complaint against us directed the Prenze attention toward us in the first place. We need to get *in*. I hope the detective's warrants are successful."

"Agreed. Maggie also has a plan." Eve explained her eventful day with the reverends. Maggie's possession of Reverend Coronado got a great deal of gasps and exclamations.

"Where is Maggie now?" Cora asked.

"I believe, if I interpreted her correctly, she's off doing reconnaissance on Arielle Prenze, her next target."

"Targeting for possession?" Antonia clarified.

Eve nodded.

"Dangerous," Jenny whispered.

"I know." Eve sighed. "But Maggie does what she wants and goes where she will. I've given up trying to rein her in. This is personal for her as well as it is for us. We've all been attacked by this family, and perhaps in watching them, she'll find the best way in."

Dr. Levi's letter was the next item of business to be shared, and Eve tried to be hopeful about it rather than frustrated about it being stolen back, focusing on something productive: "He thinks as we do that the device was trying to measure brain activity," Eve finished. "It's a reminder that if we shield, whatever read Prenze got on us, we can block it."

"On that exact topic, I've been doing some reading on stones!" Antonia began excitedly.

"My darling scholar," Eve said fondly. "You each do your part so well."

Antonia's smile was bright as she continued. "I've noticed, Eve, that you've been wearing a few significant gemstones here and there, pressing them to you in moments of strife. It's clear you're resonant with their properties. I thought perhaps we each should wear a token, a talisman of a sort, making sure we're never without a token of protection. Gran took us to a little esoteric shop to round out everything I needed."

Antonia lifted a small canvas bag from her lap and, from it, produced a thin, round circlet with a hair comb sewn at the fore to keep it in place when set into a coiffure. A smooth black oval stone was held in a delicate stamped setting of silver filigree. Everyone breathed appreciative, impressed murmurs.

"Eve, my friend." Antonia presented the circlet to Eve, whose hand flew to her heart as Antonia continued. "For the woman who gave me refuge. I was led to you, and you've never let me down in safe haven to be my true self. Your mind is what must be protected above all else, as it is you that the spirits are all most drawn to. You're the presence we all orbit, in a way."

"No," Eve insisted. "Never think of yourselves as secondary; you're not some moon, you're your own planet. Especially as my mind has faltered, especially as I've been weak. You mustn't—"

"Hush, you, this is about building more love and strength, not modesty; try to play along." Antonia laughed. Rising, she gently placed the circlet over Eve's head as if at a coronation, setting it around the braided bun where its filigree circumference fit around the pinned knot that gathered all her thick black hair at the top of her head. "This is obsidian, which wards specifically against psychic attack. Your boundaries are being tested as forces are trying to get in. Wear this on your head, at whatever angle, in hopes it will block intrusion."

Eve wasn't always sure what was simply the power of suggestion when it came to stones and their powers, but they always helped focus her and she couldn't help but think they had an effect. Just with this placed at her crown, the comb slid into her coiled braid atop her head to steady it, Eve felt a pressure ease. Her eyes fluttered closed, and she felt her busy mind take a turn for the quieter. She felt stronger, just by its presence.

Antonia turned to Cora and produced from the same bag a slender oval black brooch cut in the style of jet mourning jewelry.

"Before I left home, my aunt, the only adult who tried to understand me, knew she was going to pass. She gave me some of her jewelry, knowing I'd want to wear it and treasure it. This was hers. Jet is the stone of astral projection. For my brave girl who breaks down barriers and knows no fear," Antonia said fondly, pressing the jet brooch carved with intricate geometric patterns into Cora's hands. "May this be a help and protection against negativity and spectral attack."

Cora stared at the gift in wonder, then back at Antonia, and something ineffable passed between them.

Antonia turned to Jenny.

"For our littlest joy," Antonia declared, plucking a thin chain with a polished purple stone pendant hanging from it. "Amethyst, for protection, and for healing any ill. We have to keep you safe and healthy always."

Jenny embraced the woman who had so clearly become her big sister and bounced back apace excitedly, gesturing for Antonia to place it around her neck.

"Thank you," Eve said, bowing her head to her colleague, "for this latest development in your esoteric studies. What did you get for yourself?"

"Gran insisted that a gift of protection given has twice the power than one procured for oneself. She gave me this." Antonia pulled a chain from below the lace around her throat to reveal three round simple stones set in silver.

"Is that obsidian on either side of lapis lazuli?" Eve asked.

"Indeed. I explained to Gran that I've been seeing a forest glade sometimes, behind my eyes. Oddly, unexpectedly, a blink of an image."

"Is that not a vision?" Cora and Eve chorused the insistence of premonition.

"That's what Gran agreed, so I'm paying attention. As you know, the lapis is the stone of clairvoyance and the obsidian will boost those powers and also protect as I discern."

"Please let me know what you determine it to be," Eve said. "I have no doubt it will prove important. Thank you all for doing such good work; we're close. I can feel that we're close to something...."

Here Eve paused, and in this, Jenny eyed her. *And there's something else...* Jenny signed.

"Yes..." Eve began. "There is something else, amid our work and tasks. We cannot underestimate the power of protection in the matter of joy, peace, and time to ourselves. Prenze has been a shadow threatening our every move. To the point of violence. We can't let Albert Prenze run our lives. Tomorrow, I declare a day off. Do what will inspire and strengthen you. We are, above all, our own people with our own lives, and by God we're going to live them a moment." Eve rose and her colleagues watched her. "With that, I bid you goodnight and every blessing. I must rest lest a migraine blossom. The pressure is there."

Eve turned away and went toward the stairs before her expression could give anything else away about the excuse. While she did worry about the aura of a migraine, her need to rest had more to do with the next day, and her nerves wouldn't let her sit still another moment.

"Are you all right?" Antonia called after her.

"I am. I've a lot on my mind," Eve called back from the top of the stairs. "But nothing to worry about. Only our protections. Those are the sole focus. Refresh the wards in each of your rooms; say blessings over them and add your light to renew the vials. Rest and take care of yourselves because we're on surveillance rotations by noon Sunday."

She closed and locked her door, shuttered her windows, and undressed.

As she removed her clothes, keeping the circlet on her head, her thoughts careened concerning what the next day would bring. If there was ever a time she wanted to be left alone and protected from intrusion, it was this, and what was to come.

Mrs. Bishop, during her visit, had placed a ward at each window. They were small glass vials with cork stoppers. Eve did as she'd just advised. Cupping the glass in both hands, with a blessing of peace and resolution, Eve sent her energy and spirit into the vials in a press of light and warmth. A little glow, visible to Eve's Sensitivities, resulted. "We will not be intimidated," Eve murmured, replacing the vial at the center of each sill.

Lying back on her bed, nightdress splayed out around her in frothy layers, she thought of fire and shielded once more. And then, she let herself daydream.

Her thoughts were consumed by Jacob and the small intimacies they had shared so far: touches and caresses that were but a prelude. Then began a torturous night, but never had she felt such delicious agony.

Hardly able to sleep, countless iterations of what might happen in the park played through her mind. A hazy, dreamy, titillating selection of images paraded through her mind and imagined sensations overtook her body as she squirmed restlessly under covers, shifting her nightclothes, her body awake and yearning in ways she'd never allowed herself to feel. Jacob opened a floodgate within her, and she was powerless to arraign what had been let loose. However, for the first time in her life, a bit of abandon couldn't be safer. There was no one else she could trust to lose control with, testing limits and boundaries. Finally, Eve drifted off to sleep wondering how it might feel when they finally gave in to the inevitable.

Chapter Eight

The next morning Eve walked in a waking dream as she washed up and slowly dressed in a deep blue wool riding habit and matching capelet with black details. Looking in the mirror, her cheeks were flushed and her eyes were wide. She knew what was going to happen because it *had* to.

The habit was flattering, but as she gazed at her figure, she boldly unbuttoned the top few buttons around her throat, wrapping a silk scarf and tucking it in so that it didn't look scandalous walking out the door. But it could easily slide away…in hopes that Jacob's breath would soon be hot against her throat. She knew where she would stop. There would be no question about her virtue. Jacob was a gentleman who wouldn't think nor dare to press her.

But the possibilities of his closeness and the ways in which they may be chastely intimate threatened to make Eve faint. She didn't dare exit her room. Her face would give her away in the instant, and she didn't want to be questioned about anything. Her fellow Sensitives were too talented not to either tease or squeal about her, and she wanted none of the fuss or attention. Wishing to be left to her nerves in peace, she remained in her room, reading a police protocol manual that she wasn't paying the least attention to, until the house was still and she felt confident she was the only one left in it, save for one piano poltergeist.

Their resident angel of music, an inconsistent spirit who had given the girls several names but had settled on Cy, haunted their parlor in occasional concerts: faintly playing their upright piano, manifesting enough for just the faintest echo, this time a new ragtime tune. The rolling jaunt of the tune had Eve bouncing down the stairs and sweeping into the rear kitchen where Antonia had left Eve's primary sources of sustenance: a pot of coffee and sliced hard-boiled eggs.

In the entrance hall mirror, Eve fussed and repinned her hair once more. Glancing out the window, she tucked an arm of her dark-tinted glasses into a buttonhole. The day was bright and she needed to weather it well.

"Beautiful, Cy, what's this?" Eve called, gliding into the parlor with her coffee to see the spirit floating at the piano, charcoal-silver hands bouncing over the ivory with deft skill the truly gifted never gave up, corporeal or no.

"Why, this is the latest from Mr. Joplin!" the ghost exclaimed jubilantly. "His 'Maple Leaf Rag,' just out this year. If you ask me, this is the one that will truly make him!"

"Wonderful," Eve said, leaving the spirit with his music as she buoyantly floated out the door as if she too were a ghost.

Once outside, glancing around for any of her attendant ghosts, it appeared that every spirit was giving her space. Sometimes the dead knew the living needed moments just to themselves, and she was relieved not to have to say so.

Hailing a hack so she wouldn't arrive already tired and perspiring, Eve feared the roiling nerves in her body would shake the sense right out of her. Part of her wanted to run back to her house and hide under the covers, because really, what did she know about any kind of real intimacy? Nothing. Only the brief, fond moments with Jacob. Those had mostly been as awkward as they'd been enamored.

What did she know about…kissing…? Not a thing. She had no experience. And as someone who liked to know what she was doing, or at least appear so, Eve was mortified at the prospect of being a failure. Desire and fear battled within her, and she was glad she hadn't laced her corset tightly because breathing was already a trial. The carriage slowed to a stop.

Eve accepted the driver's help descending from the step, paid him, mumbled something about having a nice day and turned toward their appointed corner.

Her breath caught in her throat.

There he was. Standing at the mouth of the park, framed by trees, hands behind his back, a shaft of sunlight adorning his dark curls. His brilliant smile when her eyes met his nearly lifted Eve off her feet, and she moved toward him, magnetized. Dressed immaculately in one of his well-tailored black suits and black cravat, his burgundy waistcoat's flare of color made it clear they weren't at work.

Goodness, how dear, how good, how handsome he was. Fear was subsumed by his magnificence.

"Hello," they chorused as she neared him. Their unison continued with a respective "You look lovely, wonderful," and they chuckled. This time, even the blush was mutual.

Jacob bent to pick up the wicker picnic basket he'd set down while waiting. He held out his other hand for her, and Eve took it.

"It's a lovely day," Eve offered.

"A perfect day," he agreed.

"Where to?" she asked.

"Does there always have to be a plan?" he asked with a grin.

"No...I..."

"We'll know the place to pause when we see it."

As they walked along for a while, Eve wondered if he, like she, was scouting for an appropriate locale: a shaded area, a copse of trees and brush that provided privacy, a natural little hideaway where they could escape from the world...

Turning the bend in the path, they saw the spot at the same time, mutually slowing as they looked up the hill toward a little plateau away from the paths where the outcropping of schist gave way to a blanket of leaves and moss. One grand willow tree towered over a ledge that seemed to Eve like some kind of fairy bower. There was a partition in the hanging curtain of willow fronds as if a green tent held a panel open, invitingly.

They climbed the slight incline, and Jacob strode into the canopy ahead of her. Ducking in after him, she watched him set the basket down, open one side, and withdraw a thick woven blanket, spreading it out on the mossy rock for them.

Bowing, he gestured that she sit. Eve did. Kneeling beside her, Jacob withdrew a silver plate of grapes, figs, and roasted chestnuts. He then withdrew a metal canteen and two small teacups, pouring her what appeared to be a sparkling punch.

"There's just a little bit of German cordial, a blackberry schnapps, in this mix, if you don't mind," Jacob said. "I didn't mix it too strong."

"This all looks lovely, thank you." Eve removed her glasses in the shade, setting them to the side. "I should have brought something, I'm sorry."

"You're all that's needed," he replied, rising to his feet. Examining the willow tree boughs, Jacob reached up and moved a branch to the side, tucking it under a fork in another limb to close the partition like one would close a curtain, creating an entirely private canopy.

As he returned to take his place beside her, Eve quailed, thinking her heart must be audible with how hard it pounded.

"Thank you for coming," he murmured. Reaching out, he removed a grape from the stem and held it. "I can imagine it might be hard for a strong-willed woman such as yourself to allow herself to be indulged." Jacob leaned closer. "I appreciate you letting me treat you. It is not because I want to lord anything over you. I just...like the idea of pleasing you...." Jacob looked at the fruit, then at Eve's lips, then her eyes. He offered the grape. She leaned in and opened her mouth. Jacob placed the grape upon her tongue. Eve closed her mouth over the fruit, her lips lingering to kiss the tip of his finger before she withdrew. The small, seductive gesture affected him in a shudder that thrilled her. She ate, savoring the sensation, everything heightened.

Lowering her eyes at him, she managed to speak in a breathless murmur. "I, too, like the idea of pleasing you...." Plucking another grape from the stem, she held it out and he responded in turn, opening his mouth to take the proffered fruit. His beautifully drawn lips pressed against her fingertip, and it did indeed create a frisson of delight.

Taking her hand in his, he turned it over, brushing his fingertips over each line as if engaging in palmistry, divining meaning in the creases. He kissed her palm and Eve sighed. His fingers brushed the lace of her sleeve, sliding a finger under a button of the cuff. With nimble grace, he opened two buttons. Leaning in, he kissed the delicate underside of her revealed wrist, a divine sensation that made her gasp, and, maintaining the press of his lips, he looked up at her with eyes that could start a fire without a flint.

After countless breathless moments, Jacob shifted, taking her hands in his, edging her away from the refreshments, sliding closer to her, knee to knee, folds of blue gathered skirts splaying over black broadcloth.

"I confess," Jacob began carefully, "I seek a prize that has been denied us before, in any number of stolen moments. But here and now, with ceremony and celebration, I'd like to make a point of something I've been desperate to do...." He stared at her lips, gently taking her face in his hands, running a thumb over her mouth so that she had no doubt about his intentions. "May I?"

"Yes, please," Eve whispered, trembling as he drew closer, leaning in, closing the distance between them.

He tilted his head, keeping that same gentle grasp upon her face as the tip of his nose grazed her cheek and finally, tenderly, he pressed his lips to hers.

Slowly, artfully, Jacob kissed her top lip then her bottom lip, the sweetest sensation that drew out Eve's breath in a quiet little moan that parted her lips. This sound encouraged him and he pressed harder, matching the part of her lips with his own, allowing for more expansive exploration. Eve's trembling hands finally found purchase in his hair, her fingers diving into his smooth curls as she'd so often longed to do. Raking her hands through his hair, she grabbed him and shifted his head toward her neck. Eagerly he seared her jawline with a string of kisses and slight tracing of his tongue, earning another gasp.

Grasping his hands, she brought his fingers to the scarf around her throat; he did not hesitate in taking her cue. Untying the knot, Jacob slid the scarf from her neck tantalizingly slowly with one hand, his other hand bracing Eve's back for the swoon he seemed determined to evoke. In the wake of the silk as her collarbone was revealed, his lips followed the lines of her fine bones, one side then the other, then back up her throat to her chin, and then again to press upon her lips.

She melted in his hold, and he shifted to cradle her in his lap, drawing back for breath.

"We needed this day," he whispered, looking down at her dreamily as her eyes fluttered open to stare up at him in wonder.

"It's been all I could think about, this..." Eve confessed.

"After all our near misses, I couldn't just kiss you on impulse," Jacob said. "There needed to be a production, an event, because the torturous build needed a grand payoff."

"Torturous, you say?" she asked, trying to be coy, shifting her head in his lap, letting pins loosen and her hair to begin to come undone.

"Yes, you delicious tease," he breathed, his eyes rolling back as he shifted his legs beneath her.

"Is it...what you'd hoped for?" This time, any wiles failed, any hobbled ability to flirt vanished, and she asked in a tiny voice devoid of art, just a simple, aching question, hoping he'd enjoyed it.

"Oh, you defy expectation, my dear," he reassured her with a smile. "You don't disappoint. A pretty girl like you, a wise, working woman..." He chuckled, and then for the first time in all this, he hit an awkward stumble. "I'm sure it wasn't your first. I...hope I did well...."

Eve's face went blazingly red, and she tried to prop herself up and turn away, but he scooped her back into his arms again.

"Oh, Eve!" Jacob exclaimed. "It was? I was your first?"

Eve nodded, her hands darting to cover her face in a vain attempt to hide.

"Darling, please look at me," he pleaded with a little laugh, one arm still hooked around her waist, one hand gently tugging on her sleeves. She peeked through her fingers at him. His expression was so warm, excited, and adorably fond. "I am honored to be your first kiss."

Eve turned, shyly burying her face against his lapels, breathing in his scent of gentle soap, a whisper of mint, fresh and sweet. "I'm...I'm sorry if I'm not any good at any of it—"

"Oh, you are," he interrupted, folding her tightly against him. He pressed his cheek against her head, stroking her hair, murmuring in her ear. "Believe me. This is everything I've been daydreaming about."

"You're too kind to say otherwise," she said with a chuckle.

Something discomfiting overtook her, and she extricated herself, leaning back so there was a foot between them, blurting out an awkward thought before she could retract it. "Do I want to know about your first kiss?" Eve asked, almost a rhetorical question. "I'm not sure I do. The mere thought of it fills me with a shocking pain."

"Oh, come now, we must be adult about things; people have histories and pasts," Jacob scoffed. "It was with Sophie. We wanted to know what all the fuss was about, and we wanted to share the experience with a friend. But that is how we knew we weren't suited for one another, not in that way. It was a learning experience. But it had no fire."

Before Eve could react to this, Jacob clamped both hands around her waist and spun her back into a cradle hold again. He dragged his nose and lips along the slope of her neck, murmuring as he lifted toward her ear.

"Whereas with you, Evelyn Whitby"—his soft words against her temple were punctuated with sensual actions—"there is such"—his lips grazed her ear and kissed the lobe—"exquisite"—edging across her cheek, he poised his mouth over hers—*fire*. Set me alight again..." he begged against her lips.

Eve arched in his hold, entirely won, pressing her bosom to his chest as her arms locked around his neck. Boldly, she pressed her parted lips against his to truly taste him, and the crash of the kiss this time was a deep, entwining fusion as hands flew across one another's backs, nails digging in against layers of fabric, seizing and releasing one another only to rake their hands up and down arms, around waists, every clutch and release beginning new breaths that dove into another kiss.

The unraveling of neckwear was the modest limit of their dishabille, but Eve took her turn with Jacob; he was just as enthusiastic, gasping at each stage as Eve untied then slid his cravat away and covered his collarbones, throat, and top of his sternum in reverent, slow kisses.

"You are..." he purred, burying his fingers in her hair, grasping her as he shuddered from the effects of her sensuous offerings, "very good at all of this. . . ."

"You inspire me," Eve said, wrapping her arms around his shoulders, pressing her forehead to his. "I never thought I could be so affected by someone as to fear I could lose myself, but in you, I regain myself. Thank you for being a safe harbor in what is a tempest within me."

"I couldn't agree more."

Eventually they tumbled back upon the blanket, breaking apart and looking up at the tree canopy, gasping for breath, laughing, and sighing.

They took to the food and punch, cuddling close, nuzzling and gently caressing, pacing themselves from losing any more control than they already had. Setting the finished dishes in the basket, Jacob first handed over her tinted glasses, which she hooked upon the scarf she loosely retied at her throat. He then handed her an envelope.

Inside were two tickets to Carnegie Hall: the premiere of a new work by Tchaikovsky.

"My favorite modern composer!" Eve exclaimed. "Oh, Jacob, how did you know…" He pressed his lips to hers again softly then rose and held out a hand. She took it. "This has been one of the best days I've ever had…" she dared to say. "And it's not even over."

He brought her hand to his lips. "I'm so happy. And yes, I can't say I've had a better one. You are my favorite company, Eve Whitby. You…" He hesitated. "You're just the very best." A sudden, concerned look crossed his face. "Ghosts…haven't been watching us, have they? That…would be rude."

Eve laughed. "They have not. They know better than to fall out of my good graces in such a manner as to be despicable voyeurs."

He untucked the willow bough, and the door between the branches reopened.

"Wait…" Eve reached out and stopped him from stepping out onto the slope. "Ghosts may not be watching, but anyone with eyes will know what we've been up to." She drew him back into the willow-branch shade, their mutual blushes making her bite her lip and giggle as she straightened his cravat then smoothed bits of willow leaf and moss off his coat.

Her fingertips took extra time putting his hair back into a semblance of order. Pausing, her fingers toyed with a silken lock. "If you ever saw me clenching my fists around you. . ." She was breathless as she took in his handsome visage. He stared at her with a dreamlike expression. "It's only because I've wanted to run my hands through your gentle curls for quite some time."

He laughed happily.

"My turn," he said delightedly, dusting her off the same, straightening and smoothing her skirts, taking particular care to return her hairpins to a sturdy hold. As he moved behind her to tuck up a few fallen locks from the back of her coiffure, he punctuated each pin with a slow kiss on the back of her neck.

"Careful or you'll undo me all over again," Eve gasped, reaching up to straighten the centerpiece of obsidian and silver gifted from Antonia.

His arms enfolded her, and he drew her back against him. "Is that meant to be a deterrent?"

Eve had no retort, only a sigh, swaying with him and letting her head fall back onto his shoulder as their embrace lingered, arms entwined as she folded hers over his, the two of them holding on to this passion with all their strength and spirit.

When they finally exited their bower, Eve couldn't help but notice the glances of passersby who eyed them and either smiled, smirked, or looked wistful. There must have been quite an aura around them, or their flushed faces and starry eyes gave too much away.

They were en route to a host of carriages set up at the corner of the park ready to take on fares when Eve felt the air around her grow icy. Her warm cheeks cooled as Olga and Vera suddenly manifested on either side of her, just ahead of Jacob.

"Take care, Eve," Olga said. A Ukrainian immigrant, a spirit a few years older than Zofia who died in the same garment district fire, Olga carried only a simple echo of that tragedy on her spectral person: the hem of her simple work dress was burned. Olga was loyal and watchful though she very rarely manifested outside of a séance. "I don't know what else to tell you, but I've a dread I don't usually feel. There's always danger in the work, just..."

"Keep a careful eye out," Vera added, floating next to her, drawing her shawl over her bony shoulders. "I don't know any more than Olga knows, but, *Dios mio*, something feels heavy."

"I'm not going to be intimidated, certainly not today," Eve insisted, putting a hand to the obsidian on her head, taking a deep breath and shielding. Turning to Jacob, she explained that she'd gotten a warning.

"We're going to a concert," Jacob said. "There's hardly a threat in that!"

There was a line of waiting carriages, and Jacob moved quickly ahead to pay for the first one, a fine, enclosed cab with open windows and a garland across the top. The walk wasn't far, but Jacob seemed to want to make a fine event out of the whole day and Eve didn't stop him.

She sat down next to him, hip to hip, shoulder to shoulder, hand in hand. Unable to help themselves, shaded by the enclosure, they turned into another kiss. Glorious and tender. Eve never wanted this bliss to end.

Rounding a corner and trotting ahead, the carriage maintained its speed until Eve and Jacob broke away, gasping and giggling.

The carriage suddenly slowed.

"Watch out!" The driver screamed. The carriage jostled as the horse reared.

Out the window, Eve could see a man she didn't recognize narrow his eyes. A bricklayer in a dusty coat and thick leather gloves held a sharp spike of building girding in two hands.

She and the ghosts saw it the moment before it happened.

The worker, his face contorted in horror, as if he couldn't believe what he was doing, turned the pike, the sharp end heading straight for Jacob's torso.

In that moment the spirit world screamed in a terrible roar. Reflexively Eve grabbed Jacob with a burst of desperate strength and turned him to the side. The pike came around and through the open window. It dashed along her arm, ripping a length of wool and tearing her flesh, puncturing the shoulder she'd raised to block him from the blow. Blood blossomed on her shoulder and cascaded down her chest as the pike clattered to the cobblestones outside.

As she shifted, so did the carriage buck. Jacob was slammed against the side of the carriage door, hitting his head, the door flying open, and his body nearly tumbling out had Eve not already had ahold of him. She hauled him back, and his neck braced on the edge of the seat and his head lolled back onto the cushion, blood spurting from above and around his temple.

Screaming, Eve managed to direct the driver; "Take us to Dr. Jonathon Whitby at Bellevue! Fast as you can!"

The driver veered east, ringing a bell as a makeshift alarm to make way, the reeling horse lurching into a canter.

The wonders of the human body in danger, coupled with the surge of focus in trying to help another, made subjugating Eve's own riotous agony easier as she tended to Jacob. Never minding the blood all over her fine blue riding habit, she whipped his cravat from where it had been loosely returned to his neck, where just moments ago she'd showered with kisses; she bound the tourniquet tightly around Jacob's head, knotting it before sitting back, pain flowing through her again. But she was pleased to see the pressure of the bandage stanched the flow.

Swooning against the side of the hack, she needed something else for herself, so she used her own scarf for the same pressure around her arm, though lifting it and her shoulder to affix it was fresh agony.

Part of her was trying to process what happened, how it happened. Prenze was attuned to her; he had a read on her, on her whereabouts, especially, particularly, as she'd been sidetracked by the day. She'd been distracted by nerves and desire, hadn't thought to bring one of the Bishops' wards on her person, hadn't renewed her shield since the park. And Prenze just manipulated the surroundings. Just for a moment. That's all it took. One window in, one momentary lapse. That's how much danger they were in. Likely that moment would be chalked up to some accident of construction: a swinging post without proper clearance and a spooked horse. But Eve knew that it was the forces Prenze could somehow manifest that had caused the incident. But proving that...

As the city raced by, a form loomed before them outside the carriage structure, a terrible fixed point as the city flew behind. The dread presence that child spirits called the shadow man. Albert Prenze projected his image next to them, and his echoing, eerie voice was like gargled sulfur, gritty and foul. The foul projection began to coax.

"Give up, Detective. Just let go. It's best this way."

Eve felt energy drain from her as if she were a suddenly flowing water tap. The idea of giving up, giving over, letting blood flow, just resting... It was appealing. She looked to Jacob, and something changed over his body, a shimmer of silver and white. A form superimposed over his face. A luminous, greyscale version of Jacob over his living, beautiful self...

A cry surged up from the depths of her, in fury and terror.

"I renounce thee!" Eve screamed at the scourge outside, the fire in her mental and psychic shielding blazed across her vision, and she felt herself pulling back the energy that was draining away like dripping blood.

Seizing Jacob's body, she held fast.

"Oh, no...no, you don't, Jacob Horowitz, you are not going to become a ghost!"

His spirit, partly outside his body, looked around then detached, separating out to sit upon the enclosed carriage bench opposite, staring at Eve.

"Eve," he said fearfully. "Am I..."

"No! Not yet, you can't," Eve refused, clutching his body. "Stay with me. Stay here."

He turned, and his spectral eyes focused on something ahead of him, something unseen by living sight. He was at a turning point, a crossroads. His form flickered and then faded invisible, losing manifestation when traveling over thresholds.

She had to go after him. His spirit could be in the Corridors between life and death, a liminal place accessible to talented Spiritualists. She could persuade him back, but she'd have better luck if she were there with him.

The deep diving in that she'd done to try to find Maggie she'd do again, in the inelegant space of a carriage. They might arrive both at Bellevue in a slump, but they were en route to help. In the meantime, Jacob needed rescuing that she was uniquely suited to provide.

Tuning out all the madness of the surroundings speeding by, Eve closed her eyes, said Gran's benediction for descent into the tenuous realm of long, shadowed halls; she felt herself falling with a dizzying swiftness into mental darkness. Perhaps the times she'd been in Sanctuary had made this spiritual journey betwixt living and dead easier. She grew more efficient in the ability to detach body and spirit, for better or worse.

He was there, walking ahead of her, pausing to look around at the walls of the Corridors, shimmering walls that looked like deep water or endless sky, porous and yet still a boundary. The air around her was slightly less polluted than when she'd last visited their halls, but it looked like dark clouds were ahead of them.

"Jacob! Stop!"

He paused and turned back to look at her.

The vague walls of the Corridors showed shimmering, luminous images, like floating pictures at an exhibition.

It wasn't that one's life flashed before the eye before or in the process of death; there was a sequence of images, and if spectrally attuned enough, one could walk that walk of memory for oneself or a loved one.

Behind them, Eve recognized some of their moments together; other moments Eve didn't recognize, images of spaces and vistas, buildings, perhaps his synagogue, embraces with family and friends.

The closest image to them, seemingly framed in bright light, a passionate picture just to the side of their stopped bodies was clearly the two of them, arms around each other's necks, pressed together in a furious kiss. A recognizable moment, from just moments ago…

It was behind them.

There was nothing yet ahead of them. No images. Just a void. Possibilities hadn't yet been dreamed up.

And that was the most terrifying thing Eve had ever seen.

They had moments yet to make. Moments yet to live for.

"You must come back with me." She grabbed his hand, pulling him back around to face her.

"Why?" His voice seemed far away, as if in the throes of laudanum, the curious disorientation of a spirit in its first moments. "This feels nice, here.…"

She could feel the initial lethargy that so many of her operatives described, the desire to simply lull into an echo of existence.

Eve had yet to experience the moments of death and following a spirit into this place. She'd never had to, certainly not for someone she…

"No, Jacob, it isn't good to be here, you must fight to revive!"

"What's wrong, Eve?" he asked sweetly, handsome and dear, even at the point of terror. "You seem upset. Where am I?"

"You're in the Corridors between life and death, and you can't be here; you can't be a ghost."

"But you like ghosts," he said, with the innocence of a child.

"Yes, but it isn't your time. I can't let you die!"

He blinked at her then turned back toward the Corridors as if drawn.

"Is that your call to make?" he asked, his voice far away.

"Listen to me, Jacob Horowitz! You can't die"—grabbing him by the shoulders, she forced him away from the mesmerizing surroundings to look at her—"because I love you. I cannot let you go when I've only just kissed you and I want so much more with you! I want a life with you!" Tears streamed down her face. She clutched his hands. She didn't dare actually kiss him here. That's not what the moment framed as perfect in the Corridors depicted. "We have to go now; we're already endangering your body. Come."

A wind picked up around them. Faintly Eve heard singing, from what she could catch of it, in Hebrew.

"You love me?" he asked, incredulous, his voice full of joy.

"Yes, Jacob, I love you," she cried.

His glassy eyes suddenly focused with fire and purpose.

He closed the distance as if to kiss her—grabbed her around her waist—and Eve used that moment of momentum to pull. To fall.

Chapter Nine

With a wrenching gasp, the next thing Eve knew was that she was tangled in an embrace with Jacob, on a cot in a clean, white room, a gurney rolling away to the side, likely whatever she'd been laid out on, and it was as if Eve had fallen on top of him yet again, souls crashing into bodies once more. Nurses and doctors shouted.

"A miracle!" one nurse cried to the woman next to her. "I thought they both were passing!"

Her father came rushing in. "Eve, oh my goodness, what—" He carefully extricated her from Jacob and began to examine her wound. Only then did Eve realize how much pain she was in. Her legs gave way, and her father guided her into a chair beside Jacob's bed.

"Hello, Father, I'm very sorry—"

"I'm sorry for nothing now that you're safe. Let me just see how deep this is," he said, peeling back the shredded layer of her dress, over her arm and the rip along her bodice. "What happened; were you stabbed?" he asked.

"I don't know what happened. I think someone was manipulated in trying to strike us."

Jacob was delirious, but coming to, murmuring.

"I'm here, I'm here, Jacob," Eve said, trying to pull away from the examination. "I'm fine, Father. I'm sure it looks worse than it is."

"It needs stitches," her father countered. "You did well with stanching blood flow but it needs to be sewn up." He looked between Eve and Jacob and seemed to understand something. "Talk to him a moment then we'll have you both patched up. I'll get everything ready."

Her father motioned to the nurses, and they exited to prepare, giving the two a moment amid the white cloth screens. Eve was grateful for the scrap of privacy.

Eve sat at Jacob's bedside, taking his hand. "I'm right here, Jacob; it's me, it's Eve. You'll be all right."

He stared at her in wonder and hope. "You said...you told me..."

She leaned close to his ear, the act of which was agony, but her murmured words lessened the pain. "I said that I love you. And I do love you."

Jacob released a happy sigh. "My love," he whispered, and seemed to drift off into a light sleep as one of the young nurses returned. Rushing to the bedside, the nurse tried to keep him awake and lucid, for fear of aftereffects of a concussion, and he maintained a sleepy, limited responsiveness.

Eve wanted Jacob to declare his heart back to her in turn. She didn't like having been so vulnerable, having given her truth away with nothing sure in return, but that was perhaps too much to ask considering the circumstances. "Will he be all right?" Eve asked the nurse.

"From what your father said, loss of blood caused his weakness, and he has a concussion that needs to be monitored. But he should recover after rest, aches and pains notwithstanding. His parents have been notified," the nurse said. "We took his card since he's an officer of the law. It was easy to reach them; they're on their way."

Eve couldn't be sure if anyone else heard their exclamations of love or not, but she knew her heart, finally, and couldn't fight it anymore, and didn't want to. Seeing his ghost was clarion focus enough. They'd all be ghosts eventually, but not until she'd had a life holding on to his warm, living body....

But the danger, this terrible turn, his near death... It was all her fault.

The sinking certainty of just how much he was in danger *because* of her hit her like a repeat blow. Her loved ones were going to continue to get hurt if she didn't change the dynamic.

If Prenze wanted her dead, he'd likely have found a way to shoot her, though a bullet was a far clearer charge of murder than these roundabout ways he was spectrally trying to maim them and threaten them off his tail. She was likely a part of the great experiment that Dupont had warned them of. People like Jacob were in the way.

Gritting her teeth against searing pain, she stood and listed between the screens, shuffling toward the first door of the wing she could see, desperate to be somewhere alone, away from this place of pain, death and hopeful recovery, needing to think about her next move. Truth be told, she wanted to run again to Sanctuary, to be let in and to never to come out, to do all her helping of the mortal and spirit world from within, keeping everyone around her safe by removing herself physically, not psychically.

As she was about to wander into the next hospital corridor, her father called out.

"Just where do you think you're going?" Dr. Whitby said in his most fatherly tone, full of British indignance masking a distinct fear.

"I'm...fine." The lie came out as a mumble. The pain was escalating; the tricks of the body that made one feel invincible in the heat of danger were subsiding to a wave of incapacitating agony. She swayed on her feet.

Her father put steadying hands on her shoulders. "I said we were getting you stitched up, and that's what we're doing."

She squeezed her eyes shut. In part to keep back tears, in part to keep from the room spinning.

"You're still in shock. Please, just let me take care of you," her father pleaded, as if that's all he'd ever wanted to do and the dangers of their lives just kept getting in the way of it. A neutral man of kindness and diplomacy, her father didn't often take either a firm or pleading tone. It was especially important to note when he used both.

Folding against his side, she let her father collect her, her head falling on his shoulder, allowing herself a vulnerability she'd tried to block out and steel herself against since childhood. When the paranormal aspects of her life strained her relationship with her parents, she'd tried to brick a wall around her heart. But there was no need of that here. Her father had always silently understood. He couldn't pretend to know how she was haunted any more than she could know the ways in which he had been. Haunting, like spirituality, faith, and one's connection with the divine, was entirely personal, and no one's experience trumped another.

Never minding fresh drops of her blood on his crisp white coat, Dr. Whitby led Eve back toward the room she'd wandered from. She let pain overwhelm her into motionlessness as he guided Eve to a bed near where Jacob lay, the nurses washing his wounds and preparing him for stitching too. Administered a sedative by a calm nurse, she drifted off into an unsettled half rest as the sting of the stitches sent her into a pain-induced dream state.

* * * *

Eve awoke to familiar, nearby voices. Four hushed, concerned tones. Before she opened her eyes, she thought to herself how to appear composed to these people. Her mother, Gran, and Mr. and Mrs. Horowitz. They'd all met, in the most unfortunate way, but they were making pleasant small talk, discussing their mutually loved Rachel Horowitz.

Commonalities, making inroads, making connections: all of this was so important, but Eve needed to retreat from it all. Loved ones, especially in the case of Jacob, meant potential casualties.

The agony of nearly losing him, of the truth of her heart—it was all too much, and she didn't want any of them to see her awake, so she squeezed her eyes closed, but not before tears flooded out.

She wanted to stay sleeping until everyone went away. Given great talents, she was hardly powerful enough. She was only good enough to get noticed and targeted, not talented enough to have solved anything; yet anyone near her was in a radius of danger.

"I confess, I'm not sure what to think about all this," she heard Mrs. Horowitz say quietly.

"He'll make a full recovery," Dr. Whitby assured her.

"And I thank you for that, Doctor," Mrs. Horowitz said.

"Indeed," Mr. Horowitz agreed. "We are in your debt for quick work. I simply would like to know what happened here."

Jacob sat up with a groan, and his outburst made Eve's eyes shoot open, reflexive to the sound of him. He looked at her first, smiling; the physical pain on his face washed away, replaced by a certain wonder, as the dawning of what had passed between them seemed to illuminate him and if Eve wasn't mistaken, he whispered, "My love…"

It drove Eve's pain even deeper, and she subtly shook her head, mentally asking for him not to make this harder on her.

Jacob looked at his family, who had jumped to either side of his bed. "Hello Mother, Father," he said. "I don't know exactly what happened— it was all so sudden—but Eve moved me aside, from a man swinging something toward us. She put herself in the way, getting injured in the process, but if she hadn't, the pike may have gone right through me…."

Jacob looked over at Eve, and it was then they all noticed she was awake.

"Thank you, Miss Whitby," Mr. Horowitz exclaimed. "Thank you for helping him."

"We are so very grateful," his mother added. Eve could sense their genuine gratitude in equal amount as their horror at his being a target. Eve understood; she felt the same way.

Eve's mother and father came to her bedside in turn, her mother leaning down and kissing Eve's brow. "Your father promised me it's not as bad as it looks…and I believe him," she said, keeping her calm, looking between her husband and her daughter. Gran stood at the edge of the partition, between the beds, a consummate diplomat and soothing presence.

"Did you… I'm sorry, Miss Whitby," Mrs. Horowitz began carefully, "but I have to ask, was it your case that put him so in danger?"

She managed to ask without accusation, simply wanting to know the facts. Mr. Horowitz winced, as if he wished there were some other way to have asked the truth of it. But there wasn't, and the slow crack threatening to cleave Eve's heart entirely in two widened. She wouldn't lie.

"It was. I'm…I'm so sorry, Mr. and Mrs. Horowitz."

"No, no," Mr. Horowitz tried to interject, but he trailed off.

"If you ask me, when they got here, it seemed she saved his life," a young nurse said as she came by with a decanter of water. "It's like she went somewhere after him and dragged him back here. It's like he fell back into himself. I've never seen anything else like it."

This rattled Mr. and Mrs. Horowitz as much as anything. Eve grimaced. This wasn't the way she wanted her spectral dealings to be revealed, in this kind of tense circumstance. She changed the subject abruptly.

"Gran, can I come have a nightcap with you and stay?" Eve asked. "Will you tell the girls not to worry? I need your advice on matters." Wanting desperately to be out of this place, Eve slowly rose to a sitting position, her mother helping her, her father checking the bandages.

If she separated herself from Jacob and the girls, for their safety, Eve was sure she could do so with Gran's help and not be reckless about it. They could plan how to extricate her and still solve the case. Gran would know how to hole oneself away to fight a spectral battle and that wouldn't be as dramatic as her irresponsibly just disappearing.

Gran looked to her father, who nodded. He handed Gran a glass bottle of small white pills, likely aspirin for the pain. "Come by our side for dinner?" he asked hopefully.

She looked at them and said plainly, "I shouldn't. It isn't safe. *I'm* not safe."

The stricken look that this created on both her parents' faces was a palpable hit. Eve despaired; she was causing such pain all around her, and in her.

"Let me take her, please," Gran murmured.

"Yes, the two of you, again," her mother muttered. "As if the rest of us never faced danger before in our lives."

Eve sighed irritably and replied in a tense whisper, "You can't be distressed by my work and then angry when I distance you! I don't want this man to be the reason your condition comes back, Mother! This is a personal vendetta for Gran and me to fight—"

"We won't be alone; we've an arsenal," Gran interjected with implacable diplomacy before Eve could drive any wedge further. "This will be over soon. I feel it."

Natalie Whitby turned to the Horowitz family, contrite. "I'm sorry to involve you in our family drama," she said. "I've always had a hard time reconciling my daughter's work."

"As have we, with our son," Mrs. Horowitz confessed quietly. "It is difficult, sometimes unbearable, to accept a job with constant risk and not feel like you're abandoning your child to the wolves just by allowing them to do it."

"Exactly," Natalie said, as if Jacob's mother had put the perfect words to her emotions.

"But they are their own people," Mr. Horowitz added. "We cannot live their lives for them."

"Indeed. It is wise of you to remind me." Natalie stepped toward the couple, clasping her hands together and bowing her head slightly in deference. "It was a pleasure to meet you both, Mr. and Mrs. Horowitz. Your son is a treasure."

"Thank you," they responded warmly.

Coming back to Eve's bed, her mother sighed. "You should stay here and rest, on doctor's—your father's—orders. But I've a feeling you won't heed them."

"Correct. But you can help me up," Eve said, offering her parents her hands. With a tired chuckle, her father took one side as her mother pursed her lips and took the other.

Once she was standing, Gran handed her a wool cape she could throw over her mauled dress once outside. She folded it over her arm.

"I'll see you downstairs, but give me a moment," Eve said to her family, looking first at her parents and then at Gran, who gathered them gently and led them out with soft pleasantries, leaving just Eve and the Horowitz family.

Eve turned to Jacob's parents. She looked down at what they were looking at. They stared at the bloodstains on her dress as if they couldn't look away.

With a deep, shaking breath, Eve let tumble a rush of difficult words. "I…I can't decide for your son how he continues to pursue his own aspect of the case. But considering his safety above all else, I've made the resolution to separate myself. I am clearly a risk. So, if my presence means a greater threat, it's for the best.... Please tell him, *insist*, he keep his distance. I know he has open cases he'd be best to resolve with other colleagues," Eve said, and turned, fighting tears. Biting her lip to force composure, she turned back. "Please tell your son he's... the very best. And that the most important thing in all the world to me is that he be safe and happy. Thank you. Take care."

Both parents opened their mouths as if they thought perhaps they were meant to protest, or say something else, but the silence was strained and Eve smiled at them, bowed her head, and left. She tried to speed out with her usual brisk pace, but the pain slowed her. Throwing the cloak over her shoulders, she buried her face in the corner of it for a moment to dry the sudden stream of tears she could no longer hold back. She breathed in the sharp surgery smell of solvents: alcohol and iodine, like a smelling salt bringing her back around.

With no clue as to what the future held, she had to walk away from Jacob for as long as it would take. For safety's sake.

The moment she exited the white doors of the surgery wing, breathing in less sharply scented air, she noticed Gran waiting for her, calm and statuesque, her brocade burgundy tea gown a rich contrast to the stark white hall.

"The girls are in the reception area," Gran said. "I knew you'd have wanted me to send them away, but I couldn't. It isn't fair to them. Their lots are all cast in, with this precinct, and with you. If you just tear yourself away without clearance..."

Eve's sudden rush of exhaustion, concern, and perhaps even panic must have been evident on her face, for Gran continued with a stern tone.

"They're psychically tied to you, Eve, and to this work. You can't expect them not to be. None of your gifts can just be turned off when it scares or isn't convenient for you. They knew something was wrong just as I did, and came. The staff wouldn't allow them in as they said it was too crowded. I told them to wait outside. I know you want to retreat. Tell them why; give them something to do. You can be involved in separate missions, but don't you dare let one man break apart your precinct."

Gran's command hit Eve squarely, and she didn't know what else to do but nod.

As they walked down the long hallway toward an exit, Eve's side was awash in cold. "Oh, *mi corazón*," Vera said, appearing on Eve's left as Gran guarded her right. The spirit's luminous hand was laid over her heart.

"Don't," Eve snapped, hastening her stride. Her Sensitivities in a hospital—a place of pain, struggle, and unexpected loss strained her ability to reason. "Nothing of the heart. Help *numb* me. I must be steeled." Each step jarred her wounds, but she wanted to be anywhere but here.

"I had to walk away from someone I didn't dare be with." The ghost circled her as she walked. "Your circumstance was not mine, but pain is pain." She opened her arms, and Eve's breath turned to frost. "I give you my cold. You are the lady of the dead. Let the chill of us comfort you until you can make things well again."

Eve let temperature overtake her like stepping into an icebox. Steel and cold. She had work to do, no time for sentiment. She had to inure herself against psychic and emotional turmoil, harden herself against the danger of love. Of letting down her guard. No matter how much joy she'd just shared. This depth of despair was as deep as her mountain of bliss had been high.

In a white, sterile reception hall that was pleasant only in how much light came in through the windows facing the river, Eve stepped over to a bench in the main reception area where Cora, Antonia, and Jenny sat huddled. When they saw her, they jumped up, and before Cora or Antonia could hug her, Jenny peeled back the layers of her cape, revealing the blood, so that everyone would know to be gentle, as if the little girl sensed the damage before seeing it.

"Hello, dears," Eve began before any of them could offer sympathies. A harsh tone was all she could muster just to get the words out. "Because everything is being weaponized to hurt those around me, you must keep your distance. I may have to be vulnerable, on my own, to see how Prenze moves. Join the surveillance operation if you must do something. But stop if you or your environments are manipulated. Send spirits only to give me information, because anyone next to me"—tears flowed again, and Eve cursed under her breath—"gets hurt. Keep yourselves safe above all else. And keep Jacob off the case. Far away. It's my fault, what happened."

"Will he be all right?" Antonia asked.

"If he keeps his distance. Make sure," Eve demanded. "Promise you'll force him back."

"We can try," Cora murmured gently. It was she who had been the most resistant to his presence at first. But she seemed very aware of the pain Eve was in. Reaching out, Cora gently took Eve's hands, and Eve was grateful the gloves Cora wore kept her psychometry from seeing all that had just taken place. "But he's his own man, as we are our own women."

Eve bit back the urge to snap orders at them. She didn't want contention, just distance.

"I'm going to Gran's, not home," Eve explained. "Be careful. Have people who Prenze doesn't have a read on research any clues or paper trails. I can't have more blood on my hands because we got too close to a wayward monster. I'll come home to the Fort when I feel it's safe."

At this, the girls all protested at once. But Eve walked away as if she didn't hear it, drawing her cloak closer over her ruined dress. She could tell she was hurting them, excluding them, and she wasn't proud of any of it: that she'd needed them in the first place, that she'd let them get close, and now she wasn't even able to fully reject or fire them, send them irrevocably away. She felt impotent and useless, like she couldn't win and neither could they, living a half life between calling and protection.

Antonia ran after her. "Eve, please. A moment of advice." Eve stopped and turned back to her colleague. "Those flashes of what I thought might be premonitions? I'm going to follow them if I see them again. I think they correlate to things in motion."

"All right, dear, as long as you steer clear of my direct path."

"I saw a forest again," Antonia said. "And I realized it was familiar. Likely Sanctuary."

"Sanctuary may indeed need protection too. It is wise to consider. Go nowhere alone."

Antonia cocked her head. "You presume to act alone and tell us we cannot do the same?"

Eve sighed and turned away. "Do not attend *Sanctuary* alone, that's all I have to say."

Despite significant bodily pain, Eve moved quickly to the front doors to avoid any other emotional exchange. All she could see was Jacob's handsome face after their kisses, and that same gorgeous visage bloodied after the attack, two images in horrific contrast that made her sick to her stomach.

Downstairs at the patient exit of the grand brick building along the busy East River, she embraced her parents. Her father helped her mother into a carriage before returning with Eve to Gran's vehicle.

"Thank you, Father, for everything."

Both he and Gran helped her, grimacing and wincing, into the carriage.

"Take care of her, will you?" Dr. Whitby begged Gran. "Maybe she'll listen to you if you tell her to find some other case to solve that doesn't have it so out for her?"

"We'll get through this," Gran promised.

Eve wasn't feeling so hopeful for herself, but she would draw danger away from her loved ones.

"Shield," Gran commanded as the carriage rolled away. Both women did so, and Eve felt the energy of the carriage become a fortification. Staring out along the river, she wondered how to draw Prenze just to her. Gran circumvented her. "Don't you dare do anything drastic."

Eve turned to her, exasperated. "I'm letting myself go with you, *stay* with you so that I don't! Help me live apart from everything until this passes and the case breaks for the better. I'll commune with spirits remotely, and you can collect the evidence and bring it to the girls. They won't drop the case, but I need them *away*. And keep Jacob entirely clear. I'm too dangerous. Will someone promise me that?"

"What happened to the detective today is not your fault."

This time, Eve leaned against her fortress, her dearest confidante, and let loose a sob.

"He nearly died, Gran; it was so close! He was being leaned on, psychically, by Prenze, to let his spirit go. To give up. I had to go into the Corridors after him. . . ."

Gran embraced Eve as she wept. The passion of the day was her secret to keep, but she had to tell someone her heart. The idea that just hours ago they were entwined in the park... Tears pooled on her hands.

"I told him I loved him." Eve choked on the words. The searing, overwhelming truth of how much she loved him, realized in this stark turn, caused as much terror as it had joy. "With that confession, I won his spirit back; I think the truth of my heart was what did it. But I do...love him, to the point where I'm terrified. It makes me sick. I can't be the reason.... I can't bear what might happen to him."

"We'll stop Prenze," Gran reassured her.

"But how?" Eve wailed. "We're trying with finances, surveillance, paperwork that doesn't yet add up, anything we can yet use in court proceedings, and every day anything could strike us. He's not letting us get closer...." An idea struck her. She sat up, dried her eyes, and stared at Gran. "I'll host a séance. Just me. Invite him to my mind. His bait. To see what's next."

Gran sighed. "Just like your mother."

"What?"

"Not precisely, but your mother played this game, to entrap the creature that attacked your father. I never thought it would play out again. She likely senses it, fears a parallel."

"The family legacy," Eve said grimly. "But this time, I'm no longer your student. This is now between me and the ghosts, and I have the ghosts to help. Whatever the 'great experiment' is, I'm a part of it."

"I was a part of the experiment too, Eve," Gran insisted sharply. "I'm wrapped up in this just as you are. And your team, they are their own people, Eve, and they care about you."

"If I have to fire them and evict them from my home, I will! I won't have any harm come to them when I am the one he wants. The ghosts and I, we're the ones to confront him."

"Whatever he thinks about spirits, he's not giving them much credit," Gran scoffed. "He doesn't know how they can fight. For now, you must rest. Thank you, at least, for being willing to come with me. Your grandfather is away on business; he's been traveling more these days, and during this bout with Prenze, I've encouraged it."

When they arrived at the house, Gran left Eve in the parlor with some peppermint tea so she could attend to telling the very small household staff, save for the security staff Gran kept on retainer, that they were getting a few days off; limiting collateral damage.

The tea mirrored the taste of Jacob's kisses. Eve had to bite her tongue nearly to bleeding to keep herself composed.

Closing her eyes, Eve begged the spirit world's guidance and felt it rustling around her like the leaves in these sharp last days of autumn, turning brittle and whirling in winds.

Vera appeared and wafted to the parlor wall to ponder the art as Gran entered with a tea tray full of small bites and savory treasures.

"Antonia has gained precognitive visions, Gran," Eve said. "She's seen a forest that may be Sanctuary. I know Clara Bishop said she'd set wards, but we may need greater protections."

"Noted."

A roaring in Eve's ears accompanied more tea being poured into her cup. A different kind of pressure than the recent bout with the children and their resolution. Eve sighed irritably at the sudden pain.

"What is it?" Gran asked, pouring herself tea.

"There's a grip on my skull. I don't know if it's the worry of spirits or Prenze trying to worm deeper in. I'm tired of being reactive, Gran. I began this precinct without constraint. I began fearless. I want to regain that strength and return to principle. *Alone.* I have to fight back."

"So, challenge him," Vera said, floating near enough for steam from Eve's teacup to make her image waver in mist. "Provocation will throw him off. He wouldn't expect it of you."

"What sort of provocation?" she asked the elderly ghost.

"If he hates ghosts so much, why don't you do something to celebrate them? Isn't that the premise of the precinct, at least in part? You're in hiding when you shouldn't be. You're meant to help keep moving us into the light."

Eve snapped her fingers, a solution hitting her. "That's brilliant, Vera, thank you. Gran, will you lend me your newspaper friends?"

This clearly wasn't the direction Gran thought the conversation was turning, and she sat back, raising an eyebrow. "I will connect you to whoever you need, provided you've a good reason."

"I'm going to write an editorial in honor of ghosts. To reaffirm my purpose. The pressure has been building to reclaim it. I can feel it from within Sanctuary; I feel it in my head." She rubbed the back of her skull where the pain resided. "We took our name off the door to placate threats. It did nothing to make us safer. Tonight, I'll write a declaration. I want to publish a manifest of the beauty of spirit. The glory of ghosts. For all New York to see."

"Wise. And the spirit world will rally to your cry. They will respond to your affirmations. Of all the challenges I thought you might issue, this is one I can get behind."

Eve brandished a pen. "A spell must be cast, in the grand tradition of gentlemen writing letters in newspapers, defending their honor, I shall throw down a glove of spirit."

She nearly ran out and up the main stairs to the next floors.

"I'm going up to the tower for all this, Gran," she called back down. There was a heavy pause. Eve hadn't been to "the tower" in years; left alone and unfurnished since her childhood. "I'll bring it down when I'm done."

Gran came back into view at the base of the stairs, visage steeled. "Very well. Mr. Godkin. *Evening Post*. I guarantee he won't like it, but he'll do it if I demand a place in editorial. I'll leave his information on a Western Union envelope by the door. Slide it under the door when you're done, and one of my guards will run it to him. I'll call and lean on him for urgency. While you write, I'm going to check on the girls."

"And keep them out of it."

"That's for them to decide. You may be their manager, but you're not their mother. Besides, in every tale of woe and terror, keeping information from parties affected is the chief way in which people get hurt. You, of all the Gothic enthusiasts, should know that."

Eve took in her words and sighed. "Still, remind them to stay back."

"Let me handle it." Gran stepped forward to the base of the stairs, pinning Eve with her sharp eye and commanding presence. "Where is the surveillance team?"

"There's a key on my foyer table. The New Netherland. Sixth floor unless they've shifted to the fifth in hopes of a better angle."

"Very good. I'm going to make some calls. Preparedness, and all."

Eve snapped her fingers. "We'll need to engage your odd friend Mosley again."

Gran nodded. "I already planned on it. Disabling the Prenze mansion is key."

"Yes. We'll have to time that, because if we can throw him off, we can all act, Maggie too, wounding him with cuts all at once. But challenge first…" Eve trailed off, thinking about what to write. "It will have to be direct, precise, and invoking the spirit world. Ah! I need the help of another woman's words."

Descending again, Eve brushed Gran's shoulder fondly as she maneuvered past, toward the cozy library of deep colors, rich stained glass, and tall, dark bookcases. As she searched for a specific spine she knew all too well, Gran followed her and stood at the threshold.

"I am loath to leave you…" Gran said mournfully. "I fear I've done too good a job of making you an independent lady at too young an age—"

"I'll be fine," Eve said, batting her hand. "I don't plan to leave cloistered work. The tower shall be my abbey. Post guards by the door if you're afraid I'll sleepwalk."

"I'll do exactly that," Gran said and kissed her on the forehead. "Once you've gotten your writing out, rest. Take sedative in your tea if need be; it's in the master bath medicine cabinet. I'll be back soon. Psychically reach out to me in any emergency. If you don't"—Gran pointed a long, steady finger that had all the power in it of drawing a bow—"I'll never forgive you, and you really don't want to see me angry."

"I know, Gran. Go on." Eve blew her a kiss and waited until Gran turned away from the library to turn her attention to the books.

Eve let out a tense breath when the front door closed behind her. Vera must have escorted Gran out, for there were no other presences remaining with Eve. As pressure on her skull eased into a broader thrum rather than a spiking sting, she reached a breathing quietude from which she could more manageably pass through the auras of any forthcoming migraine.

"Focus on the work," she commanded herself. "It's the only thing you've ever been able to rely on your whole, weird little life." Work was the only thing keeping her from an incalculable abyss of emotion and fear.

Alone in the library, Eve scanned the spines until she fell upon her treasure: *Nineteenth Century Miracles* by Mrs. Emma Hardinge Britten, a leading Spiritualist of the century.

Britten had recently died, near the beginning of their whole ordeal with Prenze, and Eve hadn't even had time to process the fact.

"May your spirit be with me as I write, Mrs. Britten," she murmured as she opened the cover, running her finger over the table of contents she'd practically memorized as a child. *Nineteenth Century Miracles* came out when Eve was three; she'd grown up with it. Gran suggested it as a way to understand and learn from gifted experiences other than Eve's or her own.

A chapter on Spiritualism in the law and courts had been an important source of encouragement for Eve to start the Ghost Precinct; and she used it as precedent.

Some wars were won by swords, guns, and battles. This personal war would be won by the mind, pen, and spirit, working in concert.

Once she'd read a few of her favorite passages, Eve began writing from her heart:

"On the Importance of a Willing Spirit"

Greetings, dear reader, fellow New Yorkers, beings of spirit and life. I have tried all my life to bridge the eternal and the material. To make the antithetical helpful. To celebrate how much the dead teach us about life.

Emma Hardinge Britten writes in her Nineteenth Century Miracles that "Eternity and Infinity are the only words that seem, in our imperfect form of speech, to embody the conditions of spiritual existence. Time and space are equally opposite to the state of being we call 'material.' Whilst therefore, we essay to write of a dispensation which manifests the characteristics of the endless and illimitable, it must not be forgotten that we are yet denizens of a material sphere, bounded in on every side by the limitations of time and space."

And so, the universe has seen fit to provide the world with Sensitives, those of us who can make polarities palatable and be the bridge between material and spiritual.

I began hearing the voices of the dead as a child. It was admittedly maddening, but with the help of other Sensitive souls and a keen desire to understand purpose in the gift, hearing patterns in the noise proved helpful for everything around me.

I am here to tell you that the spirit world is real. It is very active in this city. And I am here, with other positive spirits, to help this city. So can you. Your loved ones aren't gone; they're a memory away. Call to them in your heart and share a bit of love. Remember life. It will lift this city up, and that's needed right now, not anyone or anything wishing to tear it down.

Leave room in your heart for the loving souls of the spirit world. You'd be surprised at what they have in store to show and share with you.

Those who wish harm upon innocent spirits, good souls lingering, I say to him: For shame. Celebrate life hand in hand with the echo of life. Otherwise the finality of death is all that you'll see.

Blessings,

E. H. W., Spiritualist, Advisor on Matters of Crime and Justice in the City, Director of the Ghost Precinct

P.S. To Mr. A. P., the gentleman returned from the grave who has threatened me and mine and all the ghosts of this city, I remain unafraid. The spirits will not go quietly. They go to peace on their own terms, not on your demand. You have been warned.

Eve put her pen down and looked at the words she'd penned. The spirit world murmured the truth of it; it was a bold, blazing dare.

She readied the envelope, sealed it, said a brief protective prayer over it, and slid the spell out the front door as Gran had instructed. What Eve could only see as a silhouette—one of Gran's hired watchmen—stepped up from the shadows of the protective detail along Gran's property line, tipped his hat to her, and strode briskly down the walk to relay the thrown gauntlet.

"Spirits help me, it's begun," Eve murmured.

The response from the spirit world was another crash of murmurs, a wave upon Eve's mental shore, the pressure in her head cresting and receding.

"Spirits, yes, you are my help, and I know you will lead the way," she said. "So please do." Instinctively, she put her left hand to her heart, her right to her mouth, and gestured both forward, signing a thank-you in advance, the gesture like a benediction.

An invigorating wind whipped around her body as if she had stepped into a vortex. She was heard. For all the time in her young life she had chafed against the spirits so constantly talking at and around her; she sometimes forgot she could talk back, bid back, request back.

"My good girl," Vera whispered before floating back against the wallpaper.

"I have always wanted to be," Eve whispered in return, in a small voice that put her in mind of the first time she'd retreated to the room she was climbing to now.

Eve climbed narrow sets of stairs to a jutting dormer corner, a square battlement in sandstone at the top of Gran's house, carrying the weight of Gothic tradition in her wake; the heavyhearted heroine withdrawing to her peak. But in those old tales, the woman withdrew as a victim. Here, Eve readied in her war room.

The tower was an isolation, which would normally have rattled her. Eve had to be content that this was what she'd asked for. She was not in danger here. Not physically. Not yet. But there were other ways in. And there would be other ways to get her out.

She took the sedative Gran gave her, thankfully not a Prenze tonic, and curled up on her childhood cot, letting the memories enswathe her in all their torment and triumph.

In the morning, her words would be published, and Albert Prenze, feeling the direct sting of it, and a city renewed in spirits, would come collect.

Chapter Ten

When Cora, Antonia and Jenny took to the surveillance rooms that same night, they were warmly greeted by Rachel, and Jenny was able to sign with her about the latest.

According to Rachel's report, painted statues were being placed into the Prenze yard one by one and hauled away, each of them some angel or devil in extreme poses of vengeance or damnation. Cora thought of Dupont's stage sets and wondered what the next drama would be. The team's arrival then allowed Rachel a bit of rest in one room and Fitton in the opposite.

Sitting with a cup of tea, Cora felt a gargantuan wrestling in her heart, the scope of which put her in mind of the biblical story of Jacob and the angel, only part of the struggle came from the stirrings of her own heart, caught in the middle of difficult discernment about what she expected from this work, from Eve, and from herself. Most of it were the forces and presences around her trying to determine what was best for those they loved.

Being at the hospital and unable to do anything was a particular agony for Cora, who felt put on this earth to fix things swiftly and efficiently. Cora chafed at being held at arm's length from the case. None of the team felt able to abide by it. Heading to the surveillance outpost in the New Netherland, Cora had left a coded note of their whereabouts on their side of Fort Denbury.

Never so aware of all the large personalities foundational to their work as now, Cora was unsurprised when Gran walked in the door of the surveillance outpost, shown there by a rather baffled bellman who wasn't sure what all these odd fellows had to do with one another.

Behind Gran walked Clara Bishop in a dark green walking dress with a wool capelet and a knot of crepe flowers and tulle on her head that she unpinned and set by the door.

"Why hello, Mrs. Bishop!" Cora said in surprise.

Clara smiled as she entered, her gold-green eyes piercing Cora first before sweeping the rest of the company. "Call me Clara, please, friends. I heeded Evelyn's call immediately. Since this man 'read' you, Cora, she was afraid surveillance may be foiled by Prenze sensing you and intercepting. So, I thought I'd do what I could to lend aid." She gestured around herself. "I'm psychically loud. Through the years I've learned to make myself louder. I can provide a certain cover. But you'll have to remember your training. I can't shield all of you."

"Of course," the girls replied at once. "Thank you for coming," Cora continued.

The moment the door opened, Antonia was clearing off the chaise so that there were more places to sit as their company grew. Ever the consummate, attentive hostess, she queried, "Clara, how can we best protect you from an epileptic episode?"

"Leave that to me, friends. The sooner you're able to find evidence against this man, the better. The tension he's causing you *and* the spirit world has become audible—a distant keening coming closer, magnifying fears and anxieties of the coming age. The turn of a century is easy on no one, least of all the Sensitive. If he harms the spirit world, woe to all of us."

It was as if she brought a storm with her words. A lightning strike flashed across the park.

Gran gestured to the telescopes. "So, tell me, what do we have here?"

"There's been some struggle," Antonia explained, gesturing for Gran to come close and have a look in. "It's clear Prenze is trying to keep his family sedated, incapacitated. There seems to be no other staff anymore. We saw a woman in what looked like a maid's uniform, with a carpet bag, flee earlier. The overwrought statues of angels and devils have been exiting the house regularly."

Rachel entered from the set of rooms on either side of their surveillance area, and Gran rushed up to greet her. She signed to Gran, who explained to the team. "Rachel says she can't sleep for the feeling everything is coming to a head."

Rachel went to the telescopes as Antonia handed fresh tea to Gran and Clara. Snapping her fingers, Rachel gestured the team to the second telescope. The lights had been turned on. Cora watched as two men in dark coats and trousers were wrestling with a now upright Arielle.

Rachel gasped. She kept her eyes on the target but signed to Gran, who translated.

"The younger Miss Prenze is overwrought. Something about taking her away. Something about an asylum…" At this, Gran's tone went deathly cold. "Damn these men. She's struggling. God, she's so frail, gaunt, hardly the picture of stunning life I saw at her party. We need to help her."

Cora watched in concern as Arielle Prenze was being helped out the door, Albert Prenze on one side, Mahoney on the other.

The air stirred. Cora could feel a shift in atmosphere, the spirit world reacting to Arielle exiting the house, disrupting the barrier Prenze had put in place.

"God if only I could get closer, to tell them to stop," Cora exclaimed. "By the time one of us runs down there, they'll be off."

"Astral projection, Cora," Clara reminded. "You're good at it already. Tell them to stop."

Turning to look at her, Cora was sure unease was written on her face as Clara continued.

"Coming from you, Cora, it will be a powerful message, directly from the police. This is a legitimate investigation and domestic disturbance. If you fear the risk of our venture here being revealed, I'll shield this location with my own psychic noise."

"Yes. I can do it." Cora's desire to prove herself far outweighed any fear of failing.

Closing her eyes, the urgency of Arielle's state focused her. She imagined peeling away a layer of herself, sending a shade ahead. Praying for Uncle Louis to guide her, she murmured an ancestral benediction. Louis's tie to Clara Bishop, his long-lost love, might sharpen the power of the moment, though she'd never say that aloud to either of them.

Cora's vision doubled, the darkness behind her eyes and the room beyond. She turned and looked; she floated outside herself a moment. Trying to fly forward, to cast herself down to the scene; she balled her fists in frustration as the world flattened. Stuck, she could move no further forward. Falling back into herself, she shuddered and her eyes refocused on the hotel outpost. *Damn.*

"Try again," Clara said patiently. "It isn't easy. Took me years to get the hang of it and even then, it's inconsistent. Think of what makes you strongest."

Cora thought about the quiet, intense moments before a séance. She called upon the strength of her ancestors who had survived so much for her to be present, wielding power, today. And suddenly, she surged forward;

she was a star hurtling in a sky. She was a bird over land. She was an unfurling tendril of *les mystères*, an instrument of the unknowable *Bondye* and His justice, His freedom.

A scene focused before her in a sharpening image like a blurred, old amateur daguerreotype exchanged for a crisp studio-made photograph. She had projected outside the Prenze mansion, across the street from the struggle. The house loomed behind the struggling trio, the brazier lamps on either side of the front door like burning eyes in a dark, foreboding face.

Two men fought over a struggling woman who clearly didn't want to be overcome by them, and this, too, made Cora's energy into a manifest force.

Cora flung a hand forward. The voice that came out of her was rich, resonant, the product of mighty matriarchs who stood their ground. "Stop. I warn you. In the name of the law, stop!"

The men abruptly halted. Only Prenze looked in her direction. Mahoney looked around. His ruddy face went white. Cora didn't trust him, and his reaction to spectral interruption wasn't helping.

"Help me!" Arielle cried out, looking around wildly. "Whatever is here with us, help me!" Her eyes didn't focus on anything. Pressing her energy forward with all her might, Cora tried to loom between the distraught woman and the men who seemed hell-bent on controlling her.

A flurry of silvery white dove by Arielle, who shuddered violently. Perhaps the spirit had actually gone *into* her. Cora had her suspicions about what just happened, and she hoped she had bought some time.

"Take her back in, Mr. Prenze, I am telling you. Take her back in," Mahoney insisted. "Something isn't right here, and there'll be a scene! She doesn't wish to be sent away, and *I* will not disregard her wishes."

Prenze growled but turned his sister around. Cora felt some relief that at least Mahoney was on Arielle's side.

"You will leave me be, brother," Arielle insisted with a newfound strength that Cora thought might have something to do with the spirit that had joined her.

Albert Prenze stormed ahead and flung wide his grand door, Mahoney bringing Arielle back in carefully, speaking soft words of reassurance to her. Going back in seemed just as tragic as going out. Cora's heart went out to this woman, even if she did have a hand, somehow, in Prenze's wrongdoings.

A scream erupted from Arielle as she crossed the threshold. Her form shuddered and shook again, and a second scream from another voice was heard in the street. A ghost peeled off from Arielle's form and careened toward Cora's projection.

Maggie. Yes, possessing the body of Arielle was Maggie's plan, but whatever device was keeping ghosts out of the mansion and those imprisoned within trapped sent Maggie's spirit right back out. She was lucky she didn't get stuck, like those who remained imprisoned below.

The door to the Prenze mansion slammed, and as it did, there was a concussive effect on the spirits. Maggie floated into Cora's projection in a collision of presences, and Cora felt her energy dissipate. In a dizzying whirl, she fell back into herself and wobbled on her feet, but Antonia was there, sturdy and steady as Cora regained her footing. She shuddered with cold as Maggie returned to the surveillance floor with her.

"Good job, Miss Dupris!" Mrs. Bishop applauded when Cora opened her eyes. The praise made Cora beam. "We could see your shadow. It certainly altered the course of the moment. Tell us about it from your perspective."

Cora and Maggie explained alternately what had happened below. Clara moved to the other side of the room as Maggie spoke, tuning out the ghost for her own health.

"It worked," Maggie exclaimed. "A possession. I can get in, just as I thought! I didn't have time to get an actual assessment, but I think I can do good and turn the tide with her. As Dr. Font said in the séance, it all comes down to Arielle, the glue of the whole family. She's gotten herself in deep; I can feel it: waves of guilt in her body as firm as her heartbeat. But I wager she'd like redemption. I need back in. But that house…it's like burning oil on my incorporeal skin! Whatever is in that house…"

"That's what Mosley is for," Gran said. "My…electrically augmented acquaintance. He'll act promptly on my call. Whatever device is blocking you, he'll blow it to pieces. Your window may be narrow. But I want her safe."

Gran whirled to the windows and shook her fist toward the mansion and roared. "Damned men committing a woman just because she's become emotional, or gifted, whatever she's become, it's unforgivable!"

Everyone stared. It was *very* unlike the poised Evelyn Northe-Stewart to have an outburst. Cora had certainly never seen it, and from the look of it, neither had Clara Bishop, a longtime comrade in supernatural arms, whose green-gold eyes were wide. Whatever had caused the pique was old, deep, and had struck a tragic nerve.

Gran must have realized that all eyes were on her in the silence. Her elegant, defiant posture deflated. Jenny drew close, teary eyed, reaching toward her while signing a question.

Their cherished elder ran a shaking hand over the little girl's braided hair. "What happened, you ask, dear heart?" She sighed heavily. "That warrants a story for another day. Let's just say that...a woman being committed against her will...is a topic I am...most passionate about."

The weight of this vague admission was heavy in the air. Cora looked over and caught Antonia's wide eyes, her hand on her heart in empathy and horror, a deeply personal reaction to the idea of being institutionalized solely on account of differences. Cora wondered what private pain and isolation each of her colleagues had to endure before finding safe refuge with one another.

The tall, gilded clock at the center of their grand parlor room struck midnight, and Jenny jumped at the sound. She went to the tea cart, organizing a fresh setting and placing used items on the lowest shelf of the cart. Fiddling with business seemed to calm the child.

"We should rest," Gran commanded, no doubt eager to change the subject.

Gran was right. Cora knew if Prenze was further provoked, into what Dupont had called the "great experiment," none of them would likely rest for the foreseeable future. She hoped that Mahoney was trying to keep peace and safety among the family, maybe even collecting evidence along the way, if he wasn't under Prenze's thrall as she distinctly feared. This was the tense calm before the storm.

The team took to whatever surfaces appealed to them. Jenny doled out small cups of herbed tea with a relaxing root infusion. Valerian extract had never worked for Cora; her mind fought it off. She'd sleep eventually, but there was work to be done first.

Through the night, while the rest of the team rested their overdue turn in beds or settees or brocade chairs, Cora opened the briefcase she'd brought with her, and at the desk near the window, turning a small kerosene lamp high, she pored over paperwork turned over to Bishop by the British bankers and looked for proof of Prenze siphoning money from the company into his personal interests after his supposed death. Once she'd placed a penciled star on all the lines that might be evidence—Alfred Prenze would have to verify, should he survive this ordeal—she sat back in her chair, pressing her fingers to the bridge of her nose.

Confident that everyone else was asleep, Cora took to a settee by the window and reached out into the psychic ether. She reached out for Eve but felt only a closed door. The pain on the other side of that door was palpable, and Cora wished she could alleviate it. She knew Eve well enough to know what the pain was about: pain that her work had hurt the detective, pain of separation from him, and the distance she thought was necessary to keep them all safe.

Wistfully, Cora thought to the very first moment she'd shown up at Eve's front door. Before Cora or Eve could introduce themselves, Cora led with her vision: "I had a dream I was working with a young woman and ghosts, our ears open on behalf of all those who can't hear or who won't listen. Are you looking for someone, Miss Whitby?"

Eve's face reflected intrigue at first by an unexpected visitor; suddenly she beamed, her pale pallor luminous, and she exclaimed with an ebullience Cora wouldn't soon forget:

"Why, you! I must be looking for you! Come in and tell me all about it."

That kind of joyous welcome, without a moment of hesitation, skepticism or second-guessing, especially from a white woman, wasn't something Cora had often experienced outside her family's well-vetted friends. The closeness with which Eve had entrusted her, rarely holding back on a thought, a hypothesis, an emotional detail, seeing her capability and talent from the first moment, trusting her with mostly coequal responsibility, had made Cora feel like she was a partner to Eve in every way. Cora had to admit privately that she'd sort of made Eve out to be her whole world when that wasn't fair. Both of their worlds were multitudes instead.

The psychic door between them felt impenetrable, and Cora hoped Eve was sleeping soundly rather than just inaccessible. She contemplated astral projecting to check on her but thought better of it lest it startle more than reassure her.

Cora never let herself be ruled by emotions, but she was well aware that when it came to Eve, everything got more complicated. The presence of the detective had only distanced Eve further. But the rest of the team had made up for it. Antonia in particular anticipated Cora's every thought, hope, or need, somehow assessing all the puzzle pieces to become the right fit.

Looking out over the darkened park, an unsettling premonition ate at Cora and she wasn't sure if it was the truth or her own heart playing certain tricks on her. She was sure that Eve closing herself off would put Eve in a greater danger than she realized. But perhaps it was just the pain of feeling that previously open channel torn away, absent, bricked up when it once flowed freely. Perhaps it was that she couldn't abide the loneliness of it.

"My sleepless, tireless wonder, heavy with the cares of the world."

Whirling around, Cora saw a handsome, luminous, slate grey face staring back at her, floating on the edge of the settee in a fine suit coat with a neatly knotted cravat.

"Quiet, Uncle Louis," Cora whispered. "Let's not wake anyone, especially your former paramour." She nodded across the room to where Mrs. Bishop was curled up upon a circular velvet pouf like a bird in a nest.

"Ah, yes"—he sighed, matching Cora's whisper—"my Clara. I died when she was still my sweetheart. Though I let her go with my blessing, to the man she *also* always loved, she'll always be my heart. I always know where she is. Though we stopped speaking long ago, for the sake of moving on, I often watch over her. But the dirge of your heavy heart drew me to you."

Cora explained her concerns about Eve and what might be next.

"I don't think she'll weather well alone," Louis agreed. "Might be the death of her. If it's what I fear, this Prenze devil wants her like a key: to open a psychic, spiritual door. Using her against the ghosts. The spirit world can fight back, on her behalf, but you'll have to as well. I know she shut you out thinking she's keeping you safe, but that man has a read on you too, Cora. Whatever he tries on her will flow to you, and to Evelyn if you aren't careful. Shield well." Cora glanced worriedly at the sleeping form of Gran, tucked in on a rollaway bed. "It takes both parties to close a channel. Pry Eve's open if you must. You'll know when."

"I hope you're right."

"I haven't spent so many years a haunt *not* to be right," her uncle said, touching a cold fingertip to the end of Cora's nose. She giggled. "I saw what you did before the mansion; your manifestation was brilliant! The Dupris line, full of invention and celestial power!"

Cora beamed. The astral projection was thrilling, and making her elders proud felt divine. "I wish Eve had been here to see it. We should be fighting side by side through this."

"Let me go to her to share your unwillingness to be set aside, circumstantially and psychically. You are her equal, as much the leader as she. She's said so. That means being as much in danger as you want to be. This life isn't for the faint of heart. I gave mine for it."

Cora reached out to his phantom hand and ran her palm over the incorporeal chill. "You did. In a fight I can only imagine was far worse than this one—"

"Different. Each metaphysical battle is of its own importance, and each of its own time. I heard my Clara say that Prenze is cracking open the tensions of the whole spirit world. It's been darkening for some time. The Corridors between life and death are murky. Polluted. Spirits have begun to be paralyzed by fears and anxieties, tensions of the coming century. We don't know what will happen when the clock strikes midnight, 1900. Many of us fear we will simply fade away, the products of a bygone era and century."

"No, of course not…"

"Think of it: your most potent assets, the precinct ghosts all are from this century, not before. The eighteenth century and earlier are no longer full-consciousness spirits, truly only shades at this point, lost to the contexts of their time, while you hold our contexts *with* you and thusly, we are held more fully in your living minds. *You* give us power to be fully realized."

Cora had never thought of it this way. She and her team still had so much to learn about the dead and their properties. The idea of losing even an ounce of her uncle's potency going into the next century sent her nearly into tears; she had to blink them back to retain the composure she sought to cultivate in his presence. Their bond was sacred. "How can we protect you?"

"We spirits are discussing this, in the ways that only we can speak and know. But it will be up to you to protect us. That's why Prenze being an enemy of ghosts is so troubling. If he starts to eliminate ghosts, much like one fright on a landing that causes a stampede, there will be a spiritual panic. I can't pretend to know what will happen. The Corridors we travel between life and death have never felt so unstable."

"Does Eve have any sense of this?"

"Perhaps. I thought Maggie and she might have discussed it, but..."

"Maggie is focused on possessing the living in this case; she may not see a bigger picture. *You* must tell Eve, uncle. She's allowing spirits by her side, just not us." Cora clenched her fists.

"I'll visit, going with my heart tied to yours. We are all a web. Only binding our threads will keep them strong. She may fall through a spiritual void, and our web must catch her."

Gran had awoken and knelt by Cora, gazing at Louis fondly, and spoke softly.

"Thank you, Mr. Dupris, for being such a valiant soldier for seventeen years. What Eve plans to do, in her editorial piece in the morning papers, is send a sweeping dose of love to the spirit world, to open the city's heart to it, bolstering and strengthening it, a challenge directly to Prenze, meant to provoke him. She hopes to create a psychic wave; you'll know when it hits. If you can be alert with us, we'll do whatever it takes to protect the living and the dead."

"Then you keep watch here, I'll do so there. Vigilance is our only friend right now, in your plane and mine."

Chapter Eleven

Dressed in her most voluminous nightdress, a gift from Gran when she was sixteen, indulging Eve in what she had dubbed a phase of "Ann Radcliffe–level Gothic devotionals," Eve settled in on the small bed she'd tossed and turned in as a child, lying in a pool of satin, muslin, and lace layers. She'd taken drops of tonic in her tea as Gran had suggested and stared out the window to the park beyond, branches climbing into a night sky heavy with storm clouds.

When psychically tied to others, one takes for granted never truly being alone. But when Eve closed her psychic doors to her colleagues, a push-and-pull before an echoing internal slam, it drove loneliness home in a sharp spike to the soul even though it was what she'd demanded.

Cora proved a particular struggle. She could feel her dear friend's indignance, demanding Eve not go too far. So loyal and steadfast, Cora was such a good woman. Eve hoped Cora knew how valued she was. Separation at such a crucial time was no rebuke of their talents.

Agonized, her thoughts inevitably turned to Jacob, wishing for all the world she could further indulge in the passion they'd just begun to allow themselves. The love she'd declared, demonstrated, allowed herself to feel despite all else... It had made them each too vulnerable. The joy of it wasn't wise.

Tears poured down her face. She didn't know what would lie ahead, if they could rekindle that passion again. If he'd ever be allowed to see her again. If he'd be willing to defy every urging of their separation. There was no assurance he'd be there for her when all of this was over, to kiss, to hold, to pleasure, to promise.... Not when she'd shut him out without any sense of when she'd dare let him back in.

Tossing and turning again, this time not from the torments of spirits but from the longings of her soul and body, just as she was about to achingly call Jacob's name solely for the delight of saying it, a cold wind enveloped her and a face came through the wall.

Eve's moan became a cough, and she wrapped the quilt around her to hide, her nightdress open at the collar. "Mr. Dupris!"

The spirit's greyscale face, generally a pleasant, handsome neutral, grinned knowingly.

"I can tell a fellow lovelorn spirit when I see one," he exclaimed. "Welcome to our distinguished club. Hold on to love, hope, and what you're living for, Eve Whitby. I come to reassure you and to warn you about what lies ahead in equal measure."

Louis Dupris explained to Eve what he'd discussed with Cora. They talked strategy and theology. Eve was both inspired and duly cautious. She drank tea and allowed herself to relax in his presence. There were certain spirits that, during her first awakening to mediumship, would just keep her company and ward off all others who wished to yammer at her. Perhaps this certifiable mystic was doing just that, because she forgot for a moment how truly scared she was and didn't remember dozing off.

Chapter Twelve

Cora woke from a deep sleep with a sudden start, freezing hands on her cheeks and a transparent face next to hers. No matter how one had grown accustomed to ghosts, they still liked to startle, and none so much as Maggie Hathorn.

"Good Lord, Maggie," Cora muttered, rising, wiping the grit of sleep from her eyes. "Don't be creepy." The spirit did nothing to adjust the lack of personal space between them. Cora folded her arms. "*What*?"

"I know Eve doesn't want the detective involved!" Maggie blurted, as if she'd been holding back a scream of gossip. "But he *has* to know why. He can't just think she's shut him out because she doesn't care anymore. I don't want what happened the last time at the soiree, when there was that terrible misunderstanding and everything was stupid—"

"Maggie, then *you* tell him. He's getting better at hearing spirits, isn't he? I'm not here to play messenger between lovebirds; we're here to nab Prenze on something we can use."

"When the next steps unfold, Cora, it's all going to go in a rushing jumble and none of us will be prepared. Two worlds, yours and mine, are on alert. I'll work from within the Prenze family. But I've a strong instinct that Jacob needs to be nearby for whatever is to come."

"Is he still at the hospital?"

"No, he went home last night. I checked," Maggie answered. "He looked toward me at the window, so he is getting better at sensing spirits, but he couldn't hear me. You should have seen his poor face. Whatever was said in the hospital must have heartbroken him."

"You weren't there with them?"

"No. I've been prowling Prenze's mansion from outside, so I know the rooms when I enter. I've tried to memorize them. Ghosts have to do things repeatedly for anything to stick."

"So you want me to go to the detective and say what?"

"That he should be with us, ready for anything. Not separated or kept in the dark. We need hearts intact. What I know about wielding power between this plane and mine, it all has to do with hearts, connection, and love. Eve's somehow lost track of that. Much like Jacob helped get Eve out of Sanctuary and come back to herself, we may need that again. If she's incapacitated, she can't yell at us for bringing him back in."

"Where is Eve now?"

"At Gran's, in her little 'tower room'—where she first came to terms with her gifts, a room that was her crucible when she was a child. From there, she's opening herself to the whole of the spirit world, and provoking Prenze in doing so. Whatever is next, there will be spirits relaying between all of you. I don't know where is best to be, but together, I believe, is wise."

"All right, then, I'll go. It's best I be the one to try to navigate Mulberry anyway; they'll get used to seeing me if it kills them."

* * * *

Alone in her corner tower, Eve woke with the sun, drawn from a heavy sleep as if pulled up from a well. She opened the door, wincing as it groaned on its hinges. Gran was downstairs; she could hear her in the parlor, humming softly, as she tended to do when nervous and trying to pretend she wasn't.

Eve looked to the coat-tree in the corner of the spare room. She needed to feel prepared. Official. As she slowly dressed in her adapted, black edition of the police matron's uniform, the stalwart look of it helped her confidence.

Patting the pocket, she was pleased the tintype was still there, that she'd kept it with her for good measure. *This battle,* she thought grimly, *may be won by emotion and the ability to control it.* In the other pocket was the knife her mother had given her when this all began and Gran had been abducted. Just in case she did end up leaving the house. Even though she'd promised she wouldn't.

But no battle could be won without some breakfast.

She descended into the parlor, where Gran, humming a refrain Eve recognized as a dreamy new piece by Debussy, had prepared a whole tray of deviled eggs, Eve's favorite, and a carafe of coffee. Gran sat in a fashionable riding habit at the tea table, light filtering over blue wool in patterns of magnolia leaves leaded in Tiffany glass that lined the bay window.

"Hello, dear." Gran gestured to the morning papers, bidding Eve take a seat before her. "Look at what you've wrought. My editorial contacts printed you in *three* morning papers."

Examining the papers, Eve tuned her psychic ear to the spirit world as she sipped the strong coffee and contented herself that the feel of it was balanced. Bidding the city to think of spirits with love was creating a far more pleasant spiritual resonance than the usual jarring chatter of the dismissed, disgraced, or forgotten. But with it too, she felt the sharp whine of discord and discontent, the wedge Prenze was trying to drive between worlds.

Before Eve even realized it, she ate the whole plate of deviled eggs, blushing an apology midbite in case Gran had wanted any. She only laughed heartily.

"I'm merely relieved you're fortifying yourself. Whatever unfolds, it will take all our energy." Gran explained what had happened at the New Netherland, the scuffle between Arielle and her brother, with Mahoney caught in the middle, no one sure where his loyalty lay. When Gran explained Cora's excellent astral work, Eve beamed.

"How brilliant. I look forward to telling her how proud I am of her when all of this is over. With this, it's clear we really have no time to waste. The pot is boiling."

"Well then, I'd best not delay in getting Mosley in place to set off the electrics. You're planning on opening yourself to the whole spirit world in a séance, then?" Gran asked hesitantly. Eve nodded. Gran grimaced. "I wish I could be in two places at once."

Eve offered her best impression of Gran's gentle scolding reassurance. "You are, Gran. Your energy is; don't doubt that now. Not to mention that's what the ghosts are for: a relay. Quicker than any modern invention."

As if to prove the point, Zofia appeared. "Ready for duty," the child said, lifting her hand to her forehead in a small salute.

"I'd like to begin," Eve stated, embracing Gran.

"You'll not leave the house."

"If, for some reason I have to, I'll be followed, will I not?"

Gran nodded.

By the front door Eve watched as Gran checked in with the men stationed within her eyeline. Elegant and powerful, Gran strode down her front walk, glancing back over her shoulder with a complicated look. Neither of them knew how many of these moments, embroiled in important things, they had left together in mortal form. The thought seemed to pain them both.

"No time for melancholy or fear," Eve chided herself, turning away.

Zofia floated close. "Chopin, my favorite musician, and my countryman, once said, 'I wish I could throw off the thoughts which poison my happiness.' It is a phrase I think of often. Do so. Throw off the thoughts that don't help. It's how I get through anything."

"You're such a help, becoming as much a mystic and muse as anything, dear one," Eve said with a smile. "And I can't imagine a better companion for this task."

The little girl beamed, her greyscale form brightening.

This whole, complicated case had begun with a warning from the spirit world: *"Don't invite anything in."*

She was about to do just that.

Each stair back up to that lonely room was a prayer. Step by step, preparing for the best and worst. With methodical precision, she set the séance table with items that she and Gran had used through the years.

Picking up a small silver bell etched with an image of Parliament's clock tower and its famous Big Ben bell within, Eve couldn't help but think back to when she'd first commandeered this piece, in her youth when Gran was describing different ways to begin a séance.

"Some use a bell," Gran had stated to little Eve, who immediately replied she wanted one. Gran returned from a parlor curio cabinet with the one Eve now held over a decade later.

"And a candle?" Eve had asked then. "I read some Spiritualists rely on candles to light their way in the channel." She'd run to her designated room at Gran's and taken the small silver tallow candleholder from her bedside table in case the gas went out.

The same small, tarnished single candleholder with its wide saucer and curved handle now sat before her, waiting. Small items with specific histories that imbued them as sacred relics were the best spiritual conduits.

She rung the bell and let the sound of the tiny, clarion ring echo in the room it faded. Striking the match, she said a quiet prayer to whatever force of love and peace was listening. Blowing out the match after the candle was lit, she watched the smoke curl away and placed the charcoal on the candle saucer and let the first drip of the candle fall on the top of her hand.

The spiritual colleagues with whom Eve already had a rapport didn't need a word from her to be summoned; just the ring of that bell and the opening of her heart was enough.

One by one, her spectral guides and colleagues arrived, filling and chilling the small upstairs room. First Zofia, then she was followed by her fellow worker Olga, who was showing up more frequently as an observer, quiet and steadfast. Vera wafted in, clucked her tongue at the sparse surroundings, making a face when she saw the cot. Eve was struck by a memory of Vera coming to her in her youth and admonishing a group of henpecking spirits to leave her be and give her space to breathe and live. That had happened here, and Eve had bonded with the old woman immediately.

They stared at Eve, and she realized she had to rally them, but she didn't have a muse of fire in her bosom like Shakespeare gave Henry V. Tired and worried, she had to come up with something nonetheless. With the same openness that she wrote the editorial, she spoke from the heart to those who had forgone eternal peace to make mortal life more bearable.

"My friends. Dear, stalwart soldiers. I don't know what's next, other than a psychological, spiritual battle. While I appreciate your presence, don't put yourselves in danger on my account. I have intentionally secluded myself from my living loved ones. At any point I want you to be prepared to do the same. Albert Prenze has been working on strategies and devices meant to rip spirits apart. Don't stand in the way of his line of fire, however that manifests. Be my relay while keeping everyone at a distance." She blinked back tears. "I'm not ready to lose any of my living loved ones today any more than I'm willing to lose my spirits; is this clear?"

The spirits nodded. As they did, the air rippled around them and Maggie was last to arrive, floating through the squat dormer window.

"My dear, while I'm always glad to see you..." Eve folded her arms and lowered her gaze at her best ghostly friend. "If you plan on entering the house to possess Arielle, you need to be there when Mosley upends their electrical system."

"I know..." The ghost darted around her like a flittering bird. Maggie's eternal ringlets bounced as she wafted before Eve, her face set in a spoiled pout. Emotional nuance hadn't had the chance to take a living root before her murder. "I just hate to leave you alone here in such a raw, vulnerable state."

"I'll be all right. Go to the house; this isn't goodbye and I'm not alone." Eve waved her off, praying that her words were true. The ghost bit her lip a moment, reached out fondly with a cold hand, brushed Eve's face, and flew off toward her designated target.

"Take care of her," Maggie instructed to the ghostly entourage.

"You take care of yourself," Zofia called after the woman she considered a sister.

Eve wasn't sure what to believe. She was alternately sure of herself, tapping into the natural-born confidence that Gran had nourished and tended like a garden, and cracking at the seams. What if what she'd built for herself sat on rocky foundations and at any moment she'd tumble apart like Poe's house of Usher?

Her ghosts hung at the periphery of the room, and she dug deeper, reached out psychically further.

"Spirits. Entities. The forces at work. Tell me. Speak to me. Whatever must be will be," she said to the air. She didn't want to invite Prenze all the way in, but it was an opening of a door of communication she'd tried to keep shut.

There was only a moment before a flurry of motion was visible outside.

The shadow arrived at the dormer window, looking in. As her enemy appeared, her ghosts receded as requested. This time, it was accompanied by the man's voice.

"Finally." Prenze's projection offered a cold smile, cruel eyes glinting behind glasses slid down at an angle, looking down his nose at her. "I only need a moment with you. It's best you don't fight it anymore. Follow," bid the voice. "Come alone. I don't want to hurt you."

"Only the ghosts?" Eve countered, narrowing her eyes.

"One can't hurt the already dead," the voice chided. "Don't resist. Once it's over I'll never trouble you again. You were designed for a unique purpose. As am I."

Eve pressed her mother's knife close on her wrist and buttoned up her uniform over the white sheath beneath. Patting her pockets, she felt a small bottle of water, notebook, money, a small bottle of various pills, a roll of bandage, and a tintype for provocation. She noted the shimmering air off to the side and knew her associates, careful to not make themselves fully manifest so as to avoid detection, would follow at a distance.

Eve prayed that the Prenze mansion, unbeknownst to its owner, was about to be thrown into chaos, clues and solutions unearthed, and those trapped be set free to set wrongs to right.

Chapter Thirteen

It wasn't many blocks from Gran's townhouse to the mansion at the center of the conflict. Maggie floated just above the low stone wall of Central Park, letting the brush and young tree branches tickle the hem of her skirts, passing through as if she were running a hand slowly over soft, supple grass. There was no friction in the spirit world, only movement, air, whispers, and a peculiar sense of time. She had to be at her most alert. A distracted soul in life, easily captivated by pretty things and pretty people, Maggie the magpie was even worse about it in death.

The formidable brownstone block that was the Vanderbilt mansion meant she had gone too far downtown, but she allowed herself a moment to stare in the windows of a second-floor room. A child swathed in silk and bows screamed at the sight of her. The mischief maker in Maggie giggled.

The earnest part of Maggie yearned for the type of experience she'd found with Reverend Coronado, an experience that she was still ruminating about, one that changed her profoundly. She'd tasted life again, and it was so very tantalizing. Now she'd cherish it again inside Arielle Prenze, someone only just older than her when she died. For a moment she might feel like herself again. But that wasn't the task. She needed access to Arielle, not her own missed opportunities and sentimentalism. The danger of ghosts was that they could grow too fond....

The Prenze mansion loomed ahead, its lights dimmed. If she wasn't mistaken, she saw tiny, sparking eyes watching from between the small bank of hedgerows the family had managed to wedge in. Around them every property line was exchanging greenery for granite and grandeur, expanding until there was hardly any breath from one mansion to the next.

"Auntie?" Maggie called.

A figure in a black gown and veil tapped a cane against the flagstones. There she was, just across the street and south a quarter block, like a haunt in reverse, trading luminosity for shadow. Aunt Evelyn would be presumed as a mere passerby; she would give Mosley a sign to trip all the wires, and whatever secondary generator the Prenze prison had in place.

"You're sure," Aunt Evelyn murmured.

"As anything," Maggie responded confidently.

Further up the block, a driver waited with the largest carriage. Antonia and Jenny had insisted upon coming and waited inside. Clara Bishop had returned home to Tarrytown to keep a spiritual ear tuned to the spectral dynamics of the area. Prenze hadn't been lurking outside of Sanctuary for nothing.

Maggie stared at the mansion. This place had done her harm, torn her apart, split her soul into pieces, and thrown it all into darkness before Sanctuary repaired her again. The thought that she might be ripped asunder again occurred to her, but like little Zofia, who appeared suddenly by her side even though she'd been told to stay with Eve, she couldn't let her own trauma keep her from the task at hand.

"Olga and Vera are with Eve. I'm not losing you again, sister," she said, reaching toward Maggie. Maggie patted her companion on the head, every touch an echo of its former power, a phantom comfort.

"But if I give you a message, you have to listen to me. If all goes to plan, I'll not be free to come and go in and out of Arielle's body. You're the best of us at a relay."

"All right," the little girl agreed, beaming with pride at the compliment about her spectral acuity in vanishing and reappearing in the right places.

Maggie nodded toward her aunt. "It's time."

Three sharp raps of the steel-tipped cane upon the slate stone outside the mansion gate. The cue.

From within the branches of the evergreens came a growl, then a hiss, then a sizzle, then a roar.

"Float back," a nervous voice insisted, waving at the ghost from between the hedges. Maggie turned toward Mr. Mosley. She'd heard Auntie Evelyn speak of this "man of current" in uneasy terms, reluctant to call upon the favors of an unpredictable soul. But Evelyn Northe-Stewart kept a motley crew of associates at the ready, specialists perfectly suited for the types of peculiar situations Eve and her family seemed destined to fall into.

"Back," he repeated before Maggie realized he could see and was talking to her and Zofia. The small, wiry man's eyes were wide and the

Tesla coils within them sparked the brightest she'd yet seen. "Float back from the direct line of it."

Maggie didn't understand, but she didn't protest and she drew Zofia away and into the street just as a carriage passed through them: another tickle of tactile object through vaporous mass, only this one smacked rather than elided, a denser mass than the caress of leaves. The horses gave a whinny of dismay at the ghosts, the carriage veering away and the driver cracking the whip to regain order.

Sparks flew up around a wooden pole on the street outside the Prenze mansion where countless wires converged.

A hum rose in the air, and though Maggie didn't have tactile hair to raise, her spectral hair stood on end, as did Zofia's, flying out all around them as if in a gust of static wind.

Another pop, bang, and reverberate thunderclap. Fireworks of sparks erupted all around the Prenze mansion, a whole bay erupting in particular from the cellar level, glass shattering and the wrought iron rattling.

In immediate response, the glow of spirits on the dark lower levels of the house brightened and blossomed to luminous silvery life from within the Prenze walls. Spirits flew from the basement in a secondary explosion of life force. A collective cry went up from the house: the distinct sound of a soul's freedom, repressed life uncorked and bursting forth. Just as the spirits began to rise to upper floors, Maggie's gaze followed, noting a haunted face.

Arielle, tired and lost, looked out her bedroom window. Perhaps she heard the cries of the freed spirits because she whirled around, eyes wide in terror, shivers wracking her frail body.

Maggie floated through the window as the whine of the electrical malfunctions died down. "I'm here to help your family."

Inside the house was pure chaos, the freed spirits darting in wild abandon. Arielle Prenze dove to hide under the covers of her bed.

Two familiar faces appeared before Maggie: children dressed in Bavarian garb as if from a folk tale. She recognized them as the brother and sister who had drawn her into the Prenze mansion in the first place; she'd been responding to their call for help.

"You freed us! Thank you!" The little boy said. "His terrible walls finally broke!"

"Who are you," Maggie asked, "and why were you imprisoned here?"

"Lab animals. The first successful test subjects," the little girl said.

"In trapping spirits," the brother clarified. "We haunted the photos after our death. Our spirits came with the photos the mortician brought, the photos you launched downstairs."

"Oh, I remember," Maggie replied mordantly, recalling what got her into all this: the day she found herself in the Prenze parlor, looking at these children. Prenze—now she knew it was Albert masquerading as his brother—had ushered everyone out and turned up his device so high she felt torn apart, like the burning or tearing away of skin, but when there was no skin, it only flayed the soul....

"We're sorry you got hurt; you were just the first soul to hear us. We didn't mean to trap you too," the little girl said, wringing phantom hands. "But you got out. Something got you out but left the rest of us there. Thank you for coming back for us. Thank you for not forgetting us!"

Sanctuary had heard Maggie's plea, but it hadn't been able to rescue anyone else from the darkness below. Maggie only had a slight recollection of the experience; it was all a spiritual murk.

"Of course. Get out while you can," Maggie said, ushering the children to the window. "Anything you can share that will incriminate our torturer, any proof, any papers, anything we can use, bring that information to the Ghost Precinct, care of Eve Whitby, you hear?"

The children nodded and floated out the window, the boy so happy about his freedom he did an aerial flip before diving away, his sister grabbing onto his hand. "He keeps a diary of his deeds!" the boy called. "You'll find everything you need in his old study upstairs, the one his brother thinks is always kept locked! Go there!"

Maggie's heart leapt at this. Tactile proof! Now to get her hands on it. She whirled to Arielle, advancing on the shuddering form beneath the covers. But before she could manifest poltergeist energy to tear back the covers and confront the woman, there came an ungodly, wretched sound, the likes of which Maggie had never heard.

Up from the floor below came a terrible scream of rage and frustration, keening sounds of misery. This is how one became a banshee, Maggie thought—a soul, tortured long enough to have lost language, and nothing else remained but pain, retaining only the capacity for wailing. Following the sound was a form, erupting up from the floorboards.

An intense face with the piercing gaze Maggie recognized as the tintype Eve found stared at Maggie, puzzled a moment, before whirling onto Arielle.

Mrs. Prenze. The dread matriarch her son hated so deeply as to despise all spirits. A tattered, bony shipwreck of a spirit.

In a violent gust, the ghost managed to throw back the covers her daughter hid under, and Arielle cried out.

"Mama?" she squeaked, the sound of a terrified toddler, not a grown woman.

"WHAT HAVE YOU DONE?" the ghost screamed, hovering over the bed like a predatory creature, white hair floating wild around her furious face like snakes in water.

"Oh no...no, no, no..." Arielle murmured, tears streaming down her flushed face. "Please, no..."

The severe spirit swooped around the room, searching, before she whirled back on Arielle, hand raised in the air like a claw, a talon ready to shred. "WHAT HAS HE DONE?"

Arielle turned to Maggie, tears in her eyes. "Help me."

Without hesitation, Maggie dove in.

The physical sensation of merging soul into body for possession was impossible to describe, and as this was only Maggie's second attempt at wholly overtaking another's body and staying put for results, she hoped she'd get less clumsy about it if it became routine.

A roaring sound then tearing pain, a sinking, falling feeling. She found her body, but as she did, Arielle spasmed on the bed, kicking the satin duvet. Maggie had been seasick once as a child, and this approximated the feeling, churning and shifting discomfort. Her incorporeal body was merging with another layer, like a heavy coat, but it wasn't a garment—it was another person.

Maggie saw through another's eyes.

"What is *wrong* with you?" the old woman cried, looming down on Maggie and Arielle as their visages merged. Mrs. Prenze's surprise was quickly masked by a venomous anger, grey eyes flashing. "What abomination is happening now?"

Maggie wasn't able to place Arielle's thoughts at the foreground of her own, but she did have the strong inclination to throw herself out of the bed and run for her life. Arielle's entire person could not be conveyed to Maggie, but she could sense her most base terrors and a crushing feeling of being trapped, as if Arielle were a woman buried alive before she'd even died.

The doors to the next room flew open.

Upon sight of the man at the threshold, the ghost of Mrs. Prenze unleashed another banshee scream.

Staring into the transparent eyes of his deceased mother, Albert Prenze's face went from controlled to horrified to furious in one malevolent swoop. His mouth fell open, and he screamed back.

Man and ghost, mother and son, screaming at one another in primal rage.

The pain was palpable. The virulence was incoherent, impossible to put into words. That these entities were enemies was undeniable.

Arielle quailed again, her thin frame wracked with a shudder, terrified of the exchange. Maggie winced within her and didn't fight the physical recoil.

"I'll be rid of you once and for all!" Prenze finally shouted.

Mrs. Prenze just kept screaming.

A fresh wail of anguish came from the next room. Another voice. Mrs. Prenze stopped abruptly at the sound and flew forward through the closed set of doors.

"Yes, yes, run to your precious baby," Albert sneered. "The only one you ever loved."

Mrs. Prenze flew out of the room, and in her wake, the rest of the ghosts that had been prisoners in the house took up where Mrs. Prenze had left off, swirling around Albert in a tornado of rage. His breath clouded around him in an icy fog.

"All right, then," Albert cried, as if he were rallying troops. "If the animals are all out of the zoo, then it's time we commence with the cleansing!"

"The cleansing..." Maggie repeated, and Arielle lumbered through the syllables.

"The next phase of the plan has been hastened by this electrical outage. I didn't plan for the prisoners to be let loose. All of it's been compounded by that stupid girl's challenge in the papers," Albert spat, glancing to the side.

The spirits stopped whirling and hovered, tense, worried, ascertaining the next moves.

Albert Prenze swiped at the air. "Go on, get out! I'll rid myself of you soon enough!"

The remaining spirits flew away, many with curses on their lips, several with prayers. Maggie thought they'd all need both.

Maggie directed Arielle's gaze to follow in the same direction of her brother's eyes, and she saw a model sitting on a corner desk, a cardboard diorama like a designer would craft for a stage production as an instruction for dimensional designers and carpenters.

At the center of the model were small figures standing on a familiar replica of two great Gothic arches and a vast span across a river. To the side was a small, thin wire and another simple arch that put her in mind of Sanctuary and the entrance to that spiritual enclave.

"Out from under the great arches, oblivion will fly." Maggie recalled the cryptic message they'd received during Dr. Font's séance.

Whatever was about to happen, it was about to happen on the Brooklyn Bridge, with another wire going off into the ether to Sanctuary's gate. If they hoped to wage a counterattack, it would have to be waged in both locations.

A bridge to burn, severing two sides of a world. Maggie threw Arielle's arm forward, pointing at the model, turning toward Zofia's ghostly form, an indication that the girl needed to relate what was shown there.

"Go," Maggie murmured hoarsely through Arielle's parched throat. "Tell all our allies. Out from under the great arches, oblivion will fly. Protect and intercept both places."

Zofia nodded, eyes wide yet defiant. "Then let it be so."

Maggie felt a shudder of fear that came most certainly from Arielle, for Zofia's defiance bolstered Maggie. Whatever Arielle knew about what was to come, the idea that the spirit world wouldn't be passive but would fight back wasn't something that Arielle felt prepared for. A life of being submissive to men seemed to have narrowed Arielle's sense of possibility.

Albert grabbed Arielle, peering deeply into her eyes. "What's gotten into you?"

At this, Maggie just giggled, wanting to yell, "Me!" but her laugh only caused a burble from Arielle's numb lips. The maniac must have drugged the woman. Coronado was a smooth and elegant joining. This was like a marionette with tangled strings and jumbled limbs.

"I can't rely on you in this state," he growled. "I'll have to lay you down with Alfred."

"No!" Arielle and Maggie joined forces to speak, indignant. "This state is *your* fault."

"I thought you'd fare better with all the fireworks against the spirits if sedated," Albert countered, "but you're not acting like yourself."

Maggie could feel Arielle's panic, wanting to say what had happened, but Maggie didn't allow for it, her spirit stronger. Arielle had been weakened by control Prenze had lorded over her for too long.

* * * *

After the spiritual melee had overtaken the Prenze mansion, Antonia rushed out from the carriage that Gran had left for them all, an escape vehicle if there was danger.

"Gran," she said breathlessly. "I just had another vision. The forest again. I recognize it now. The arch. It's Sanctuary. And I saw *you* there, and all around you a great light." Antonia blinked back tears. "What I saw is beautiful and terrible in equal measure...."

Zofia appeared on the street.

"There are two attack sites, all wired up," the little girl explained. "One is Sanctuary!"

Antonia and Gran looked at one another, Jenny watching from the carriage window.

"You're tied to Sanctuary, Gran," Antonia said. "If that's a place spirits consider safe, it needs all the protection it can get."

"What about Eve?" Gran asked worriedly. "She's still conducting a séance from my house, yes? While guarded?" Gran asked.

Zofia nodded. "I'm going to tell Cora and the detective too, all hands on deck."

* * * *

From within the Prenze mansion, another man stepped quietly into view as if he'd been lurking at the threshold just beyond, listening. Sergeant Mahoney. Maggie remembered Eve saying he'd initially given her trouble but then saw sense. Whether he would prove ally or hindrance was yet to be seen.

"Let me take care of her, then, if she's not seeming herself," the officer said. "Why don't you go and do whatever it is you plan to do and I'll look after them."

"Keep them here," Prenze growled. "If you need to sedate them—" Prenze plucked out a tonic bottle from his breast pocket.

Suddenly, at a lumbering run from the next room, another body flew forward.

Alfred Prenze, greying hair mussed and distressed, hair askew and jaw slack, came running at Albert and knocked him over, the bottle flying to the side of the room and shattering in a green splatter across the champagne wallpaper and oozing down the lower wood paneling.

Mrs. Prenze the ghost followed Alfred and flew around her now tussling sons who wrestled on the parquet wood floor. The leaner, sharper Albert quickly got the better of his incapacitated twin. Mahoney tried in vain to pry Albert off but couldn't keep a grip.

"Leave my best boy alone, Bert!" the old woman cried. "We were better off when you were dead!" At this, Albert Prenze snarled and threw his brother aside, where he groaned against the floor.

"Now, now," Mahoney said, helping Alfred up. He stumbled back, brushing himself off. The sergeant turned to Arielle. "Are you all right, Miss Prenze?"

All Arielle could seem to do was blink at the officer. The only words Arielle could manage were "I'm scared." Maggie prompted Arielle to more. "I want to know what's going on."

Albert Prenze was brushing off his suit coat, muttering. "Don't play stupid. You've been as supportive of ending ghosts as I am. And it's overdue." He stormed out, and Maggie forced Arielle to stand and try to follow. Mahoney tried to block her, but she stumbled past him. She caught her balance at the threshold, gripping onto the wall.

"All right, Eve Whitby, queen of the dead!" Albert called from the landing as he charged down the stairs. "I'm coming for your reign."

Chapter Fourteen

Upstairs in her tower, sweat dripped down Eve's temples as her body shook and her fingers trembled. Reaching for a glass of water with her good arm, her injured arm still smarting and throbbing, she drank messily, spilling it down her chin, closing her eyes to keep the room from spinning as a migraine shoved its miserable way in too.

Keeping an open channel for this length of time was taxing to Eve to this point of nausea, but it was the only way to gauge the effectiveness of her editorial.

From the morning on, as papers had been delivered and the city took to the pages, Eve could feel an additional opening. The channel widened. The response was positive. The spirit world warmed to her appreciation and call for engagement. The living thought of those they'd lost and strengthened the bonds between worlds.

But just as this feeling crested, there came a sharp crash. As if the river grew too wide and suddenly overflowed its banks, breaking a dam.

One of the things Eve hadn't anticipated was muddying the Spiritual channel, the reality of which Lily Strand and the Sister-souls of Sanctuary had specifically warned against. There was resistance. What had felt like a pure channel was now getting foggy, full of silt and sediment.

For all the swell of positivity and affirmation Eve's editorial created, there was rejection and denial too. Not everyone would agree with her, and she couldn't expect everyone to. She could taste disapproval on the air, a bitter tang.

Prenze wasn't the only one who wanted to reject ghosts. It was a reaction from the collective unconscious Eve hadn't bargained for. Just as the spirits were nervous about the coming age, so was the city worried about its future. Entrusting part of its spiritual welfare to the dead was hardly a comfort for many. Prenze likely deemed her blasphemous.

Like a spot of black growing before her into a shadow, there was the astral projection she'd been expecting.

Outside the tower window floated a dark silhouette, glasses slightly askew, hat at an angle, eyes still as piercing and vitriolic. The streaks of silver hair that had grown in around his temples flared out in mad tufts. Eve liked to think, by the look of him, that he was unraveling, but she didn't know if she could use that to her advantage or if that would make her situation all the more precarious.

Did you or your minions have anything to do with the electric? The figure sneered. The voice was disembodied, like her mind was manifesting it just outside her ear. It was not the way she heard spirits; this was infinitely more disconcerting. It was too close. Insidious.

"I don't know what you're talking about," Eve said, and she held up a paper with her editorial at the fore in front of her face. The shadow growled, the sound terrifying Eve, but she tried to make sure it didn't show on her face. But when the paper was ripped away from her by unseen hands, just the force of projection and power, pages falling torn at her feet, she jumped.

How dare you, little girl, came the indignant message slithering through her mind like an unwelcome insect in her ear. *How dare you challenge me? Proud fool. You'll come with me and we'll see who's the better mind. It's been a fun game to determine. I faced down death by industrial fire and came back with great power. You're a child.*

Eve swallowed the insult. "Leaving someone else to die in your wake, then," she countered, trying to get him to admit his responsibility for the body that had been assumed his.

That was...unfortunate. An accident of timing and too eager artists. But it provided advantage. Come along; we've much to advantage together. An incorporeal shove of her wounded shoulder forced Eve to her feet, garnering a hiss through clenched teeth. *Ah, that's right, you've a little bruise.... Such accidents of timing, yet again! Cooperate and we'll keep you clear of others.* Prenze's laugh echoed in her head. Eve wanted to scream a curse but bit her tongue and let herself be led.

Lest he think she was deliberately throwing his game, Eve tried to find the right balance of fight and resistance. The industrial disaster that set him on this path drove him to desire power, to reign supreme in mental prowess, so she would let him think he had a greater hold on her than he did. She could feel the gemstones she'd kept in her pockets heat up though she'd had to leave Antonia's circlet of protection behind; it would have drawn too much attention. She pressed the knife sheathed at her arm against her ribs, just to feel that it was there.

Descending the stairs, Eve asked the looming presence where he wanted her to go.

To the most mystical of structures: an arch.

Worrying for Sanctuary, she tried to keep her mind clear of *that* special, solitary arch. There were thousands of arches in the city, in all kinds of buildings and squares, that could be anywhere.

"Tell me about what happened to you. How you became so powerful," she prompted, hoping flattery would get her somewhere.

His form followed her through every window as she descended, a black pall floating, inescapable.

I nearly died. Some people see God in that moment. I saw nothing. But at the crossroads, I was given a choice. I accepted what was rightfully mine and came back like God, my mind opened by death. But I don't want to be haunted anymore. Now I can do something about it.

He was leading her out the front door. Surely this was ill advised on his part, Eve thought, walking slowly. Gran's hired security would see her and follow at a distance as had been instructed.

But, glancing side to side, they were nowhere to be seen. That wasn't something she'd accounted for.

A carriage sat at the end of the walk that Eve didn't recognize. When one of the hired hands from the door approached the top-hatted driver, the man showed him a paper and waved him off. The guard walked away looking similarly dreamy.

Eve wasn't the only one being controlled, clearly, and because she'd opened herself so fully to the spirit world, she was a walking ghost herself.

Early in the understanding of her gifts, when she didn't know enough not to open too wide as she was doing now, she had experienced that she could easily pass unnoticed or unseen. Because she walked with ghosts, sometimes she took on their passing qualities, if too much in their world. Shifting somewhat invisible hadn't been so much of a liability until now, when she needed someone to notice if things got ugly. No one was noticing her now.

Eve felt the world fall away, her breath short as she approached the waiting carriage, a hulking black compartment that looked more a prison cell than a comfortable ride.

The spirit world was anxious; the voices that she could usually pick out were all a nervous, whispering, chattering, nail-biting mass. She wanted to speak to the driver, who was staring forward on his bench, dazed and detached, but like a nightmare where she couldn't scream, so was she unable to reach out. She'd let Prenze too deeply in and overestimated her ability to control her shield, and underestimated his effect upon the environment around her.

Get in. Prenze's voice was sharp in her ear. Another nudging push nearly tripped her on the walk. She grabbed at the wrought iron gate, but her hand missed the handle. The carriage door swung open, revealing a dark, empty interior.

The interior appeared smooth, oddly reflective. Strange.

Eve tried to pull further away from Prenze's mental press, but in trying to do so, like a tug-of-war, she stumbled forward, losing ground and falling against the side of the carriage.

Get in.

Her step inexorably lifted to the baseboard, and her head ducked under and in. Her body fell heavy on the bench inside, jostling her bad shoulder and she groaned in pain.

The compartment door slammed shut of its own accord, and upon closer inspection, she saw the material, that strange, reflective quality on every surface, was metal.

A buzzing arose around her. The hairs on her arms and neck stood on end; any hair not pinned to her coiffure floated around her.

It dawned on Eve in a slow horror that the walls of the carriage were electrified, pulsing in a manner to keep the ghosts out. Eve saw Zofia try to float into the carriage, but the little girl's spirit bounced back as if repelled. Zofia hissed and waved her hand like she had been scalded. The most terrible look passed over her little face: a sense memory of the fire that ended her life. The electricity burned her, and Eve watched an old trauma overtake the young ghost.

Opening her mouth to shriek and rail against such a cruelty, the words died in Eve's throat as what felt like an unseen hand clamped around the back of her head and shoved to the side, dashing her head against the door in a sickening thump.

With an explosion of pain, there was only darkness, cutting Eve's renunciation to the quick.

Chapter Fifteen

"Is Detective Horowitz here?" Cora asked the patrol officer stationed at the Mulberry Headquarters entrance. The officer shrugged. "He was injured in the line of duty yesterday, but as he is the most diligent of men, my guess is he's already back to work. I'll check his offices myself if you don't mind." Cora held up the card, her finger placed pointedly beside Governor Roosevelt's signature of clearance. "I know the way."

The officer held up a wide, calloused palm. Cora sighed. "I've been to see him before and you gave me, and him, similar resistance. It's exhausting. Don't obstruct an ongoing case," she said simply, holding her head high. "Just because you don't like us won't deter us; it only slows us down from good work, the results of which will benefit *all* the force. We're not going anywhere, so it's best you adapt and get used to us."

He frowned, lowered his hand, and took the latch off a wooden gate. Cora passed through, allowing a strained breath to exit her lungs once she was out of sight down the rear hall.

A knock on the doorframe of a dim, narrow office had the detective looking up from his desk, desperate and hopeful. A wide-brimmed hat mostly covered the bandage over his head, but the corners of a nasty bruise and scrape across his forehead were visible in the lamplight.

When the detective saw it was Cora, she could see a flicker of disappointment cross his face. He was surely thinking it was Eve that had come to call. But he recovered immediately with a genuine smile, and Cora did feel he was glad to see her as well.

There was no artifice, no games about Jacob Horowitz; he was all kind heart and diligence. Moment by moment he softened Cora's heart that had been predisposed to think him a rival for her position as most important to Eve and the precinct.

"Miss Dupris, what news? May I ask, where is Eve, how is she? When I woke in the hospital, she and her family were gone. My parents said she..." He swallowed hard. A distinct anguish worked across his face so openly that it drew Cora forward. "She left saying she didn't want to...*see* me or work with me again. That can't be true, can it? After we've been through so much? After we..." His face colored and he looked away.

They must have shared some kind of moment of passion before the attack. Cora could tell the poor man was reeling. She wanted to reassure him but didn't know how.

"Eve doesn't want you near her after being specifically targeted so violently. What happened is so terrible; are you feeling better? I was there at Bellevue to check in on you both, but the doctors didn't want all of us crowding everyone."

"Apart from headaches and a few dizzy spells, I'm all right," the detective said. "Thank you for your concern." Setting his jaw, he leaned forward and continued. "My parents said Eve went so far as to remove me from the case. She has *no* authority to do so as she has *no* authority over my rank. I won't abandon what I'm working on, and I won't abandon *her*. I don't know what she thinks—"

"She thinks she's trying to protect us," Cora interjected with exasperation. "She's done the same thing to me, trying to distance her own team, being stubborn again. She's trying to spectrally force his hand, to reveal whatever he has planned, like challenging an old courtier to a duel. She's so old fashioned sometimes. Trying to keep us away from the confrontation is daft. Why have a precinct and a department? She should have just been a hired Pinkerton if she wanted to act like a vigilante."

Cora and the detective both folded their arms and huffed in frustration, then looked at one another and chuckled.

"Then we are agreed, we'll not let our dear lady go on as some lone and reckless firebrand," the detective said. "Where is she?"

"She is tending to spiritual matters from a room in Gran's townhouse. The papers today began the challenge; I don't know if you saw."

The detective shook his head. Cora plucked the latest paper from a pile on the corner of his full desk. His workspace was stacked with papers, letters, books and notebooks, the sign of a man on constant intake, diligent work, and thoughtful process.

Just then, they were joined by another man who stood at the threshold, the same officer who liked to give Cora an uneasy time in the reception area. He looked utterly baffled, verging on angry. Cora clenched her fists.

"Why would you, of all folks, *Has-no-wits*, get a package from Scotland Yard?" the man squeaked. "Not just from Scotland Yard, but how would Chief Inspector Harold Spire know your name?"

"Chief Inspector Spire!" Cora lit up and made a pointed exclamation, driving the point of rank and prestige home. "He worked with my parents, under commendations from the Queen herself; he's brilliant! You couldn't have a better man on your side, Lieutenant Horowitz!"

The officer questioning them now turned his shock to Cora. Horowitz came out from around the desk with a confident smile. The detective's calm competence and Cora's own family history with the respected police chief stood strong against this officer's hateful air that underestimated them as much as it marginalized them.

"Officer Portman, I *asked* Chief Inspector Harold Spire for his help on a related case. You'd be surprised, if you'd let yourself be resourceful enough to ask a man with more experience for his assistance, how far you might get. Thank you for bringing it to me. If I'm right, it's his casebook on a suspicious suicide related to our case."

"He…sent you his *casebook*?" Portman whispered incredulously.

"It pays to be polite and trustworthy," Horowitz replied with a winning smile, reaching out for the package.

Portman handed it over, shook his head, and walked away. Cora exhaled, half sigh, half laugh.

Horowitz moved to close the door partway. "Shall we have a look?" he asked, eagerly opening the paper-wrapped package. A black leather-bound notebook with a letter slid into his hand.

He read aloud, moving around the room as he spoke. Cora noticed that he winced from pain at certain steps but seemed too excited to sit still.

Dear Detective Horowitz,

My best wishes to your colleagues. Any friend of Evelyn Northe-Stewart is a friend of mine. I am glad you wrote; you confirm my suspicion that there was something off about the suicide in the Prenze tonic laboratory and the burned body left behind. May you find something useful in this that can put your pieces together and perhaps stitch together a few of mine. I'll retrieve it from you when you're finished; keep it as long as you need.

*In the front you'll find my numbers to send wires; call or visit if you're
in the country. If you can tie up the burned loose ends that led nowhere
in England, I'll heartily commend you. Give my regards to all Evelyn's
associates, please, and good luck. Cheers.*

Yours truly, Chief Inspector Harold Spire

At this, Horowitz nodded deferentially to Cora. The missive brought
unexpected tears to her eyes. She missed her family so much, a fact she
generally tried to repress. Spire worked with her parents when they first
fell in love, all while fighting a violent cabal. Beautiful things can thrive
amid terror and violence, in direct defiance of it, a lesson Cora had learned
young and one that they all needed now as much as ever.

"I promise to do right by you and everyone involved," the detective
replied to the letter as if the chief were in the room with him. His energy
certainly was imbued into the casebook.

The detective moved to open the book when a burst of cold air overtook
them all and Cora's vision was filled with Zofia's face floating before
her, wide eyed and concerned. Baffled, Horowitz suddenly shivered,
turning to Cora.

"The big bridge!" the little ghost cried. "Gran and the girls have gone
to Sanctuary. Because Prenze wired something to Sanctuary's arch that
can threaten the portal. But Prenze is forcing Eve toward Brooklyn, to
the bridge for something worse! None of Gran's guards have been able to
follow! She's all alone!"

Cora repeated the spirit's words as she said them.

Hearing Eve was in danger, everyone ran for the door.

Chapter Sixteen

Maggie only had a moment in the Prenze mansion to herself, and while she wanted to use Arielle's body to try to stop Albert, enough of Arielle's instinct gave her pause.

The ghosts had flown out. Alfred had lost consciousness again in his room, and his mother's spirit was fussing over him in a pattern she must have overdone in life.

"I need you to help me, Arielle," Maggie tried to say, but her voice could only translate to a mumble from Arielle's tongue. Still, the woman had to hear her. "Please. We don't want anyone to get hurt anymore."

The weary, bleary woman only laughed hollowly.

Show me something I can use, Maggie bid her host, one mind to another. *I'd like to do this with you willingly, but I'll force you to move if you won't. Spirits said something about a study upstairs?*

Maggie found herself lurching out of the room and down the end of the hall opposite. A wooden balustrade divided, going up a level or down to the front entrance foyer in a grand, winding slope. Above, golden light shone down from a bay window.

Shaking in mind and body, Arielle was a heady mix of sentiment and fear. Maggie reeled within her as though she were seasick, every step a trial.

What don't you want to face up there? Maggie asked her.

"Everything," Arielle replied. A lifetime of regret in one sad, raspy word of confession.

Tears leaked hot onto Arielle's cheeks. Maggie ached at the feeling. It had been so long since she had felt the warmth of breath, the salty sting and heat of tears. So bittersweet, this blending of life and death. Shame was as heavy as her tread.

He is not a good man, and it has clearly affected you, Maggie continued in Arielle's mind. *You are not to blame for his misdeeds.*

"Oh, but I am. We all play our part...."

At the top of the upper-floor landing a door appeared to be boarded shut at eye level. Arielle was leading now. She fumbled for a key behind the board, unhooked it from a small peg on the underside, and unlocked the keyhole, ducking under the slanted board, the back of her coiffure knocking against the underside, shifting the copper-red braid at the back of her head lopsided, hairs tearing on the rough wood.

Inside, bookshelves were half-empty, covered with dust and cobwebs. Light filtered in from an umber stained-glass window in geometric shapes.

Rather than pressing the woman about what was here or what they would find, Maggie tried to enjoy the sensation of being corporeal again, even if it felt a bit like puppetry.

Shuffling forward, Arielle pressed a lever, and the rear bookcase opened like a wall. Maggie felt her whole being flutter with a thrill of delight at a secret passageway. One benefit of dying young was that things that proved exciting as a child never ceased to enthrall. Maggie might have grown more wary, but simple pleasures of magic and mystery remained.

The room beyond was pitch black, electric lights dashed by Mosley's interference. Arielle ran her hand along the side of the wood-paneled wall until she found a knob and turned. Fire flickered to life in brazier sconces across the room, the old gas fixtures still working.

"I insisted we keep the old pipes at the ready against unreliable newer technology," Arielle stated proudly.

Maggie took in the chilling rectangular anteroom, all dark-paneled wood and tortured-looking forms. A sculpture stood at the center of each wall, robed figures with arms reaching upward as if for mercy. Figures in Purgatory or Hell. Maggie could nearly hear them crying out. Perhaps she did. Perhaps the statues were haunted, just like Dupont's stage production and his chapel of reliquaries, still restless dead to be soothed.

Maggie forced Arielle's hand to gesture to the figures. *What are those?*

"The first art Albert ever commissioned from Mr. Dupont. Years ago."

Before Albert staged his death? Maggie clarified.

"Yes," Arielle replied. The drugs Albert had administered to sedate and keep her from interfering must be wearing off as she seemed more lucid. She stood before a wax figure of a tortured woman, bare chested, clawing at herself and the sky. "At the beginning of Albert's macabre interests, he began assembling artists of like mind."

Arte Uber Alles? You do know the association led to the deaths of many, Maggie replied in Arielle's mind. She could feel the woman recoil, shame and panic flooding her body. *I'm not interested in implicating you, Arielle, if you can help me and my colleagues put a stop to all this.*

The part of Arielle interested in self-preservation rallied. She spoke quietly. "I...thought his intentions were entirely pure, that he was concerned with sanctity of spirit, that he wanted spirits to go to Heaven, not lingering here in pain. I understand now he wasn't interested in healing. But in controlling. *That* I should have known."

Still staring at the figures, something chilled Maggie to her core. Those weren't *just* statues.

You must understand what we're dealing with. See what I saw, my new friend, Maggie said to her host, mind to mind, and let her thoughts wander to the stage set in the theatre district when the spirits of children superimposed themselves onto infernal set pieces to show Eve and her team where parts of dead bodies were hidden in each statue of the elaborate set.

Arielle now saw these four bodies in the room not as sculpture, but as they truly were: an active crime scene of desecration. Above the heads of the figures were wisps of eerie light, like old engravings of little fires above the heads of prophets, demarking fire of holy spirit. Only this was the flicker of dying embers. Unlike the souls of children that had recently been set to rest, whatever pieces of life left within these statues belonged to souls that were so long detached and kept away from what unsettled them that they'd begun to entirely fade. Not potent enough to cry out for help.

Arielle choked back a sob and turned her body away. Trembling to the point of her knees nearly buckling out from under her, she ambled toward the smooth-lacquered ebony desk trimmed in gilded, Grecian patterns.

What all happened here? Maggie pressed.

"You'll hate me if I show you," Arielle whispered to her possessor, leaning her fair hands on the dark desk's edge for support.

"I come not to hate, but to help," Maggie countered, bidding Arielle hear her out loud, hoping if she heard it on her own tongue, she'd believe it.

Behind the desk, in lieu of a fireplace, floor-to-ceiling bricks appeared a fireplace shaft. But the bricks were odd—not clay, but metallic.

"What's this?" Maggie pressed. Arielle quailed. Maggie forced Arielle's hand into a fist.

"Before he built the downstairs prison for spirits... Here he began torturing Mother's spirit, several years ago. Bricked her ghost up behind electrified bricks to keep the spark of her spirit contained. Like Poe's Fortunato behind Montresor's mortar. For the love of God."

Her body sunk heavily into the leather desk chair as Maggie shuddered in her body, recoiling from the description of torture, thinking about how Albert ripped her own soul apart for Sanctuary to piece back together. She opened her mind to the memory and let Arielle see it, feel it. Feel the pain, the darkness, the fear. Maggie kept the memory of Sanctuary to herself.

The woman cried out. "I'm sorry, spirit, I'm sorry," she begged the spirit within her.

My name is Maggie.

"I'm sorry, Maggie."

"You may not think of us like the living." Maggie ground out through Arielle's clenched teeth. "But we were. We still are, just not in the way the world can comprehend, nor legislate, nor protect."

"It was, at first, for the love of God," Arielle explained, fresh tears spilling down her cheeks. "Albert and I were always close. Mother always said too close. I hated how cruel she was to him so I tried to love him enough for all of us. But I guess it wasn't enough. Like Albert, I did think the persistence of ghosts was unholy, and I tried, with Albert, to stop those women, the ones using ghosts like they were some sort of service."

My auntie Evelyn, you mean? Maggie pressed. *And my best friend Eve? Those gifted women who do so much for the living and the dead?*

"I always thought communing with the dead was wrong, evil."

Do you think I am evil, Arielle? Maggie asked. *If I were evil, I'd be here tormenting you, not trying to help. Take a moment. Feel my heart. Search my mind. We're a lot alike, Arielle, women of privilege blinded by the wrong things. Seduced by dark forces. That's what killed me. I don't want it to hurt you too.*

In a strange, swirling moment, as if the two women were swept into a waltz through time, scenes were shared of mistakes and missteps, bending to the will of those who held uncanny power over them rather than thinking for themselves on their own terms.

Maggie watched a potent memory: Arielle threw her arms around Albert who had snuck into her rooms to see her in secret, begging her to keep the fact that he hadn't died a secret. He placed a tonic for sleeplessness by her bedside. Only much later would she realize he was slowly poisoning her to keep her compliant and out of the way as his obsessions escalated.

In turn, Arielle watched as a young Natalie Stewart, a year before Eve would be born, held Maggie in her arms as she died, in a dining room covered in blood, as the dark cabal Maggie had unwittingly assisted fell apart around her. Maggie remembered there'd been so much she'd wanted to say to her friend before her body failed that night.

Maggie's ghostly tears fed Arielle's living ones.

"I never hated ghosts," Arielle murmured in a plea. "I thought we needed to let spirits pass on and go to Heaven to help them, not contact them to linger. Though I doubt Heaven's where Mother would have gone." Arielle shifted into her mind again for the next part, looking around as if frightened she'd be overheard. *Mother was too hateful, too spiteful for Heaven.*

It was as if the mention of her summoned her.

The screaming returned, that terrible banshee wail. The woman's fine gown had gone to tatters during her imprisonment, along with a floating mess of wild hair and scraps of satin, glistening black pits for eyes bearing down on her daughter and her possessor with brute force and searing cold.

"Get out, get out," dead Mrs. Prenze shrieked, "get away, get away, you wretched little brat, get OUT.... What good have you done to MY house but squander it?!"

Ducking away from the raging spirit, Arielle fumbled beneath the center desk drawer for something, her fingers closing around a small key and prying it loose.

Your proof, Arielle said internally. In these moments, Maggie was no longer the driving force, and all she could do was offer energy and support as Arielle shied away from the lunges of her mother's ghost.

Maggie admired her host in this moment. Despite being screamed at by the ghost of Mrs. Prenze who rent the air with icy talons, swiping at Arielle's hair and face, Arielle managed to open a desk drawer and fumble past papers and glass vials with marks of poison on their labels.

You'll have to come back for the rest of the papers, they'll likely be telling. But this...

Arielle finally pulled out a black leather-bound journal. *You'll want this.*

Clutching the volume, Arielle ran.

Her body far more responsive than when Maggie dove in, the entwined souls tore down the flights to the ground floor entrance foyer where Mahoney was trying to help Alfred Prenze into a chair, a pool of vomit on the fine rug.

"No, stop, I must get out and follow Albert," Alfred mumbled. "I have to stop him from hurting more people.... I have to help...."

"You are in no state to do so, my friend," Mahoney said gently.

Ignoring them both, Arielle went to the front armoire and threw a russet-brown wool riding coat over her day dress, tucking the leather-bound journal into a deep interior pocket.

"Just where do you think you are going?" Mahoney asked wearily, as if he'd been fighting all day with exhausting children. Maggie could feel Arielle hesitate, so she helped supply the response.

"Where do you think? Help or get out of the way!"

Arielle threw the door open, blinked at the bright light of day, finally free, and kept running.

Chapter Seventeen

Eve walked in darkness. Regaining a sense of herself only in sound, a crying child. One by one her senses returned. Vision finally arrived. She stood in the hallway of a large house with no lights on, only moonlight through tall windows with every shutter open and creaking in a high wind that gusted against shuddering panes. Beyond was a sleepy New York that seemed less built up than she remembered. She didn't recognize the grand home.

The last thing she remembered, she'd been thrown against the wall of a carriage by Prenze's manipulation. She was, for all intents and purposes, unconscious. But where *was* she now? This was like no psychic journey she'd ever experienced before.

She passed a little boy in a room with two beds, two sides of the room identical to each other. One of the beds was empty. In the other sat a boy, in a white nightgown, stock still, bright red hair mussed, a frightened look on his young face.

There was crying from the end of the hall. Eve was drawn to it and looked in: a miserable looking alcove with one narrow window and an empty wardrobe with no doors.

"What did I tell you?" a sharp voice yelled.

"To stop inventing nonsense," the child repeated morosely.

"To stop being *stupid*. Pray to God he makes you smarter, like your brother." The woman shoved him toward the door. "If you don't quit your fantastical ideas you'll be sleeping in this closet for the rest of the week."

She raised her hand as if she was about to strike him. He ran back to his room down the carpeted hall and slammed the door.

Eve followed toward it and moved through the door as if she were a ghost.

"I think they're good ideas, Albert," the other boy whispered. "In fact, I think we could make a whole business of your tonics and cure-alls. Just keep it to yourself."

Albert said nothing, just climbed into bed and crawled under the covers, turning away from the brother who was clearly concerned for him.

Albert and Alfred Prenze as children. How was she watching this memory? The malevolent Albert had truly gotten into her head. With his level of psychic connection to her, albeit an unwelcome bond, perhaps when she went unconscious, she had slipped into his unconscious mind? An unexpected merge?

The scene changed. Eve stood in the corner of a lavish parlor draped in black crepe and filled with vases of pungent lilies. A man was laid out in finery with his arms crossed over his chest. A wake. The two boys, a bit older, were staring at the body before them. To their right was a pretty little flame-haired baby in a white lace dress set in a pram. Mrs. Prenze, tall and severe, looking older than she likely was on account of her harsh face, gripped each twin's hand tightly.

One of the boys—Eve couldn't really make out who was who—was sniffling quietly.

The woman seized each of the children's hands and placed them on their father's cold face. Each boy whimpered.

"Your father is dead and that's that," the woman scolded, her voice rising. "No crying for the dead!"

The baby in white lace began to whine.

She whirled toward the pram and screamed. "NO CRYING FOR THE DEAD!"

A sharp, dizzying shift in vision and the scene changed. Partially.

Eve was staring at the same room. Some of the furnishings of the gilded parlor were different, but the room was again draped in crepe. The two boys were now adults. The differences in personality became clear: Alfred had a softer face that was pensive and peaceful: Albert was hard and harsh. Arielle was a young and lovely thirteen or so, wide eyed and vulnerable. All were dressed in black.

Before them lay another body.

Mrs. Prenze. She even died with a scowl on her face.

There was a tense, dreadful silence between the siblings.

Suddenly, Albert screamed at the body. "NO CRYING FOR THE DEAD!" Abruptly, he turned on his heel to leave the room.

A ghost shot up from the body in a move so sudden it made Eve gasp.

Mrs. Prenze's greyscale body, her transparent form swathed in the widow's weeds the undertaker had dressed her in, flew up above her body and turned toward Albert as Arielle's hands went to her mouth in a shriek. Alfred's mouth gaped open.

The newly risen spirit flew after Albert as he ran to the door with a moan of despair, her shrill, berating tone like nails on a chalkboard. "YOU UNGRATEFUL WRETCH!"

Eve followed the ghost and Albert, but at the threshold of the parlor, everything changed again. She was plunged into a long corridor that was entirely dark ahead, save for the slight silhouette of Albert, lit by a building in flames behind them, framed by a doorway.

The hall they were now in was a distinct one, a psychic precipice Eve had been in often of late. The Corridors between life and death that opened up to anyone at a particular crossroads. This was the day Albert nearly died.

"I want to be free," he pleaded to the empty hall. Eve found it striking that there were no framed pictures on the Corridor walls indicating distinct moments of Albert's life, only the faint flicker of fire behind them vaguely illuminating a misty darkness.

Suddenly Albert put a hand to his head, and Eve felt a sympathetic pang in her own. A different pain than that of a blow. A specific tearing, rending feeling. She knew it well. It happened to her when she was young and her psychic gifts first took over her awareness, obliterating all else.

Then, the air of the Corridors spoke in an eerie chorus:

"You want power you feel you were denied, do you not, Albert Prenze?" The collective unseen voices made for an unnatural sound. Eve didn't trust that it was human; it sounded like an elemental force given capacity for speech.

Gran had always told Eve to be careful if the Corridors ever spoke, and never, *ever* accept if the Corridors offered something. It was like eating something in the underworld: it would prove binding and never for the soul's own good. The Corridors were a place where souls could easily be tempted to darkness before they searched out the light.

"Yes," Albert gasped desperately. "Give me what I deserve."

"Then go," the seething murmurs chorused. "See what you can do with it...."

Still clutching his aching, expanding mind, Albert turned back to the threshold, toward the living, toward the fire, his eyes falling on something. Eve watched as he bent to examine a wooden crate set just at the edge of the portal toward death.

Inside the crate was a makeshift box with a spool of paper, wires, and graphing implements. The early great experiment. Propped against it was a medical journal boasting bold queries as headlines:

Can we map the human brain? Can we chart a sixth and psychic sense? Are we merely a sequence of electrical charges or do we have Patterns? What does our mind possess?

"I will possess control," Albert murmured, sweeping the box into his arms as he rushed out from the Corridors into the burning building. Eve followed as if she were attached to him. Heat flashed across her face and body. Out of the corner of her eye across a smoke-filled factory floor, she could see a figure choking and falling to his knees. Albert, coughing, escaped onto the second-floor landing as the flames crested without helping the man behind, the body that would be left in his wake.

As he was about to hobble down a metal set of stairs to a loading landing, Albert turned to Eve.

"You," he sneered. His face could have been handsome if it weren't so hardened and weighted down by bitterness. "You're not welcome here," he said, and pushed her down the stairs of his memory.

Eve fell as though she were falling down a pit or a well, falling away from memory and back against the hard wood and upholstered fabric of the present carriage, her consciousness crashing against the pain erupting in her head.

Lifting her hand, she felt the large lump where she'd been cast against the side of the carriage and a narrow gash that was slightly bloody, although coagulation slowed the flow. She gritted her teeth as she raised her injured shoulder. Putting her cuff to the small gash, Eve pressed to stanch it fully, hissing at the sting and throb. Otherwise she seemed intact.

Opening her eyes slowly, she cried out at the face that floated before her: Albert Prenze still projected his presence just on the other side of the carriage window, a rivulet of her own blood intersecting the pane from where she'd been knocked against the corner of the frame. She put her hand to the sheathed knife but stopped. It would do no good against a mere projection.

You intruder, his presence growled.

"*You're* the one who wanted hold of my mind," Eve muttered. "Don't blame me if it wanders. Just because you lived through pain doesn't mean you can inflict it on others. You were given an opportunity, granted psychic gifts on the doorstep of death. Just think of all the good you could've done with it. Instead you just left a man to die and increased your own misery and that of others."

Prenze's image just laughed and faded. She hadn't banished it; he simply disappeared. Eve wasn't sure she wanted to know why.

The metal walls of the carriage still blocked out the ghosts beyond from coming too close, though nothing could keep little Zofia from maintaining a watch at a safe distance, floating as the carriage slowed in downtown congestion.

Lining up behind other fine vehicles outside the bridge side of city hall, the carriage stopped. No one came for her. No one stepped down from the driver's perch. She tried the door. It was locked securely from the outside by some sort of device. Average hired hacks and hansoms had no such impolite trappings.

Glancing out the window past gaslight streetlamps not yet lit during the bright midday, Eve noticed the side seams of city hall. Like so much of New York, it was all façade and positioning. The building's face was marble and beaux arts finery while the back of the building remained plain, its 1811 designers foolishly thinking no one would bother to be anywhere uptown of it, especially not near such a derelict district as the former Five Points. That infamy was gone; the gilded age consuming every scrap of the teeming island at the center of the world, and nothing spoke of its dizzying appetite as much as the great landmark ahead.

It was impossible not to be in awe of the inimitable New York and Brooklyn Bridge, no matter what.

A stunning web of wire rope sloped gracefully to the brown granite and limestone towers set with two enormous, pointed arches. The vast, suspension bridge was unmatched, a wonder of engineering and the vision of the Roeblings, finished thanks to the steadfast effort of Emily Roebling, one of Eve's inspirations. Countless New Yorkers strolled its pedestrian walkways.

The double Gothic arches of the behemoth, the tallest man-made structure on the continent, seemed to hold up the bright sky as if the clouds were the clerestory of a cathedral. What a magnificent stage for her antagonist to set his scene. What did Prenze want with Eve here?

The permits they'd found in the folder at the viewing parlor, Eve remembered with a sinking feeling. City permits for an art exhibit.

Was she about to be on terrible display?

Loud and abrupt, a barrel organ erupted into a clattering, eerie tune not meant for such a machine at the mouth of the pedestrian landing. The instrument and its grinder, a cloaked figure, were bordered on either side by the immense arches set out into the river, and suddenly the beauty of it all loomed as a threat.

Eve placed the tune clanging from the organ bleating at the bridge approach; it was one of her favorites, a pavane in F-sharp minor by Gabriel Fauré. Written a decade prior, the tune was known to waft into her head more than any other. It was an intimate, particular personal detail Prenze couldn't have known, and that terrified Eve more than anything yet had.

She gripped the carriage door again, but this time, with a pinging, metallic click, the door swung open.

That's it, whispered a snide and sneering Prenze. Eve prayed she could unsettle and overturn his haughtiness. *Come, it'll all be over soon, just as you dared, so go on.*

A sign at the mouth of the pedestrian walkway proclaimed the arrival of a temporary exhibit:

Welcome to The River Styx! Cross at your leisure or peril and reflect upon your life!
Art installation courtesy of Arte Uber Alles

Her mind remained wedged open, unable to reclaim her shielding. Nudged along, she felt as though her body was being carried in the eddy of a current. Stepping out onto the wooden slats of the bridge promenade, watching the buildings fall away below, a tenth of a mile passed before she was over water and nearing the great Gothic suspension towers.

Couples, families, tourists, and workers strolled across the promenade in a range of immaculate finery to sooty work clothes, looking at the beautiful sculptures of angels and seraphim placed at intervals.

To Eve's horror, she recognized the sculptural style. Dupont's figures, just like he'd made for the stage set: sculpture in the manner of reliquaries. What the passersby couldn't know was that each figure held bits of dead flesh inside. Some might wear actual skin, others bones, organs, hair, each a token taken without permission, each a work of haunt.

These statues represented more restless souls and unfinished business, hence the ache at the back of her skull, the constant whispers at the corner of her mind. But with these works now exposed, where were their spirits? Trapped, most likely. Hopefully not for long, if Maggie had her way and Mosley ruined his systems, but she couldn't be sure.

A few workers in suspenders and shirtsleeves were wrapping bits of wire across the railing. The bridge was made of wire rope, so much so the wire could wrap around the earth, designers were proud to boast. What was this additional wire needed for?

You… murmured a reply in her mind. *This is all here for you, my dear….*

The hairs on the back of her neck rose as something bored into the base of her skull.

Turning slowly around, the sight before her made her blood run cold.

Above her and coming closer, a man floated in a black suit coat and cloak, hanging among the diagonal stays and vertical suspender cables, a fearsome spider in the web of wire rope.

His smile was fixed like a mask, his eyes bright and hard, glasses slightly askew. Prenze's projection had never been stronger or more unnerving.

A man began walking toward her, his feet solidly on the wooden planks. In a dizzying optical shift, the projection retreated as the man strode closer.

Body paralyzed, time slowing, Eve stood stock still as Prenze, the actual, physical man himself, approached and stood a mere foot away from her. The projection of his energy merged with the man in a sickening, disconcerting fusion of dimensions, his mask of a clenched-jaw smile unchanging as he regained himself.

"What do you want with me?" She asked.

"Nothing unusual," Prenze replied calmly. The sound of his voice just before her and not against her ear was a relief, though his proximity was cause for alarm. She put her hand back on her forearm, ready to withdraw the knife if need be. "You're just here to do what you always do, Miss Whitby. You're here as a service to the dead."

He tried to nudge her forward with a physical hand on her shoulder, but she dug her heels in against the edge of the wood. "And what would that be?" Eve figured if she could buy time, to keep him talking, then she could strategize a plan of escape and any of her ghosts watching could find ways to help. Zofia had removed herself from view, which was wise, but she wasn't sure who was on her side.

"To talk to spirits," he replied simply. "Come, let's take in this art installation, shall we? Can't make a scene if you're already in a scene!"

The sculptures were placed at forty-something-foot intervals along the bridge's walkway, pedestrian flow keeping to the right coming and going but pausing in clusters and knots of family and friends taking in the harbor view and the installation.

Hired guards, Pinkertons from the look of their uniforms, stood between the statue intervals as if they, too, were part of the exhibit. Each had a tray in their hands with faux coins and a small sign marked "For Your Safe Passage." The coins representing passage across the river Styx, the principal of Greek mythology's five underworld rivers the dead might pass over. Everyone was bid contemplate their mortality high above the East

River current. It only played into Eve's plea to make the spirit world that much closer to touch.

The sky was so beautiful, the river so busy, the promenade so full of life. The ever-climbing skyline of New York—Manhattan and its boroughs, both inspiring and hard to fathom, the large and small scale—was all in view, from the teeming docks to high-finance rooftop spires gleaming in sun like cathedrals of commerce.

Passersby along the promenade, tucking their parasols under arms lest they be turned inside out in the wind, top hats held by the brim, murmured toward Eve and Prenze in their black clothes, gesturing and complimenting the immersion of all the "performers" with their tokens of travel, their payment to the boatman, as they contemplated the sculptural visages of disquieted forms.

The spirits of the city were equally intrigued by this display. Each statue had a throng of spirits floating around it, examining it, their transparent bodies silhouettes from a range of decades and cultures, imprinted against the sky like dimensional cameos with light shining through. Several spirits, their frock coats and dresses trailing away into wisps of vapor, tried to take the prop coins, looking at the offerings wistfully as if the tokens might return them to the shores of the living, their hands passing through the platters, gently rearranging the offerings.

The art had drawn out the delighted living and the luminous dead in equal measure, mortality contemplated on the stage of man's greatest feat of engineering far above the dynamic metropolis. It would be utterly poetic if it weren't so spiritually threatening.

"Keep moving," Prenze murmured. He wasn't touching her, but she could feel her body pressed as though a hand were clamped on her shoulder, pushing. "Toward the tower."

When she turned back, looking up at Prenze's cruel face defiantly, he loomed over her. She could feel his mesmerism pressuring her to engage, to reach out to the spirit world she was so awash in. She closed her eyes and pushed back against the impulse.

"What do you *want*?"

"To end ghosts' unholy reign of terror on this city. And I admit, I want to expand my influence and thrall over the living. Is that too much to ask?"

He laughed. Whatever he had once been—once a scared, sad and mistreated child, then a hardworking chemist and innovative businessman—exerting power now was the goal, the broken child trying to reclaim a dominance he felt was owed him.

Slipping her hand in one of her jacket pockets, she felt for the tintype of Mrs. Prenze. She'd use it to unsettle him at the right moment. It wasn't all ghosts he hated, it was just his mother, Eve intuited; but *any* ghost represented his childhood torment. All the vast wonders his expanded psychic capacity had offered and he'd gathered no nuance? Made no new discoveries of the wonders of the spirit? Eve pitied as much as feared someone so fixated on one violent retaliation. She and her team were each an example of how to live a haunted life more fully and meaningfully.

However, righteousness didn't free her. Trying to turn on her heel and run, she was quickly whirled back around again by psychic force. Eve had no experience in the kind of physical compelling Albert was exerting. She tried again to shield, but the wounds on her temple and shoulder throbbed instead. He was too far in for her to shield with any effectiveness. Even her hand was immovable, unable to unsheathe her knife after all.

Ahead, set up against the formidable stones on the right side of the vast western suspension tower, sat a black-lacquered wooden dais topped with a carved wooden throne trimmed in gold. All this must have been made in tandem with Dupont's stage work, a culmination of the elusive great experiment.

Above the dais, a few feet above the apex of the throne was a golden diadem tacked to the stone, a floating crown with wires trailing away from it. Behind the throne was a whirring, circular dynamo, powering an electrical current that attached not only to the throne, but Eve could see bright new copper wiring tracing up and over along the whole of the bridge, wire upon wire, upon wire.

"The Pretty Girl with the Electric Mind," read a plaque at the base of the platform.

To the side of the throne, under glass, sat a familiar object: the monitor box that had been placed outside her office to affect her engagement with spirits before Mosley blew it down and Jacob had taken it to Bellevue for examination. Here it was again, stolen from the doctors, repaired and in working order. As she approached, she noticed the graph, the ticker scrolling out graphite markings from a needle, reading more rapidly, a peak and valley, an undulating line. It sensed her fear; or, in fact, it was recording it. Perhaps even amplifying it, she couldn't be sure.

"What is all this?" Eve asked, folding her arms.

Prenze smiled that disturbing mask of a smile. "You're the most gifted medium of your age, Miss Whitby. And that isn't, as I've realized, a lie or hyperbole. I tested your grandmother who is a known *legend,* but you… your readings were quite literally off the charts. I've never seen someone so open to ghosts. So utterly drowning in them," he said with distaste. His eyes, perhaps once bright and engaging, seemed clouded by cataracts of hate. "You're just *covered* in them. They swarm around you. Like a disease. It isn't right, Whitby. You spread *contagion*."

Movement drew her eye to the monitor, the pencil making wide swaths along the ticker tape. She could feel the spirit world's agitation. Whispers and murmurs, shouts even, were all coming at her as swift as the biting breeze, autumn shifting toward a distinct chill, the changing seasons and the ice of spirits entwined. She glanced away from the monitor to the harbor below, boat whistles suddenly mirroring banshee screams, the harbor noise traded for the clatter of the dead.

"I've made adjustments to this device that was placed outside your office to gain readings on you, and your spirits."

"Blocking them, you mean—"

"Not entirely. Many of your associates still got through. I learned a lot. Now I know how to cast your net, your signature, for the widest impact."

The barrel organ grinder was making his way across the bridge; the unsettling tune seemed to crescendo as Eve's nerves mounted.

"Step up, please," Prenze said, taking her hand and, with his walking stick, pressing it against the back of her knee, forcing her to bend. She stumbled forward and onto the small dais, her knees crashing against the foot of the throne. "To your seat. Come. You cannot fight this."

He hoisted her up and sat her down. She closed her eyes and tried to push back, to shield, to reject his hold, but her body felt numb. A low-grade vibration pulsed across the seat of the throne, which she realized was a plate of metal, mildly electrified. Once she was seated, Prenze gingerly set small metal discs in place, one on each temple and one tacked with a theatrical adhesive to the center of her forehead—her third eye.

Wires flowed from the discs and toward the bridge where they wound around the thick wire rope, wiring her into the thousands of miles of wire coiled across the structure. It seemed clear the wires were meant to amplify her mind. Once the spirit world was entirely open, truly open, that is.

In her editorial, in hopes of a show of force, Eve had bid the spectral city open itself to goodness and fullness, to declare itself. For the living and the dead to rejoice in the presence of ghosts. They were all the more visible. Now, all the more vulnerable. Somehow, she'd played right into his hands when she'd hoped she was shaking a spear and appearing formidable as a unified spiritual front against him.

The low-grade current made her teeth chatter and made her slump as if lifeless against the throne. Her body was unresponsive, but her mind raced.

With horror, she thought about the additional wire servicing paperwork routing from New York to Tarrytown. There was another wire tracing its way to Sanctuary. She had warned Clara Bishop, advising her and Gran that the forest glade was in need of protection, and had told Antonia to follow her visions, which surely warned of the same concern, but was that enough now, when whatever burst of electricity she'd be a part of, would arc its way there?

From the back of the dais, Prenze brought out stanchions with a velvet rope and corded off an area around them, nodding to one of the hired guards who then set up a similar barrier, indicating that the area Prenze and Eve took up could only be witnessed at a significant arm's length.

Movement out of the corner of her eye drew Eve's attention: her operatives, including their quiet Olga, along with Vera and Zofia, were floating just beyond the wide curving tube of the greatest load-bearing cables of the main suspension.

Withdrawing a black scarf from his interior coat pocket, Prenze unfurled a few specific objects that made Eve queasy. He'd been to her workplace to take her sacred items.

He placed her séance bell, Cora's painted box of matches, and her office tallow candle next to her on the wide arm of the throne. "No one can say I stole your séance materials if you have them," he said, leaning in toward her with a smile.

The insidious power-play of it all: he'd gotten to Gran, to her, to Cora, to her operatives, to the reverends. He'd loomed at her house. At her parents'. He'd gotten into her office. He'd gotten into her head. Her ears. Her life. Tried to hurt—no, *kill*, her love. He'd swiped at everything that meant anything, trying to destroy it all. Eve had never felt such fury or boiling hatred in her entire life. Perhaps he hated her just the same, for all the things he never had.

She spat in his face.

The smile unchanged, he used the black scarf to wipe the spittle from his nose and cheek. Still smiling, he struck the match and lit the candle.

He picked up her bell and rang it, a clarion, resounding tone that seemed to carry, in Eve's mind, across the whole harbor.

"Go on. Call your work to order."

He turned a knob near the wires, and she felt a surging, painful snap. The metal buttons on her uniform sparked. Wisps of smoke came up from the buttonholes, and Eve let loose a panicked gasp before he turned down the knob again.

"Call your work to order," he repeated. "I've calibrated the amperage perfectly, for the best long-range effect. But you'd best get on with it, as women have a lower tolerance level to prolonged current, so call your work to order," Prenze bid softly in her ear. "Open."

She wanted to swing her fist and punch him right in the insidious mouth, but she couldn't move her arms; the current had seen to that, weighing her down, tethering her where she sat.

Eve was too in tune with the spirit world to ever be fully closed from it. The sound of the bell was an instinctual opening, a drawing back of a curtain, connecting to the spirit world was muscle memory tied to the ring of the bell, and Prenze was counting on it. The sounds of the rushing wind, an opened door, an unlocked gate, all followed. She was connected to the dead, and they to her. As inextricable now as ever.

"Spirits, hear us…" Prenze hissed like a snake, aping her séance opening.

He turned on the electricity, and Eve felt her body shake more boldly, felt her teeth snapping together, felt any scrap of physical control leave her.

Every wire, cable, metal part of the bridge, all seemed alive and pulsing. Joints sparked. A string of colored lights and little paper lanterns along the bridge's length lit up, buzzing and flickering with the pulse of Eve's heartbeat, the sparks that the increased electricity manifested created small explosions of glittering silica dust of many colors that trailed out from the lanterns like firework streams. The crowd gasped and cheered at the unique visual effect.

The spirits did too, reactive to the pretty fireworks, but to Eve's horror, every spirit that touched the bridge, whatever spirit might be near a metal support or floated within any of the web of wires and cables, their form faded away. Dissolving like wisps of smoke blown by a swift breath. The tiny gasps of delight the ghosts had exclaimed while watching the show soon turned to stifled spectral screams.

Where the spirits went, Eve couldn't guess. The electrical force magnified by the wiring of the bridge was disassembling the spirits near it, whether the souls could amass ever again was a part of the divine mystery she couldn't be privy to.

"Get away, spirits…away from the bridge," Eve cried, her tongue thick in her throat. She was parched, dizzy and nauseous.

Prenze seemed delighted by her panic and leaned in to plead in a sickening, saccharine manner. "I want in. Now let me in. Let me see what you see. Let me walk your walks." He reached out as if to touch her temples.

Eve closed her eyes and sent what shielding she could muster out from her body in an explosive capacity, hoping she could sever the tie, close the door, shove him back. "I…renounce…" She couldn't manage to speak the full rejection, but her energy burst from her like the slap of a hand.

Prenze rocked back from the force of her shielding, but rather than being put off, he smiled that terrible smile again.

Her shielding blow was directed overbroad rather than specific, magnified by the wiring. Her radiant energy created a psychic wave that furthered the electrical charge. She could see it on the air, a transparent, cresting, outwardly surging, sluggish tide that glittered with Tesla-coil edges.

The lightning tendrils of psychic power consumed the nearest floating spirit, a young ghost that wore a long robe, the wispy form dissolving into mist with a little cry of surprise, like blowing a tendril of smoke and seeing it disperse. The forked tongues of the electrical edges of this psychic, electric tide paused for a moment, its pace slowed by consuming the ghost, but then continued to spread.

Vera floated in proximity to this epicenter, and the old woman's eyes widened as she saw the wave begin to crest over the edges of the bridge and reach out toward Manhattan, hungry.

"Run," Vera cried, screaming to the spirits of the city. "Run! Keep away from the sparking light!" The woman gestured behind her wildly. The spirits heeded her, fleeing in careening, airborne speeds. Vera floated in place.

Zofia wafted to her side and wrapped her arm around the old woman's torso and closed her eyes, standing as if they could stop the flow or at least slow the wave down from the rest fleeing in terror and buy them time and distance.

"No!" Eve cried.

Vera tried to remove Zofia from a clinging grasp. "No, *mi pajarita*," Vera lovingly scolded the floating child at her hip. "I lived a full, living life, a second one in death, I'm ready, you are not. Run to safety, you know where to go."

Zofia struggled to keep hold as Vera tried to disentangle her. Olga's form appeared on the air, always the big sister who swooped in when order needed restoring. The adolescent ghost wrested Zofia free with a gentle, Ukrainian admonishment. Picking up the child she'd taken on as a ward, a fellow casualty from a garment district fire, Olga nearly threw the little girl away from the encroaching spread, putting distance between them.

Throwing her arms around the old woman as if to shield her from any pain, Olga turned to see the Tesla-coil tendrils work their way up her skirt, leaving nothing behind. The current slowed, surging around them as it encountered their forms, pausing to take them apart as other spirits fled. Olga was the first to disassemble, Vera's light merging with her own, and soon their clutching images were only vapor, then a bright shimmer of light, then simply part of the hovering clouds.

Eve's throat was raw, choking a cry, as further away Zofia screamed, weeping, hands clenched in her slightly singed dress. The little ghost ran away from the consuming tide, as it began spreading again, toward a small, dark point in the air.

In the distance, between two heavy clouds, a shape seemed to grow in the sky: a small Gothic arch. But the clouds obscured it as the wind picked up across the whole of the harbor, and even Zofia's form was lost behind mist and vapor. Eve didn't know where she'd gone, but she prayed it was somewhere safe that only a spirit knew.

"You can't...take...m-my spirit family," Eve mumbled. The rattling of her bones and chattering of her teeth drew blood as she bit her tongue; she had no control to keep a stream of bloody spittle from dripping down the side of her slack jaw.

"But I can. I am..." Prenze applauded. "You're doing so well...." He turned to the harbor and shrieked, "NO CRYING FOR THE DEAD!"

The only thing Eve could think to do to try to stem the tide, to try to reroute all the energy bent on dispersal of spirit, was to drag it down with her to murky depths. The Corridors between life and death were as much of life as they were of spirit. As this energy wouldn't harm the living other than perhaps a slight shock or sting, she hoped the dead could take shelter from dissipation in the meantime.

With the last of her physical control, closing her eyes, Eve said a private benediction known only to her and Gran and let herself slide under into darkness as if slipping beneath the surface of a great body of water.

Life was unpredictable and cruel, but in death, the spirit should have more control as to when to move on, an idea Eve took great comfort in. As she tumbled into darkness, waiting for the metaphysical floor of the Corridors to catch her falling spirit, Eve mourned her colleagues.

Vera and Olga should have been able to choose their times to say goodbye, not in an abrupt spiritual sacrifice. Being so tied to her spirit colleagues, Eve could feel the immediate absence, the utter silence of those once vibrant energies. Wherever the wisps went, Eve could only beg the divine mystery of all that was beyond their reach to gather the essence of her friend and hold it in eternal, beautiful, peaceful light.

But she had to still fight, to warn every spirit to brace itself. Everything of body and spirit existed in a balance, the reality of which only the most dedicated Sensitives could truly grasp, a subtlety lost on Prenze's vendetta.

He had forced her to create an imbalance, used her power to hurt others. She wasn't going to do that again.

Her fall into darkness had never taken so long and the Corridors had never felt so foreign. The rising murk she'd first encountered at the beginning of the search for missing and unsettled children during the first brushes with Prenze's great experiment was now even thicker, as if she were floating in ooze and smoke.

Eve hoped that by slipping away into the Corridors it could somehow detach her from being a conduit of destruction, but her mental and physical state was so addled, she didn't know if she was making anything worse or better. Time was lost to her. All she felt was raw pain, every nerve singed and flayed. She tried to stay conscious, but the darkness of the Corridors was so soothing.

Dangerous, this precipice. Gran had often warned her of this place; when the Corridors seemed like a place to sleep, it was a place one wouldn't wake up from. In this walkway, souls often got lost. Jacob nearly had been—confused and misdirected. She thought of bringing him back to himself when the injury had knocked the spirit right out of him.

"Jacob," she whimpered, wishing for all the world she could just curl up in his hold and rest there, indefinitely, at peace, warm, safe, and in love. Folding her arms around her chest, she sank to her knees on the cool, murky floor of this liminal space and closed her eyes.

At some point, she roused to the distinct feel of hands on her shoulders, shaking her, demanding she wake up. Prenze's angry voice was growling her name. Good. Let him rail. She wanted to sleep. Forks of lightning flashed across her closed eyes; the current had made her a Tesla coil from the inside out.

He wanted further into her mind. But he didn't know the Corridors. He was a bully and a coercive mesmerist, but he did not have her gifts and could not go all the places she had experience going. Yes, he'd been in them during his own near-death experience, but he couldn't know how to slip between the cracks of life and death as Eve had become accustomed to in her work of late.

Her diving into the Corridors was stalling for time, yes, but Eve didn't know how much longer her body could hold out against the current. Prenze was varying the levels, keeping it shy of fatal, though there was only so much a body could take. He did seem to be trying to skirt murder charges, even if he was the proxy for many deaths.

If one was at a precarious threshold of physical vulnerability, as Eve was, this walk between life and death was generally, in Eve and her family's experience, full of framed moments, slivers of memory, hope, happiness or poignance, frozen in static pictures on the liminal walls of an endless hallway; the art of a life on display for the purposes of reflection. As she'd seen with Jacob. But here, the walls had gone dark. Everything of life and death had been hiding from Prenze this whole time. Perhaps that was for the best.

Just as she felt herself beginning to fade into a sleep from which she might never awake, there was a ring. A distinct, glaring, irritating ring. In sequence. A telephone. She opened her eyes and focused on an object.

Out of the dark pool ahead rose a telephone box floating in the darkness.

Eve slowly got to her feet, drifted to it, picked up the bell, and whispered hello.

"Hello, Eve," came a familiar voice, still distant, crossing between life and death. Lily Strand, calling from Sanctuary.

"He's here.... He wants in, don't let him," Eve whispered.

"I know, dear heart. We know," the deaconess assured her. "We have help from your dear ones, here with us now. Your Antonia disengaged the wire. We'll be all right. But you? You're very precarious. Shield and let go."

"But the shielding just disassembled Vera and Olga—" Eve wept.

"It won't again. The spirits are no longer in play."

"I'm sorry I—"

"Hush, child, I couldn't have known, when my soul cried out in hopes of protecting a lost child, finding you through the modernity of a telephone wire of all things, how this would come to pass. We wander life's labyrinth until great forces nudge us away from dead ends toward the right path. We are prepared. You're a product of *now*. We're a product of eternity. Go *live*, Eve."

There was a click on the line, and then the telephone dissolved into mist.

"But what do I do..." Eve whispered into the darkness, having never felt so lost.

Eve was seized. Not by darkness but by familiar hands, and she was whirled around to see a concerned face.

"Cora!" Eve exclaimed. The brilliant woman had found her by astral projection.

"Eve, I have to pull you out. You're in far too deep."

"But Cora, beloved friend, be careful; you could get lost here too," Eve cautioned, looking around for a path forward. "I fear I've fallen deeper than I can find my way out of. Please don't get lost here too, on my account...."

Cora cupped both hands around Eve's cheeks.

"As mad as I am when you try to take on the whole world all on your own, I can't stay angry because you do it out of care. It's noble, but maddening." Cora stepped back and gestured to herself. "I'm a projection, but you won't be alone for long. Just hang on. In the meantime, take care of your mind." Cora gave her a shove.

The process of falling back into herself began again in a sickening tumble.

She wondered what Cora meant by not being alone for long; her heart lurched at the idea of Jacob coming. Her aching body longed for his touch: a soothing, all-encompassing salve. If she ever felt safe enough to see him again, she'd let him hold her for hours, days even, to restore her.

Praying the rest of the spirits she loved had all somehow weathered the blast, she had to trust Lily Strand and listen to Cora. She fought back up toward the surface of life.

In returning to herself, vibrating pain rousing her back, she knew she couldn't amass her own energy again, not in shielding as Lily had instructed, nor in reaching for spiritual contact. Prenze's ultimate cruelty was that her efforts of protection were used against her. Did he plan to just roast her slowly with low voltage until she collapsed, spent, charged to a crisp? The amperage was now a light cyclical thrum, but her nerves were so exposed her skin felt raked by coals.

Her eyes fluttered open as her hands shifted onto her lap. The candle wax pooled on her knee, a burned spot on the wool, the bell was upturned, her hand was inching toward the pockets sewn into the waist gathers of her jacket. For the moment, Prenze was nowhere to be seen.

The sky had entirely cleared of spirits. Eve had never, in her memory, seen the skyline, the harbor, without them. She had to blink to believe her eyes. While for Eve and any ghost, the bridge was an apocalypse; for most New Yorkers, the day remained pleasant and the sky striking.

A shadow fell over her face; then a cruel smile came back around into view.

"Are you ready to reach out once more?" Prenze asked quietly. "You can't have gotten all of the spirits. More will come if you ask nicely. Then we'll banish them like all the rest."

"This one too?" Eve mumbled as she withdrew the tintype, shaking violently even though the current had let go.

Prenze's eyes widened in surprise; then his face contorted into hatred. "Where did you get that?!" he growled. "Yes, most certainly that one, *that one's* why there's all this! Why we're going to wipe the whole city free from the dead!" He swung his hand in a violent gesture across the harbor.

It was as if just looking at the image of Mrs. Prenze summoned her in a banshee wail of righteous fury as Eve's and Prenze's attention were drawn to a knot of Pinkerton guards and a cluster of protesting people some yards toward the mouth of the walkway.

Her heart surged at the sight of Cora, gesturing toward the Gothic tower, but her colleague was pushed back by a Pinkerton guard. Sergeant Mahoney tried to calm the situation, but the guards still argued. Several New York police hired by the event seemed confused as to which loyalty they should attend.

Above them all floated the ghost of a wild-haired woman, eyes dark pools of fury, in a tattered gown that had once been fine; but now the fabric looked like it had been shredded to pieces by the old woman's sharp nails. Whoever was in the right or wrong concerning the Prenze family now, the matriarch *was* terrifying.

Whatever spirits had been open and drawn to Eve's call, Mrs. Prenze had not been among them. Instead she made quite an entrance at the mouth of the approach, her wail as intense as the shrillest train whistle.

One woman, shaded behind a parasol, scurried around the melee and made a direct line, an odd, disjointed run, toward them. Another tall, lean figure in a black frock coat edged around behind her, face and head shaded by a large-brimmed black hat. The wiry figure made Eve's heart surge with hope.

A harpy shriek was bearing down upon them as if no amount of charge would stop her. Even despite her trembling form, Eve held on to the tintype, her own bond with the object tethering the spirit in a channel that mere zaps of electricity couldn't disperse. Albert Prenze likely hadn't accounted for the fact that the ghost he most wanted to kill, his own mother, would be the hardest to drive away. The pain, anger, and fury between them had forged an unstoppable haunt and worn a psychic groove to the bone.

"Brother," Arielle cried from paces away, moving awkwardly. "End this. Stop now! I can't protect you anymore. I won't. Alfred knows all. Punishment is up to you."

Horrified, Prenze stared back and forth between his younger sister and the screaming, translucent form of his mother, arms out, claws raised.

The stanchions kept the crowd at bay, but some watched in wide-eyed fixation at the intense play being performed before them, oohing and clapping alternately. Eve couldn't be sure if anyone saw the ghost above or if onlookers might think it was some elaborate stage effect.

Suddenly Albert ran toward the side of the bridge, and Eve couldn't tell if he was about to fling himself from its side or was just looking for escape. He grabbed hold of a switch that had been rigged to the suspension cables and moved to turn the dial, but his mother's ghost dove at him, and the force of her knocked him back onto the planks.

She stopped screaming and began crying, folded over him in wispy scraps and tatters like gnarled branches of a windswept tree bent over a weary body.

"I'm no good at showing care," the ghost cried. "I never was. But if I thought it would drive you to all this...I'd have tried to do better...."

"Better isn't in you! Leave us be!" Albert howled. "Go to Hell," he cried, scrambling toward Eve. His hands fumbled across hers as he reached for the levers and settings, knocking the candle and bell aside where they clattered to the planks before spilling hot wax on Eve's hands. The tintype slid from her hands, which had turned into sudden claws in the pain of the increased voltage.

"Come away, Mother," Arielle cried. Having gained swiftly on them, she dove for the tintype image before it fell through the cracks in the boards, but Arielle caught it, the sharp side of the image slicing her finger.

Prenze had turned the current higher than before, and Eve was sure she wouldn't survive it this time. Her body shook with a fresh violence. Mrs. Prenze returned to her screaming and flew back as if shoved by the current, tatters of her gown flying away into mist. Eve lost sight of her as another form swept toward Eve in a swirl of black fabric.

A fist came barreling toward Albert Prenze's face, and the man was knocked back cold onto the planks, a spurt of blood spilling onto his cloak, head lolling to the side.

The resulting cries of the crowd and guards telling people to keep moving were drowned out as the current crested in Eve's body and her eyes rolled back in her head. As she was barely managing to murmur, "Help," strong arms scooped her up and out of the dais, yanking away all the wires, tearing off the discs with swift pulls and a hiss of pain as the electricity stung her liberator.

With a swift kick, her rescuer knocked the monitor box from the throne where it crashed to the planks.

She was entirely at the mercy of whoever had struck Prenze and now held her tightly, whisking her away from the dais. Limp and barely conscious, Eve found the hold familiar and her racing heart skipped beats as tears leaked from her eyes, hope and need surging in her soul.

"Evelyn Whitby," Jacob Horowitz murmured with loving admonishment in her ear.

"Jacob," she murmured achingly, her deepest desires answered by his voice, by his covetous hold. "M-make sure the e...lectric is off...."

With her still locked in his arms, Jacob bent down to disengage the lever of the dynamo. The dreadful whine and crackle of the turbine subsided.

Moving with Eve to the interior side of the tower, he sunk to his knees
with her, leaning against the rough stone.

"I don't care if it's dangerous! Do you hear me?" He insisted. "I refuse
to be banished from your side."

Clutching her to him, cheek to cheek, breath hot against her ear, he
uttered a prayer of thanks Eve recognized as an offering for surviving a
great hardship: *"Barukh ata Adonai Eloheinu, melekh ha'olam, hagomel
lahayavim tovot, sheg'molani kol tov."*

"Amen," Eve offered weakly.

Her childhood time spent in prayer with Rachel made this prayer of
thanks all the more resonant as it reminded her of the times when she'd
felt most spiritually at peace, and here she was with the man who made
her soul rejoice. His ministrations took away pain; his touch healed. He
drew back to look at her, and just the sight of him made her weep in relief,
processing all the pain and fear. She didn't know if they'd won the day or
just a respite, but for this moment they were conscious and Prenze wasn't.

Jacob cupped her face, staring in horror at the blood and saliva
pooling down the side of her chin, reaching for a handkerchief, wiping
the gore away with such gentleness, staring into her eyes, ascertaining
her state and strength.

"Do we have enough..." Eve mumbled, fighting for words, trying
to rally. "Even with all this, the coercion...hard to prove, because I
went...willingly...."

"He *hurt* you, Eve," Jacob cried, anguished, "and could *easily* have
killed you! All the money and tricky lawyers in the world can't refute the
level of malice and madness here."

Arielle Prenze knelt before them and reached into an interior pocket
of her coat, presenting a black bound book. "Take this." She handed the
journal to the detective. "It should illuminate the rest of what's been
speculated—putting your pieces together."

Jacob took it and slipped it immediately out of sight into a breast pocket.
"Thank you, Miss Prenze. Are you all right?"

Arielle rose, smiled uncannily, and walked away.

"Maggie," Eve called after her, "are you..."

"Shh..." Arielle said over her shoulder as her face shifted ever so
slightly, a little luminous rustle within.

Eve almost chuckled, but it turned into a wracking, painful cough. The
smell and taste of copper overwhelmed her, and she gasped for fresh air.

Jacob cradled her closer, moaning in abject horror at her pain. His
generous heart, operating with a level of empathy that might put him in

the capacity of a Sensitive himself, appeared nearly undone. "What were you thinking going it alone!" Jacob cupped her face again, brushing hair from her eyes before pressing his forehead to hers.

"I can't bear to lose you," Eve gasped, tears leaking again onto her cheeks. Jacob gently wiped them away. "I'd rather be miserable, devastated, lost, alone without you than be the cause of your suffering, injury, or worse."

"That isn't your choice to make," Jacob declared. "I'll take my chances with you any day instead of a brokenhearted half life. The job is dangerous, you no more so than the job. Don't fight me, Eve. Love me. Like you said you did. Unless that was a lie?"

"No, I do…" Eve sobbed. "I'm so scared. I love you so much, it hurts. Worse even than any of this—I've never been so terrified to lose something."

"How did you think I felt when I learned you had shunned me, told my parents you wanted nothing to do with me, kept me out of your plan, put yourself on a suicide mission? Even if you thought it was 'for my own good'? What if I'd done that to you?"

"I…I didn't know what else to do. Don't be angry with me," Eve pleaded.

"I'm not angry; I'm beside myself," Jacob exclaimed, his hand hovering over her body. "Just like you came after my spirit when you saw it leave my body, I could…I could *feel* you flagging, your spirit separating out, nearly torn to pieces. I wasn't next to you to help, and it was agony. Please. Don't push me away again."

He pressed his forehead to hers again, murmuring against her lips. "You have changed me irrevocably, Eve Whitby. You can't turn me away when I have become so cleaved to you, my treasure. I love you with all my heart. Love me, as you said you do, and let me love you."

At this confession, Eve gasped, the jarring pain of the electric replaced by a shudder of pleasure. He drew back again to stare into her eyes. Her angel: the closest thing she'd ever known to a heavenly sort of happiness. Nothing had ever made her feel as alive as this. He was right. It was worth the risk. If he indeed felt the way she did, she couldn't reject him. Neither would ever recover. They'd live, but forever haunted. Ghosts weren't just spirits. Ghosts were also the heart's roads not traveled.

Eve gathered what strength she had and reached up, bringing him down to her lips. She murmured her assent. "Yes, Jacob. My beloved. I will. For you…for the love in my heart I can't possibly deny or forget…I will do anything."

"Thank you," he exclaimed. "Thank you, beloved." Embracing her fully, he sealed their compact with the tenderest of kisses.

After a sweet, breathless moment, he drew back. "Can you stand?"

"Jarred to the bone, I thought my skin was rattling off. I doubt it. Am I still shaking? It feels like I am."

"Slight tremors. Come on, then," Jacob hoisted her up toward the dais. They saw that Prenze was stirring, so Jacob placed Eve on the neutralized throne and blocked her with a wide stance. The sight of her torturer rousing made Eve shrink back, but Jacob raised his fists to have another go at the wretch before he could stand.

From the other side of the tower, jumping over the stanchions, Mahoney came swiftly between them and seemed to be helping Prenze up. The waking man seemed happy to see the officer at first, but then there was a struggle.

"Sergeant, what are you—" Horowitz stopped as he saw the officer forcing a vial of green liquid down Prenze's throat. The man sputtered before going entirely limp from sedation and fell back to the boards.

"Taste of his own medicine," Mahoney replied. "Pulled from the stores he was using to control his household." He nodded his head at Eve. "Miss, I hope you didn't suffer too much." The officer stared down at Albert in disgust. "Between what you've all seen and what I've seen, we've enough. We've enough to try him."

Horowitz patted his coat pocket. "In addition, we've his journal thanks to Miss Prenze and Chief Inspector Harold Spire's Scotland Yard case notes on the body presumed his."

"Very good." Mahoney clapped his hands.

"Thank you, Sergeant, and I'm sorry to have doubted you," Eve said quietly to the Irishman, "But I wasn't sure what side you were on."

"That was intentional," Mahoney replied. "Albert revealed himself to me, and then the fool thought he had me under mind control. But as I said, when I gave up the drink, I promised myself and the spirits of my wife and child I'd never give anyone or *anything* that power over me. So, I played along."

"Brilliant," Eve murmured, before a wracking cough took her. Jacob stepped up to the side and soothed her aching back with a gentle, massaging caress.

"We'll book him," Mahoney said, reaching down to cuff Prenze, "but we've only a bit of time to hold him unless we formally charge him."

"Assault of a city official," Jacob stated. "Eve isn't an officer in the traditional sense, but she is a public servant Roosevelt himself signed for." The detective shook with rage as he described what had happened. "Prenze drew *blood* from Eve. Even if his fancy lawyers dare say Eve came here of her own volition. It got out of hand, beyond all reason and sense. The devices and testing link him to the abduction of Evelyn Northe-Stewart. He tried to coerce you too, Sergeant: another charge."

"I'll testify, but I'd rather you keep Arielle and Alfred clear of it. They were victims in this, and if anything's to blame, it's from turning blind eyes, not active participation."

Mahoney took a step closer, looking around.

"Even though I'm sure it was her helping Albert in the funerary warehouse where Gran and I were first experimented on?" Eve countered, following Mahoney's eyes to Arielle, who had gone to stand further up the approach, staring out over the harbor.

Looking at the tintype of her mother, Arielle seemed to be conversing with herself. Maggie must be giving her instructions.

"He *did* control her," Mahoney said, balling his fists. "Preying on her piousness in his delusions of Godlike powers, the wretch."

"We'll keep her out of it once we've built an irrefutable case," Jacob declared.

The passersby remained cordoned off, but Cora finally fought off guards keeping them from "the art and performers" and hurried to their colleagues' side. Behind Cora, keeping a respectful distance but a sharp eye, Eve noted that the good officer Fitton had arrived to help. Jacob's friend and a stalwart, unfailing help to their cases, he must have received a call and hurried to attend it. Jacob stepped aside to allow Cora clearance, and she rushed to embrace Eve warmly but carefully.

Cora didn't get to say a word before Eve demanded: "Where's Gran? Antonia? At Sanctuary? What about Jenny—"

"Zofia told Jacob and me, as we rushed from his office, that they were rushing toward Sanctuary," Cora replied. "Antonia's vision: the wiring was there too; we had to split up—"

"Good. I fear for *all* the spirit world, it's so vacant here," Eve said, wincing with pain and raw nerves, glancing nervously at the harbor. Busy with boats and life, it remained empty of spirits. "Vera and Olga are gone...."

Tears flowed again as Eve relived the sight of their last moment. "It's my fault, I was trying to shield against Prenze, but it magnified an electrical blast.... They stood in the way to buy time so that Zofia could run. I... doubt they can reassemble. I'm praying Sanctuary created a safe haven for other souls, until the ground is safe for those that wish to haunt."

Cora nodded, biting her lip.

"I am deeply sorry for your loss, but don't take on guilt," Jacob said quietly. "You couldn't have known what his devices would do; you were doing what you'd been trained to do to protect yourself and others."

"Exactly," Cora agreed.

"I'm just sorry I didn't get to you sooner," Jacob explained to Eve. "There was massive confusion between the guards and hired police at the mouth of the approach. They tried to stop the group of us. In hindsight, I shouldn't have paused to show my badge; I should have just rushed this stage when I saw it. Cora and Fitton brilliantly caused a scene so I could slip by the barricade. Thank you both."

Fitton, who had joined them during Jacob's explanation, nodded acknowledgment. The two clapped one another on the back in appreciation before Fitton began examining the scene and taking notes.

"I know why you did what you did, Eve, letting this play out," Cora said, edging closer to Eve, scrutinizing her, trying to determine if Eve was hiding any deeper injury from them. "But I thought you'd promised Gran you wouldn't leave her house. I'm angry with you for letting yourself get hurt."

"That makes two of us," Jacob added.

"But the court of New York does not accept spectral evidence since the advent of seventeenth-century witch trials," Eve countered. "We had to get to the point where he drew living blood. I hadn't thought I'd be left entirely unguarded and without resource, but it makes my case all the more compelling."

"Thank God for ghosts letting us know where to find you," Jacob said.

"I'll get Centre Street to come collect all the statues, wire, and boxes for evidence," Fitton said.

"Yes please, and if you could have any wire that doesn't belong to the bridge cleared," Eve begged the diligent officer who had been such a boon to the case. "That's very important."

Perhaps the spirits would return if they felt it was safe. She prayed Prenze hadn't been successful in driving them all away for good. What had become of Mrs. Prenze, Eve couldn't be sure. The electrical surge seemed to have torn her apart from what Eve could tell in the melee.

"I'm going to stay here, Eve, if that's all right, to help Fitton clear and catalog things," Cora said. "Then I want to get psychometric reads on Prenze, likely while en route to prison."

"Do you need help?" Eve said, struggling to sit up.

"No!" Cora and Jacob both chorused.

"You're going to rest," Jacob commanded.

"It's a wonder you survived. Let us each do work we're called to do," Cora declared.

"Does anyone need a stretcher?" Fitton asked Eve, glancing over at the prone Albert. Mahoney hoisted Prenze over his broad shoulder in an impressive fireman's carry.

"Stretcher or..." Jacob held out his arms. Eve moved toward him as he smiled, again scooping Eve up, pressing his lips to her forehead in reassurance and gratefulness. She wound her arms around his neck and held on as tight as she could. "Then let's be done with this," the detective said, carrying her away.

Exhaustion overtook Eve. Finally feeling safe for the first time in a long time, she nodded off until she was aware of being lifted into a carriage, heard a door shut, and was jostled into another covetous hold.

Eyes fluttering open, she saw that Jacob still cradled her as an open-air hack carried them uptown. They were halfway to her house.

"I think we should stay close tonight," Jacob said quietly. "I see no reason now why your home shouldn't be safe, but I will feel better if you allow me to help stand guard alongside your colleagues. I don't know what mental powers Prenze will wake up with."

It was a solid point, and it was true she'd take any excuse to stay near to Jacob.

Nuzzling close, she kissed the hollow of his throat and pressed her ear to his strong heartbeat.

"Thank you..." she murmured against that comforting thrum. "My whole life has been dealt in spirit, in realms beyond my body. I was so scared of being separated from you, body and spirit, it shocked me, the depths of emotion. I haven't known how to be *whole* as a living woman, but you...just here in your hold, you bring me back to life."

He bent and kissed the crown of her head. "You've done the same for me." Brushing her hair from her cheek, he tightened his grip around her, pressing her head to his heart. "Literally and figuratively. I've always felt called to my work, but you call me to *life*."

"If the ghosts have all gone somewhere for peace and safety," Eve said, "it would behoove me to remember that I still live. I live here." Looking up at him, his beautiful eyes spoke volumes of passion and promise. "And I want to enjoy every minute I have with you...."

He arched her up into a hungry kiss. While her world was tactile, she would appreciate every sensation, grateful for the opportunity to touch, to feel, and to fumble toward love.

Once arrived at Waverly Place, Jacob helped Eve up to her door with an arm around her waist. The lights were dim. The detective removed his hat, and Eve now saw it had been concealing the damage he still bore evidence of: a bandage affixed to the stitches on his head, and the remaining bruise across his forehead and temple. He was surely dealing with significant lingering pain from his injuries, but he'd entirely hidden it, valiantly.

Once inside, Eve looked around for signs of her team but found only Rachel Horowitz sitting with tea in the parlor next to a stained-glass lamp as she wrote in a notebook.

Looking up as Jacob helped Eve in, Rachel jumped to her feet and rushed to set extra pillows on the settee for Eve to sit and lean against.

Are you all right? Rachel signed, looking at the two of them in horror. *What happened?*

"I am all right now." Eve nodded, gesturing to Jacob.

Jacob added, "And I am all right thanks to Eve's intercept. But it's been a trying few days."

Rachel embraced both of them. Eve didn't want to go into all the electricity and pain, or any of the previous attacks, but she did want to get Rachel's read on the state of the spirit world. Glancing around, Eve noted that even the usual house haunts were absent.

I'm the only one here. Rachel intuited her thoughts. *Your mother let me in. I explained you were still working a case so she didn't ask questions. I wanted this to be a safe space for the team to return to, and to be an intercept for spirits to relay messages.*

Eve posed the most important question on her mind. "Have you seen any city spirits since this afternoon, Rachel? Any usual haunts outside? Has your spiritual channel changed?"

It's quiet, Rachel signed, gesturing all around her and to her head. *Too quiet.*

Eve pursed her lips. She wanted to hold a séance but didn't have the energy. If any lingering effects of Prenze's experiment were somehow still in her system, she didn't want to do additional damage. She'd done enough. Grateful she still had gas pipes, she doubted she'd ever switch over to electric after this.

Closing her eyes, she only had enough energy left in her to reach out to one asset.

"Margaret Hathorn." She tried to summon her best ally. "Come talk to me. I know you're busy with Arielle but…"

There was no answer. Eve sighed.

"In the morning we'll call the reverends for an exorcism," Jacob said. "I can't imagine taking over Arielle Prenze was something Maggie wanted to do for too long."

"I can't imagine Reverend Coronado would mind obliging," Eve replied with a grin, recalling how much the previous encounter seemed to affect both spirit and clergyman.

Rachel poured Jacob and Eve tea while they shared some of what had happened.

"If Gran had been there on that bridge"—Eve shuddered—"she'd have tried to put herself in the way. I am so glad she went to Sanctuary instead. Bless Antonia's vision. It's my hope that Sanctuary is playing a part in the protection of all spirits."

"In the morning we'll take a look at these," Jacob said, reaching into his coat pocket and withdrawing two bound books. Arielle's offering: Albert's diary, and something else. "Before Zofia burst into my office," Jacob explained, "I was given this casebook."

Eve reached over and took the second book, reading Harold Spire's letter to the detective. "Chief Inspector Spire! Gran worked with him; you're wise to ask his advice. This will be an enormous asset. While I know Prenze will never be able to be tried for the torture and dispersing of souls, he can't be let to abuse the living anymore either."

As she eagerly began perusing the pages, Jacob chuckled.

"In the *morning*, Eve, not now. Prenze nearly made a dynamo out of you. You *must* rest."

"I…" She looked up at him then at Rachel, who mirrored his stern look.

"But I am rather, *energized…*" she said with a sheepish smile.

Jacob groaned at her poor attempt at humor. "Drink some tea, at least, will you?"

"Yes, and an aspirin. They're in a bottle by my bedside, if you don't mind?"

Jacob went for them, and Eve blushed at the idea she was sending him off to her room, watching him go, savoring the look of him: determined and strong, striking in any state. The only thing that could pull her away from looking at Spire's casebook and Prenze's diary was the prospect of being alone in a room with Jacob Horowitz. Rachel was staring at her, looking bemused.

Gesturing after Jacob and back to Eve, Rachel inquired about the state of things. *I was worried about you two after the Thalia gala. The Veils said you were very upset when you left. Did you and Jacob have an argument?*

"It was a misunderstanding," Eve explained. "When I saw Jacob with Sophie, so close and familiar, I thought they were courting and I just… panicked.…" Her face went bright red. Glancing at Rachel sheepishly, she added, in sign; *Because honestly, I'm helplessly in love with him.*

Rachel beamed. *I know.* At this, Eve bit her lip, her blush brightening. Rachel chuckled.

I remember them both, she continued, *Jacob and Sophie, from my youth. Before I moved to the Connecticut Asylum to learn sign and our families lost touch. They cared deeply, but I knew, as did the spirits, that those two were meant only for dear friendship.*

Eve welcomed Rachel's reassurance, having thought she'd never be able to forget the sight of Jacob's handsome face looking so lovingly at such a beautiful woman. But jealousy was a warped, foolish demon Eve wanted nothing to do with.

He loves you too, I can see it, Rachel signed. *Confirming something the spirits said to me long ago, about you. About your future.*

Before Rachel could elaborate, Jacob returned with two small white tablets, holding them out for Eve.

She took the pills from him and clasped his hand as she did, looking into his eyes, hoping her gaze showed him the truth of her heart: that she did want to go forward, fearless and with hope....

Just then, a roaring, piercing pain struck Eve's skull. A shriek awoke within her, and she didn't know if the sound was hers or another soul's cry that echoed in the room. All the pain she'd experienced at the bridge swept back over her body, starting with the crown of her head and overtaking her whole body with a vengeance.

"Prenze woke. I can feel him," Eve ground through clenched teeth. "The *anger...*"

Albert, in his dread astral projection form, was looming over her head, reaching out for her neck as if he held a reaper's scythe. "Get out," she growled. Looking to the table where Rachel had lit candles, she focused on the tips of the flame as inspiration for her shielding; but his anger anticipated her, lashing out in his own swift, psychic blow. The aspirin rolled away as Eve's eyes rolled back and darkness descended once more.

Chapter Eighteen

Evelyn Northe-Stewart had tried not to panic when her carriage sped away from the city and her granddaughter. The spirits were urging her toward where she needed to be; it was very clear. Antonia and Jenny had been supremely focused, quiet, listening on the journey. Gran was impressed with their studious fortitude. They'd discussed Eve briefly, as Gran tried to explain her strategy, though the vagaries clearly unsettled the trio deeply. Focusing on what they could control, they tuned themselves to the energy of the sacred space ahead.

Antonia, quite brilliantly, had taken a quiet initiative, after seeing how their foes affected spirits via electrical manipulation, to learn about the power lines and what companies serviced what area in the boroughs and beyond. When they arrived at Clara Bishop's house to apprise her of the Spiritualist guard they were keeping not far from her property, Antonia suggested Ambassador Bishop call the local service company. Under the guise of contracting digging and construction in the surrounding acreage, he bid the power company shut down nearby lines for the remainder of the day, encouraging any affected parties to contact him directly. He'd pleasantly mesmerize anyone concerned into not minding any inconvenience.

Once the mechanical threat was neutralized, it was their purview to tend to the spiritual.

Now they were outside of the Sanctuary arch, and everything was very quiet. Unnaturally so.

The three had brought a picnic to the arch that Clara had packed them while her husband cajoled with the local utilities. She remained home, as getting that close to a parting of the veil was a guaranteed epileptic seizure. But she promised to listen for disturbances and to pull positive ley line energy, routing a different kind of "wiring" than Prenze could ever have fashioned, compensating with ancient light if things grew dark.

For most of the day, as they picnicked before the arch and listened to the chatter of any passing dead, all of it was general murmuring, familiar to any Sensitive. But then there was a distinct shift. A rush of noise and then nothing, just as they'd had the last of their tea cakes. Even the dead leaves on the rustling trees had gone silent.

Too quiet, Jenny signed to Gran, who nodded.

She rose, still in the black widow's weeds from earlier—it suited their mission—and placed her hand on the arch.

Gran's fall was swift and instant.

All she could hear was "She's here! Our benefactress! The one whose heart built the door!"

And then she lay on the floor of a beautiful cathedral. Above her head soared innumerable Gothic arches.

Joyously she realized it looked like the Cathedral of Saint John the Divine was meant to look. A behemoth Gothic wonder that hadn't yet been completed, it was just getting started in upper Manhattan, the mere hope and darling of her heart, the life's work of so many, here made manifest. She gasped in delight. The nave was enormous, the altar expansive and bordered by carved wooden choir rows, the front rose window huge and blue, each petal signifying one of the Beatitudes. The rear ambulatory let in more light, the chapels of patron saints all lending their stained-glass glory to the Gothic whole.

"How is this possible," Evelyn breathed, and music answered.

Angelic sound swelled around her: all women's voices, a sacred tune Evelyn recognized as that of the great Hildegard, inspiration to women who sought to be seen and heard. The light, the *living* light of her twelfth-century visions, brightened around the great space poised to become one of the largest Gothic cathedrals in the world. Long after Evelyn would pass from this mortal coil.

A woman in a blue Episcopalian deaconess habit peered down at her before helping her up from the stone floor. "Evelyn Northe-Stewart, the legend herself," the woman said, guiding her to a nearby pew and sitting down. "Hello, I'm Lily Strand. I imagine Eve may have mentioned me."

"Yes, I'm so grateful to you, and for this place to look like *my* church..." Tears flowed down Evelyn's cheeks. "I knew I'd never live to see it finished! Thank you...thank you for this."

"It was your steadfast faith, even when everyone else in your childhood hurt and rejected you, that created this portal. The least we could do is let you see this future."

"I fear for the present," Evelyn said gravely.

"Don't. You've done well to protect us by shutting down the wires. What you'll need to do is shield yourself and your psychic friends. Because we're going to fight back."

"And Eve?"

"She'll survive—"

Evelyn shot to her feet. "What do you mean, 'she'll survive'?"

The deaconess rose too, walking Evelyn toward the vast front door of the ponderous space. "I mean exactly that. I've checked on her. She's not alone."

"But she's still at the house—"

"What's important now is the protection of a whole city's worth of spirits, making sure the psychic wave Prenze created stops here with us, the levee. We strain at capacity, but we will hold for safety."

"Where are all the spirits of this Sanctuary, then?"

"Hiding," Strand said. "Those who enter here will first see the sacred space they most want or expect to see. The truth of this place lives in the recesses. We've not time for a tour. Go, sit with your fellows. Keep watch like all the women who have kept watch since time began. Go with our heart and our thanks, and when the trumpet sounds, brace yourselves."

Lily Strand flung open the great door, and light beyond blinded Evelyn. With a gentle shove from the deaconess, Evelyn fell back, but as she did, the world opened.

For one brief moment she thought she glimpsed every shadow of Sanctuary, and beyond, into the Corridors, past the Corridors into a more ancient place even deeper into a stone purgatory, into the land some called the Whisper-world, all the levels and layers and labyrinths open to the dead. One yawning, gaping moment when everything seemed vulnerable. But it had to be an illusion. One could not get to the mythic Whisper-world from Sanctuary. She had been expressly told by spiritual agents she met in her youth that those gates were shut.

And yet, the whole of the spirit world had become to Evelyn's eye a great, yawning maw, a widening scream and at the center of it, a terror. A hulking, undulating shadow that filled Evelyn with dread. As it pulsed, so did it grow. The spirit world feared it too, and Evelyn's empathetic Sensitivities were overwhelmed. Her heart faltered in her chest. She was no longer the young warrior she once had been. She didn't want to die like this, falling away from the Heaven she'd been so desperate to see finished—

"Wake up." A whisper fluttered over Evelyn's eyelids, and she felt as though she struck ground. With a moan, she opened her eyes to see Jenny staring down at her, Antonia at her elbow.

And then there was a loud, clarion trumpet blast. Evelyn couldn't be sure who or what heavenly host sounded it, but she knew the onslaught was coming.

"Shield!" Evelyn cried, bolting up to grab and cover Jenny with her body as if blocking her from a blast, cradling the child as she'd done over Eve when first embattled with her gifts.

In a freezing immersion, the forest clearing was gone and the women were drowning in spirits.

Chapter Nineteen

"Take me home," the tintype had whispered to Maggie, seeing through Arielle Prenze's eyes near the mouth of the bridge, once she'd given the detective Albert's journal. The edge of the metal plate was bloodied from Arielle catching it roughly during the tumult on the bridge.

The mouth of the stern woman in the image actually moved, and Maggie realized what had happened. Mrs. Prenze had gone into the object, what was left of her. She wasn't the manifest whole spirit, but there was enough of her to command attention and possess an item with her essence. Perhaps, Maggie and Arielle thought in tandem, the blood made for that much more of a spell. It wasn't the first time that woman had drawn blood, Arielle admitted to herself, and to Maggie, and the weight of abuses twisted knots in the woman's stomach.

Arielle Prenze, possessed by Margaret Hathorn but not entirely overtaken by her, as the two had reached an accord of companionship within one body, returned to a darkened house as her mother bid. Maggie wasn't done with the Prenze family or the mansion yet. Arielle turned on the gas lamps in the front hall, and glass sconces leapt to a frosted golden life, the pipes still installed and at the ready. Even though electricity had been implemented, many fine homes maintained both, just for good measure. As she took to the stairs to find Alfred and see if he had recovered from Albert's drugs and toxins, a great wailing roar took over the sky and the temperature around her plummeted drastic degrees.

What looked like a wave of silvery light swept over the house, a tsunami of eerie, luminous vapor. Arielle's hair was blown back, her body wracked with shivers.

"What's happening?" Arielle asked the spirit within her, terrified.

I think the spirit world is taking revenge, Maggie replied in Arielle's mind.

"Will they come for me?" Arielle said in a panic. "I did help Albert in the beginning. I did think I was doing the Christian thing, by trying to move spirits on, but I see now it was torture. I see now it's best to let spirits be. I'm sorry…" she cried to the air.

If they're not causing harm, that's usually best. But it is complicated, as I can see that there were tortures you and your brother lived through, in life and through your mother's spirit. I can't say I wouldn't have wanted her gone too. But the way he went about it… I wish you'd all have called an exorcist instead. I know a very good and handsome one.

As the luminous wash of spectral energy passed over Arielle, the tintype of her mother began to glow, and the form of Mrs. Prenze lifted from the frame, a dimensional projection of the face below.

"I should have found a way to care for you better," Mrs. Prenze whispered. "I see that now. Can that possibly be enough?"

"It helps," Arielle said.

"Will you tell him that? Albert? It may ease him. It may not. I would like to be done with this anger. With this restlessness."

"I will tell him."

"I would like to rest."

As the spectral tide flowed, Mrs. Prenze, the wisps that were left of her, lifted from the image and into the current.

"Goodnight, Mother," Arielle called.

"Goodnight, Elle," replied a whisper that blended into the wash.

The tintype went still. Arielle bowed her head. She set the tintype on the mantel of the parlor and said prayers over it, for herself and for the spiritual river flowing past her. A cold caress of luminous silk as it passed over her, the flow of the dead in an airborne torrent was uncannily beautiful, profound. Something she'd never forget. Whenever it reached Albert, he'd have far less of a peaceful time of it, but at that point it would be justice.

* * * *

In Eve Whitby's parlor, Jacob dove to catch Eve's falling body lest she strike her head against the wooden arm of the settee.

"What's wrong," he cried, cradling her. "Is she under a psychic attack again?" He looked around as Rachel did, but even to her trained eye nothing was there.

Rachel lifted a finger to tell him to give her a moment and closed her eyes, reaching out her hands in front of her as if she were feeling for a wall. As Jacob held Eve, Rachel bent near Eve's head, looking up at Jacob, and nodded. She gestured toward Eve's mind and made a motion as if something was trying to get in.

"The Bishops taught us shielding. Maybe we can shield for Eve too?" Jacob offered.

Rachel nodded eagerly and stood, pulling a hand-shaped pendant from around her neck, clutching the hamsa as she mouthed a prayer. He joined in the *Tefilat HaDerech* with her, a traveler's prayer, as good as any, as Eve's mind was indeed traveling uncharted waters.

Jacob wrapped his arms around Eve's shuddering body tightly, clutching her head against his. "Come back, Evelyn Whitby," he demanded. "I'll not have you taken again. No one shall have power over this mind but herself!" Jacob declared to the air around them. Closing his eyes, he took a deep breath and released it slowly.

Rachel held her hands out as a shudder of power and fortitude expanded through Jacob; she could feel his energy lifting up Eve, enswathing her.

"Wake, Eve," he urged. "Return to us. To your power. Your control. Come home."

The response was immediate.

Eve sighed as her eyes fluttered open, and she stared up at the man she adored. "My brilliant love...your light and strength pulled me from the depths!"

Jacob beamed. "I'm so glad it helped."

"You always do," she sighed happily, reinvigorated. "Thank you both," she said, making sure Rachel knew she was just as appreciated, their efforts both helped her fight back the clutching darkness she hadn't wanted to fall victim to again. "I could feel Prenze trying to slither back into my consciousness. But he was weakened by the day. He'd gone so long without censure I'm sure he thought he'd just slip back into the shadows again after all this."

With a deep breath, Eve sat up and cried, "I renounce thee!," pushing her hands up as if shoving away unwelcome presences. The gas lamps flared as if directly responsive to her calling forth elemental forces, and Eve felt certain the collective shielding did exactly what it was supposed to do this time; a muse of fire.

"Finally." She tapped the center of her forehead. "A bit of peace and quiet!"

Zofia appeared before Eve in a sudden sweeping motion, all cold air and moonlight in her ethereal form.

"Dearest little one!" Eve cried, reaching out and through her as if to hug her.

"Fondness soon, Eve, but now, right now, plug your spectral ears," the girl exclaimed anxiously, and motioned to Rachel the instruction, tapping the center of her grey, transparent forehead just as Eve had done and then putting fingers in her ears, signaling the need to block and protect her third eye and all Sensitivities. Rachel nodded.

"What's happening?" Eve asked the ghost.

"Prenze lashed out against the whole spirit world," Zofia explained. "It is lashing back. You will be overwhelmed. I must go and scout." She disappeared again.

Eve turned to Jacob, reaching up to touch his face.

"We must shield again, just as you did a moment ago, Jacob. How brilliant you were! In the darkness I felt your embrace pull me away from his violence, your blessings sustaining me. I felt my feet underneath me again, representing how you ground me. Right now, we must shield not only from malevolence but from the world of wraiths entirely. It will get very loud in here, even for someone who is spectrally adjacent such as yourself."

Jacob nodded and went to the bottle of headache tablets he'd brought down and offered a fresh pair. Eve took them and swallowed with cooled tea.

Eve heard it before anyone saw it. "It's coming..." she murmured. "We should sit."

Everyone did, just in time for a wave of silvery light to crash over them as if a dam had burst, covering them in cold air that blew their hair back and swept around them in a torrent. The flood lasted a few moments, and the assembled company stared at it, following it to the door and looking out as it swept over the park, collecting more light from the memory of the bones there, and onward downtown, toward its target.

Chapter Twenty

There came a shriek from the most recent occupant of the Tombs prison, groggily rising to his feet, coming to in a foreign, unwelcoming cell of stone and murk.

"How dare you," Prenze growled, and reached out toward the woman that had been in his mental grasp earlier in the night. But Eve wasn't there. She'd gotten away and he'd ended up here.… Yet he was still tied to her. He shoved his way back into her psyche.

He gained sway upon her, dragging her under, but she retaliated with fresh strength. She was now surrounded and supported by others. He had no one. Bitterness rose again in him, and he felt his consciousness entirely knocked back into his body as that young bitch cast him out as if he were a demon. Well, then, perhaps he'd act like one.

Prenze's fresh shriek of rage was followed by the most incredible rising racket: a thundering, tearing, rending, ravening roar that would become legend among inmates.

The sporadic gas torches blew out as if from a great breath. Their pilots would need to be relit lest the gas poison the air, but in this moment the paranormal had taken over and the mortal world was no longer their own. The resulting light that replaced the flame was a luminous silver wave. A dam had burst, and spectral light flowed like water.

The roaring wave poured over the inmates, many of whom shivered and saw nothing, several of whom cried out in fear, a few of whom laughed as if in hope of release. But the silver river pooled and swirled, creating a vortex around Prenze in his stone cell with a cot in the corner where he cowered in his fine suit coat.

"I was done with you! I banished you!" Prenze cried to the wave that was drowning him. "Back, you unnatural wretches!"

It wasn't one ghostly voice that spoke to him. It was a spectral force, a coalesced army of souls, collected sentiment coming through in choice words curated to address his specific wrongs and what the ghosts of New York, and any other spirit he had wronged anywhere in the world, intended to do about it:

You could have used your near-death moments to see the divine and make a brighter world. Instead, you used powers granted at that precipice for spite and pain. So then must your gift be revoked. You do not deserve it. Be then as you were. We close the spectral door to you but open you to all the suffering you've caused.

The light swirled around his head, and he clutched at it, as if trying to peel back an invisible foe. He screamed. A vein in his forehead bulged. A rivulet of blood ran from his nostril.

Collapsing onto the cot, his eyes rolled back in his head.

The scream brought no guard. Screams were common in the Tombs.

Albert Prenze went silent and curled up on his cot as if shriveled and deflated, his world suddenly, painfully small, the weight of consequence crushing the air out of his lungs.

* * * *

Zofia returned to Eve's parlor in a burst of cold and enthusiasm. "It's over!" she cried. "It was amazing. There was a whole river of spirits, everything Sanctuary had protected flowed back over the city! And somehow," she said excitedly, "everyone took Prenze's powers away!"

"When I was attacked by Prenze, en route to the bridge," Eve shared, "I lost consciousness, but in doing so, because of being controlled, I had access to *his* mind and memories. I saw so much of what made him hateful." She fiddled with a fresh cup of tea as she explained those unnerving moments.

"He was dealt a cruel hand, yes, but also his choice to live in the pain and exacerbate its effects rather than reject it is where he lost his way. I saw his near-death experience. I was *with* him in the Corridors between life and death when he gained his abilities. I heard that space offer him power. He accepted it as if it were owed him. I suppose what the spirits give, the spirits can take away if the gift is squandered."

Zofia floated close as if relishing in a secret. "Exactly! And after all that, the best part? Prenze can still *see* ghosts; he just can't do anything about it!" She giggled a bit maniacally before sobering. "Serves him right for disappearing my family," she said, transparent tears suddenly glistening in her greyscale eyes. "It's my fault, though, Vera and Olga were trying to save me—"

"None of that, little one," Eve cautioned. "They'd have done it for any spirit, for the whole of the city, buying it time. You know that. They're at rest. Peace. Not as any of us planned, but peace none the less. There is nothing of their energy the sky won't welcome as a gift."

She hoped that was true. In her heart, she felt they were resting after a long, hard life and afterlife of good deeds.

You're very impressive, Eve, I'm so glad your mind and body could withstand all that has happened, Rachel signed, tears in her eyes. With a smile, Eve rose to her feet and moved to embrace Rachel.

"I live blessed by so many talented people and spirits in my life," Eve said, squeezing Rachel's hands before withdrawing a step. "All I know how to do is to try to always do right by all of you."

Eve wobbled, and Jacob was right there behind her, steadying her with hands firmly on her waist. "Careful," he said gently.

Eve threaded her fingers through his, and, pulling on his arms so to draw him against her, she leaned back against his shoulders and breathed deeply.

Looking at the lovebirds with a knowing smile, Rachel took the teapot and motioned toward the rear of the house, exiting to refresh tea and giving them a moment alone.

Eve turned to face the man she now was no longer afraid to say she loved, winding her arms around his neck as she spoke.

"The pressure that, for weeks now, has been drilling into my skull, has finally released its torturous grip," Eve said. "I haven't felt so good in weeks. Save for the day in the park… Because *that* day… Before everything went wrong, *our* day was ecstasy—"

They crashed together in a furious kiss, one devoid of the careful hesitation that happened during the injuries on the bridge, ignoring their still-flaring aches and pains. This was a kiss of release: rough and passionate, made from all their hopes, their fears, and the searing depth of their desire. Jacob sunk with her onto the settee again and only drew back when they heard Rachel's step in the hallway.

They breathed raggedly and smiled at one another with dazed grins drunk with adoration.

"I am so glad you're feeling better." Jacob adjusted his skewed clothes and straightened hers.

Rachel entered the parlor with more tea and another smile. Eve knew she approved of them, so she didn't feel she had to hide anything; she was among family.

"It's like the spirits took the pain away in the torrent, and whatever they did to Prenze cleared away whatever hold he still had on me." She clapped her hands and darted to the séance table where the Prenze notebook and Spire's casebook sat lying open.

"Let's get this case together," she said, taking one of the notebooks in hand.

"Eve!" Jacob laughed. "You have to rest."

"We have to *charge* him," Eve insisted, "and with solid grounds, before they release him, no matter the effects of the spirit world. And believe me, when one suffers migraines, when it finally leaves, it's like dawn breaking and energy fills you. I could work for hours!"

Jacob sighed and chuckled, placing his hands gently on her shoulders and bending to kiss her on the head then sitting down beside her. "I'd be angry with you for such bullheaded determination if I didn't find the quality so attractive," Jacob said.

Eve turned and signed to Rachel what the notebooks were and continued with an invitation: *Would you like to get a read on them, for clues on the page and with the scope of your Sensitivities?*

Rachel eagerly joined them, and the three lost track of time, poring over notes and making their own, until each of them fell asleep face forward on the séance table.

Little Zofia kept watch, diligent, loving, and all the brighter a manifestation for all her work on behalf of the living.

Chapter Twenty-One

Eve groggily awoke on her settee at dawn, a stiff pain in her neck, her mind blank as to where and when she was. She listened for her team and tried to extend her abilities to sense them, but she felt no one and saw no ghosts. The world remained disconcertingly quiet. She assumed Cora must still be downtown, Antonia and Jenny still with Gran. Perhaps they'd stayed with Clara in Tarrytown. No one was there, save one beautiful man stirring across the room.

"Good morning, Eve," Jacob said from the chair where he'd been sleeping, sitting up as she did and rubbing his eyes. "I'd have moved you to your bed, but I didn't dare be improper and as Rachel had fallen asleep too—I awoke to see her with her head against that Queen Anne chair there—I just couldn't bear not helping you to something a bit more comfortable than facedown on the table."

"Thank you," Eve said, taking in the sight of him.

He'd set his frock coat on the back of the chair. His cuffs were undone and his white collar, smeared with a bit of Eve's blood, was open with his similarly spattered white neckwear hanging untied aside black suspenders. His disheveled and unbuttoned look created a sensation in Eve that felt like nothing short of a sudden, drastic fever. She didn't know whether to be frustrated by how overwhelming her emotions for this man were or impressed by what he evoked.

His somewhat impish smile made Eve realize she was staring—gaping, actually—and she blushed and looked away, still unused to the idea that it was all right to be smitten, overwhelmed, hungry. It was still very new to have admitted they loved one another....

He rose to his feet and walked toward her, pausing at a console table where Eve had placed a silver bowl of small mints as parlor favors, placing one in his mouth. Séances often tired Eve's throat, and she liked to have little lozenges and candies around as an aid. She hadn't thought about the practical uses of awaking to a lover and wanting a more pleasant kiss.

"Don't be embarrassed," he said, reading her entirely all too well. "You make me feel the same. You...affect me." He knelt at her side. "To the point I can't stand it. I've just had to be more practiced at not showing what I feel; it is unseemly." He lifted up a second small mint. Eve opened her mouth. He placed the mint on her tongue. She again kissed the tip of his finger as she had done in the park, little marks of seduction.

"You can always show me how you feel," Eve said, lowering her eyes.

He accepted the invitation and kissed her deeply, their hands getting ever bolder with one another, until the phone rang and they broke apart with a little moan.

Rising to pick up the phone, when Eve lifted the bell she heard a less familiar voice in a very familiar cadence.

"Eve, darling, it's me, Maggie, well, Arielle Prenze, but I'm still here. Can you bring the reverend over to get me out? I think I've spent too much time in Arielle. I think we're a bit stuck. Thank you!"

The click of Maggie hanging up, clumsily, in Arielle's body, was jarring, her request presumptuous but already expected, and it jolted a laugh out of Eve.

"Well?" Jacob prompted, assembling himself.

"Time for an exorcism at the Prenze mansion."

* * * *

Once a call had been made to the reverends, Coronado tried to hide his excitement at the prospect of being haunted by Maggie again but Eve could hear it in his voice.

Rachel, who was needed by colleague of hers on a trying haunting a few states away, signed to Eve a goodbye and a promise that she would be here for her as things progressed with Jacob, as an advocate and resource. Eve was aware she and Jacob couldn't court indefinitely without answering to each of their parents, and she had no idea if anyone would be amenable to an engagement should it go that far. There was much to discuss, but for the moment, she just wanted to enjoy having allowed her heart to open to passionate love.

The detective and Eve set off for the Prenze mansion, leaving a note for any of the team who returned and wondered where they were.

"I made a call about a warrant," the detective said as they hired a carriage waiting at Washington Square Park. Both of them were moving slowly, worn and bruised, and weren't up for their usual brisk walks or jostling trolley rides. "But an invitation *into* this mansion is far better."

Their aches and pains were eased by shifting into a warm, covetous embrace during the trip uptown.

They were taking their time crossing up the walk to the Prenze front door when it opened.

Alfred Prenze, looking rather green, awaited them at the threshold to show them in. Alfred's general predisposition toward kindness meant Eve wasn't jarred by looking into such a similar face as her tormentor. This face was ill, tired, and baffled. It held nothing of the contempt she'd fought against. Eve's Sensitivities were well aware of Alfred's differences, his softer energy, and wearied—if not a bit cowardly—heart.

"She's upstairs. Follow me. Thank you for coming. The reverends are already here. With everything we've been through, I confess I never thought an exorcism would be part of it."

Eve hesitated on the landing of the second floor, turning back to Alfred.

"How are you, Mr. Prenze?" Eve asked gently. "I can imagine this is overwhelming."

"I…I don't know. Albert drugged me, and evidently has been doing so for weeks, so my memory is hazy. But I hear he hurt someone, trying to get to the spirits. I told him long ago to give up his animosity. But he never really listened to me. I never knew what he was on about. I saw Mother's spirit; we all did. But she didn't bother us like she did him. She must have cracked something open in him, and the more he railed against ghosts, all ghosts, the more he saw them and was haunted by them."

Eve's tone was grave. "It was us he hurt. The detective and I. Nearly caused our deaths. I hope you can help us with making sure he hurts no one again."

"I'm very sorry. I'll do what I can. Arielle told me she gave you Albert's diary? I have no idea what is in it, so please ask if you've questions. He may have painted me in a bad light too, so be advised he's never been the most reliable of narrators."

Jacob, who had stood by Eve's side, stepped down a step toward the pale, weak Alfred. "While I can't blame you for wanting to protect yourself, sir, with all due respect, I do wonder about your turning a blind eye to something obviously wrong with the accounts. I have the ledgers and an accounting of the London merger, done just before Albert's 'death.' A high clearance in Scotland Yard and an ambassador here opened some doors for us, and I can't imagine you'd have built a successful business if you were this open to or unaware of vast sums clearing from the company stores to a predatory artist circle."

Alfred sighed. "Before he died, Albert told me he'd been supporting a charity he cared for a great deal. After his 'death,' I kept the money going, I suppose out of a sense of guilt, out of honoring his memory. I didn't know what they did."

Eve bit her tongue so as not to mention Dupont's transgressions, Mr. Zinne's blood used for paint, the artist who had gone missing the night Albert died who stood in for his corpse, abandoned as the warehouse burned. All of it would come out; it didn't have to right now. She motioned to Jacob, and they walked up the stairs as Alfred shuffled away, muttering to himself.

The reverends, each dressed in their black suits with white clerical collars, were already sitting with Arielle in the wide room Eve and Jacob knew from their surveillance position.

Reverend Blessing waited at the back of the room with a slight smirk on his face as Coronado sat at the side of the bed, holding Arielle's hand and gently praying over her.

"I fear I have a fever, Reverend, tell me, am I warm?" Arielle asked, prompting the reverend to place his hand to her forehead.

"A bit. You've been through an ordeal. You'll be better soon," Coronado assured her in his light, elegant lilt of an accent born of his youth in Mexico City.

Jacob hung back with the bemused Blessing to ask his thoughts on evidence and mental states of the family. The floorboards creaked as Eve approached the supine woman, and both Coronado and Arielle looked to the foot of the bed.

"Eve!" cried Arielle at Maggie's prompting.

"Miss Whitby!" Coronado rose and came to clasp Eve's hand in his. "Are you all right? I heard—"

"Yes, I am recovering, but the more evidence we find in this house, the better I'll be."

"Just give me a moment, Eve," Maggie said through Arielle, her cadence and intent clear. "I'll be right with you. But I need the good reverend's help a bit more, please." Maggie flung Arielle's hands out, reaching for Coronado.

"Yes, Margaret," he said, instantly by her side again, taking up Arielle's hands, but it seemed clear the reverend saw beyond the body to the soul that had taken up within. It was as overdone as a vaudeville melodrama, but Eve couldn't help but be warmed by the connection.

Early on in Eve's friendship with Maggie, the ghost becoming Eve's best and only true friend, the spirit had noted her only regret about life was that she'd never truly had a romance. Not a good, pure one. She'd been taken advantage of but never held dear. What was happening now was dear.

"I just need a little momentum. Perhaps you can pull me. Draw me to you, dear Reverend?" Arielle's mouth murmured, but it was clear Maggie was the one asking to be drawn to the handsome cleric.

Everyone in the room save for Coronado turned away, as if they were all listening to something deeply private that they shouldn't be.

"Is she better?" Alfred Prenze asked from the doorway, a ledger tucked under his arm.

"We're almost there," Coronado said brightly. He was the most affable, radiant man Eve had ever met; there wasn't a soul who could look upon his utterly gorgeous face and not see his kindness, lighting him from within.

"Good," Alfred murmured and shuffled to the detective, handing him the ledger. "When I awoke from my stupor, Arielle showed me Albert's office, the back room I thought was locked and forgotten. This was in the safe, tucked behind bonds. But I think this ledger will draw the last connections you need, noting accounts and withdrawals. The accounts... life savings, everything those poor artists had in his deluded organization. Drained. He was a vampire, Albert. Once he drained the money, he let those sad, lost souls fade away, using them to advantage. His thrall is a cancer. He was always testing the limits of people, but I never thought it was as drastic as all this. How do we prosecute that quality? How do we stop his mesmeric persuasion?"

"I've been told the spirit world saw to the removal of his powers," Eve replied. "He's now an average soul who must face justice. And, despite all his efforts, he still sees ghosts."

Alfred nodded wearily. "I see. Let me know what you need. In the meantime, I'm going to get Prenze tonics back in the business of trying to ease suffering, not creating it."

He shuffled away, and Eve hoped he had the strength to make good on it.

"All right, then," Coronado said gently, pulling on Arielle's hands and murmuring a benediction in several languages, as if for good measure. Arielle's hands gave way to silvery, luminous hands and Maggie was pulled up and out and floated now before the reverend, her head bent toward him as he looked up.

Arielle lay back and drifted into an immediate, peaceful sleep.

The reverend now stood face-to-face with the spirit that had asked for him.

"Hello," they both murmured, a reunion of old friends, something stirring in their souls that transcended this moment, time stopping for soul mates. Eve had never witnessed anything quite like it. Maggie and Coronado were far more forward than she had been, being so affected by Jacob, yet they didn't seem awkward.

All of them, Jacob included, seemed to have a better, more sensible relationship to infatuation than Eve did. She still felt as though she was fumbling and flailing whenever she looked at the man she loved. Glancing at him, she saw him staring at Coronado, who appeared as though he was holding thin air. He was. But the spirit there was just as powerful as touch, in her own right.

Jacob came close to Eve and touched her on the elbow, leading her away from the tender moment. "Let's search the premises while we still can." Blessing nodded at them, gesturing they go on. If he was uncomfortable, he masked it by a serene patience.

They found Albert's room, the torture devices against ghosts, and another device like what had been placed outside Eve's office: prime evidence that would be added to what Fitton and his associates gathered on the bridge. They then descended to see the prison lined in metal.

"While it proves his cruelty, I know his actions against the dead cannot be prosecuted, nor can anything I witnessed inside his head," Eve said, reaching out to touch the smooth metal wall. The phantom sensation of electrocution vibrated over her, and she withdrew her hand with a hiss.

"Still," Jacob said, taking notes in his leather-bound casebook, "this builds a profile we can bring to an Alienist to explain. Courts are warming to Alienist testimony these past few years."

Eve nodded. "Whether they'll warm to a Spiritualist is yet to be tried. I'll need every precedent this century has offered."

Maggie floated across the threshold of the basement toward Eve, looking rather pleased with herself. "Well wasn't that an adventure," she said with a laugh. "What a beautiful soul." Before Eve could ask Maggie to clarify who she meant, she continued. "Arielle, poor thing, is now sleeping soundly. Having endured quite the reckoning, she's earned a rest."

"We all have," Eve agreed. "Come, let's go home. I *must* see Gran and the girls."

"Oh, I can't bear another minute of this house," Maggie said. "This prison was the first place I was transported to. The pain in this room continued to tear me apart. Only my prayers got me out; Sanctuary heard me and drew me to it. Now let's hear what Gran has done with it."

As they exited, Maggie was humming a waltz and flouncing about in the air ahead of them.

"*You're* chipper," Eve murmured with a knowing smile.

Maggie glanced between Eve and the detective. "*You've* finally stopped ignoring the obvious, I see. Good. You're very good together, you two, so don't disappoint me," Maggie declared before vanishing into a hedgerow.

Chapter Twenty-Two

Gran, Antonia, Jenny and Cora were all in Eve's parlor when Eve and the detective returned to Fort Denbury, and the joy was palpable. After rounds of embracing, each had stories to tell about the past day, about the wires at Sanctuary and what the spiritual explosion looked like from their end.

Eve and Jacob agreed not to tell Gran everything, for fear she'd never let Eve out of the house again without having employed a *hundred* guards. Even so, Gran looked at Eve with such scrutiny she feared the woman would uncover everything regardless. She had to promise Gran many times that she was all right; only begging Cora to share her news of the Tombs shifted the focus.

Cora took a stiff drink of port before speaking. "I...touched Prenze while he was still unconscious, while Fitton was securing him in the Tombs. I saw many last moments. He often liked to watch who he coerced toward death," Cora said, shuddering and downing the last of the glass. "Zinne. Font. Drained or poisoned. There were a few glimpses of others, less clear, it became a blur; but the names that were a part of our cases stood out the most. It was the control of it, I suppose, his watching the expiration."

"There was an unhealthy obsession with death, I think, that was formed from his childhood," Eve said. "Things I saw when his mind was too open to me. I'm sorry you had to face the nightmares of what he became in so direct and visceral a fashion."

"Fitton saw how affected I was and offered to take a walk with me along the harbor and share all the details of the case I found relevant. He's a good man."

"The best I know," Jacob agreed.

"I think it is always wise to walk with a person of kindness after having witnessed and felt such a person of cruelty," Cora said. "I would have come home, but I wasn't far from one of my cousins and I stayed with her. Not a lick of paranormal ability in her and I think I needed the fresh air. I knew you were..." Cora glanced at Jacob and back to Eve. "Taken care of."

"I don't feel abandoned." Eve laughed. "I pushed you all away anyway."

"And you won't do it again." Cora lifted a finger toward her.

"I won't. Forgive me?"

"Always," Cora replied, embracing her.

"Thank you for *everything*, my rock, my unfailing soldier." Eve kissed Cora's temple.

Smiling, surprised, Cora did the same. "We live what we were born for."

"That we do," Eve stated and moved to Gran, who was staring out the bay window. "You're far away, Gran. Are you all right?"

"It pains me I wasn't with you. I know you're not telling me everything."

Eve took Gran's empty teacup and handed it to Jenny, who swept forward with a fresh one, the little one always attentive, especially to Gran.

"If Sanctuary had been harmed, I'd never forgive myself," Eve countered, handing her the tea. "Neither would you. We had to be separated. I stand by that."

Gran seemed unconvinced, frowning. Eve knelt before her, all elegance on a Queen Anne throne, and looked up at her, speaking directly.

"Please don't act like you're still the warrior you were with Mother. There are things you can't withstand now. There are things that might have killed you today were you not where you were." Gran's frown deepened, and Eve changed the subject. "Did you go in? Did you meet Lily Strand in Sanctuary? Did they hail you as the heroine of the portal, the reason it's tied to that arch?"

Here, finally, Gran smiled. "It was glorious. It was Saint John! Finished and...everything my heart could have hoped for. And I *did* meet Lily, guide and guardian. She was mysterious, and protective of the spirits, which I understand. She pushed me out before the spirit deluge. We were so exhausted after that we stayed with Clara and Rupert, to be close if the spirits needed us to return." Her hand fluttered over her heart. "I could feel you were...safe. But still—"

"Gran. We have to split up the team if we expect to get anything done." She leaned in and whispered in her best friend's ear. "Besides. It earned me time alone with Jacob."

At this, Gran laughed. "I knew he'd never agree to part from you, and it does my heart good to see it."

They both glanced at Jacob, who was looking over at them but hastily looked away as if pretending he hadn't been trying to listen in.

"Don't be nervous, dear boy; it's only good things," Gran called to Jacob. He strode toward them, pausing at the samovar to pour Eve a fresh cup of coffee and handing it to her.

"My constant hero," she murmured, taking it.

"Yes, my hero too," Gran added. "While I know you're holding back details, I assume you think for my benefit, I am grateful for your not leaving Eve alone as she'd demanded."

He offered his most disarming smile, the kind that had weakened Eve's knees from the start. "I will always respect your granddaughter's wishes unless those wishes put her in grave danger, in which case I will respectfully navigate my way around them to ensure her safety."

Gran embraced him with a laugh.

Forever drawn to a lively parlor, Cy appeared at the piano—his altar. Soon jig, hymn, and popular song filled the room with clairaudient melody. Music issued from the spirit world sounded far away but nevertheless lovely, carrying a poignance that music from live hands couldn't evoke or imitate.

Antonia had utilized meditative time in the kitchen to a delicious result, and fruit tarts were enjoyed heartily over more tea, coffee, wine, and liqueur.

Everyone was chatting excitedly in the parlor save for Jenny, who was contentedly sketching a field of flowers. More often than not, her sketches were scenes of death, morbidity, or some message from the beyond that chose her as a channel. If she sketched pretty things it meant she was at peace.

Bringing a sweet treat to the console table near her, Eve kissed her on the head and whispered, "That's beautiful." Jenny smiled and shaded the wings on a butterfly.

Eve looked around, her soul full, content. For what might have been the first time in her entire life, inside her heart and spirit, there was balance. Leadership and allowance. Shared responsibility. A willingness to accept risk on all sides. Dare she say she was excited for what was next?

Jacob stepped up to her side once more. "It seems all is well," he said. "We've a trial to prepare, more than enough to convict, and more than enough time to manage it. In the meantime..." Jacob reached in his pocket and handed Eve tickets. Carnegie Hall. Tomorrow night. A Tchaikovsky encore.

"Oh, Jacob," she murmured. "How did you find time amid saving my life to replace our concert tickets?"

He chuckled. "I had them already, Eve. When you agreed to go to the park with me, I bought several, for the rest of the year, so I'd always have something to tempt you with."

"You don't need tickets to tempt me, Jacob," Eve said under her breath. "I think we proved that...."

Jacob sighed gleefully as if that was just what he'd wanted to hear.

Maggie wafted in the window, floating over to kiss Eve, then Jacob, on the cheek with a cold peck. He blinked rapidly and turned his head. While he had grown more attuned to the appearance of presences, he couldn't pinpoint them. But the temperature was palpable. "Did I...just..."

"Get a kiss from a ghost? Yes."

"He's very handsome, Eve," Maggie declared, offering a devilish grin. "You know, if you like, I could always practice kissing him so that he gets even better about sensing ghosts."

Eve brandished a finger in Maggie's incorporeal face. "You brat. Stick to your reverend."

"Oh, I will," she declared and floated over to a line of cordials in delicate flutes that Antonia had poured. The ghost tried to stick her tongue into one before Antonia admonished her with a squeal.

"But I miss cordial as much as anything in life!" Maggie cried with a pout, sticking an incorporeal finger in the open decanter and touching it to her tongue, a tiny droplet of red liqueur dispersing in vapor. Antonia swiftly corked the decanter, but Maggie just pursed her lips and stuck her finger through the side of the bottle and did it again.

Jenny laughed louder than Eve had ever heard come out of her mouth, Zofia floating at her side, giggling along with her.

A pang for Vera and Olga pierced Eve's heart and sobered her. She wished with all her heart they were there with them. Then a thought occurred to her she couldn't ignore.

"Now that we're here, reunited," she said to Jacob, "I've an instinct to hold a séance, now that it's safe. Do you mind?"

"Go ahead. This is your calling. I stand by in support, and at the ready."

She touched his face. "You are sublime. Everything I could hope for." He took her hands in his and kissed one then the other. Eve sighed, delighted by his every ministration. "I am so grateful for you," she murmured before turning to her friends.

"My dears," Eve called. The separate conversations all paused as colleague and spirit turned to her. "I'd like to hold a séance, reunited here with all of you as the great threat of our current cases is neutralized. He obliterated all else. But there surely are other voices that have needed us. There are surely injustices we need to follow. Will you join me?"

She raised her hands, and the mediums of the Ghost Precinct glided to their chairs as if drawn in a dance to their circle.

Cora brought forth the séance items Prenze had stolen and left on the bridge.

"Thank you for collecting them," Eve murmured.

Cora nodded and offered blessings in French; then she struck the match, lit the candle, watched it leap to life, and blew out the match, interpreting patterns in the smoke.

Eve gestured for Antonia to ring the bell. She reached forward and did so, the clarion call to service.

Jenny turned her sketchbook to a blank page for automatic writing, ready for those who did not wish to manifest voice. *Dear spirit world,* she wrote.

"Dear spirit world," Eve echoed. "We have been through so much together. I am sorry for the ways in which I faltered. Show us what you hope for us in triumph. Guide us toward what we were forced to neglect. What of this oft-troubled city needs us most?"

The Ghost Precinct and its remaining operatives looked at one another, with excitement and resolve, as air grew cold and their hearts warmed to the entrance of spectral friends bearing tidings of good work to be done.

Acknowledgments

Special thanks to my editor Elizabeth May and the Kensington team for enthusiasm and support along the way! Alexandra Kenney and Lauren Jernigan, supreme publicity mavens, you are so dearly appreciated, thanks for all the help, facilitating and signal-boosting. Thanks to Lou Malcangi for the *amazing* cover art!

Deepest of heartfelt appreciation to my fantastic, thoughtful and incredibly helpful sensitivity readers Brina Starler, Elizabeth Kerri Mahon, Sebastian Crane and Ashley Lauren Rogers. You are stars in my sky.

Endless thanks to my agent Paul Stevens with Donald Maass, thanks for guiding my way.

To my incredible family, I couldn't have a better support system in all the world. Love you more than words. To my birthday-twin Marijo Farley, thank you for always being there for me no matter what.

Empyrean appreciation to my Torch and Arrow business partner Thom Truelove for meticulous, swift and thoughtful research and brainstorming, you're a wonderful resource to say the least.

Spooky thanks to Andrea Janes, founder and CEO of Boroughs of the Dead. Not only is it a pleasure to work for Boroughs of the Dead, acclaimed ghost tour company here in our beloved New York City, but I'm so grateful that you seek to honor the dead as I do and can never resist a good haunt and all the history it brings in its wake. Thank you for all the support and signal-boosting through the years.

Thank you, spirit world. I feel you. I know you. I will always tell your stories. Let us continue to be a luminous force.

Thank you especially, dear reader.

Blessings and Happy Haunting!

Meet the Author

Actress, playwright and author **Leanna Renee Hieber** is the award-winning, bestselling writer of gothic Victorian fantasy novels for adults and teens. Her novels such as the Strangely Beautiful saga, and the Magic Most Foul trilogy have garnered numerous regional genre awards, including four Prism awards, and have been selected as "Indie Next" and national book club picks. She lives in New York City where she is a licensed ghost tour guide and has been featured in film and television shows like Boardwalk Empire and Mysteries at the Museum.

Follow her on Twitter @leannarenee, or visit www.leannareneehieber.com.

Keep reading for an excerpt of the second book in the Spectral City series!

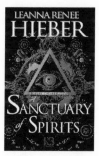

New York, 1899, and the police department's best ally is the secret Ghost Precinct, where spirits and psychics help solve the city's most perplexing crimes . . .

There's more than one way to catch a killer—though the methods employed by the NYPD's Ghost Precinct, an all-female team of psychics and spiritualists led by gifted young medium Eve Whitby, are unconventional to say the least. Eve is concerned by the backlash that threatens the department—and by the discovery of an otherworldly realm, the Ghost Sanctuary, where the dead can provide answers. But is there a price to be paid for Eve and her colleagues venturing beyond the land of the living?

Searching for clues about a mortician's disappearance, Eve encounters a charismatic magician and mesmerist whose abilities are unlike any she's seen. Is he a link to mysterious deaths around the city, or to the Ghost Sanctuary? Torn between the bonds of her team and her growing relationship with the dashing Detective Horowitz, Eve must discern truth from illusion and friend from foe, before another soul vanishes into the ether . . .

Prologue

Manhattan, 1899

Monsieur Dupont, career undertaker and director of a Manhattan viewing parlor for the dead, considered a postmortem body the most beautiful treasure. For him, the tired cliché of an undertaker being obsessed with death was transcended; he rejoiced that the dead made him feel so alive.

The dead were the key to the kingdom of heaven.

His craft had started innocently enough. Locks of hair. The obsession progressed. Other tokens and trinkets were next, taken and procured with exquisite care. Subtle trophies.

No one would know or see. No one could. Grief was such a strange, ever-changing beast, but one constant remained: no one ever noticed *all* the details of a corpse. No one would notice if some small thing wasn't exactly as it had been, as death had already made the familiar strange.

Memory rewrote itself. He'd seen the proof of it time and again. The dead were transformed and made perfect by their loved ones. In that perfection it was just so lovely, so sacred, so beautiful to take a small scrap of that elevated, exalted existence...

So, he began. Tokens of his little saints made into sacred objects. Tiny souvenirs from the world's most innocent: children. Taking something from a child was the most sacred of all transactions. Procured and placed into sacred vessels. Surely no one would mind. Their bodies were photographed for posterity, and a souvenir was taken in private just before the body was taken to the grave.

No one but the ghosts, that is. Spirits of children noticed what was gone but didn't understand.

Then there was Ingrid. *His* Ingrid. The child that by all rights should have been his if fate hadn't been so cruel. Heinrich Schwerin, thinking the girl was actually his, had interfered and ruined everything. He took the little girl's body, presenting her dressed and anointed as a saint and giving it as a gift to an orphanage when worship of her should have been done in private. A promising apprentice gone mad. None of it had gone to the grand design. As a divine architect, Dupont had lost control of the lamb that wandered from the flock and had to be fed to the wolves, never knowing the child he'd gone mad over wasn't even his.

He stared out the third-floor window of his viewing parlor and watched as boisterous theatre folk tumbled from their boarding house. There was such life in this city, and to juxtapose it with constant death was high art. He took on the sorrows of those who did not wish to, or could not, greet death in their own homes. He took it on for them, an extension of his undertaker role. Wakes were usually done in the home, in the downstairs parlor, but for those who couldn't bear it or didn't have a suitable place to host an entourage for days, his viewing parlor stood in for home. Families could consider calling their parlor instead a "living room" because he was displacing death for them, banishing it from their doorstep.

Thankfully, the spirits had been banished from his.

The best thing about meeting his business partner Montmartre at a lecture about the mapping of the human mind three years prior was that the man had devised a way to keep out the ghosts. The children floating outside the window, pointing at what had been left behind in Dupont's cabinet of treasures, simply didn't understand. He'd tried to explain it to them, but if children had a hard time grasping divine mystery in life, it was even more hopeless after death. He wished he, like most people, didn't see ghosts. He supposed his ability was an unfortunate symptom of a profession in death.

Montmartre had devised the ghost barricade, but out of the corner of Dupont's eye, he could see them marching around the exterior of the building like striking workers on the line. He couldn't allow their constant parade to distract him, so he stared at a fresh child laid out on the slab and dabbed rouge on cold blue cheeks.

He feared his careful enterprise would be revealed after all the nonsense with Ingrid. Part of him relished the edge of danger. Part of him wrestled to regain a simpler life he'd left behind once his mind had been opened to the grander possibilities of his artistic rituals. What was it his friends would say? *Arte Uber Alles.* Art above everything.

Turning to another work in progress, a waxen sculpture standing against the wall, he affixed a hint of color to the lips of the new seraph that adorned a pedestal of the stage set. So very realistic. He stared at his work and swelled in pride. No amount of danger could dull this rush.

He stared at the lovely little faces. He would make saints of them all.

There was a knock at the door. He scowled, put down his tools, and went to answer it. His stomach twisted with dread when he saw the tired face he'd once found sweet, years ago, when she'd worked as his maid. But now she was a troublesome card he had to strategize how to play.

"What did you do to my daughter?" the mousy-haired woman demanded, barging past him into the entrance foyer, her wide eyes full of rage. "And *why?*" She shrieked. Whatever beauty she'd once had was now sunken by grief and pierced by the sharp knife of poverty.

"Shhh, my Greta, my love," he murmured. "You've come back to me. Now we can grieve, together…"

He clutched her passionately, forced her to acknowledge him. Their past. Their little Ingrid. Their illicit child. He held Greta as she cried and tried to soothe the wildness of her sorrow with sweet nothings.

The thought occurred to him that they could try again. She could be his Eve and he could build something new, with all of his prizes collected in an Eden of his design. Perhaps, finally, he could feast with all the saints…

Montmartre wouldn't like it. But that man had his own agenda, and Dupont planned on leaving him to it.

Dupont seized Greta roughly. "Come with me, and we'll make hell a heaven."

Chapter One

Union Square
Manhattan, 1899

"Maggie." Eve Whitby waved at the distracted ghost who floated before her, a transparent, greyscale and luminous form. "Answer me. How could you, of all spirits, simply disappear? And what brought you back?"

"I *am* dead; we do that sometimes, you know. Vanish," Maggie said with a laugh. She turned and began floating north, in the direction of the train depot where they were headed. The wraith was a visual echo of the lovely young lady she'd been in life, dressed in a fine gown of the early eighties.

"Don't you be flippant, my dear," Eve chided, lifting her skirts and hurrying after the specter, running directly into the cold chill of her wake. "We've been distraught for weeks," she continued with a shiver. "We knew you'd never leave without telling us! We couldn't even catch a *trace* of you during our séances!"

The dark-haired man taking long strides to keep up beside Eve cleared his throat.

The generally drawn pallor of Eve's cheek colored. "I'm sorry, Detective." She turned to him without breaking her pace. "I forget you can't completely hear or see our subject here."

Tall and lithe, with a neatly trimmed mop of dark brown curls that bounced in the breeze, dressed in a simple black suit with a white cravat, Detective Horowitz, in his midtwenties, was as sharp in wit and mind as he was in features. The angles of his face curved and softened as he smiled. His ability to shift from serious to amused was as swift as it was attractive.

"I'm catching pieces here and there," he replied, "but to be honest, I'm more enjoying the looks you're getting from passersby, averting wary, disdainful eyes behind hat brims and parasols."

"Oh." Eve batted an ungloved hand, caring not a whit for the fine details of sartorial propriety, as gloves often got in her way of tactile experience important to her work. "Mad folk walk New York streets daily and no one stops them; it's one of the glories of the city—minding one's own business!"

Horowitz laughed and kept pace.

The three angled along bustling Broadway as it slanted up ahead of them, the ghost at the fore, dodging passersby with parasols and weaving past horse-carts, careful to mind their droppings. Eve grumbled as the stray foot of a businessman's cigar was lifted by the wind onto her shoulder, and she brushed off the embers before they caught the thin wool on fire. She wore an adaptation of a police matron's uniform: a simple dress with buttons down the front, but in black, having donned constant mourning in honor of those she worked with and for, the spirits of New York.

The detective didn't seem to hold Maggie's interruption against her, despite the fact that he'd been leaning toward Eve in a near-kiss when the spirit's incorporeal form had appeared between them. That the detective even *entertained* the idea of a ghost was a blessing. That he could slightly see and barely hear fragments from Maggie was incredible progress. Just weeks before he'd been a confirmed skeptic. Perhaps Eve's Sensitivities were rubbing off on the practical, level-headed detective. The idea that she might be able to draw this man further into her world was an equally thrilling and cautionary prospect. Eve reeled in more directions than one.

Maggie Hathorn had been Eve's dearest friend since childhood, the most trusted spectral asset in her Ghost Precinct since its recent inception, and the spirit didn't seem to be taking her own disappearance seriously. Yes, ghosts often came and went as they pleased. But they were generally creatures of habit with particular patterns of haunt. Eve's Ghost Precinct of four mediums relied on the constancy of their stable of specters, Maggie at the core. Until she'd vanished with no word.

"If the Summerland draws you and you wish to go, Maggie," Eve said earnestly, reaching out to the floating figure and touching chilled air, "just tell us. I love and need you, but I know I mustn't keep my dear friend from her well-earned peace."

"Oh, my dearest friend." Maggie turned and reached out. A transparent, icy hand brushed across Eve's cheek. "None of this was about wanting to go but wanting to *stay*, to help. But come, there are details I can't trust myself to remember. I'll take you to where the Sanctuary left me. You can't go in, but you of all people should know where I came out." She turned and resumed her float. Eve and the detective tried again to keep up.

The spirits that pledged themselves to Eve's Ghost Precinct promised they wouldn't go on to the Sweet Summerland, as the Spiritualists called their idea of a heavenly plane, without telling their coworkers. It was a way of ensuring that the delicate channel between the precinct Mediums and the spirits did not tear itself into injurious pieces. An open, psychic channel to the spirit world hurt if torn away and not properly shut. A wounded third eye could never properly heal. It had injured Eve when Maggie had been ripped away. It seemed the spirit hadn't thought of that. Eve swallowed back a reprimand that would seem ungrateful considering how glad she was to see her dead friend.

"Eve, who *is* this gentleman trailing you?" Maggie waved an incorporeal hand toward the detective. "Have you started hiring men since I've been gone?"

Eve shook her head. "Detective Horowitz and I have been consulting on strange cases that have unexpected, intersecting patterns. He's been a critical liaison for the department and a valuable friend."

"To be clear," the detective added, looking vaguely in Maggie's direction as they continued uptown, his gaze focusing and losing focus as if he faintly caught sight of her spectral person then lost her again. "I do support Miss Whitby and her precinct, even if I don't always understand it."

The public at large didn't know about the existence of the small Ghost Precinct, technically part of the New York Police Department. The few lieutenants and sergeants who did know thought the whole thing preposterous. "Full of hogwash," Eve had overheard one day in Mulberry Headquarters. The fact that the Ghost Precinct was made up of women didn't help the force's estimation, and it had been Eve's hope that Horowitz championing them would help win over some colleagues. The ones who didn't similarly judge him for being Jewish, that is.

The unlikely trio made the last fifteen blocks to Grand Central quicker by jogging over an avenue to catch an uptown trolley line, hopping on the next car that clanged its bell at the stop.

Maggie looked around with fierce interest in every sensory detail as the trolley dinged along, her luminous eyes taking in every storefront and theatre. The venues grew grander as the blocks ticked up their numbers. The ghost seemed to study every horse and cart, carriage or hack; every passerby, be they elegant or ragged, watching the shifting sea of hats along the sidewalk, from silk top to tattered caps, feathered millinery to threadbare scarves, forms dodging and darting like fish in a narrow stream.

Eve saw it all pass around and through the ghost, her transparent image superimposed over the tumult of midday Manhattan.

"I've missed you," the specter murmured to the metropolis. Eve didn't hear New York reply, but she felt it in her heart. When one genuinely loved the city, the soul of New York took note.

Watching Maggie watch New York was a study in eternal eagerness. Love kept the good spirits tethered to the tactile world. Moments like this were Eve's lesson about life taught by the dead: drink it all in, the chaos, the tumult, the bustle of existence and its myriad details as much as possible, as one's relationship to it all could change at any moment.

Once inside Grand Central Depot, a noisy, dark, crowded place filled with glass and trestles, soot and steam, a building dearly overdue for an upgrade to a full station, Maggie gestured toward a particular platform.

"Transit is with us, and if we're quick, you can be back within the two hours I quoted," the ghost exclaimed, wafting up train-car steps on the northern line. With a screeching rumble and a billowing burst of steam, they were off. Eve and the detective took a small bench at the rear of a car before pausing to consider whether it was wise to trust the demands of an excitable ghost.

Greenwich Village, Manhattan

Three mediums of the Ghost Precinct waited for their manager to return, sitting primly at their séance table on a crisp late autumn day. Hands clasped together, they were ready to begin. The lancet windows of their rear office had been cranked wide open to hear the clamor of New York City meld with the rustle of falling leaves and the constant whispers of the dead.

Cora Dupris, Antonia Morelli, and Jenny Friel had been left alone at the Ghost Precinct offices after having given their leader, Eve, a bit of a hard time about leaving again on a whim with the detective to whom she seemed to have a growing attraction. They knew that to wait for her to begin their séance would waste a precious opportunity for new information regarding the many loose ends of their cases. The three young mediums came from vastly different backgrounds and circumstance but were brought together by their gifts and calmly began their ritual of communing with the dead.

Cora, Eve's second-in-command, a year behind her at age eighteen, struck the match.

"Good spirits, come and speak with us, in the respect of your life and your cares in this world. Is there a spirit who would like our attention?

We still seek our friend Maggie. We still seek answers for that which remains unsolved."

Two ghosts appeared, their transparent, greyscale forms fully manifest on either side of the table. The two girls, little Zofia and the elder Olga, were immigrants from Poland and the Ukraine who had died in the same garment district fire years prior. Their spirits, most keen on keeping other young people from similar fates or myriad abuses in the vast, churning, industrial behemoth city, quietly stood watch over the proceedings as devoted spectral assets to the Ghost Precinct. Zofia chose to remain a consistent haunt; Olga chose to manifest only during séances. Both girls were silvery, luminous, with dark charcoal hair pulled back from their sharp-featured faces. The darkened, singed hem of their simple dresses was the only reminder of how they'd died.

The appearance of these precinct assets—ghostly, serene faces staring at their living friends—heralded the opening of the spirit realm to mortal ears.

There was a rushing sound through the room, in an ethereal echo, as if a great door had been opened.

"There's a host of children," Zofia said, uneasy. "And they've been wronged somehow."

"We are listening," Cora responded, speaking loudly to the spirit world as a whole but nodding at Zofia to make sure the girl knew she was heard and understood. So often spirits spoke, trying to help the living, and were ignored.

A thousand whispers crested around the mediums like a tidal wave, a jumble of woe, impossible to make out one word over the next. Little Jenny clapped her hands over her ears. Antonia, her tall, wide-shouldered body sitting starkly still and bolt straight, winced. Cora released a held breath carefully, slowly, as if she were lowering a great weight onto her delicate shoulders, untucking a handkerchief from her lace cuff to dab at the moisture that had sprung up on her light brown brow.

There was another sound, a scuttling behind them, though they could see nothing. They felt presences they could not see. Ghosts were unpredictable in the ways in which they manifested. The scurrying sound, accompanied by the same wash of urgent whispers, swept over to the locked file cabinets against their rear wall.

The young women turned their heads very slowly.

Just because one worked with the dead didn't mean they couldn't be frightening. Spirits were often creatures of startle and shock.

The precinct file cabinets flew open.

All of the women jumped.

"But we don't even have all the keys," Cora said, wondering how the ghosts could possibly have unlocked the dusty old wooden cabinets filled with incomplete and shoddily taken case notes from earlier decades of corruption and disarray.

Below one of the four desks scattered about the long room, the center drawer creaked open of its own accord. Then another desk's drawer. Then a third. Papers rustled, and a few flew out. Then a few more.

Jenny edged over to the seventeen-year-old Antonia, who held her long arm out for the little girl who had become a surrogate sister, and the child tucked in against her. Antonia kept herself calm and collected, for Jenny's sake if nothing else. The little girl didn't need to sign, or write a note to be understood, her small form shook, making Antonia hold her all the tighter. The child didn't need to have any further traumas added to her condition of selective mutism.

"Spirits, what do you wish to tell us?" Cora demanded, finding her voice.

"And why this display? You've never been the sort to give us poltergeists!" Antonia exclaimed.

"Find us..." came a murmur that consolidated from the voices, the words racing around the room in a freezing chill, though no spirits could be seen to have made the declaration. It came from the fabric of the air itself, repeating again, in aching earnest. "Come find what we've lost!"

Made in the USA
Middletown, DE
18 July 2020

12553068R00144